FIRST BLOOD

First published in 2011 by MP Publishing Limited
6 Petaluma Blvd. North, Suite B6, Petaluma, CA 94952
12 Strathallan Crescent, Douglas, Isle of Man IM2 4NR

ISBN 978-1-84982-116-2
First Blood

1 3 5 7 9 10 8 6 4 2

Book & Cover Design by Maria Smith & Dorothy Carico Smith

    Rayner, Claire.
        First blood / Claire Rayner.
        p. cm. -- (A Dr. George Barnabas mystery)
        ISBN-13: 978-1-84982-116-2
        ISBN-10: 1-84982-116-X

        1. Women forensic pathologists--Fiction.
        2. Detective and mystery stories. 3. Medical fiction.
        4. Suspense fiction. I. Title. II. Series: Rayner,
    Claire. Dr. George Barnabas mystery.

    PR6068.A949F57 2011   823'.914
                        QBI11-600145

A CPI Catalogue for this title is available from the British Library

Claire Rayner

FIRST BLOOD

A Dr. George Barnabas Mystery

For Kim Ismay,
the sixth Rayner,
with love

Acknowledgements

Thanks for advice and information about death, detection and motor cars, due to Dr. Trevor Betteridge, Pathologist, Yeovil District Hospital; Detective Chief Inspector Jackie Malton, Metropolitan Police; Dr. Rufus Crompton, Pathologist, St George's Hospital, Tooting; Dr. Hilary Howells, Anesthetist; and are gratefully tendered by the author.

1

"Good God!" Sheila Keen said and stared at him in horror. "Are you telling me he's a woman?"

"You got it." The mortuary porter was enjoying himself hugely. "Not a he. A she, that's what he is. Dr. George Barnabas. Female of the species. You needn't have bothered with the coffee tray, need you? Not unless you've gone funny in your old age and going in for a bit of let's be friends!" And he laughed and went away to make coffee for himself, deeply pleased to have got his own back on the old cow for the way she'd complained about him to the former department head, just because he'd been a bit off-hand with a couple of relatives who hadn't given a damn about the stiff anyway. It was just as well old Dr. Royle had been finishing his last week at the time or he'd have made things hot for him, Danny, and Danny liked things quiet and peaceful around the place. Mortuaries, in his estimation, ought to be quiet and peaceful places, especially mortuaries which he was in charge of. Except when he could make Madam Sheila Keen mad. Then it was worth putting up with a bit of a row just for the pleasure of watching her simmer. She might be the senior technician in the lab, but so what? He was the boss of the mortuary which was the most important place in the whole of the path. department.

Left alone in the consultant's small office, which was, unusually, shiningly tidy and scented with fresh coffee, Sheila was indeed simmering. How could they have lied to her so over in the Dean's office when she'd gone to hang around the secretaries and ask questions about Dr. Royle's successor? They'd always been a catty pair, but how could they have been so hateful as to let her get it so wrong? How could they have expected her to think that a person called George was anything but a man—an unmarried one at that, or he wouldn't be moving into the residency the way he had. *She* had, dammit all. Sheila sniffed hard, picked up the coffee tray and took it out to the main laboratory. To hell with the secretaries and to hell with the new consultant. She was certainly not going to let any female think that she, Sheila Keen, was there to make coffee for her, head of the department though she might be. Jerry could have the coffee—he at least was a real man even though he was one grade lower than Sheila herself, and therefore usually to be regarded with some contempt. Though not all the time…

"Did you know that the new man was a woman?" she demanded as she slapped the coffee tray down beside Jerry, who was curled up over his bench with his head down over a set of slides. "Named George and a woman. I ask you!"

"Ah!" Jerry said sympathetically, not lifting his head from his microscope; he had to keep it very carefully focused. It was an antique model, and he always insisted on using it, however much the others accused him of affectation. "Disappointed, are you, love? Well, never mind. Plenty of fish in the sea…Have you got the follow-on set to this lot? Umm—double A nine two seven three?"

"Look for it for yourself," Sheila snapped. "I'm not here to wait on you, you know. Do your own running around." And she snatched up the coffee tray again and bore it off to her own corner to sit there and drink it grimly, determined no one should benefit from her efforts to be nice but she herself.

Jerry sighed, abandoned his microscope and went to find his set of slides. On the way back he went and stood behind Sheila, and tickled the back of her neck surreptitiously. "Don't get gloomy, sweetheart. She may turn out to be quite a decent type. You never know your luck. And it's not as though old Royle was such a gift, is it? A right old misery, he was. I'm glad to see the back of him, personally."

Sheila shook her head irritably, but not so much that Jerry would be distracted from his attentions to her neck. "Oh, you don't understand. Not at all. She'll try to push me around and give me orders—"

"She wouldn't dare," Jerry said. "I'll see to it that she doesn't."

Now Sheila did turn to look at him thoughtfully, but he backed off and laughed.

"No, you don't, sweetheart. Don't go getting ideas again. I'm not for you. I've told you, what we are is best friends. Let's not spoil it with anything else. It didn't work last time you tried it on with me, and it won't now. Don't let's ruin a beautiful relationship with sordid old sex."

"I don't know why I put up with you," she snapped. She got up and, sweeping up her coffee tray, went away to the small kitchen at the back of the lab, leaving Jerry to amble back to his own place. The other two technicians in the small lab, both pretending to be immersed in their own work, made commiserating faces at him as he passed their stools. Quiet fell again, broken only by the faint hiss of the centrifuges and the rattle of the agitator with the samples from the cardiac clinic.

After a while Jerry stretched and yawned. "Does anyone else have any gossip about the new incumbent?" he asked the air, and Peter, the older of the junior technicians, his head still down over his own work, only grunted. But Jane was ready to stretch her back too and stop for a while.

"Not a word," she said cheerfully. "It wasn't till I heard Sheila tell you that I knew it was a woman. Nice, that. Make an agreeable change. At least Sheila won't moon after her."

"Poor Sheila," Jerry said absently. "We'll have to find her a bloke somewhere. It's all getting a bit too obvious."

"If she can't have you—and Heaven knows why she should fancy you—she wants a senior consultant. Nothing less would do for *her*," Peter said, sniffing loudly, and Jane winked at Jerry.

"You'd have had a tiger by the tail if you'd managed to get anywhere with her when you tried," she said. "You're much better off with your nice little physio."

"Hmmph," said Peter, and went on working.

"Pity, really. She's not a bad old soul, Sheila. Just so damned *anxious*," Jerry said.

"She'll be really sick over this new one." Jane giggled. "She had it all worked out, I'll bet you. Cook him nice little late dinners, offer to do his notes for him—poor bugger wouldn't have known what hit him."

"Well, it'll have to be me who cooks the new one nice little late dinners and does her notes for her, won't it?" Jerry said and Peter sniffed more lusciously than ever.

"So what else is new?" he jeered. "If it isn't Sheila leching after every new pair of trousers that walks in here, it's you slavering over every skirt. The pair of you make me sick."

"I dare say it's those salmonella samples," Jerry said kindly. "You've probably been licking your fingers again. Oh, shit. That sounds like the Professor. Heads down, children."

They were working with great absorption when the door opened and the boom of Professor Dieter's voice, which had alerted Jerry, came clearly over to them. None of them looked up as he came in.

"And this, of course, is the main lab, though I think you saw it when you came for your Board…"

"Mmm, yes," his companion said and stood looking around. Jerry, at the sound of her voice, lifted his chin a little and, grateful yet again for his old microscope, twisted its mirror to give himself a rear view, diminutive and distorted, but still a view. And took stock.

She seemed to be tall. That was a plus. A man as lanky as Jerry got tired of jokes about girlfriends having to be put up to it. This one could look him in the eye, yet he'd have no trouble seeing down her cleavage. He squinted to see how she measured up in that department, and was frustrated, because she was wearing a heavy bunched topcoat and had her hands in her pockets. A very disguising garment, a topcoat, he thought, I'll get a better view when she gets into her lab whites; and looked at the rest of her as she went on staring around.

Curly and dark. Nice, that. A little untidy to look at, but then it was blowing a gale outside; the old tiles on the roof had been rattling all morning. He looked at her face then, and was just in time to see her pull her hands out of her pockets and put on a pair of glasses; big round glasses with rather dark rims and he shivered happily. Women in glasses were always so sexy, in his experience.

Professor Dieter was still booming on, something about the rather dilapidated state of the labs and how hard it was in these times of cutbacks to get all the work done they'd like and how if they got their Trust status in the next round it might be possible to manage a little money to improve the working conditions, as well as the staffing levels, but meanwhile he hoped she'd cope as her predecessor had so well. Jerry went on studying her through his mirror, and then went a sudden scarlet. She had spotted him and was looking coolly back at his reflection with her brows raised. He reached up and turned the mirror back into position and began to fuss with his slides.

Professor Dieter was introducing her now. Sheila had come out of the kitchen and Jerry looked at her out of the corner of his eye and was amused; she had powdered her nose and applied fresh lipstick and her frail blonde prettiness was greatly enhanced by the way she'd fluffed up her soft hair. The newcomer might be a woman but there was no way Sheila Keen was going to let herself down by not looking her absolute best. Not bad for an old 'un, Jerry thought pityingly, aware as always of the fact that he, at thirty-four, which was old enough, God knew, was still five years Sheila's junior. She could have been quite toothsome if only she weren't so intense.

"How do you do?" Sheila said with gracious charm as Professor Dieter made the introduction. "Ah, Dr. Barnabas, yes."

"Hi," said Dr. Barnabas and put out her hand, and Jerry thought, American? She's a bloody American! And this time turned around to look.

"And this," said Professor Dieter, "is—er—is..." And he looked blankly at Jerry, for all the world, Jerry thought with irritation, as though he were a stray puppy who'd wandered in to pee on the floor.

He shifted his gaze from the Professor's rather pale face and smiled at Dr. Barnabas. "How do you do, Dr. Barnabas. I'm Jerry Swann. Technician. Mostly blood, some histology, general purpose really." He shot a glance at Sheila who was hovering in the background. "Deputy," he said smoothly, "to Miss Keen. I'm in charge when she's not here."

"Hi," said Dr. Barnabas again, and surveyed him with, it seemed to Jerry (who found it was a hopeful sign), some amusement. Her eyes, he saw, were a strong dark brown and her face was—well, interesting. Not pretty, but interesting. Big eyes, big mouth, big nose. About thirty-five, he thought. Not bad for a consultant's post. It'll be her first. "Good to meet you."

"Good to meet you," Jerry said with some fervor as Professor Dieter took her off to meet the two juniors and also Danny Roscoe, who had emerged from his fastness in the mortuary ostensibly to deliver a message to Sheila but actually to hover at the door with a deference that deceived none of the laboratory staff who knew him. His personal radar was very effective; he always knew where and when to put in an appearance and, what was more to the point, when to be invisible. Now was a good time to be seen, and he smirked as Professor Dieter introduced him and Sheila looked furious. Pushy was the word she most often used about Danny who, in her estimation, thought far too highly of himself.

Professor Dieter took Dr. Barnabas away to introduce her to the rest of the staff in the other laboratories, Sheila Keen leading the way as was her right as senior technician. Jane and Jerry immediately started to compare notes as Peter, with obvious scorn, went back to work and pointedly refused to join in. Which made both the others even more outrageous.

"What do you think, Jerry? Is she to be filed under 'Beddable' or 'Forget All About It'?"

Jerry was judicious. "Hard to be sure. Wears glasses, which is always such a turn-on for the discriminating man."

Jane wrinkled her nose in disagreement. "But she doesn't take much care about how she looks. No make-up to speak of. But she's available, that's the best bit, surely? She's got to be unattached. She moved into the residents' quarters, so Sheila said, didn't she? That's why she got so excited when she thought George Barnabas was a fella."

Jerry shook his head. "I doubt that means all that much. Probably worked somewhere right outside London before, and hasn't got a place here yet."

"No." Jane was very definite. "If she had a chap, whether a husband or a posselque, they'd have found somewhere to be together, a hotel even, if they had to. She certainly wouldn't have settled down all virginal in that dump over the way."

"Posselque?" Jerry was mildly diverted.

"Person of Opposite Sex Sharing Living Quarters," Jane recited. "Didn't you know that?"

"I do now. So if there's no posselque that means she could be a sinbad."

"I'll buy it," Jane said, after a moment.

"Single Income, No Boyfriend, Absolutely Desperate. I could do all right if she is. Make-up or no make-up, she does wear glasses, after all—"

"Will you two shut up?" Peter roared, no longer able to maintain his cool disdain. "You sound like a pair of rutting rabbits. For God's sake!"

"Do rabbits rut? I thought that was stags," Jerry said, as
Jane giggled.

"Everything ruts," she said. "Even old Peter. Except for
poor old Sheila..."

"And I hope Dr. Barnabas," Peter snapped. 'So that we can
get some peace around here. It'd make a nice change, that.
Very nice indeed.

George Barnabas watched the Professor stride away across
the courtyard back to the main hospital buildings. Not until
she was sure he wouldn't turn around and come back again did
she relax. He'd been fussing around her ever since she'd got
here this morning and she'd become more and more irritated.
It was right and proper of course that the Dean should be
interested in a new consultant but he didn't have to make quite
such a drama. She felt like a new over-rich child at a fancy
school being hauled around by a snobbish headmistress, and
that boded ill for the future. The main reason she'd applied
for this post, even though it was in such a dump of a hospital,
far from the well-kept splendors of the elegant Scottish place
she'd come from, was to be free of the burden of constant
supervision and watchfulness.

Being a registrar had been interesting, of course, and she'd
had some excellent experience, both on the hospital path. side
and the forensic, but never the real freedom she'd hankered
after. The job at Shadwell's Royal Eastern Hospital (what was
it they called it? Old East?) had seemed to her to promise that:
the advertisement in the BMJ had stressed the autonomy of
the appointment, the importance of being able to organize the
combination of hospital and forensic work and to work with
minimal support, because the post, the advert had admitted
smoothly, was for a single-handed consultant; and so she had
applied. She'd never thought she'd get it, of course. At just
thirty-five, and with only two registrar jobs behind her, she had
to be well down the list for a consultant post, she'd told herself
when she'd come up to London for the interview. But clearly

no one better had fancied working in such a dismal part of the world. And that was why she was in.

And I wish, oh I wish I'd never heard of goddamn Shadwell! she thought now as she pulled off her heavy topcoat and threw it at the hook on the back of the office door. I knew it'd be a poor neighborhood, but Jesus, not this poor! She sat at the desk and thought broodingly of the walk she'd taken last night after she'd dumped her bags in the gloomy room they'd assigned her in the residents' quarters. It had been raining, but that had never bothered her in Inverness; there the rain had been soft and agreeable, scented even. Here it was cold and harsh and reeked of diesel and the river and human dirt; and she had plodded through the dull streets, past the anonymous blocks of flats and the littered yards and tried hard not to think about Ian. Just as she was trying not to think about him now.

But she had to give up because it was impossible to keep him out of her mind, and she sat now glowering at the closed door, thinking about Ian very hard indeed. How could the man be such a bastard? How could she have been so mad over him for the best part of a year and not know he was a bastard? That was the thing that hurt almost the most. She'd thought he was wonderful: not just a great lover and fun to be with; not just a fine brain and fizzing with the sort of ambition that made him lively and exciting all the time, whatever they were doing; but a caring person, one who understood her and her feelings and hopes and ambitions. But when it had come down to it, he'd turned out to be—well, a bastard. One of the worst sort.

He'd had the chance of a job in London too; he was a good surgeon and had a marvelous CV; he'd even been head-hunted by a private sector set-up where he'd have made a lot of money—which was very much part of his ambition—and got a lot of kudos too, because they could have fiddled him an NHS consultancy as well. But would he see it that way? The world'd explode before he would, she told herself, with bitter tears filling her throat and making her eyes feel hot and dry. The bastard…

It had been so surprising, that was the thing. She'd told him, burning with excitement, how she'd got the job; had gone hurtling from the airport to the hospital in a very expensive taxi, instead of a bus, just to get to him sooner; had gone rushing into the medical staff common room, expecting him to cheer as loudly as he could, expecting him to get excited about taking up his own offer from London so that he could come south with her; and what had he done? He'd stared at her, unsmiling, and said baldly that he'd never expected her to get the job; that he'd encouraged her to go down for the interview just to get the itch out of her system; that he wanted a wife, not a competitor in his own house; that if she wanted the marriage they'd been talking about she'd settle for a registrarship until she started having babies, and after that it wouldn't matter anyway. And when she'd protested, had told him that there was no reason why consultants couldn't have babies, he'd told her coolly that she was being too damned feminist for his taste these days and she'd better make up her mind what she really wanted and choose accordingly. The only comfort there'd been in the whole rotten mess was his clear astonishment when she'd told him she had chosen and was taking the job. He'd stared at her with his mouth open, literally. There'd been some pleasure in that for George; but not for long. He'd just listened and then had closed his mouth, nodded and said flatly, "Well, that's that," and had turned and walked out of the common room. And that had indeed been that.

And now here she sat in a rotten East End of London slum in the middle of a battered old hospital that no longer had the glow she'd seen around it when she'd come down for her interview and there'd still been a loving Ian in the background and the world had seemed full of happy possibilities. She was a consultant, sure, but big deal. She was head of a department that had no registrar or houseman attached; only the promise of such appointments as and when the hospital could afford them. Some consultancy that was! She was furthermore all alone in

London without enough money to get a place of her own to live in, not in this outrageously expensive town, with not a friend in the whole lousy city. Ever since she'd come to Britain from home ten years ago, she'd worked anywhere but London, so she had no London contacts. She'd done her forensic training in Liverpool (and what a great city that had turned out to be! She still missed the buzz of it, and the people she'd known there) and her house and registrar posts in Scotland. That had been a great part of the world for an eager new forensic pathologist. Lots of work, lots of opportunities to indulge her passion for probing into other people's deaths, and therefore their lives, lots of chances to deepen her knowledge and her abilities. But no chance to make London-based contacts. Yet she had felt herself ready for London. What she hadn't thought was that getting there might turn out to be a recipe for a deeply lonely life. Now she feared it would. Being an American in Britain hadn't mattered so far. She'd gone to Inverness via Liverpool and her various jobs with a golden reputation, and leaving the family behind at home all that time ago hadn't turned out to be all that painful. People in the North had been friendly and within a month of getting to Inverness, of course, there'd been Ian—Oh, shit, she thought and got to her feet. I'd better start doing something, anything, or I'll get maudlin. I might even miss my mother and want to go home to Buffalo, and that really would mean I was in the pits.

She put on the clean white lab coat set waiting for her over the desk chair and began to prowl around the office, looking in drawers and cupboards. She wasn't impressed. Someone had clearly gone to a lot of trouble to tidy up, but what was there wasn't worth the effort. There was no decent equipment, not of the sort she was used to, certainly, and only the most battered of what there was. The chair by the desk swiveled crookedly, and the desk itself was scored with dents and scorched all around the edges with cigarette burns. The window was clean but looked out on to a far-from-attractive view of the main courtyard, with its criss-crossing of glass-roofed walkways and the inevitable litter silted around the stanchions that held them up, and the uneven and unpleasantly shiny walls that framed the window were painted in a grainy and depressingly thick green. She sighed deeply and thought about the staff to whom she'd been introduced.

The pretty little woman seemed pleasant though a bit watchful; but that was natural enough. No one relaxes their guard when a new boss turns up till they know whether it's safe or not. The long lanky young man with the thick bush of springing yellow hair had looked cheerful if a bit on the randy side, and the others—well, she'd get to know them in time. As long as they weren't all madly attached to her predecessor, and resentful of her newness, she'd be all right. She got on with most people pretty well, after all. Except Ian, an inner voice whispered, but she ignored it. She'd go now and have a wander, talk to them all, get the feel of the place.

The door opened after a perfunctory knock and the fair-haired woman looked in. She was smiling, a triumphant sort of grin that George found alarming, as though George had done something nasty to her, and the woman was about to get her own back. A silly thought. She dismissed it and welcomed her, pushing her glasses further up her nose and smiling widely. "Oh, yes, do come in. Sheila, isn't it?"

"Yes," Sheila said and smiled even more widely. "I've got a message for you. They've just brought a body into the mortuary. The coroner's officer's down there waiting for you. Want a PM right away, please, because the courts are jamming up, they've got so much backlog, and they want to get the inquest in as fast as they can, while they've got a slot."

"Oh, right." George got to her feet. "You'll have to show me the way to the mortuary, I'm afraid. Professor Dieter never got that far. They never do, do they? Always keep out of the nasty places if they can. Can someone go over to my rooms and get my instrument case? I like to use my own gear when I can."

"I doubt you'll want to use anything good on this one," Sheila said, and her voice was creamy with satisfaction. "Drowned. Been in the water well over a week, according to the river police, who brought it in. Very far gone, it is. Stinks to high heaven. Nasty for your first one here, isn't it? Well, there it is, that's the way it goes. I'll show you the way. Danny's down there getting ready. Even he's not best pleased about this one, so soon after lunch, and it takes a lot to get under old Danny's skin. He's dealt with more nasty bodies than you and I have had the proverbial hot dinners. But I dare say you won't mind." And she beamed beatifically and held the door open.

2

"It's for Barrie Ward," Danny said. "You know—named after J.M. Barrie. The kids' ward. They should ha' called it Peter Pan really, but there you go. But the meeting isn't happening there, anyway. It's to be in the Board Room in the old building there on the far side of the third block. You can't miss it."

"Why do people always say that when missing it is the easiest thing you could possibly do?" George said, pulling off her rubber gloves and throwing them into the bucket, and Danny snorted and at last took the cadaver away. She took a deep breath of relief.

It had been one of the nastiest George had ever had to deal with and at first she hadn't enjoyed it at all, and neither had the coroner's officer. Almost before she'd made the first examination, once they'd got the clothes off and they'd found the wallet in the pocket of the jacket with its still legible suicide note and clear identification (the man had been an accountant who, it seemed, had been overenthusiastic about investing his clients' money and had lost large amounts of it), he had announced that he was quite content to leave her to it, would see her again soon, and goodbye for the present. And had fled. She'd wished for a moment that she too could escape the unpleasantness of it; but then, as she got on with the job, the work had taken over and the last remaining shreds of queasiness had gone. But they had come back after she'd finished and she'd had such a job closing the abdomen. The tissues had deteriorated to such an extent it was inevitable there'd be problems, but she'd managed it (to Danny's grudging approval, she knew, because he'd been a good deal more respectful to her after they'd finished than he'd been when she'd started) and then made her notes—the man had died of drowning after taking a heavy dose of a hypnotic drug—and only then did the awareness that the object on which she'd been working had once been a breathing human being come back to her, and that had brought back the nausea.

Now she stripped off her gown and apron and began to scrub her arms and hands, enjoying the sting of the water on her skin and the heavy reek of the soap. A shower and shampoo and complete change of clothes was indicated too. In future, she'd make sure she kept a set of the necessary things here at the mortuary so that she could get herself cleaned up and comfortable without having to go over to her room to shower. She should have thought about that this morning.

Danny came back and began the sluicing that always followed an autopsy, and shouted above the noise of the water, "You'll be going to the meeting about the kids' ward then?"

"Do I have to?" George began to collect her notes and the cassette tapes she'd dictated, and her camera and its pile of pictures. Danny had looked askance when she'd told him it was her normal practice always to take Polaroid photographs of her autopsies, just in case one day she wanted to do a book of some kind, muttering about old Royle never having done that and no one had never had no complaints, seeing as how the police took their own if there was any call for them. She registered the fact that her predecessor had clearly been either a lazy or a rich man. She knew lots of pathologists who took pictures of their more interesting cases, mostly because they, like herself, had vague plans some day to write, for pathology textbooks could be extremely lucrative. Well, perhaps Dr. Royle hadn't had any need to consider pecuniary matters. She, however, was very interested in improving her finances if she

could, and if investing in a few Polaroid pictures could lead
to such improvement, take them she would, no matter what
her mortuary attendant thought. But in fact she knew that
because of the way she'd handled this unpleasant first case, she
had Danny very much on her side; from now on he would be
willing to accept anything she did with equanimity. So perhaps
it was no bad thing her first corpse at Old East had been so very
nasty; it had certainly served to make at least one of the staff
show a proper respect for her.

"Oh, that's up to you, of course." Danny was scrubbing
furiously at the marble slab, covering it with Festival, the
concentrated disinfectant that gave the place its odd fruity
smell. "Not for me to say. Mind you, it's one of those things
they're all on about—getting cash for the kids' ward. There's
never enough for all the things they want there. The latest's a
pool for the physios to use for the rheumatoid arthritis cases,
after they've built the new ward block. That'll cost a bomb.
But getting it! Well, there'll be some very fancy footwork over
it, you mark my words. Everyone who's anyone around Old
East'll get themselves involved."

"Politics?" George said, lingering to watch the small busy
figure. Maybe now was the time to recruit her first ally. She'd
worked in hospitals long enough to know how important they
could be; making sure you had them among the secretaries
and orderlies was as vital as having them among the senior
consultants and ward sisters. "Is that what you mean? It could
be a good step for me? I'd be glad of advice."

Danny stopped scrubbing and leaned on his bunched fists
on the slab. "Well, since you're asking, doctor, I'd say yes, it
would be. From all I hear, they're all mixed up in it, from top
to bottom: consultants, nurses, as well as a few fancy outsiders;
the lot. It's all wrong, I reckon, having to go to charity to raise
the money for fixing up the children's ward. Supposed to be
the NHS, ain't it? Some bloody NHS when you got to go
around with a beggar's bowl to give the kids a decent place

to be in when they're ill. Anyway, that's how it is these days. Much good the bloody election done us, eh?" He brooded for a moment and then nodded at her, starting to scrub again. "If I was you I'd go along. You might as well meet as many of the buggers at one time as you can. Begging your pardon..." He threw her a sharp little glance under his brows to see how she'd react to his lèse majesté and, when she laughed, grinned widely. From now on, George told herself with great satisfaction as she assured him she'd do just as he advised, and went to her office, Danny's my man.

She gave her cassette tapes to Sheila, so that they could be passed on to Dorothy, the woman in the typing pool who dealt with the path. lab's secretarial work, and told her she was about to go over to the medical residence for her shower and change. The smell of the cadaver lingered in her nostrils and probably about her person too; the sooner she cleaned up the better.

"I wish I could have had a chance to talk to everyone properly this afternoon," she said. "But that took a long time. These tricky ones do."

"Nasty, was it?" Sheila said with some relish. George lifted her brows at her. "To start with. The coroner's officer certainly thought so. Went very early. But it was really too interesting to be unpleasant. It's amazing what survives in these immersion cases and what doesn't. There was a note in the pocket that was still legible—admittedly it was inside a wallet, but all the same—Anyway, it makes it clear it was a suicide, and he'd taken a handful of a hypnotic before he chucked himself in the river, and some of the pills were still visible in the stomach, so that should get it through the inquest fast enough. But the skin..." She shook her head. "The degree of maceration was really—"

"I dare say," Sheila said hurriedly. "Well, I must go. Got a rehearsal tonight—the hospital show, you know, for the children." She began to collect her things, and George looked at her sharply. This was in marked contrast to the positively joyous way in which she'd announced the arrival of the body in the mortuary and for a moment her heart sank. Dammit, the woman was hostile. She'd been pleased to see her faced with a dirty job. George sighed. Someone else to coax around into the allies' camp. Why the hell had she ever come to Shadwell? Why the hell didn't someone hang Ian up by his sleek blond hair and tickle his feet till he screamed for mercy? Why—

"The children," she said. "I think I've heard about that. There's some sort of thing tonight, isn't there?"

"Yes, a reception for a few of the locals. We're biting their ears as hard as we can. Are you going?"

"I thought I might. It'd be a chance to get to know a few people around the place."

Sheila was looking thoughtful. "I could come and introduce you to some if you like. I mean, our rehearsals can't start properly till it's over, because some of the more important people in the cast have to be at the reception for the first little while. If you like, of course. I don't mind."

She was elaborately casual but George sniffed her eagerness. She wants to show me off, she thought, pull me around like a liner behind a tug, her property. I've met her sort before. She opened her mouth to snub her but then thought better of it, remembering the need for allies, and instead said meekly, "That would be very kind of you."

Sheila actually bridled, lifting her head and shoulders with a little moue of self-satisfaction, and George was amused. A harmless enough creature after all, she thought. Needs attention the way babies need milk, that's what it is. And smiled at her with as genuine a warmth as she could conjure.

"Do tell me who'll be there. Just so that I don't look a complete nerd. What sort of locals are they? The Mayor and so forth?"

"Possibly. He does come to quite a few things. But he's not so important as the ones with money."

"Are there ones with money around here? From what I see it's the pits. I mean, the poorest of the poor live here, right?"

"Wrong." Sheila looked pleased to be able to contradict her so flatly. "You have to see beyond the end of your nose in these parts. We're on the edge of Docklands here, Dr. Barnabas. There are flats—" She stopped and then went on with kindly patronage: "Apartments, you know, that cost enormous amounts. They've got as many bathrooms as they've got bedrooms, even if there are six of them, and marble kitchens and heaven knows what else." She nodded with a sort of pride as though the affluence of the Docklands apartments conferred credit on her personally. "Oh, there's plenty of money in these parts, take it from me."

George forbore to make any comment on the fact that she was well acquainted with the idea of homes that had as many bathrooms as bedrooms and said only, "Well, you never can tell, can you? So you're getting the sort of people who live there to come in. Are they all that much interested in helping? In my experience rich people like to get real value for their charity dollars. You know, fancy balls and showy bonanzas where they can wear their diamonds."

"Oh, but we've got the Oxfords," Sheila said, and seemed to glow. "They're not like that, and the sort of people they know aren't either. They get a very nice class of person supporting our events. It's the Oxfords who are in the cast of the show— well, Richard is, at any rate." She dimpled as she said his first name, clearly relishing the intimacy. "You know who Richard Oxford is, of course."

"Waal," George said drawling with as deliberate an imitation as she could manage of her New England mother's voice, "can't say as I do…"

Sheila swelled happily, delighted to be relieving her ignorance. "Richard Oxford, the novelist? You must have heard of him. He's hugely famous. He wrote Devil's Eyes Down, and The Cattermole Variations—that was a fabulous film, wasn't it, Richard Gere, super—and of course the best of the lot, I think—so does he, actually, told me himself—Morning of the

Darkest Night. Oh, yes. Everyone's heard of Richard Oxford."

George could not deny that she had. She had in fact read one of his books once in Corsica. She'd found it left behind by another English-speaking visitor and, for want of anything else to fall asleep over on the beach, had picked it up, and to her own surprise enjoyed it. It had been an adventure tale involving Arctic exploration, deposits of gold discovered under the pack ice and a battle between Americans and Russians to get it; a lot of preposterous nonsense really, but immensely readable and absorbing. She'd read it all through one long hot day and been sorry when she'd finished it. But then, after she'd gone home, she'd come across an article about him in the Guardian in which he revealed that he never stirred from his flat in Docklands to write his adventurous epics, set though they were all over the world. "Wouldn't be caught dead in the Arctic," he'd said cheerfully, "let alone the Mojave Desert or the Brazilian rain forest," where he'd set several more of his books. "A great researcher, that's what I am," he'd told the journalist, "with exceptional knowledge of the London Library." George had read the article, furious with herself for having been so taken in by the man's book. She'd actually believed some of the stuff he'd written, thought he had to be describing scenes he'd observed with his own eyes. He'd made a fool of her; and after that she hadn't made any effort to read more of his books.

Now she said only, "Oh, yes. That Richard Oxford. You said the Oxfords. There're a few of them?"

"His wife," Sheila said. "Such a glamorous woman, you've no idea. She's Felicity. I don't know too much about her, except that they've been married for ages. But they live quite—well, busy lives and she has some sort of business of her own apparently, so naturally they aren't in each other's pockets. It caused a bit of gossip, but I don't listen. It's none of my business." She looked down her nose, trying to display virtuous horror, but George wasn't in the least convinced.

"What sort of gossip? Tell me."

"Well…" Sheila mimed reluctance but not for long. "She's supposed to have had affairs, you know the sort of things people say, and I've heard that Richard got mad about it and—well, I never found out really. The gossip stopped fairly quickly. It was a year or two ago. Anyway, I don't know more than that." It was clearly a painful admission for Sheila but she carried it off with aplomb. "The thing is, I see most of Richard. He's very active in our drama group, and does so much to help us. He's in our show. Did I tell you that?"

"I'm not sure," George said diplomatically. "So, he'll be there, and his wife. Who else?"

"Hard to say. The consultants, of course. They always turn out." Sheila giggled. "I think they have to. They're sort of expected to. It's very important to Old East to get the children's unit properly up and running. It's been madly shabby for far too long. Anyway, I'll point them all out tonight. Introduce you and so forth. If it'll help."

"Oh, I'm sure it will," George said with a pretty show of gratitude. "I'll meet you then, shall I? Just tell me where and what time."

The room was extremely handsome, George thought, and for the first time since she'd arrived at Old East found something of which she could genuinely approve. It was in the administration block, housed in the original Georgian building which had been the first hospital almost two hundred years ago; a massive double cube of a room with faded blue and pink and green paint on the plasterwork panels of the walls and the elaborately molded ceiling, and a vast turkey carpet in subdued shades of red and brown and blue to highlight them. There were spindly chairs and tables in mahogany and fruitwood that belonged entirely in the period, as did the long Governors' Table. For this occasion it had been pushed from its normal central position under the elaborate glass candelabra to the side of the room to be spread with the inevitable crisps and peanuts and Twiglets as well as wine and bottles of water. What was it about meetings of intelligent people in England, George asked herself, that they couldn't be held without the accompaniment of these over-salty, usually stale bits and pieces that created thirsts that couldn't be quenched on the amount of wine provided? She thought nostalgically of the sort of event this would have been back in Inverness, where more substantial food would have been on offer, together with much better wine and probably whisky; and thoughts of Inverness brought her perilously close to thoughts of Ian and back even further to memories of her parents' parties for the faculty of her father's university, with their great bowls of dips and crisp home-baked biscuits and canapés, and she felt a thick melancholy settle on her. Maybe it had been the big mistake she'd made in the first place, leaving Buffalo to come to the UK. And then wanted to shake herself with irritation, for who could possibly be homesick for a dump like Buffalo, for God's sake, even when they were in a dump like Shadwell?

"Well, now." Sheila was back at her side with a glass of white wine clutched in each hand. "Here you are. Now let's see who's here." And she looked around the room with a sharp and considering air.

George sipped the wine, which was warm and slightly vinegary, and, resolving to abandon it as soon as she decently could, followed Sheila's gaze. Some of the people she did recognize: the three people who had been on the Board when she'd been interviewed, and she trawled her memory for names. The stocky one with the petulant expression was Keith Le Queux. Genito-urinary? Yes, that was right. He was talking to the rather thin man who had asked her sharply about her own health and then said little more. He was Agnew Byford. Hearts, she thought vaguely. I'm not sure but I think he's the senior cardiologist. And then there was the only woman who'd been there, a good-looking person of perhaps forty, maybe less; it was hard to tell because she tended to frown rather a lot in a harassed sort of fashion. She was clearly as preoccupied now as she had been on the day of the interview, because she was the only person here in her white ward coat; plainly about to rush off again. At the interview, George remembered, she'd been sympathetic and concerned about her housing problems in London if she got the job, and George had warmed to her. She obviously knew how tough it was for women to be consultants. She had been in her whites then too; and George smiled to herself. Maybe it was a way of not having to wear good clothes to work. A little white starch covered a multitude of sartorial sins.

The woman had seen her and came over. "Hello, it is Dr. Barnabas, isn't it? I'm Kate Sayers. We met when—"

"Of course," George said and held out her hand. "As if I could forget. You were kind. Worried about me having to live in the residence."

"Now you're in maybe you can see why," the other said drily. "I lived there myself for a while and hated it, though it's not as bad as it used to be, believe it or not. There's so little money around for non-essentials. And doctors' comforts are very low in the list of essentials, I'm afraid, Dr. Barnabas."

"Call me George," George said as Sheila hovered beside them, clearly annoyed at not being included in the conversation. George, aware of that, turned and smiled at her. "You know Sheila Keen? From the lab? She's—"

"Of course," Kate said. "Everyone knows Sheila. She's the one you call if you need something done in pathology in a hurry or the reports haven't come through in time for a clinic. And she's the best person we know for stirring up the typing pool."

Sheila wreathed herself in smiles and bobbed her head. "Well, I do my best."

"And do it well. But then women always do, don't we?" Kate looked at her watch and made a little sound of exasperation between her teeth. "It's no good. I can't hang around for the speeches. Got three kids on dialysis. And I so badly want them to have their own special pediatric beds instead of being mixed up with my old daddies! I'd have liked to put in a special plea for them. Oh, well, another time, I suppose. Glad to have another woman here, George. Why George, by the way? Not that it's my business, of course. Short for Georgina, is it?"

George sighed softly and shook her head. This always came up eventually; it said a lot for Kate's pleasant manner that George didn't immediately hate her for asking.

"I was named after my grandfather. He insisted that my mother's first child was given his name exactly, or he wouldn't leave any of his money to us. So, I'm George Postern Barnabas, and that's all there is to it."

"I hope the money was worth it," Kate said and grinned. "You must have had hell at school."

"I did, and yes, it was worth it in the end. It put me through medical school and a good deal of postgrad as well, including my forensic course here in the UK. So the old devil got his comeuppance anyway. He only did it because he didn't like women, and never forgave my mother for being one." She laughed then. "We won, though, Ma and me."

"Didn't you just. Hell, I must go. The speeches are starting. See you around. Glad you're here. You were worth fighting for, I'm certain." And she touched George's sleeve and went as the room, now rather full of people, settled to an uneasy half-silence.

Worth fighting for? George wondered. Had it been so difficult to persuade her fellows on the interviewing Board that George Barnabas was the right person for the pathology job? Had Kate Sayers pushed for her because she was the best or because she was a woman and Kate felt the need of female reinforcements on the staff? It was a sobering thought, and not one designed to inflate the ego, George thought ruefully, as she made herself listen to the speeches.

It was routine stuff, lauding the skills of the brilliant medical and nursing staff struggling to cope in inadequate premises, begging all present to put all they could into the fundraising which was now moving into its second phase at a time when the recession was biting even deeper. "Only a million left to raise," the speaker said brightly. "We can do it." And everyone applauded politely and looked unconvinced.

George stopped listening to the words and started studying the speakers, leaning over and asking Sheila in a whisper who they were when she needed to. Sheila was only too happy to tell her, in an equally subdued tone, so that by the time the talking ended on a last impassioned plea from Professor Dieter, the Dean, George had a pretty clear idea who everyone was.

There were various local businessmen and representatives of Trusts, and George dismissed them from her attention. The ones who mattered were clearly those standing close to the Dean, Richard and Felicity Oxford. They'd been introduced already by Professor Dieter, who had treated them with obvious deference, and that had fascinated George. There had been nothing deferential about the Dean when he'd shown her around the hospital and introduced her to her department. Now, amid the shuffling as the people grouped around the microphone rearranged themselves, she could study them both more clearly.

Felicity was a good-looking, extremely elegantly dressed woman with primrose-yellow hair which she wore plastered close to her skull and then pulled into a rich smooth bun at the back; an old-fashioned, indeed period look that made her very striking. A strong face, George thought, with heavily marked bones. Got some Norse in her somewhere, she decided, remembering her year of work in anthropology and the extra papers she'd done on racial characteristics. She could have been a Scandinavian princess in a third century saga.

The man at her side looked far less well made, but none the less was equally striking. He looked blurred where she looked sharply defined. His chin was softened to a jowliness with equally soft but well-shaven and talcum-dusted cheeks, and beneath his rather muddily gray eyes there were pouches of drooping skin. His hair was a strong iron gray, thick and bouncing, and he was wearing a pale gray suit that shone almost silvery in the light thrown by the candelabra above his head. He had a perky crimson bow tie and a matching waistcoat, which was well displayed by his non-chalant one-hand-in-trouser-pocket stance, and George thought, He knows exactly how to make the best of himself; and was a little repelled by the calculation of it all. And then was amazed at herself. Why shouldn't he be self-aware? With his fame it was obvious that he must spend a lot of time in public situations like this, being looked at and pretending not to care, or even to notice. He had every right to stand any way he liked. She was being irrational, and she straightened up and looked at him attentively as he took the Dean's place at the microphone and began to speak. But it was a moment or two before she could stifle her feeling of dislike and concentrate on his speech.

"... This hospital has always mattered to me and mine," he was saying. "Haven't I lived here for the past twenty years and never gone further than a cottage in the Cotswolds?" There was a ripple of approving laughter. Clearly everyone knew his much vaunted travel-adventure books were based on total fantasy and didn't mind in the least. Perhaps I'm just a bit pompous? George thought. What does it matter, after all?

"That's why I'm working so hard with all of you to raise the necessary funds." He had a good voice, well pitched, with, in true London style, a hint of a nasal accent, and he knew how to use it. "I want us here in Shadwell to have the best children's ward in all London. Our children deserve no less. As you all may know, my wife and I'—here he made an expansive gesture in her direction and she bobbed a pretty little mock curtsey—"are producing a little show—music and sketches and so forth, with both local talent and a few of my professional friends..." And he reeled off a string of names of very well-known actors and television performers in a studiously casual manner. "So I do hope as many of you as possible will buy tickets and join us. The details are on the handout sheets you'll find by the door as you leave, together with covenanting forms for your donations." He smiled with conscious charm. "Don't let our children down. Please. They can't appeal for themselves, but I speak for them. They need you. We all need you. Thank you so much." And he stepped back to a warm spatter of applause.

He was followed by the hospital's Chief Executive Officer, Matthew Herne, another very self-aware man in a rather too-well-cut navy blue suit and shoes so highly polished they made George blink. She thought, Ex army, you can spot them anywhere, and was childishly pleased with herself when, as part of his own appeal for funds, he threw in comments about his days in the Services, helping to enthuse the troops, as he was hoping to enthuse his listeners today.

He was followed by yet another administrator, this time the one mainly responsible for the actual plans of what was to be done in the children's unit. He put them through a tedious ten minutes of looking at almost indecipherable ground plans and artists' rather exaggerated impressions of how the finished work would look, as George went on learning from Sheila who among those present were hospital people.

There were several: an untidy and rather round woman who was the psychiatrist, Barbara Rosen; a handsome tall creature with lots of Byronic curly hair who was, Sheila said in a yearning whisper, Dr. Neville Carr, so nice and caring, a real darling; and, in pride of place today because it was her specialty that stood to benefit from the proceedings, the pediatrician, a severe woman in her fifties with pepper and salt hair cut in a hard fringe that did nothing to improve the jutting effect of a strong nose and chin. "They call her Judy sometimes," Sheila whispered. "Cruel, isn't it?" And George nodded and looked at Sheila and both of them grinned. Susan Kydd really was remarkably like Mrs.. Punch to look at.

"There's Lawrence Bulpitt," Sheila continued. "He's neurology. Bit of an experimental type, likes to come down and pick up this and that in path. You'll get to know him fast enough. And the rather fat man there, he's Gerald Mayer-France, general surgery; and that untidy one is Toby Bellamy, he's the gut man; and Peter Selby, who's ENT, and—"

"I'll never remember them all," George said and then relaxed as the last little burst of applause ended and the audience shimmered into movement, heading back for the drinks table and, some of them, for the door. "I'll get to know them eventually. But thanks for the run down."

"My pleasure," Sheila said. "I'll have to go now, though. Mr. Oxford's actually coming to the rehearsal tonight, you see. We're only chorus and so forth, we're not famous like the real performers, but all the same..." She laughed a little breathily. "It's all rather exciting. So, I'll see you tomorrow..."

She was itching to get away, watching over George's shoulder as the Oxfords made their way to the door, talking to the Dean and Matthew Herne as they went. She was clearly longing to be with them, looking for the chance to chat directly to the great man himself; and George was amused. She's a star-screwer, our Sheila, she thought indulgently, remembering one of her mother's more astringent remarks. Likes to chat up the most important people wherever she is. Well, it's a harmless enough foible. And she patted Sheila kindly on the shoulder and said, "You go. I'll be fine. See you in the morning." Sheila threw a grateful glance at her and darted away.

George stood looking down at her glass, still full of the vinegary wine, made a small face at it and turned to put it back on the table before escaping herself, and almost bumped into a man of her own height, with a rumpled suit, a shirt that looked as if it had been introduced to a hot iron only in the most perfunctory manner, and a cheerful face under uncombed hair which was thick and the color of dust in long empty rooms. He laughed at her and held out his hand for her glass.

"Isn't it horrid? Come down and have one with me. I know a place where the beer's good and they sometimes have a bottle of good Vouvray on the go if you insist on wine. They do great ham sandwiches too. With the crusts on, thick and solid. You might as well. There'll be shepherd's pie in the canteen and they make it with shepherds who've been dead a long time."

She blinked, startled, and he held out his other hand. "I'm Toby Bellamy," he said.

She concentrated on what Sheila had told her and remembered. "Ah, guts."

"Precisely. Which means I know what's good for 'em. So, coming to my favorite pub? It's a civilized one. No juke-box."

"I like juke-boxes," she said, a little nettled. He had an air of self-satisfaction that reminded her of Ian and was not at all attractive. He seemed to realize there was something wrong and looked anxious, his face crumpling a little. And that was nothing like Ian, and she thought, To hell with it. And said, "But why not? Yes, that'd be fun."

3

George was sitting at her desk working over the previous day's reports when the door was pushed open without even the usual perfunctory knock. She looked up with a frown. She'd been finding it hard enough to concentrate as it was. Last night's casual drink and ham sandwich at Bellamy's favorite pub had turned into a late session of loud laughter and even, heaven help her, Karaoke singing (she blushed to remember it now), which she'd enjoyed enormously, but which had meant she'd woken this morning with the sandy-eyed awareness that she'd slept for far fewer hours than she should have done, and a disagreeable internal sensation that told her she'd had rather more food and drink than had been good for her. The last thing she wanted now was interruptions.

It was Sheila, looking ruffled, pink and excited all at the same time. She beamed at George with breathless pride and said quickly, "So sorry to bother you, Dr. Barnabas, but it's Mr.—"

"It's all right, Sheila." The voice came from behind her and was loudly authoritative and clear though there was a thickness about it that was unpleasant. "I can speak for myself, thanks."

George knew she knew the voice and couldn't place it for a moment, but then remembered. The man who had spoken so eloquently at the meeting yesterday. Last night he had sounded smooth and placatory; now he was arrogant and a great deal too sure of himself. At once the anger she had felt against Sheila for interrupting her melted and reshaped into protectiveness. "I'm busy, Sheila," she said. "So perhaps you can ask the—er—gentleman to wait. I'll let you know when I'm available—"

But he set Sheila aside as casually as if she'd been an inanimate object and came into her office to stand in front of her desk and smile at her, one hand held out in a friendly gesture. She looked directly at him and ignored the hand.

"Richard Oxford. Do forgive me for barging in on a busy woman, but I have a string of appointments in Town—you know how it is. I just wanted to fit this little chat in before I got too deeply into my day. I'm sure you'll understand." He looked over his shoulder briefly. "Thank you, Sheila," he said pointedly and Sheila gave a little gasp and closed the door behind her before scuttling away with a clatter of excited footsteps.

"I too have a great deal to do," George said crisply, and got to her feet. "So if you'll forgive me perhaps we can make an appointment that will suit us both and—"

"This won't take a moment." He had pulled the other chair from the side of the room and now sat easily, leaning back with crossed legs. "As you'll see, I waste no time in coming to the point. I just want to talk to you about any special needs you may have here." He flicked a glance around the room, clearly sneered at its shabbiness and dismissed it, all at the same time. "I may be in a position to see that you get anything you need. Extra equipment. Materials. Money, even." He smiled, widely, and the thickness of his face that she'd noticed last night seemed to increase as the jowls melted together into heavier folds and his eyes hooded with the pleats of sagging eyelid that hung over them. "Not that that's so easy, but it's surprising what can be possible if it has to be."

She sat down again, damned if she was going to stand in front of him. "Look, I'm not sure why you should think you can come in here and—"

"Oh, as to that." He waved a hand vaguely. "You don't really understand this place yet. But you will, you will!" He leaned forward confidentially and at once she leaned further back in her own chair. He didn't seem to notice. "You see, I have a deep and abiding affection for this place. Yes. A deep affection. Always have had, you know. Living here as I do, so near, I raise funds for dear Old East. Quite large sums. Been doing it for more years than I care to remember. The truth is, Old East would be in big financial trouble without my efforts. Roehampton Hospital has that television chappie raising their funds, and Old East has me. But you were at the meeting last night, so you know who I am and what I do."

"Was I? And do I?"

"Oh yes. I saw you there." He smiled at her even more widely and small crevasses appeared in each cheek and she thought, sickened, The bastard had dimples once and still tries to use them. "I never miss a thing, you know. Novelist's eye. I see everything, store it all up, keep notes." He dimpled again but she didn't respond, holding her face as unsmiling as it had been since he'd barged in, and for the first time he seemed aware that he was not as welcome as he had assumed he was. "You'll find that I'm very much part of Old East," he went on a little sharply. "The Dean—Professor Dieter, you know—and the admin side, they understand my role as fundraiser-in-chief. Just as their predecessors did. I've been here for many years."

"Really?" She was sharp herself. "Inasmuch as an NHS hospital has to have such a person, of course."

"Oh, this one does, and never think otherwise. In fact every hospital does these days. All that socialist claptrap—it's obvious a hospital has to get its funds wherever it can. Once we get Trust status, of course, it'll be easier. I'll be a non-executive member of the Board'—he produced a little crow of laughter—"non-executive by label, that is. In fact I'll do a great deal more than the paid staff, just as I always have. But that's by the by. I just wanted to tell you that I could be of help to you, with your co-operation, in providing your department with all sorts of useful things." He turned his head to one side like an enquiring bird and again showed the crevasses in those powdery cheeks.

"What do you mean, co-operation?" she said bluntly and he shrugged, clearly amused.

"Who can say? It depends what's going on, doesn't it? I might need support in some way, with a Board matter, perhaps."

"That won't concern me."

"Oh, it might, it might. You may find yourself a member of the Board. Many of the staff will be, of course. Executive members. And you're the head of pathology—"

"It's a very small department. It's unlikely. And, anyway, the hospital isn't a Trust."

"Yet. Its time will come." He got to his feet. "But think about it. Let me have a list of items you might need, by all means. Once we've raised all the money we need for the children's ward, who knows where we may be turning our attention next."

"Well, let's see the children's ward finished first, shall we?" She looked at her watch. "And now, if you'll forgive me…"

He got to his feet. "My dear girl!" He was beaming. "I'm grateful to you. I hadn't noticed how time was running on and I'm at risk of being late and that would never do. So discourteous to one's appointments, hmm? Well, glad we were able to have this little chat. You can find me when you need me. Just ask Sheila, or, indeed, anyone here at Old East. They all know me. I'm part of the fabric of the place."

Again he grinned at her and this time, to her relief, went. She stood there beside her desk rubbing the hand he'd shaken on her white coat, feeling it dirtied in some way. He was as nasty a man as she could remember meeting; and the whole discussion had been ridiculous. The last thing she'd do if she needed anything for the lab, she promised herself, would be to use his fundraising services. She'd rather have a car trunk sale of all she owned. And she went back to her reports. Oh, the politics of this place! Every hospital was political, of course it was, but this one seemed to be showing itself as more devious than most. Well, she'd learn whom to trust and whom to avoid, in time. Right now she had at least identified the one to put on top of her avoidance list.

The crocuses in the scrubby flowerbed in the small courtyard at the front of the admin building startled George. How could they be there so soon after Christmas? It certainly seemed only a matter of days since she'd arrived at Old East in the third week of January; yet here were spring flowers. And then she thought, working it out, But it's been at least six weeks, and was even more startled. Six weeks; it didn't seem possible.

She went on around the flowerbed to duck in under the walkway that led towards the main ward blocks. She didn't usually spend much time in the wards; when they needed someone to do something fairly trivial from path. she'd tell them firmly that since she didn't have either a registrar or a houseman, they'd have to settle for one of her blood-letters, and even the most intransigent of the consultants—like Le Queux—had learned that she wouldn't come running just when they crooked their fingers, however senior they were. She might be a consultant without any medical support staff (yet, she thought wrathfully; Professor Dieter was being really impossible about the problem but she'd lick him!) and a very recent and young consultant at that, but she was still a consultant. But when it suited her she didn't mind going to consult on the more tricky ones, and today's was a very tricky one indeed.

That's why I'm so willing to be clinical today, she told herself as she hurried through the cold gray morning; this case really is very difficult. Bad enough the poor little devil had lost so much of her colon to Crohn's disease; to have battered her liver with an overdose of paracetamol had been the act of a madwoman. And she smiled a little wryly at the thought. Perhaps she isn't that mad; would I like to be twenty-three with nothing but a life of invalidism and nurturing an ileostomy bag to look forward to? Maybe I'd have tried to throw myself away if I'd been in her shoes. Anyway, that's why I'm going to ICU. She has the most alarming liver-function results any of us have ever seen in a living creature; she ought by rights to be dead, but she's still hanging on and that's fascinating. The fact that she's Toby Bellamy's patient is beside the point, it really is.

Toby Bellamy; she let herself think about him. He really is great fun. He might look scruffy and seem vague about ordinary daily matters but he's got a sharp mind and he's funny. Men who make you laugh are incredibly attractive: you believe you could actually live with them for a lifetime—

She pulled herself back from the thought. For an intelligent, educated, highly professional and well-motivated woman, she really was behaving in a most absurd fashion, she scolded herself. And then thought furiously of Ian. It was all his fault. If he hadn't turned up and made her start thinking in such a sentimental fashion about marriage and housewifery and family building such ideas would never have entered her head. But because he'd talked that way she had suddenly become aware of her age, and the number of healthy child-bearing years she might have left to her. Articles in the tabloid papers that littered the medical common room and in the women's magazines she saw at the hairdressers that wittered on about biological clocks running down suddenly seemed not only of enthralling interest but of deep import. I'm thirty-five, she thought now mournfully, as she cut across the adjoining walkway which would take her past Green block to Red block and the intensive care unit. Thirty-five. If I got pregnant now, I'd be in the high-risk group. I'd be an elderly primip—Oh, the hell with it! People have babies at forty and gone and they do fine. But that's only five years down the line, does that mean you'd have to settle for just one? And—

She walked faster in an attempt to leave the stupid thoughts behind, knowing she was being childish to label them stupid when what she meant was she didn't like them; and then saw Kate Sayers coming towards her from the X-ray department and grinned widely to welcome her, relieved to have company.

"Are you coming to ICU as well?" George asked. "I hear they've put out a three line whip on the Bellew girl."

"Um. She's been dialyzed twice already this week. Kidneys are playing up badly. But I think they'll do, if the rest of her does. How's the blood picture?"

"Like Jackson Pollock," George said. "All over the place. A complete mess. I think we could stabilize her, mind you, given time. It all depends on how long they can keep the liver going, let alone the heart."

"Mmm," Kate said abstractedly and they turned left as they reached the way that led to outpatients. Beneath their feet the lines of different colored paint that showed the routes to the various parts of the hospital were so scarred and faded it was hard to make them out, and George, looking down at them, thought, They look the way I feel. Not sure where they're going or why.

Behind her Kate suddenly yawned, a great jaw-cracking grimace, and George looked at her sympathetically. "Emergency last night? It must be hell, that. Like being a junior again only you're a bit older and not so able to survive on nil sleep. It's one of the reasons I went into pathology, hating to be dragged out of bed at night. I'm useless when I am."

Kate shook her head. "No, it's not that. I don't get hauled out for work that often. David Mount's a good registrar and takes the burden off. No, this was Penny. She's got chicken pox and spent most of her night up and shouting about how she itches."

"Penny?"

"My four-year-old. The little one's probably going to get it too, and then, heaven help me, with Oliver away—"

"He's a doctor too?"

Kate shook her head, and looking at her George could now see the weariness. Her eyes were pouched and reddened and her skin a yellowish color. "No. He's a journalist. He's in the Balkans right now, on that reconstruction conference. So I can't even lean on him."

They'd reached the entrance to Red block but George hesitated. Kate stopped too and looked at her enquiringly.

"Is it so difficult?" George said abruptly and Kate quirked her head in puzzlement. "I mean, being a wife and mother and all that and a full-time job here as well?"

"Difficult?" Kate said and stared at her with her slightly bloodshot eyes looking a little remote and glassy. "Difficult? I'm not sure what the word is I'd use, but it certainly isn't difficult. Bloody impossible, more like. But there you go. I manage it somehow. It's only for a few years, I suppose. Till they get past this awful stage of getting one damned bug after another. They'll be at school eventually and it's got to get easier. I'll tell you this much, it's made me much better at dealing with patients' parents. I know what it's like." She shook her head and managed a grin. "By God I do," she ended feelingly and held the door open. "Well? Shall we go and see what we can do in ICU?"

The consult went well. The girl was improving, by some miracle. Her liver was ticking over tolerably well, now that her blood was being carefully dialyzed, and they'd got her fluid balances and medication the way they wanted them. She was conscious more often now, Toby Bellamy reported as they— Kate and George and Agnew Byford who was offering a cardiac opinion—clustered around him and looked at the notes. All he needed now was to see how they could push her a little faster, without damaging the progress they'd made already.

Byford started talking about her cardiac output and Toby listened and then joined in, arguing a little pugnaciously. George watched as the two men went at each other with some heat, and tried to be objective about Toby. Did she really like him as much as she suspected she did? In fact, was she getting rather too emotionally involved? It was an almost impossible question to answer, she decided, and that meant all she could do was take her time. Make no decisions either way in a hurry, her deep inner voice murmured, sounding very much like her mother. You only make terrible mistakes.

Kate went away at her usual speed once Toby had assured her that he could deal with the dialysis at present, though she promised to check later that afternoon. Byford, muttering a little, went too, and George made for the door. She'd done her job, assessing the blood picture and advising what the next steps should be, and now she wanted out. She disliked intensive care units; always had. They seemed to be so ambivalent somehow; although there were patients there was none of the humanity and warmth of the ordinary wards, where people filled the big spaces with clutter and noise and smells and their complaining voices, for these patients were inert and silent; nor was there the cool scientific calmness of the laboratories with their glittering equipment and humming, rattling, hissing machinery, even though such paraphernalia was here too. ICUs fell unhappily between the two stools and that made her uneasy. But Bellamy, who had returned to the bedside, called quickly, "Hold on, George!" and after a few words with the nurse, who was adjusting the intravenous lines, came over to her.

"I wanted to talk to you," he said. "Got a moment for some coffee? There's usually some in the office." And, not waiting for a reply, he took her elbow and led her into the small room which adjoined the main ICU and looked out into it through a wall-sized window.

He fussed over coffee cups as she sat perched on the desk, and again she tried to look at him dispassionately. He was wearing ICU whites, a short-sleeved white shirt over white cotton trousers that were too tight for him. His buttocks showed hard and shapely through the thin fabric and she felt a little frisson crawl across her belly, and looked away. But all she could look at were his arms, which were just as shapely and well muscled and had a drift of hair that had a golden tinge to it into the bargain, and that didn't help at all. She lifted her eyes and tried to concentrate on somewhere safe and chose the back of his neck, beneath the white theatre cap that barely contained his rough hair, and that was even worse. The nape of his neck was soft and curved a little under the curls like a child's, with a deep cleft that bore warm shadows, and she thought helplessly, Goddamnit, I really fancy this guy! and took the coffee cup he brought her feeling more than a little shaky. Maybe it was more than being anxious about running out of baby-making time, after all. My God, but I'm fickle! Two months ago I was devastated because one guy dumped me and here I am aching to get into another one's pants. And I thought I was in love with Ian! It just goes to show you something, but I wish I knew what it was…

"You're looking very sorry for yourself," Toby said. "Lost a pound and found a penny?"

"Mmm?"

"Never mind. It's quaint old English. You'll learn it eventually."

She didn't look at him, feeling absurdly elevated at being so close to him, but stared down into her coffee cup and tried to sound lugubrious. "Oh, I've just been trying to fight City Hall. And getting nowhere. After all, why should I do any better than anyone else? It still makes me mad, though."

"Argument with the Professor?" Toby was sympathetic.

"It's not much to ask for! Jeez, every other consultant in this place has a registrar, but me, I don't get so much as a houseman!"

"But you send out some of your work to washerwomen, don't you? That's why they're so mean with you."

"What? Washerwomen?" She was puzzled.

"I thought that a lot of your stuff went out to the forensic labs," he said. "Doesn't it?"

"There's enough pathology work for the hospital to justify a registrar, even a houseman, but the bastard won't let me have—"

Toby sighed. "You'll never understand the corporate mind. And Professor Dieter's as corporate as they come, take it from me. That fella's so keen on doing things the way the powers that be want 'em, it'd make you sick. Got his eyes on the Department of Health if you ask me, and a knighthood. Fancies himself right at the top of the administrative tree. And I know exactly what he's thinking about you and a registrar."

"Then let me in on it!" She was sardonic, and now able to look at him. The embarrassment of her earlier thoughts about him was diminishing as she relaxed. "It could help me."

"It's easy." He perched on the table beside her, and she could feel his arm warm against hers and the embarrassment came thundering back like a stampede of very eager buffalo. "He knows the forensic side of your week's work is funded by the police and the local authority and that some of the lab work—the bits you send off to the forensic labs—is paid for that way too. That means it's not the hospital's business, right? Well, he can extend that none-of-our-business-is-it? to the whole of your time and convince himself that the hours you put in on your forensic work here have nothing to do with the hospital either—which means that those hours belong here. In other words, he counts your work hours as nine to six, all for the hospital, even if you have three hours of that for forensic. So you can do your own registraring in the time you're doing forensic, on account of you're not doing it for the hospital. Get it?"

"That's crazy," she said after a moment. "It makes no sense."

"Don't tell me that. Tell the Prof.," he said cheerfully.

"I've tried telling him any number of times." She shook her head a little wearily. "It's like talking to a wall. He's charming, he's concerned, he wants everything to be perfect but he can't extend my establishment. Fancy way of telling me to get lost. He's useless."

"Never think it. He's bloody clever, that man. If anyone can run with the fox and go riding with the pink coats at the same time, he can. Don't underestimate him. Listen, why are we talking about a boring old fart like Dieter? I want to talk about something else."

"Because you asked me why I looked sorry for myself."

"Well, forget it. Try him again tomorrow. You never know, he might be having a bad day and you could wear him out. Chinese torture method. I want to know whether you're coming to the show tomorrow night?"

"Ah, the show," she said. "That."

"Yes, that. Are you coming?"

"I hadn't planned to," she said and then laughed. "To tell you the truth, I'm sick of the sound of it. Everyone keeps on and on about buying tickets and there are those posters everywhere, it's so *boring*. If I could have my druthers, I'd rather go some place else."

"You're just bloody-minded," he said equably. "Never mind. You'll enjoy it'

"I will not. Anyway, I'm not going."

"Oh, come on! You've got to. I bought you a ticket."

"More fool you then. I didn't ask you to buy one for me. If I'd wanted to, I'd have bought my own. I've worked hard at saying no. I've had Sheila Keen driving me crazy and I'm damned if I'll—"

"I know. All the same, come with me. There's a party afterwards for the cast and their hangers-on and the booze'll be free. It's been donated by some off license down the road and they tell me they've sent some pretty good stuff. And we can laugh at the luvvies poncing around being Frightfully Famous Actors, and have some fun. And you never know, maybe people'll get smashed enough to say things to each other they really mean, instead of being polite all the time. This place is a maelstrom of intrigue, you know! Half the staff hate the other half, and everyone hates the Prof., and he never shows who he hates—I tell you, one of these days there'll be mayhem done. And this show's as good a setting as any other! So come and see the fun."

"It's like that in every hospital. I don't see why this one should be any worse than any other. Hospital parties always end in rows."

"Just you come and see for yourself then. Prove me wrong, if you like."

She hesitated. "I told Sheila Keen I wouldn't."

He stared at her and his face was a little crumpled. "Hell, George, what is it with you? Here I am asking you out, and all I get is you bleating about Sheila Keen! Are you trying to tell me you're gay or something? It's not the impression I've had so far!"

"I'm trying to tell you I'm well mannered," she snapped furiously. "If I refuse to go to something when one person asks me, to accept the same event from someone else is hardly polite. And I was raised to be polite. As for any other reason—"

He burst out laughing. "Oh, you're so funny!" he said. "Listen, George, the whole hospital knows about Sheila Keen! She's man mad—makes a play for all of us. And she'd understand better than anyone if you told her you were going with me. Then it wouldn't be going to the show, it'd be going out with a bloke." He leered in a somewhat melodramatic manner. "And that comes first."

"Oh, does it?" George said wrathfully and got to her feet. "Like hell it does! I don't play those sort of games, mister; I don't need to, take it from me. And you don't have to put down Sheila that way, either. If I go to the show, I go because of her, and not with you. Even though you do wear trousers of a sort!" And she slammed her coffee cup down on the desk and headed for the door.

She heard him calling after her as far as the main door to the ICU as she went storming out. She would go to the lousy show, boring though she was convinced it would be, in spite of what he'd said she'd go just to show him. With Sheila Keen. He could go to hell.

Which was why she was in the back row of the most expensive seats when the whole fuss started.

4

Not, of course, that she was with Sheila at all. She sat there at the end of the row, slumping as low in her seat as her height would let her and simmering with irritation. Sheila had sold her her ticket with great delight and then said cheerfully, "I don't know who'll be sitting next to you, because someone else is selling those, but it might be somebody you know."

"What?" George had said, appalled, and Sheila had opened her eyes wide at her. "Won't that be your seat? You're only in the first bit after all, aren't you? And I'd thought you'd want to watch the rest."

"Oh, but I have to stay backstage," Sheila said, pitying her lack of understanding of the way show business worked. "It would never do for members of the cast to be wandering about front of house, now would it? But it's great you'll be there. It'd never do not to be, actually. This one really is madly important, it's not just to raise money, you see, it's the publicity that'll help us get even more money. They're sending a TV crew, they say, because of all the big names we've got!" And she went twittering away to sell more tickets, leaving George feeling as though somehow she'd been made a fool of, and having to face the unpalatable fact that if she had, she'd done it herself.

All around her the place hummed with chatter as people came drifting in and greeted each other and changed seats to be with their friends and fussed over programs. The audience split into two obvious groups: the outsiders dragged in by members of the charity committee who had bullied and cajoled them for months, which included people who wanted to be on good terms with the hospital—suppliers of goods and services, local GPs and others of that ilk; and those who were part of the hospital and who had been even more strongly bullied and nagged by committee members to support the event. A few rows behind her Jerry and Jane sat with their heads together giggling, and around her there was a scatter of uniforms from all parts of the hospital: nurses and physios, porters and orderlies, and even a few patients in dressing gowns and slippers. It was certainly an egalitarian affair, George thought, which has to be some sort of comfort. At least it'll be interesting looking at the audience, even if the show itself is cruddy. Which she was sure it would be. She'd sat through enough benefits of this sort in too many other hospitals not to have a low opinion of their quality.

Behind her someone touched her shoulder and she looked around a little warily, wanting to avoid being seen by Toby Bellamy if he had arrived in the audience already, only to find herself looking up into his face. She was furious with herself because she felt her own face redden.

"So where's your little friend, then?" he said and grinned. "You might just as well have come with me, mightn't you? It'd have been no fun to sit here on your own."

"I'm hardly on my own," she said frostily. "The people who are taking these seats'll be along any moment, I'm sure."

He stretched his legs awkwardly and managed to climb over the seat beside her and sat down.

"That's Sheila's seat," she said. "After she's done her bit she'll be wanting it."

"No, she won't. You won't get her out here when all the glamor-pants brigade are back there." And he jerked his head to where a stage had been set up with red plush curtains at the far end of the room, which was the main canteen, stripped out and suitably rearranged to make a space that would seat four hundred people. "And anyway, these are my seats." And he patted the empty chair on his other side. "I bought 'em last week, from the chap who runs the catering department. He's on the committee too. So you see, you could have saved yourself ten quid."

"I didn't want to," she said still icy. "I wanted to contribute as much as anyone else—"

"Oh, George, do let's stop! I didn't mean to step on your toes. You really are very touchy, you know! No, don't look at me like that. I apologize, I apologize. I was rude, I was clumsy. God help me, I was sexist. I admit the error of my ways. I'll never do it again. Now let's forget it, please, let's, hmm?"

She sat silent for a while and then sighed. It really was all rather silly after all; such a fuss over a seat for a concert she didn't even want to be at; and she made a face and said a little gracelessly, "Oh, all right."

"That's better!" He beamed at her. "Now, do you have a program? I have, look."

She took it, grateful for something to cover her embarrassment, and pored over it. It was the usual sort of thing; several pages of ill-printed advertisements for local businesses, many of them offering special discounts for hospital staff; a page of children's names and photographs, all of whom purported to be fervent supporters of the appeal; lists of people who had to be Thanked for Making This Evening Possible. Then at last there was the list of items they were to see and hear: under the care of Richard Oxford, Famous Author and Lecturer who would compère, a well-known if rather second-rate TV comedian would tell them jokes; an even more second-rate pop singer would regale them with her latest hit ("I wonder if she can really sing?" Toby murmured. "Or will she be miming to a record? I hope so and I hope it's cracked."); and a couple of extremely celebrated actors would perform a famous sketch to do with photography. There was a magician; the hospital's own Choral Society ("God help us," said Toby. "I've heard them practising." And George, who had heard Sheila practising alone in the office said nothing but privately had to agree with him.); and what promised to be the hit of the evening, a shadow operation to be performed by a group of the medical students who were currently seconded to Old East from their parent hospital on the other side of the river.

"At least we won't get Classical Golden Alltime Hits on the pianoforte," Toby said and George snorted with laughter and pointed to the small print, which promised interval music by Chopin, Puccini and Mozart played on the piano by Mary Shepheard LGSM, who even George knew was one of the domestic supervisors who had been working at Old East for the past fifteen years, just to fill in until her music career really took off. They both laughed and at last George felt relaxed and glad that their spat was over. She really did rather like him, which was annoying in lots of ways but undoubtedly made life more interesting; and she settled down to enjoy the show.

Which was taking its time starting. The audience was getting restless now, and George glanced at her watch and then raised her brows. "I thought it was supposed to start at half past seven? It's almost eight."

"Mmm?" Toby had been staring across the rows of chairs to the far side where the Dean was sitting with a tall woman wearing a shapeless outfit in deep purple with a bright red shawl and a good deal of heavy folk-design jewelry hanging about her person, and Matthew Herne, whose companion was a woman so well dressed and glossy that even from this distance she looked like a catwalk model. Sitting beside her, and looking as striking as ever, Felicity Oxford sat very upright, wearing the starkest of high-necked black with white flowers twisted into her great rich bun of hair. She looked spectacular; George had noticed her as soon as she'd come in, and been amused to see how many pairs of eyes followed her every movement.

She had also wondered how someone as handsome and clearly capable as Felicity could even begin to tolerate the likes of Richard Oxford. She'd tried not to think about the man since he'd barged into her office all those weeks ago, but now, looking across at his wife's serene face (was it too studied and controlled a serenity? It was hard to tell at this distance), she wondered again. Well, who could ever say what attracted a woman to a man who was essentially a pig? Hadn't she herself been ears and elbows in love with that bastard Ian—

Hurriedly she dragged her mind from that dangerous road and said, "They're running late."

Toby jumped and turned to look at her. "What did you say?"

"It's getting late." George tapped her watch. "They'll be slow clapping any moment." Even before the words were out of her mouth someone right at the back began to stamp rhythmically on the floor and in a matter of moments the low chant had started, ragged at first but gaining strength. "Why are we waiting, oh, why-hy are we waiting…"

Toby peered at his own watch and then looked back at the people behind. The chant was spreading now and some of the audience was shushing the complainers. The edginess showed the two different groups of the audience clearly; people from outside were being polite and well behaved about the delay. It was hospital staff, the younger ones, who were being restless and rowdy, and at the front of the audience the Dean stood up and looked back in a minatory manner. But it made no difference, for the lighting was such that it wasn't easy to recognize the people in the back rows and this emboldened them. The noise went on.

The Dean went hurrying over to the side of the stage, peered around the curtain there and then disappeared behind it, and someone at the back shouted, "Hell, if he's singing, I'm not waiting!" which got a louder laugh than it deserved.

The curtain trembled, moved and half opened. The Dean stepped out. A loud ironic cheer greeted him and, by holding up both hands, in one of which was a radio microphone, he appealed for quiet as the lights flickered, increased and then faded in the main hall and came up in front of the curtain. He looks devilish, George found herself thinking as the glare from the footlights accentuated the bones of his face and made the eye-ridges look over-developed and the eyes deep and dark. But then the light changed again and it was possible to see him properly. He looked concerned without being over-anxious, and at the same time competent and in control. It was as though his very pose and facial expression were capable of bringing order out of chaos, peace out of uproar.

And indeed he did seem to have enough authority for that; the sound died down and the audience sat expectantly as he lowered his hands and spoke into the microphone.

"Ladies and gentlemen, we do regret the delay in starting this evening's performance. There's been a small hiccup—well, we imagine so. Unfortunately, our master of ceremonies, Mr. Richard Oxford, has been detained and, much to everyone's regret, is unable to be with us at the moment. So we feel we must, albeit sadly, start without him and hope that perhaps he'll be able to join us later. Now, you all have your programs, so you won't need me to tell you who everyone is and what they're doing. We'll leave it, as I'm sure you'll want me to, to the great talents who have come to help us tonight to entertain us and raise much-needed funds with no more introduction than this…" And he began to clap his hands. After a moment the audience joined in as the Dean walked backwards to the side of the stage, still clapping, and jumped down with a nicely lissom air as the curtains parted and the comedian came on to stamps and whistles and shouts.

"If they can do without him now, why did they ever ask him in the first place?" Toby muttered into George's ear. "Stupid old sod's probably sprawling at home drunk again and forgot he was due here at all."

"Does he drink that much then?" George whispered as the comedian held up his hands for attention and the noise died down. "Enough to lose his memory?"

Toby shrugged. "I don't know. Maybe. I was just guessing."

He turned his attention to the stage and George, glancing at his profile in the light from it, was puzzled. He'd said that Oxford was at home drunk with such conviction she'd been startled. When they'd talked in the pub that evening after the meeting on her first day at Old East, he'd been very entertaining about all the people in the Board Room but had said nothing about Richard Oxford. She had assumed then he knew nothing more about him than she did herself, but just now he had sounded as though he knew the man intimately. She should have asked him after Oxford came to see her. She hadn't because first she wasn't sufficiently interested in the man to talk about him, and second because she had in a strange way been embarrassed by him. Silly really, she thought, and tried to pay attention to the comedian instead of thinking about Oxford.

Her attention flagged rapidly, though most of the audience seemed to find him hilarious beyond measure, for they laughed and applauded a good deal. She began to watch the spectators instead, as she had promised herself she would. They were much more interesting.

She looked at the woman beside the Dean, glittering a little as light caught her profusion of silver and gold jewelry and thought, I know her face from somewhere. I wonder who she is? Then she was distracted by movements at the side of the stage, which she could see just beyond their profiles. The side curtains were twitching and someone came out and went quickly up the side of the audience to disappear through the big door at the back, followed by another little flutter of the curtain as someone else peeped out and stepped back. Still looking out for Oxford, she guessed, and then as the laughter rose again to greet one of the comedian's blue jokes, couldn't help it. Not thinking about Oxford was impossible. "Do you suppose he's ill?" she whispered to Toby.

"What?" Toby seemed vague and blinked at her. "This bloke? He's not very funny but I don't think you could blame it on any sort of pathology—"

"Idiot! I mean Oxford. Does he have any health problems? Heart or something? He's got a rather puffy look. I thought when I talked to him that—"

Toby looked away. "Couldn't say," he said and began to applaud as the comedian told one more sexy joke and bowed his way off stage so that he could come back and be applauded even more loudly. "I know nothing about the man."

"Oh, I thought perhaps you did. You sounded so certain about him being drunk."

"Well, it's a reasonable guess," Toby said vaguely and shook his head in disgust. "This so-called comic really is the worst ever, isn't he? Here's hoping the next act's a bit better. What is it?" He took the program from her lap and began to read it.

The pop singer appeared and talked at some length and almost totally incomprehensibly about her "noo' single, a pronunciation which sounded interestingly exotic in the middle of a speech made in an impeccable cockney accent, while a great deal of amplifying and noise-making machinery was set up behind her. Then she launched herself into a very loud rendition of said single, which George found painful to listen to, unlike the back rows of the audience who shouted approvingly to accompany her. Beside her Toby sat and stared, seeming not to be listening; a remarkable feat, George thought drily, considering how the place was shaking. Not until the singer had finished her first song and was bowing to the applause which, though it was abandoned and enthusiastic, came as a relief, could she speak to him again.

"I get the feeling there's a considerable drama going on," she said. "Someone went out a while ago from backstage and just came back and then someone else came out to talk to the Dean and he's gone off. I wonder what's happening?"

"Maybe he's going to take over the show," Toby said. "Will you put your hands together for our next act, ladies and gentlemen, Our own, your own, your very own, the one and only Professor Charles Dieter FRCP and half the rest of the alphabet, who will now enthral you with his account of the structure and function of the Bundle of Hiss in healthy hearts as examined in vivo, the wonder of the century, the performance of the age! Roll up. Roll up!"

"Well, if you're just going to be silly," George said. "I won't bother to mention anything else I happen to notice."

"I think I know why you're a pathologist," Toby said as the singer on stage started on a high-pitched and apparently heart-rending ballad which at least had the virtue of being only half as loud as its predecessor.

George said, "Oh?" blankly and someone in front of them looked over her shoulder and Toby hissed at her, enjoining silence. But when the applause came at last at the end of the song she nudged him and said, "Why?"

"Why what?"

"Why am I a pathologist?"

"Hmm?"

"You said you knew why."

"Oh. Yes. Because you're so damned nosy. You have to know everything that's going on, right? Me, I watch the show, for what it's worth, but you, you watch what's going on on the sidelines. Interested in the happenings behind the scenes, more than in what you can see on the stage."

The singer started again, this time accompanied by the hospital choir, with Sheila standing bang in the middle and mouthing her words very clearly as she beamed with the brightest of gazes at the audience, and George sat staring unseeingly at the pop singer in the tight black leather skirt that barely covered her buttocks and felt a little frisson of pleasure. This man was more than just good to look at and physically interesting. He actually was perceptive, despite his unpleasant remarks yesterday. He had of course assessed her with total accuracy. She had always been more interested in what was hidden than what was visible. Her mother had despaired of her when, as a five-year-old, she had cried at the death of her pet rabbit, not because the creature had turned up its paws, but because she wasn't permitted to cut it up and look at its insides. She'd always been like this over everything, more interested in snooping into restaurant kitchens than in the food they put in front of her, more fascinated by the machinery of a vehicle than the way it performed. And he'd realized that. She felt warm; and needed to say so.

"You're a clever bastard," she said, as soon as the singing stopped and the pop singer went off stage to loud cheers, leaving the choir to shout its composite head off with great energy for the next three numbers. "You notice more than you want people to think you do."

He laughed, looking at her sideways. "Got you bang to rights, did I, guv'nor? Thought so. But it's not that difficult. There're really only two reasons why people go into your specialty."

"Indeed?" She was defensive. "Is that so? Do tell me."

"Because they're women."

"Because—Are you just being a shit again?" Some of the pleasure in him diminished. "Using cheap digs and—"

"Not at all! I'm just being observant and practical. Women like the specialty if they have kids. It's one of the few that never gets you out of bed in the middle of the night, and works office hours. Like dermatology. That's the other cushy option. So, women go for it—"

"You're wrong on one count for a start," she said, suppressing her memory of what she'd told Kate Sayers yesterday about the paucity of night calls in her specialty. "It does get you out of bed at any time. Murders need a forensic pathologist on the spot and murders show up outside office hours. I was called out in the wee small hours in Inverness dozens of times. It hasn't happened here yet, but I've no doubt it will."

The audience was moving, standing up to go for drinks and cigarettes as the interval took over, and he stood up too as she led the way out of their row. "I didn't know that," he said. "That you're forensic. Was your predecessor?"

"Yes. The posts here always have been combined. Because of being near the river, I was told. Lots of funny deaths. Well, if not lots exactly, certainly more than average."

"I can't remember working in a hospital where the pathologist was also the police one."

"There! An interesting experience for you."

"No need to be patronizing! After all, why should I know? You never told me."

"Why should I? You never asked me. So I never said."

"Murders." He stood still for a while as other people, laughing and chattering happily about the singer and rather rudely about the choir, eddied around them, and she looked up to see him staring at her with an appraising look.

"Does that bother you? Some people find it a complete turn-off"

"No," he said after a moment. "Not a turn-off at all. You're good company, George, and I could get very attached to you, stink of formaldehyde or not. It's just that I didn't know—"

"Does it make a difference, knowing that I'm a part of the legal structure and the police state?" she said lightly.

He thought about that with apparent seriousness. "I never thought of the job that way," he said. "Police state..."

"Oh, of course not, klutz! I was making a bad joke. But I do have to work with the police if there's a murder. I thought there'd be a few more down here than we had in Scotland, but in fact we've had none yet. A few suicides and suspicious deaths that turned out to be accidents or natural causes, you know? But a real murder—nothing of that sort yet. You never know, though."

There was a little flurry of people as someone came pushing towards them through the crowd, and it parted, a little unwillingly, to let Professor Dieter through. He was frowning but his expression smoothed as he saw George. "Oh, there you are, my dear. A quiet word if you don't mind." He detached her from Toby, throwing him a vague dismissive nod as he pulled George out into the corridor. "Dr. Barnabas, I'm sorry to have to drag you away, but we feel—well, some of us feel—that really it might be as well if before we involved any—Well, the thing of it is that we were worried about Mr. Oxford. So unlike him to let people down, you see. He did the dress rehearsal yesterday, assured us all we'd see him this evening and when he didn't arrive—well, we sent someone to find him. His wife was most insistent we should. She was most concerned. And he's come back and—and the man's dead, I'm afraid. Lying in bed, looks perfectly all right but quite dead, according to Bell—he's the chap we sent. Experienced porter, you know. I don't suppose he's wrong. I'm on my way over there and I'd value your company if you wouldn't mind. Before we call in the police, don't you see? Which of course will have to be done."

He had started to move away, and she caught his sleeve. "I'll just—hold on a moment," she said and went back to Toby, who was watching out of the corner of his eye, clearly consumed with curiosity.

"I'll have to go. Emergency," she said quickly. "Sorry and all that. See you tomorrow, I dare say." She was pulling on her coat, which had been on the back of her seat, and he began to help her into it.

"Accident? One of the murders you've been missing, then?"

She stopped at that and looked up at him. "Murder? I haven't the least idea till I get there. But you never know."

5

There were blue lights flashing ahead of them as the car turned into the narrow street, and Professor Dieter spoke for the first time since they'd got into the car. "Shit!" he said loudly.

George peered at him in the dimness, amazed. "What?" she said blankly.

He threw a sharp sideways glance at her and grimaced slightly. "Sorry about that. Forgot myself."

"That's OK. It was just…" She looked ahead as he maneuvered the car towards the blue light and the figures she could now see in the shadows around the vehicles, and said, "I thought you said you wanted to see Mr. Oxford without calling the police? I mean, why should they be called? Is there anything at all to make you think—"

"I'm as much in the dark as you are," he said, switching off the engine. "I didn't call them. I understood from Bell that there was nothing at all unexpected, apart from the fact that the man was dead in his bed, and he came straight back to us, so why these people are here I can't imagine."

He was out of the car now and she followed him along the street as he pushed his way through the little knot of people with the sublime assurance of one who is used to having others always make way for him. It was enough to make them fall back until he got to the double arched doorway that led into the block where the Oxford flat was. There a tall and extremely young-looking policeman stood and barred his way. Dieter looked up at him sharply and snapped, "Please make way."

"No, sir," the policeman said. "No one to enter here. Sorry, sir. Are you a resident?"

"No, I'm Professor Dieter from the hospital. The Royal Eastern. I've come to see what has happened to my—to the man who—to Richard Oxford."

"Sorry, sir. Can't come in here. Not right now. The Soco's up there and—"

"Soco?" Dieter said.

George leaned forward and spoke in his ear. "Scene-of-Crime Officer." She looked over his shoulder to the policeman, and said more loudly. "I'm Dr. Barnabas. Forensic pathologist. Here you are." She held out the identity card with which she'd been equipped when she'd started her job at Old East. ("Just to make sure you don't have any problems getting where you've got to be, doctor," the coroner's officer had told her; and because it was a cold night and she had her heavy overcoat with her, she was able to use it, since it lived in the pocket.) She felt a small glow of satisfaction as the policeman looked at it, then at her, and gave it back to her with a slightly stern nod.

"That's all right, miss—doctor," he said. "You go ahead," and as she passed him moved back into position to exclude Professor Dieter.

George looked back over her shoulder at his outraged expression and took pity. "He's with me," she said. "Assisting." And after a moment the policeman nodded and stood aside.

They climbed the stairs in silence, though she could feel Dieter's anger almost as a tangible thing, and schooled her face. It would be too easy to laugh at the way the man was reacting to the wounding of his amour propre, if he needed to be so aware of his status, who was she to make life difficult for him?

The flat was on the first floor. They stopped as they reached it and she looked around. There was money here, no question. The lobby was as thickly carpeted and picture-hung as a private drawing room, and equipped with elegant furniture: a small sofa that stood with its back to the wall between two of the large number-bearing doors that led into adjoining flats, and on the other side a pair of handsome matching armchairs flanking a long table on which stood a vase of fussily arranged flowers. The flat door to the right of the flowers was wide open and a policeman stood just outside in the hallway. The one next door to Oxford's remained closed, but the other two on the opposite side were ajar, and the occupiers were peering out in some alarm; and as George and Dieter arrived a man in a dark suit beneath a black raincoat was coaxing them to go back inside.

"Nothing to see here, now," he said. "No more fuss at all. Sorry you've been troubled. Goodnight—do lock up carefully." And reluctantly the neighbors closed the doors, leaving the man in the raincoat to turn back towards the door of the Oxford flat. He frowned sharply when he saw George and said with a marked lack of warmth, "Can I help you?"

"Pathologist," George said briskly. "Dr. Barnabas." And again held up her card.

The man frowned even more and looked at her card and then at her. "Ah, Dr. Royle's successor, are you? Who called you, doctor? No need to have done that. Soco would agree, he's just finishing off. It's clear enough, no call for you; or you, sir." He looked enquiringly at Dieter.

"This is Professor Dieter from the hospital," George said. "He's with me. No need for me, you say? And who are you to tell me that?"

"Detective Sergeant Dudley, doctor. From Ratcliffe Street nick."

"I see. And you've already decided there's nothing here to investigate?"

"Oh, not at all, doctor." He opened his eyes widely at her in mock innocence. "Of course there's something to sort out. Two things in fact. One is what the poor sod in there died of. And the second is who the chap was that set off the burglar alarm which was what brought our chaps out."

"Burglar alarm?" Charles Dieter said. "There was one in this flat? Did someone hear it?"

"Not that sort, sir. It's the sort that's connected directly to the nick. A lot of the people in these flats have the system. A bell's no use in a block of flats, is it? Time you've gone around 'em all to find which flat's started the bell going, your villain's gone. And you've upset all your neighbors for no purpose. So, they have this sort and someone triggered it tonight by unlocking the front door without deactivating the alarm in the usual way."

He turned to George. "Not that we think he did any harm. The Soco reckons he had a key to get in, and came in as normal as you like. But he didn't know how to switch off the alarm, so it went off down the nick. Soco says whoever it was looked in the living room and the kitchen, then pushed open the bedroom door, walked in and stood by the bed and looked, didn't touch nothing and went away and locked the door behind him. Or her. But there's no way he or she did anything to the bloke in there. No sign of any trouble, for a start. He's just nicely dead. And no time for anyone to have done anything anyway. Soon's that alarm showed the patrol car was on its way here. They couldn't have missed the chap leaving by more'n a second at the most."

"It was Bell," Dieter said.

Sergeant Dudley quirked an eyebrow at him. "Sir?"

"Our head porter. Very good chap. Came to see if Oxford was all right, saw he wasn't, and thought he'd better come and get me. Which is why I'm here. But look here, how can you be so sure what happened? All this about your—er—Soco saying exactly what Bell did. How can he know?"

"The sergeant looked at him witheringly. 'Because he's a scene of crime officer," he said.—"Because it's what he does, 'n't it? Looks at traces at the scene, works out what happened."

"Oh," Dieter said and George jumped in before he could say more.

"Why is there a Soco here anyway? Were you so sure there'd been a crime?"

"Fair point," Dudley said. "No. He happened to be in the nick when the shout went out. So he came with instead of goin' home to be called out again if it was necessary. He's like that, Joe Sturridge is. Thinks ahead. Anyway, this time it wasn't really necessary. Ah—" and he turned as another plainclothes man came out of the flat.

"Right, it's all yours," he said. "Like I said, I don't think this is one for CID. I'll tell uniformed branch and they'll take over, eh?"

"Well, I'm here," Dudley said, with a slightly lugubrious note to his voice. "So I might as well make life easy all around. Perhaps you'd like to come in, sir." He had turned back to Dieter. "And we can sort this out."

Dieter moved towards the door and George started to follow. Dudley looked at her over his shoulder. "No need to bother you, doctor," he said firmly. "They'll get this chap moved to your mortuary soon as they can, and I dare say the coroner and you'll sort it out there, eh? It'll be a PM, of course, seeing it's unexpected. Or I imagine it will be?" He looked at Dieter. "If this chap—I mean, did you know him well, sir? Did he have a history of illness? If he's been seen by his doctor this past day or so then of course no need for any—"

"I didn't know him that well," Dieter said. "Not at all. He was a—a sort of colleague, if you like. Helping us at the hospital with a special appeal for the children's unit."

"Oh, yes, that." Dudley looked interested. "We're collecting for that at the nick, aren't we?"

"I'm delighted to hear it. Anyway, as I say, Mr. Oxford was due to compère a concert for us tonight and didn't arrive. So, naturally, we were concerned, and since he didn't answer his phone, his wife was most anxious. Said he'd never go out and not turn on his ansaphone. So I sent Bell to see what was what."

"Wife, sir? Oh dear. She'll have to be told, then."

"Well, yes, of course."

"Before she comes home. We wouldn't want to have her walk in here and be shocked."

"Oh, no need to worry about that. She won't be coming here," Dieter said.

Dudley looked at him sharply. "How's that? Not on good terms, are they?"

"They are on excellent terms," Dieter said repressively. "As far as I know. They choose not to live in the same place, that's all. As I understand it. As I say, I'm not particularly close to them."

"Interesting," Dudley said. "Well, we shall see. Meantime, as I say, perhaps you'd like to come in and explain in detail about this chap Bell coming here with a key."

George again followed and again Dudley looked at her forbiddingly. "Really no need for you, doctor. If there's to be an inquest you'll get your body in good time."

"Hey, I'm not that hungry for bodies," George said tartly. "I'm not hanging around out of some sort of excitement, you know. But, like you and your Soco, I'm here, and there's a good deal to be said for seeing a dead body in the setting where it got to be that way. If you don't mind, that is." And she looked at him with a dangerous glint in her eye. He seemed to recognize it for he hesitated, then shrugged, and led the way into the flat.

It was undoubtedly a rich man's home, George thought, looking more expensive than even the outside lobby would have led her to believe. The place had clearly had a great deal spent on it; the entrance hall was wide, so wide that it looked as though the adjoining flat had been plundered for space; and then she saw the second main door further along and realized that she'd hit a homer. This flat was indeed a combination of two, making it extraordinarily spacious. It was paneled throughout with very pale, almost blond wood, and the carpet was a rich Persian one that glowed in the warm light like a basket of jewels: emeralds and sapphires and rubies. Beyond the hallway, there was a long drawing room, and it was there that Dudley led Dieter. The furniture was big and soft and deep, the carpet was even softer and deeper, and the curtains and upholstery were in a very fine white leather. There were two or three large fiercely modern paintings on the walls and a great many flower arrangements of great skill, but the whole room was dominated by a pair of pillars that stood on each side of the vast double windows which looked out on to the dark gleam of the river and the lights of the buildings upstream. The pillars were gleaming even more richly than the lights, for they were gilded, and George touched the surface of one of them and thought, with some awe, That's gold leaf. It really had to be the most amazingly sumptuous room she'd ever seen.

Dieter looked around with a wooden expression, and the policeman said sourly, "Juicy, eh? How the other half lives. Begging your pardon, sir. Seeing he was a friend of yours."

"I told you," Dieter said a little absently, still looking around. "He was more a colleague. Hardly a friend. Good God, that's a Jackson Pollock!" And he went and peered more closely at one of the paintings. "It must have cost a fortune."

"If you say so, sir," Dudley said, clearly unimpressed by the tangle of color and line. "Now, if you wouldn't mind just sitting down here and telling me about the events of this evening as you remember them…"

George wandered off quietly. Out in the hall she looked at what was probably the kitchen door, hesitated and then couldn't resist looking. It was all she'd expected: an expanse of white and black marble, the most coruscating of chrome fittings and an array of kitchen implements dangling from a central bar over the cooker hob and the sink, which were in an island bang in the middle, that would have done justice to a five-knife-and-fork Michelin Guide restaurant. She closed the door softly and turned to what was obviously the bedroom one, and pushed it open.

Light was blazing everywhere, in the center of the ceiling which was completely mirrored, on an elaborate chandelier and in the many sconces arranged in extravagant patterns on the walls. The sconces were as golden as the pillars in the drawing room, their lustre reflecting softly on the figured silk that hung on the walls from floor to ceiling in deep oyster-gray folds. The bed itself, an extremely large round one, was dressed in the same color sheets and covers, and stood on a central dais over which a wide coronet, again with a coating of gold leaf, hung from the ceiling bearing floor-length drapes of translucent oyster tulle. The carpet again was the softest she had ever stood on and the room smelled faintly of flowers and herbs.

She looked around in disbelief and wanted to laugh. She'd never seen anything like it, ever, not even between the pages of the most ridiculous of glossy lifestyle magazines. It was like every harlot's fantasy rolled into one, she thought, and shook her head in amazement.

The bed was what mattered, however, and she moved across to it and stepped up on to the goatskin rugs that covered the dais to stand beside the bed and look down on its occupant.

He lay with his head turned slightly to one side, the face towards her, in the very center of the bed, large though it was. The pillows beneath his head were large and round and covered in oyster satin slips, arranged in a sort of armchair, so that his arms were supported on them as well as his head. The indentation of the head was such that it was clear the pillows were very soft, and she reached out and touched one. Down, she thought. Very costly down. Both hands were resting on the top silk sheet, in a relaxed and easy pose, and the pyjamas he was wearing, in a toning but deeper oyster, were also of heavy satin. He looked comfortable and undisturbed. If it had not been for the pasty yellowish color of the face and the half-open eyes which stared blindly up at the artfully arranged tulle drapes, he could have been merely sleeping.

But he wasn't sleeping. Even without touching him it was clear that this was a very dead man. But she touched him all the same. Hands cold.

And very stiff. She picked up the hand, or attempted to, but there was resistance. Rigor, she thought, and wished she had her equipment with her. She'd need to check the body's temperature as well as the ambient temperature to estimate the time of death, but till then at least she could be reasonably sure the man had been dead between eight and thirty-six hours. Yet it was too wide a margin to be really useful.

She lifted the covers and looked at the rest of the body. It too looked peaceful, with no signs of any undue disturbance. He didn't even seem to have tossed and turned much in his sleep before he died, if it was his sleep he died in. But why am I being so doubtful? she asked herself, staring down at the expanse of satin. It's obvious he did. We'll probably find when we talk to his GP that he had some sort of heart problem. He certainly looked pasty enough the last time I saw him. And she looked at the face again and noticed that the puffiness seemed to have gone. Well, she thought, maybe he had a good night's sleep before he popped off. That'd make him look as well as he does, and she felt a little giggle rising in her like a bubble. It was a tendency she'd always had, and needed to control. This was no time for levity.

She touched the belly and then one of the legs and they confirmed her original estimate of the time that had elapsed since Oxford had died, and then, after a moment or two of struggle, managed to turn him slightly to one side and looked beneath the pyjama jacket. There were the patches of bluish-red hypostasis, the post-mortem staining that was to be expected, and she let the body fall back to its original position, and stood considering.

Heart failure? It looked as though it might be. Certainly it wasn't any sort of carbon-monoxide poisoning; there'd been nothing cherry-pink about that staining. Another sort of poison? It was possible...

She pulled herself up and looked around the room once more. Why should she start to think this way? Was it that she wanted some sort of excitement to be found here? Could it be because of Toby's comments about pathology being a "cushy option?" Did she want this to be murder so that she could prove to him how important a person she was, and how valuable her job?

She shook her head at her own foolishness and looked at the table beside which she was standing. A crystal decanter of water and a glass, clean and dry. Nothing else. She considered looking in the drawers and decided she'd better check first with the sergeant; it wouldn't do to touch what she shouldn't, just in case prints were to be taken. Though he'd said, hadn't he, the Soco, that he'd finished? That it wasn't a job for the CID but the uniformed branch. No need for fingerprints. But still she didn't touch anything. Not yet.

She stepped down from the bed dais and prowled a little, looking but not touching. A bookcase full of Oxford's own titles, but with a few rather notorious erotic works tucked in among them. A small bar, open to view with crystal glasses and bottles arranged on mirrored shelves. How flaky can you get? she thought, looking at it. It's the sort of thing that'd make my mother look away in embarrassment, priding herself as she did on her excellent taste. This time George would have had to agree with her.

There was a door that led off on the far side of the bed and she opened it. The lights were on here too and the room blazed with brightness, for every surface that could be was mirrored. Of course, the bathroom, and she went around it, hooking her forefinger gingerly into the frames to open them: medicine cabinets loaded with all sorts of tubes and bottles. They would need to be looked at, though at first sight it all seemed commonplace enough. Vitamin pills, painkillers, athlete's foot creams, hemorrhoid treatments, cough medicines, eye drops, the usual detritus of a modern man's bathroom; and she closed the doors and was glad she didn't have to sort it all out. Or at least I won't unless we find something is odd about this death. But again she had to shake her head at her own unscientific thinking and made her way back to the drawing room. She left the lights on in the bedroom and bathroom. The GP when he came would have to see the chap, and he'd need light. Anyway, she didn't want to leave the dead man alone in the dark. An irrational thought, but there it was.

In the drawing room the sergeant was leaning back in his armchair, with the telephone clamped to his ear. Unsurprisingly, it was one of the most recent of designs and looked absurdly fragile in his large hand. "Are you sure?" he said and listened.

George looked at Charles Dieter who gazed back at her and lifted his brows in the sort of expression that pretends to be saying something but conveys nothing, and she looked back at Sergeant Dudley.

He was still listening glumly and then said, "Well, fair enough. I'll put a constable in overnight and you can come as soon as you're able. But if, as you say, you haven't seen him— mmm—Well, I'll speak to you tomorrow. Thank you, doctor. Goodnight."

He hung up and looked at George. "Looks like one for you after all, doctor," he said. "That was the GP. We found the number on his list." He lifted up the white leather-bound book he had in one hand. "Says he hasn't seen Oxford as a patient for over a year, that he knows nothing at all about his health on account of the fact the man insisted on taking himself to fancy Harley Street types who never write letters and there's no way he's coming out at this time of night to see a body that wouldn't see him when it was alive. No point, he says, seeing as he couldn't sign the certificate anyway. But he'll come tomorrow for the look of it. Maybe. So there you are. We'll have to get him shifted after that to you, right? And then you can tell us what he died of. Or tell the coroner, that is."

"Fair enough," George said. "The sooner the better. Tomorrow's a fairly full day. I'll book it in anyway. Meanwhile, has anyone checked all that stuff in the bathroom?"

"What stuff?"

"Oh, pills and potions of all sorts. Herbal mixtures, cough stuff, skin creams—it's all there. Someone ought to check, just in case."

He looked at her for a long moment and then shook his head. "Let's wait to see what your PM shows us, eh, doctor? Then we can start worrying ourselves over the bathroom, if it's really necessary. Well, thank you, Professor. No need to bother you again. I'll have to talk to your man Bell, of course, just to keep it all tidy, but it's clear enough. The man went to bed after setting his burglar alarm, died in his sleep, and the good doctor here'll let us know why in due course, and Bell set off the alarm when he came to see why the fella wasn't with you as promised. The wife gave him the key, so it's all above board. Now, I suppose it's the matter of the wife. Shall I tell her, or…" And he looked invitingly at Charles Dieter.

He sighed. "I suppose I will," he said unwillingly. "Better me than a—Well, better me, perhaps."

"Yes, well," the policeman said, a little nettled. "We're trained, of course. But I dare say you'll do it better than an ordinary copper like me, hmm? Well, goodnight to you both. We'll look forward to getting your report, doctor."

"You shall have it," George said and then stopped suddenly and said, "I'd better go and switch the lights off in the bedroom. No need to leave them burning all night."

"Yes," Dudley said, turning back to the Professor. "By all means. Professor, there's just the matter of phone numbers. I'd better have contact numbers, if you don't mind."

George went into the bedroom again, walked straight through to the bathroom, and put her hand around the door to switch off, though she remembered to use her handkerchief over her fingers before she did it. After all, you never knew…

She came back to the bedroom to do the same there. But on the way she stopped and stepped up on to the dais again to look down on the dead man. She didn't know why, or even whether she was looking for something, but felt the need to do it. She let her gaze move across the pallid rather thick-looking skin, the half open eyes, the rigid muscles just showing under the pouched neck, and then turned to leave.

And yelled. Standing at the door of the bedroom was a man in a track suit with a sweat band around his forehead. He was pink and perspiring and looking around the room as casually as if it were a shop he was considering coming into.

"Who the hell are you?" she managed, moving a step backwards. He was tall and burly, and for a moment she felt a shiver of fear. "If you don't go at once I'll shriek the place down. There's a policeman in the next room and—"

He stared at her and then back at the room, and, moving easily with both hands tucked into the wide pockets on the front of his track-suit top, walked calmly forward. And she stared at him with dilated eyes and did the only thing she could.

She screamed at the top of her voice.

6

She didn't hear them come running because of the thickness of the carpets everywhere and for a sick moment she thought he was going to come directly towards her where she still stood beside the dead man. She was deeply, genuinely frightened. He was a big man with heavy muscles on his legs and chest and arms, clearly visible through the soft damp fabric of his track suit, and there was a smell of power about him that made her own muscles harden with tension. But he bypassed her and went to the other side of the bed to stand and look down on Oxford, just as Dudley and Dieter arrived breathlessly at the bedroom door, with the uniformed man who had been outside the front door right behind them.

"What the devil—" Dudley was shouting and then he stopped short as he saw the man beside the bed. "Oh," he said.

George stared at him and then at the interloper. "For God's sake, do something! This guy just walks in here and—"

"Evening, Guv," Dudley said and looked over his shoulder at the uniformed man. "You go back to your place," he said curtly. "No right to leave it."

The young policeman looked sweaty and anxious. "I thought it'd be all right, sir, seeing it's—"

"You heard me," Dudley said curtly. The young policeman took off his helmet, shook his head, rubbed his damp face, put it on again and went, and Dudley turned back towards George.

"Jesus Christ!" she shouted. "What's the matter with you? Is this the way you always run things? Let anyone wander in and then—"

"This is Dr. Barnabas, Guv," Dudley said, not looking at her. "Took over from Dr. Royle. This is Detective Chief Inspector Hathaway, doctor."

She turned her head and glared at the man in the track suit and he looked back at her with a cheerful grin.

"Never thought a pathologist'd get so uptight, even if said pathologist was a female," he said. "Glad to meet you, Dr. Barnabas."

"Do you always work in that sort of plain clothes?" she said icily. "It's no wonder you startled me. It's not what you'd normally expect to see at the scene of a crime."

"Crime?" Dudley said and came forward. "No crime here, doctor. We agreed, didn't we? It's just a run-of-the-mill affair."

"You had a Soco here," she retorted. "Which surely suggests—"

"Simply that we were doing what we should," Dudley said smoothly and looked again at the man in the track suit. "Burglar alarm went, Guv, we came, found the body, took no chances. But it's all sorted. We know the whys and wherefores, and once Doctor here does her PM at Old East tomorrow we'll have a cause of death too. All straight up."

George was furious. That she'd made a fool of herself by overreacting was bad enough, but it was worse to have to put up with this sort of unspoken rudeness from goddamn cops; and she spoke without stopping to think. "I don't know how you can be so sure there's no crime," she snapped. "Until I've reported on the body, you know nothing."

"Like I said, doctor," Dudley said smoothly. Too smoothly. "After you get the body over at the mortuary and do the necessary—"

"It's not going anywhere until I've done all the examination I want to do here," she said. "I've only been able to make a cursory one, and that's not enough. So you can send for my equipment, and I'll let you know when you can move the body. It's up to me and I'll decide when I'm good and ready and no sooner."

"Now, look here, doctor!" Dudley was nettled. "It's midnight! What do you want to go making all this fuss for when we can send the body over to the mortuary first thing in the morning and—"

"No." She was implacable, pleased to see the glint of anger in the man's eyes. She'd show them for making a fool of her, even if she had prepared the way by making such a stupid fuss in the first place. "Now. I don't care what the time is. Things have to be done properly."

Dudley opened his mouth to speak, but Gus Hathaway was too fast for him. "I think we have to listen to Dr. Barnabas, Roop," he said. He had a rough voice with a rumble in the bass and a decided London twang, and George found herself thinking absurdly, That's an attractive sound, and then glared at him.

"I mean right now," she said, daring him to argue with her.

"Then right now it'll 'ave to be, won't it?" he said amiably. "Roop?" He looked at Dudley, whose face was thunderous. "Send someone to Old East to pick up Dr. Barnabas's kit, will you? Seeing she forgot it."

"I did nothing of the sort!" she almost shouted. "I had no idea we were going to be dealing with a crime."

"*If* we are," Hathaway said and smiled at her with the same irritating cheerfulness. "No evidence at present, o' course, according to my lads. Still, we got to look, don't we? Yes. So off you go, Roop. No 'anging about. With a bit of luck we'll get this sorted by dawn."

George was already regretting her impulsive behavior, and, as she caught Dieter's eye and saw that he too was far from happy at the thought of the night being dragged out any longer, almost opened her mouth to retract; but she couldn't

do that, now now, and said only, "I can manage on my own.
You go back, Professor. No need for you to hang around." She
managed a malicious little grin. "Only these policemen here.
If that's what they are, come to think of it. I've been shown no
IDs, after all."

"Oh, for God's sake," Dudley said disgustedly. He turned
and went. "I'll send for your gear. In the lab, is it?"

"In the cupboard on the right-hand side of my desk," she
said. "It's always there for an emergency. As I say, we didn't
know that this was one."

"Well, you've made damned sure that you've made it into
one," Dudley said. "When there's no reason."

And Professor Dieter looked at her with a slightly
accusing gaze, and she lifted her hands in a sort of apology
to him. "I'm not saying there is now. Just that there might be
circumstances—"

"Well, I'm not waiting around to find out," Professor Dieter
said with a sudden brisk air. "I have a heavy day tomorrow. I
suppose you'll be able to get transport back, Dr. Barnabas?"

"No need to worry about that." Gus Hathaway had moved
from the bedside and was now sitting in a low armchair in front
of the open fireplace. "We'll see the doctor gets 'ome safe and
sound. Good night, Professor. Thanks for your assistance with
this matter."

"Yes, well…" Dieter said. He nodded at Hathaway and then
at George and went. The two of them were left alone.

"I'll bet you're sorry now," he said in a conversational tone
after a long pause. "Doesn't do to get mad, does it? Causes
more grief to yourself than it causes others, sometimes. I found
that out a few years back. But there it is, we all 'ave to learn."

"Don't you dare patronize me," she blazed in fury and he
laughed.

"Oh, come off it, ducks! That's the in word, 'n't it? Patronize.
Feminist claptrap. You got mad because you misjudged a
situation, and anyone could ha' done the same. You wasn't to

know who I was, so you made a bit of a bish. Well, there it is. It 'appens. It'd make more sense if you said as much now and let us all go 'ome to our beds, don't you reckon? Better than trotting out that feminist flim-flam. Patronize!" And he laughed, deep in his throat, a cheerful burring sound that again she liked. But her fury was greater than her liking for any sounds he might make.

"I see no point in discussing this," she said icily. "I have my doubts about this situation. As the pathologist on this patch I'm entitled to make my own clinical decisions. If I think it necessary to do an examination here, then do it I shall and—"

"Oh, we all know that. Try and stop you! I was just trying to persuade you to stop yourself. But if you don't want to..." He shrugged. "We can sit it out without any trouble." He looked at his watch. "Well, as soon as old Roop gets back with your kit, I'll be on my way. I only dropped in as I was passing." He laughed again. "That's why the outfit, ducks. I was on my way home after my evening constitutional. Saw the lads, had to pop up and do a recce, didn't I? Well, of course I did, you'll understand that, I'm sure. Seeing you're so keen on knowing the facts about everything, you'll understand someone who's got the same sort of attitude. Ah, here's Roop."

"Do you have to call me that?" Dudley growled, trying to keep his voice down so that George wouldn't hear him. "You know I—"

"Sorry," Hathaway said cheerfully and in full voice. "I forget. Here's Rupert then. Got the gear for the good doctor?"

"It's on its way. And so's Mike. He can sit in on this."

"Not you?" Hathaway said and quirked an eyebrow at him. "Thought you'd want to stay here with the doctor and see it through. It'd be a pity to miss out on the excitement, after all."

"What excitement?" Dudley said. "Anyway, I'm in court tomorrow, with the Hobson affair. I'll need all my wits about me for that. Mike can take over. He's on his way. He's picking up the gear as he passes Old East. Shouldn't be above ten minutes or so."

"Well then, we'll be on our way, shall we?" Gus Hathaway got to his feet and smiled at George, who was now sitting on the edge of the dais, her arms folded around her knees. "There's Bob Dennison on the door. He'll keep an eye on things till you're ready to go. Good night, doctor. Glad to have met you. I'm sure we'll meet again from time to time." And, absurdly, he pulled the sweat band off his forehead with a little flourish, as though it were a hat, and the curly hair that it had been constricting sprang out into a tight bush as he sketched a sort of bow. She glared at him and said nothing. They went, and she heard the rumble of their voices as they left the flat and went away down the stairs. It had been a long time since she had felt quite so sorry for herself—or quite so angry with her own impetuosity.

There really wasn't a great deal she could do with her examination. And the fact that she suspected that Gus Hathaway, if not Dudley, had known this perfectly well didn't help. But she did it, doggedly and carefully, as the detective constable, who had introduced himself to her a little shyly as Michael Urquhart in a soft Scottish accent that she found very comforting, stood silently at the foot of the bed and watched her.

She checked the body temperature first. A more accurate idea of the time of death must surely be useful; the rigor mortis assessment was never enough.

She thought carefully before checking the rectal temperature and opted for the deep nasal route backed up by a reading from deep in the ear, rather than the more common rectal one. It would, she felt hazily, be more seemly, and anyway easier than having to manhandle the body on to its front. Not for the first time she was grateful for the pocket-sized electronic thermocouple Ian had given her for her birthday last year; it made her work a lot easier, for using a normal thermometer in

these circumstances was very difficult. It was not until she'd
completed the temperature readings and carefully logged them
that she realized she'd thought of Ian for the first time without
a single pang, and was pleased about that. But she didn't
linger on the satisfaction; the examination itself was much too
absorbing.

She worked in contented silence, checking not only the
body's temperature but that of the bed and the room itself,
and photographing every step of the way. By the time she'd
completed her superficial examination and logged all the
observations and measurements of the degree of postmortem
staining, rigor mortis, and the rest of the minutiae, she had a
full tape on her dictaphone, a little pile of her Polaroid pictures,
and only a few unexposed films left. Almost on an impulse
she moved around the room, taking pictures of the bed, the
way the body of Oxford was lying in it, and then finished off
with pictures of the contents of the bathroom cabinets. All
the time she dictated notes about what she saw, and Urquhart
watched and listened to her in silence, clearly puzzled. But it
wasn't until she had finished and closed the cupboards and the
bathroom door that he spoke.

"I've never seen the doctor at a scene take the pictures," he
said. "Is this a new way of doing things?"

"I wouldn't take them if there were photographers here,"
she said. "But there aren't. They don't think it's necessary
and me, I'm not sure. That's why I wanted to do a preliminary
examination of the body here, instead of just waiting till I got
to the mortuary."

"Oh, is that it? Yon Rupert told me it was that you wanted to
show Gus Hathaway you were not about to be pushed about."

She reddened. "I never heard such stuff."

"You didn't?" He sounded disappointed. "I thought it would
be a great thing if she does, the doctor. No bad thing at all."

She finished packing her kit and looked up at him sharply.
"Why? Is he troublesome?"

He leaned against the wall, his arms folded, clearly settled in for a nice chat now he'd started. "Not exactly troublesome. He can be a bit sharp, if you take my meaning. Not to deny downright nasty sometimes, but then so can we all. No, it was just I thought…Well, of course, he's the Guv'nor, but now and again it's no bad thing for a man to listen to others, is it? But when we try to come up with the odd idea, it's a rare day he'll pay us the attention we ought to be getting."

"Ah," she said. "He ignored you?"

"That he did. I saw as clear as anyone that the lad couldna have done it—this was the matter of the robbery down at the bonded warehouse in Wapping, you'll understand—but would he listen? He wouldna, no matter what I said. But in the end when it was shown I was right, well, would he say I'd done right? Indeed he did not. Just said that intuition was not enough, he only cared for hard evidence. Well so do I, but there's a deal to be said for using your gut feelings, now, isn't there?"

"Yes," George said a little absently and then lifted her chin. Why shouldn't she try to pump him? He seemed willing enough to talk and there was no one around to listen, after all. "What sort of a man is he?" she said. "Apart from not liking hunches?"

"What sort? Well, verra full of himself, to tell you the truth, though I'm sure you'll no' tell him I said as much! But he is, and there's others'll tell you the same."

"Does he usually follow his own men when he's off duty? I imagine he was off duty tonight, seeing he turned up here in a track suit."

"Oh, he was off duty all right. But he only lives three doors down the street, do you see? So he couldna help seein' all the lights and the lads when he came home. I dare say I'd have come in lookin' about too, if it had been one of my neighbors that was involved. He doesna usually meddle when he's off duty, I'll give him that."

She lifted her brows. "I didn't know policemen made enough money to live in places like this."

He laughed. "Oh, they're not all as fancy as this one, these flats. This is a double one for a start. No, he has one of the smaller ones. But all the same, he does have a deal more money than the rest of us. Inherited a fortune, he did."

"Oh, did he now? What sort of a fortune?"

Matt grinned. "Fish and chips."

"Fish and…"

"I laughed too. We all did. And he gets verra verra verra angry when we do. But we canna help it. His old dad owned a chain of fish-and-chip shops all around the East End, and when the old man died the Guv got the lot. I'm told it's over five hundred thousand he came in for, and still earning. The shops are doin' fine, d'ye ken." He shook his head admiringly. "I'd no' work if I had that sort of siller, would you?"

"I don't know," George said, and tried to see the man who had so alarmed her when she had first clapped eyes on him as a substantial heir, a rich man. She couldn't. He was a policeman and policemen were never rich. "It's different for me, maybe, I love my work. I'd do it whatever happened."

"That's what he says," Urquhart said and sighed. "Me, I just dinna comprehend it. Are you finished then, doctor?"

"Mmm? Oh, yes. Pretty well." She looked around the room again and nodded. "I'll do the rest at the mortuary tomorrow. I'll call the coroner's office as soon as the body arrives and get the go-ahead. I take it you'll move it quickly."

"Nine o'clock tomorrow. After the GP comes over. Not that he'll be much good: not seen the bloke for God knows how long, according to Sergeant Dudley," Urquhart said with some briskness, now that the end seemed to be in sight. "He said not tonight, too expensive."

"Too what?"

"It'll cost more to shift the body tonight. Overtime," Urquhart explained. "Got to think of budgets these days, don't we? And it's not as though this was a murder, after all."

"How do you know it isn't?" She was combative again.

He stared at her. "Sarge said it wasn't. Rupert, he said."

"Well, he isn't the Angel Gabriel, you know, with a gift of divination into everything," she said tartly. "No one can say what Oxford died of till I've done my examination. Tomorrow. So don't you go jumping to conclusions. And you can save the GP an unnecessary trip too. If he hasn't seen him for a long time he can't help now. Tell him to send his notes to my office, please. First thing. Right. Are you going to drive me back?"

"We are. I've to call in to the station when we're ready for a car," he said.

"Call in? You mean there isn't one down there?"

"No need to waste a car waiting for us," he said cheerfully. "Like I said, budgets are tight. But he'll be back soon enough. You go on down, doctor. I'll secure the premises here and call in. I'll no' be that long."

She waited for him down in the street, yawning a little now, for it was well past two in the morning and fatigue was creeping up on her. Out here under an indigo sky blushing at the rim with the lights thrown by the buildings that edged the river, the air smelled fresh and clean, for all it was dank with the thick tang of the river and its sludge, and she was glad to breathe deeply and rid her lungs of the smell of roses and herbs that still filled her from the bedroom in the over-decorated lush flat upstairs. There had been something deeply repellent about it, once the first glamor of the look of the place had faded. It had had an air of decadence, a whiff of nastiness, that had nothing to do with the presence of a rapidly cooling body, and it was good to have left it behind.

She turned to look up at the building's façade and noted even more features that showed they were expensively built; the trim on the balconies; the tropical hardwood frames to the windows; the general air of not-a-penny-spared; and thought again about the unpleasant Gus Hathaway, he of the interesting voice and rough manners. She'd never had to deal with a rich cop before. It could be odd working with this one. She'd have to make damned sure that though they'd started off badly he didn't get the idea she was someone he could push around, half-millionaire though he might be. And somewhere deep inside her spirits lifted at the thought of coming battles. It was always more interesting when there was a bit of an edge to a working relationship, she told herself. She watched a car come around the corner, its blue light winking, with deep gratitude. It really had been one hell of a long day.

7

Everyone was early the following morning. When George walked into her office at half past eight Jerry and Jane were already sitting with their heads together chattering busily, with Sheila hovering around them, clearly torn between wanting to join in and her status as senior in charge, as Peter sat and listened, clearly fascinated but not deigning to speak.

"Good morning," George called and they all—even Peter—turned and looked at her expectantly, like children waiting for lollipops when their mother comes home from shopping, and she laughed at the sight of their eager faces. "So, what's new?"

"That's what we want to know," Jerry said. "We've been buzzing with it. We gather old Oxford's gone to the Happy Adventure Playground in the sky."

"There's no need to be offensive," Peter muttered and Jerry flicked a look at him.

"If you think that's offensive, wait till I really try. So, Dr. B., is there any news? Did you find out—"

"I have to ring the coroner's office," George said. "The body'll be here at some time after nine for the autopsy. Then maybe I'll know a bit more."

"Oh, Dr. B., don't!" Jerry got to his feet and came over to her, his head turned to one side in his familiar wheedling manner. "Do be a darling. Let us in on it. What do you think? You must have some idea! Did he get himself done over by a bit of rough trade? Or did he just expire of allround decadence and an overdose of ambrosia in his bath of asses' milk?"

She looked at him sharply. "Now, why should you get ideas like that?"

"You only had to look at him to see what an oddball he was!" Jerry said. "Jane and I thought so ages ago, didn't we, Janey?"

"Leave me out of this," Jane said promptly. "It's you does the talking, me who does the listening. You know that."

"Well, he did." Jerry was unrepentant. "He'd got—had—one of those spongy faces, you know? Hands much too soft and smooth, like he had a manicure every week, probably from some terribly precious lad in glitter earrings and lurex socks, and the sort of body that made you think he pampered it to the top of its bent. Am I right? What's his place like?"

George knew she shouldn't. She'd worked in Britain long enough to know that the hierarchical structure of hospital life was important. Consultants didn't usually gossip with their staff, even their junior medical staff (if they had them, she thought sourly), but she still had enough of the relaxed American style about her to find it hard to be aloof; and now she pushed the hesitance away. After all, they might have information she'd like to hear.

"I suppose I have to say it was on the decadent side," she admitted and Jerry let out a little whoop of triumph. "Or maybe it's just that I'm not used to that sort of—well, opulence." She described the flat, and they listened with total absorption. Even Peter gave up his pretence of lofty indifference.

Jerry sighed with satisfaction when she finished. "I knew he was that sort. He had to be. The clothes he wore…Did you see that suit he had on the last time he came to a hospital meeting, Jane? Sort of silvery with a sheen on it. One of those unbelievably expensive materials—mohair, is it?"

"Vicuña," Peter said unexpectedly and reddened as Jerry looked at him. "He's got—he had a vicuña overcoat too. I touched it once. Amazingly soft. Even more expensive than mohair."

"Maybe that was why he was killed," Jerry said. "For his wardrobe."

George looked at him sharply. "How you can jump to the conclusion that he was killed is beyond me. I wouldn't say that until I'd done the autopsy, so how can you?" And she buried the memory of her own conclusion-jumping last night.

"I can see it all," Jerry said with relish. "Picks up a bit of rough trade, takes him back to the flat, plies him with costly drink, chap gets above himself, takes a machete or a kitchen knife or some such to him—"

"Phooey," George said loudly. "He died peacefully in his bed, as neat as you like. Probably the night before last, going by body temperature and the degree of rigor."

"Oh, well then'—Jerry was unabashed—"some remote poison unknown to medicine. He picked up a sailor, that was it, and the sailor—"

"Shut up," Jane said. "He was a married man, for heaven's sake. If he picked up anyone it'd be a prostitute. A female one."

"Either way, what does it matter?" Jerry said. "And don't you jump to conclusions, Jane. Married men like a bit of the other sometimes, you know. They're not all like me, solid masculinity all the way through, with never a hint of anything nasty."

"There's nothing nasty about people who happen to be bisexual or homosexual," George said sharply. This was the sort of prejudice she loathed as much as she hated color prejudice, and it chilled her to hear such talk coming from Jerry.

He had the grace to look uncomfortable. "Sorry, Dr. B. I didn't mean it. Some of my best friends and all that. But you have to admit this is exciting. It's not every day someone as close to the hospital as Oxford is—was—goes and dies in mysterious circumstances. Let me have a bit of fun with it, do! It beats screening gut washings five times over."

"Apropos of which, you ought to be working," Sheila said, but made no effort to get the day started. She turned to George, her eyes bright with curiosity. "I suppose he could have committed suicide, couldn't he?"

"If he did, I don't see how," George said. "Until I do the autopsy I can't be sure of anything. But there was no note, and nothing beside the bed that shouldn't have been, either. A carafe of water, as I recall. Nothing else."

"It wouldn't surprise me if he had," Sheila said. "Poor devil."

"Oh?" George had turned to go back to her office but now she stopped and looked at Sheila with interest. "Why?"

"Well, it's her, isn't it?" Sheila had everyone's attention now and was clearly enjoying it. "She'd be enough to drive any man to despair, the way she goes on."

"Oh, magic!" Jerry said. "Do tell. Why? What? Where? What have you dug out, She?"

"Nothing that isn't common knowledge for those who have eyes in their heads," Sheila said tartly. "That wife, she's like a—a bitch on heat. Anybody's."

"She doesn't look like one," Jane said, giggling. "That hair!" And the clothes she wears—she beats him hollow. They must have spent a fortune between them. Did you see that thing she had on last night? That didn't come off any common-or-garden peg, believe you me."

"It was a Vivienne Westwood," Sheila said. "You can always tell. And I meant her behavior, not what she looks like. She looks all right," she added grudgingly. "No one could say she doesn't."

"She's a knockout," Jerry said. "Of course blokes go buzzing around her, what do you expect? Looking like that, and rich as hell besides. That's always sexy."

"I don't mean anything like that, either. I'm talking about..." She hesitated. "Well, it's the way she is with people. The sort she's interested in. She just sort of eats them up. I mean, I've seen her before. It used to be the Professor."

Jerry gaped at her. "Prof. Dieter? You've got to be kidding."

She shook her head. "It didn't go far. But she was after him, no question. I don't know what changed it but then she stopped. You have to remember I saw her a lot, both of them really, at the meetings and then the rehearsals for the show. Which was all spoiled." She brooded for a moment over that and then went on. "Anyway, it's not the Professor now."

"Oh?" George was puzzled. Hadn't Professor Dieter told Sergeant Dudley last night that he wasn't close to the Oxfords? Yet here was Sheila saying he'd had an affair with Felicity. Idle gossip, perhaps, built on nothing much in the way of real knowledge, like so much hospital talk? Or...She looked at Sheila and said casually, "Well, if it isn't the Professor, who is it?"

Sheila didn't look at her. "Toby Bellamy."

George felt a jolt and was startled more by that than by what Sheila had said. Toby Bellamy was after all only a friend, and a very recent one at that. He flirted a little, that was all, nothing to take seriously. But clearly she had taken him seriously; if she hadn't, why the jolt?

Jerry covered the hiatus with his excitement. "D'you mean the gastro chap who keeps on about helicobacter? He keeps sending me biopsies from his endoscopy clinic looking for it."

"That's the one," Sheila said. "Last night, after you went, Dr. Barnabas, and before Bell told Danny and it got all over the place that Richard Oxford was dead—"

"Oh," George said. "Then she didn't have to wait to hear it from the Professor that her husband had died. He said to the police that he'd tell her."

"What? Oh—no. Like I said, Bell told Danny and he told everyone." Sheila was irritated at the interruption. "Anyway, as I said, as soon as she heard, she came straight over to him, and the way she went on—well, it was obvious."

"What was?" George couldn't help it.

"That there was something there. She talked to him in that way people do, you know. Sort of close and intimate, and he listened with his head bent and looking into her eyes, and, well, you could tell."

Yes, you could tell, George thought. He talked to me like that. I rather liked it. Bastard!

"And then, when everything was over, she went on to the stage herself, would you believe it, and she said that her husband had died suddenly, and that was why he wasn't here, and she wouldn't want people to think he hadn't cared enough to turn up, that was why she was telling us."

"Good God!" George said. "She did that? Surely someone else could've—"

"That's what I thought. But who was there? Professor Dieter had gone off with you and I suppose she didn't fancy Herne doing it."

"She looked incredible," Jane said. "Just standing there in front of the red curtain in that amazing black dress with all the flowers glinting in her yellow hair—"

"She looks sort of buttered, doesn't she?" Jerry said and snickered. Jane ignored him.

"—and she spoke in a very dignified way and, do you know, people applauded her. Then she just walked off and put her hand into Toby Bellamy's elbow and he led her out. She walked all the way with her head up while they applauded. It was quite something."

"It sounds a bit theatrical," George said a touch spitefully.

"Oh, it was," Sheila said. "Amazing performance."

"I'm sure it was," George was sardonic now. "And then what happened?"

Sheila again threw her one of those sideways glances. "I don't know. She went off with Toby Bellamy and we all went home. No after-show party, or anything. I'd been looking forward to that, too."

"Never mind, ducky," Jerry said. "I'll take you out at lunchtime and we'll have a private party."

"I can imagine."

She looked at Jane. "Have you got those slides ready for Neville Carr yet? He wanted them for this morning's teaching round."

"Almost," Jane said. She slid off her stool, went back to her place and sighed.

"All right, all right, O Big White Chief," Jerry said and sketched a salaam. He returned to his own bench. "Ever onwards shall I plod with my helicobacters. Wish me luck."

"And for heaven's sake use a proper microscope," Sheila said. "You can't get the full definition on that old wreck."

"Don't say such things in front of him! You'll hurt his feelings." Jerry patted the microscope. "He never lets me down, you know that. And anyway, I haven't got one of the others."

"Then where is it?" Sheila said wrathfully. "You had one on your bench yesterday, didn't you?"

"I think so. I was using this one all afternoon. I imagine someone from the other lab must have come and borrowed it. They often do."

"They don't need to any more," Sheila said. "We got three new ones last month. God knows we had to wait long enough for them. I'll sort it out. Peter, those sensitivities are needed for this morning's clinic, so you'd better get them out of the way first."

The day swung into action as George went slowly back to her office to sink a little heavily into the chair behind her desk. The excited energy that had filled her when she woke this morning after only five hours' sleep had vanished, to be replaced by a deep inertia and a sense of emptiness, and that puzzled her. Because she'd been taught all those years ago by her mother that there was no sense in sitting wallowing in bad feelings, you had to think them out of the way, she pondered on that. And knew perfectly well why she felt as she did.

It wasn't that she really cared all that much about Bellamy. It wasn't like Ian (and again she managed to think of him without undue discomfort; after only six weeks, too! She must have a shallow heart, she told herself a little sadly) but it had been fun.

The thing is, she thought, I like to be admired. Most women do, she knew that. But for herself it was more important. Never having been one of the people at high school who got chosen for anything interesting in the cheerleader or prom queen line, she'd settled long ago for being labeled always 'the clever one'. To discover, as she had at some time in her first year at med. school, that some men found a lively intelligence attractive had been a great moment for her. But the basic uncertainty created by those schooldays spent in the back seats while other people necked joyously in the front had left its mark. Any man who fussed over her, she thought now with some gloom, was one she liked. Well, that had to end. She'd chosen a bummer last time, no doubt because she'd been flattered out of her mind, and she wasn't going to do it again.

Except that I already have, she told herself, remembering how much of a jolt it had been to discover that Toby Bellamy had a special thing going with Felicity Oxford. I already have, goddamn it. And I'm going to reverse it. That's the end.

And she looked at the clock and reached for the phone. Time to get some real work done. If she concentrated hard, she could do it.

The death, the coroner's office told her, had been reported to them and the autopsy could go ahead. The documentation was on its way, with the coroner's officer, and they'd be grateful if the job could be done as soon as possible so as not to keep Mr. Constant hanging about.

"I have other things to get out of the way this morning," she told them crisply. "And I can't start this job till…let's see, I can start at noon. No sooner."

"That'll be fine," said the clacking little voice on the phone. "Thanks for your help."

She hung up feeling irritated again. Why? They hadn't been awkward. It was she who was prickly this morning.

She settled to some of the desk work that she'd left from the day before, but she'd barely picked up the first piece of paper before the phone rang.

"Dr. Barnabas?" the voice said, a little thin and tense. "Er—George?"

"Yes?" He sounded familiar and yet...

"This is Charles Dieter. Are you all right this morning?"

"Oh!" Clearly his own late night hadn't agreed with him. "I'm fine, thanks."

"Well, what was it? Have you decided?"

"I haven't done the PM yet. I really can't say."

"Oh! I thought—when you insisted on staying last night—that perhaps..."

She was glad he couldn't see her. Her embarrassment was, she knew, written all over her face. "I just wanted to do all the necessary checks," she said as smoothly as she could. "But I won't have any firm answer for a while yet, I'm afraid."

"Pity," Dieter said gloomily. "I've got Felicity Oxford to keep informed."

"Yes," George said non-committally, remembering what Sheila had said about the Professor and Mrs.. Oxford. "So sorry."

"Well, can't be helped," he said. "I'm sure you'll let me know as soon as you can."

"Of course," she said. "The coroner's usually quick in his decisions." She sat with the phone in her hand for a while after he'd hung up. He really has been rattled badly by Oxford's death, she thought. To sound as uptight as that...Well, he'd have to wait for the PM like everyone else. And that reminded her. She jiggled the phone rest and rang down to Danny in the mortuary to tell him of the coming body and the booking for noon. He grunted and said he had to come up and get the register if she didn't mind and he'd get the details then, and snapped the phone down in a way that made her even more irritable. Ill-mannered creep, she told herself wrathfully, and when he did come in, an hour or two later, glared at him.

"It's him, is it, what's coming? Oxford?" He looked at her lugubriously. "Well, it'll make a full circle, I s'pose, seeing as he's been hanging around this place for years. Mortuary must ha' been the only place he never put his nosy old head into, and now he will." And he made that soundless shake of his shoulders that passed for laughter with him.

"Yes, it's Richard Oxford," she said, her head down over her work. "You can take the register. It's over there—and take my kit down with you, will you? I used it last night and it needs cleaning."

"So much for all his concern for the kiddies' charity campaign," Danny said, picking up the register and the kit. "He really scuppered it last night, didn't he? We was going to go around with the bucket to get some more cash, but after that wife of his got up and said he'd been and gone and died, there wasn't a chance." He sniffed rather disgustingly. "Just shows you."

"Shows you what?" George was too irritable now to watch herself. Normally she let Danny's outrageousnesses pass over her head. It was important to be on good terms with him and that meant not rising to the bait. But this she couldn't let pass. "It wasn't exactly his choice to die when he did, I imagine, and I'm sure if he'd realized how much it might affect the collection at the concert he'd have been more thoughtful."

"Well, yes." Danny seemed oblivious to irony. "Like I said, it could ha' fetched in a few bob. And even that'd help. It's not that it's growin' that fast, the fund, no matter what we do. Sales we've had, and sponsored walks to work we've had, and all sorts, and it never seems to grow by more'n a hundred or two. They got to be doing something wrong with it."

"No doubt," George said and let it go. What was the point of ever discussing anything with Danny? He made for the door, but before he could open it, Sheila was there, her head poking around the frame.

"It's too bad," she said. "No matter what we do, it makes no odds, it still happens. This one'll really put the cat among the whatsits, though. I mean, twenty thousand they cost, or so I'm told. Each of them."

"What?" George squinted at her in puzzlement.

"The new microscopes." Sheila came right into the room to stand there with her arms akimbo, red in the face with annoyance. "It took three years, I swear to you, to persuade them up in the office we needed them, and now this! I haven't had them more than a month, I swear to you, and now this!"

"What?" George said again. "You'll have to explain yourself."

"They've taken them back," Sheila said. "Would you believe it? It seems there's a fault in them or something. At twenty thousand a time? The man came yesterday, Barbara in hemo. said, took all three of the new ones, said they had to go back to the factory for checking because of some errors or other. Now here am I with a load of work and not enough 'scopes to do it. Even after the hospital spent all that money."

"What did you do before last month?" George asked.

"We were doing the best we could with the old 'scopes. Terrible old things they were, and—"

"And where are they now?"

"In the stores," Sheila said. "I think. They said something in the office upstairs about trying to sell them but I didn't want them cluttering us up here, did I? Not once I had three good new ones."

"Then you'd better contact the stores and see if they're still there, and pray that they are." George got to her feet as she heard a large vehicle stopping outside and feet scraping on the concrete driveway. "You can manage with them till the others come back."

"But they're so old and—"

"Jerry manages very well with an extremely old one," George said firmly. "So you'll have to do the same. I'll look into the matter of the return of the new ones as soon as I get the time. Right now I have an autopsy to think about. Danny, go on down. I'll be right there. OK, Sheila?"

Sheila looked at her a little sullenly, with an expression that threatened more argument on her face, but George stood and stared at her, and at length her authority won. Sheila made a grimace and went back to the door. "All right," she said. "I'll try. But don't blame me if there are errors and the consultants complain. It won't be my fault, it'll be—"

"Yes, I know. The manufacturers. Look, get out the paperwork for me, will you? I know the original stuff will be in the purchasing office, but we must have some sort of documentation here. Let me see it and I'll call the purchasing office and—"

"Don't waste your time with that lot. Asleep from June to January, and snoozing the rest of the time."

"Then I'll call the manufacturers direct. Either way, I'll sort it out. On your way, now, Sheila. I really do have to do this autopsy."

Sheila stopped at the door and looked back at George with a totally new expression on her face; a kind of awe. "It's one thing when they come in and you don't know them, isn't it? But it must be funny to do an autopsy on someone you've seen walking around alive not all that long before."

"It's never funny to do an autopsy," George said as repressively as she could. "But they have to be done. I'll see you later about the microscopes." And she walked past Sheila down to the mortuary to perform the last and most drastic surgery that Richard Oxford would ever have.

8

Danny was holding court down in the mortuary when she got there. He had an electric kettle and quantities of tea bags, sugar sachets, milk portions and biscuit packets he'd filched from the hospital canteen tucked away in his cubby hole and liked to ply visitors with his brews. Using the mortuary as a sort of café was highly improper, George felt, but she had more sense than to object to a time-honored practice; and if he could enjoy his tea while surrounded by deep drawers containing very dead bodies that was up to him. She had to admit other people seemed serene enough about their silent companions. The police and the coroner's officers were regular guests of Danny.

Now he was sitting with Harold Constant, the coroner's officer who most frequently attended at Old East, perched uneasily on his small table while he told his hair-raising tales of unpleasant autopsies at which he'd assisted. Harold, experienced as he was, looked grateful when George arrived and stopped Danny in full flow.

He scrambled down from the table and brushed biscuit crumbs from his chin. "Morning, Dr. Barnabas. All very unexpected, this, isn't it? Mr. Porteous'll be very taken aback when he discovers it's Mr. Oxford."

"Oh?" George's interest sharpened. She had to admit it was as Sheila had said, rather funny, in the sense of being odd, to be about to perform an autopsy on a person so well known to so many people around Old East. One of the bulwarks against the natural repugnancy all human beings feel when faced with evidence of their own mortality in the form of other dead humans is anonymity, she had long ago discovered. This body had none at all, and the thought of having to cut into the soft pampered flesh she had known in life, albeit briefly, was disagreeable. "The Coroner knew him, then?"

"Everyone knows—knew him around here. Very involved in the community, Mr. Oxford." Danny shook his head. "Quite a loss he'll be. He was always generous when he was asked to contribute to anything."

"Well, maybe his wife'll continue the pattern," George said. "I imagine his death will leave her well provided for, looking at their flat."

"Oh, it wasn't theirs," Harold said. "She lives right up in the West End, she does. It was his. Didn't you know that?"

George couldn't resist pumping him, and put on a look of innocent surprise. "Oh! That's a bit—well, it's not what married people generally do, is it? How could I have known that? How do you, come to that?"

"Oh, everyone knows it." Harold looked pleased with himself. "It's just you're new on the patch."

"I'd ha' told you if you'd asked me, Dr. Barnabas," Danny said smugly and George threw him a look but didn't answer. There was no point.

"Well, it's not quite noon, but I suppose I can start now. Are we ready, Danny?"

"Near enough," Danny said. "He's on the slab, and I've done up your kit."

"Right," George said. "Now, identification. You doing that, Mr. Constant?"

"I could do, but I've got a document here…" He dug into his briefcase. "His wife came to the flat this morning to do the necessary before he was shifted. So that'll be enough, won't it?"

"If you say so." George had changed into her cotton suit on her way down, leaving her clothes in the shower room, and was now putting on a heavy rubber apron before picking up her gloves. She checked her pockets for her dictating machine and the small Polaroid camera: they were there, of course; she'd put them there herself. "So we'll get going."

"Aren't you waiting for the police?" Harold said.

She turned back from the door to the autopsy room. "Why? You're here. That's all that's necessary, isn't it?"

"Well, legally, yes, but they told me they wanted to cover this."

"Who did?" She was frowning. Bad enough she'd caused such a fuss last night with the police. She really didn't want to have to face them again so soon.

"I did."

She turned and there he was, standing in the doorway and looking at her with his brows up. He was wearing a heavy overcoat over a crumpled blue suit. His hair was sleeked hard to his head this morning, quite unlike the bush of curls it had been last night, though it was clearly trying in places to escape whatever gunge he'd put on to control it. His rather round but well-shaped face looked rosy and healthy with the bite of the cold morning he'd left outside.

"Oh," she said and turned away.

"Morning, Mr. Hathaway," Harold Constant said with a deferential note in his voice. "We haven't started, of course. I was just telling Dr. Barnabas we'd have to wait for you."

"You weren't going to wait though, were you?" Hathaway looked at George who had pushed the door open and was almost through it.

She looked back at him coolly. "No," she said, letting the door swing back to blot him out of her view, and marched over to the slab and glowered down on the pyjamaed figure that lay on it. "Nerd," she muttered under her breath. "Creep."

"What's that?" Danny lifted his head from his own contemplation of the body.

"Not a thing," she said savagely. She stretched her neck and relaxed her shoulders consciously, before glancing at the clock and hooking the dictaphone out of her pocket and clipping it to the front of her apron. She'd had the case adapted to make that possible so that she could dictate while keeping her hands clear; she'd always enjoyed gadgetry of all sorts, and fixing this one had given her a great deal of pleasure. Then she pulled out the camera and checked it had its full complement of film and that the spare packs were set ready.

"Eleven forty-five February 26th," she said into the dictating machine and at the same time took a shot of the whole body. Behind her the door of the autopsy room opened and she felt Hathaway come in. Harold Constant was already in, at the side, leaning against the wall with his arms folded, and Gus Hathaway joined him. She saw out of the corner of her eyes that he'd shed his overcoat and had shrugged into a white overall, clearly wanting to protect his clothes from unpleasant smells. Huh, she jeered inside her head. With a suit like that, he's worried?

She nodded at Danny who began to remove the body's clothes and put them in a plastic bag. She took more photographs, of the whole body, of the head, and of the hands, dictating all the time and then looked very carefully, using magnifying lenses, at the skin to search for any evidence of punctures that would suggest he'd had injections. There were no such marks, and she made a note of that. There was nothing else to report at this stage; just the body of an over-nourished white male, aged... she looked at Harold Constant and paused while he checked his identity document and told her promptly that he was—had been—fifty-seven. Then the measurements. She always liked to have lots of these, even more than was called for in the usual protocol laid down for an autopsy, and she measured him from crown to soles, then the chest and belly dimensions and several more, with Danny's grunting help. He also had to help as she took samples from all the body orifices, nasal and throat swabs (could he have had a sudden overwhelming infection? Possible) and even from the ears, since she was nothing if not thorough, and finally a rectal swab as well as a sample before at last setting to work proper, pulling her trolley of instruments closer and picking up the big knife. From now on she had to concentrate even harder.

She worked swiftly, with big sweeps of her knife, as Danny stood by watching unperturbed ready with his dishes to take the viscera to the examination table, and whistling softly between his teeth. Harold and Gus Hathaway murmured to each other from time to time and at one point she looked up and saw Hathaway's look of distaste, just as she lifted the abdominal viscera into clearer view and away from Oxford's carcase. His expression was quite wooden but his mouth was set so firmly she could see a thin white line above his upper lip, and she thought with satisfaction, There, that'll show you! Though quite what it was he had been shown she would have been hard put to it to say.

As she worked it became ever clearer to her that this man had died peacefully. There was no evidence of any bruising, only hypostasis, the post-mortem staining that was quite normal; there were no signs in the carcase that there had been any gross disease. A good deal of microscope work would be needed to identify anything that might be there, she told herself.

The same applied to the brain. Once the skull was off and she could see it clearly there was no evidence of any hemorrhage or loss of blood supply to a particular area. Finer dissection would be needed to be sure of that, but certainly on first inspection he hadn't had a stroke.

The room was silent now except for the hiss of the running water on the examination table as Danny prepared it, and when she turned away from the carcase, having completed her dictation and her photographs there, her empty stomach announced protestingly and remarkably loudly that she'd had no breakfast and it was now well past lunchtime.

Hathaway grinned at her. "Take you out for a sarnie after, if you're good," he offered. She looked at him witheringly and got on with her work. Harold laughed a little uneasily and began to talk about the last case the two of them had attended together. Hathaway responded cheerfully enough. Clearly he wasn't going to allow himself to be put out by her display of bad temper, and that made her feel even more bad-tempered.

She went on, and slowly her heart began to thud against her chest in a heavy, dispiriting fashion. She really had made a considerable fool of herself. All the evidence she was seeing in this man's body pointed the same way. A peaceful expiry as the result of heart failure. There was no evidence of previous disease in the heart or any of its adjacent structures to suggest why it should have failed, but she knew perfectly well that that was not unusual. A heart can choose to stop simply because it is ready to stop; perhaps a fault in the conduction system, she told herself, perhaps a sudden immune response, who could say? She certainly couldn't.

At this stage. Slowly she finished: dictated the weights and dimensions of the organs as she dealt with each one; taking her materials for histology; making certain the body fluids had been collected; blood; urine; stomach contents (very meagre; he hadn't eaten for some time before he died); all of which confirmed her original idea that he had died in his sleep in the small hours of the morning after having been in bed for several hours, and at last turned away from the examination table and washed her hands for the last time beneath the running water before pulling off her gloves and switching off the dictating machine.

"Well, doctor?" Hathaway said with great geniality. "Can you give us a cause of death?"

"Heart failure is all I can say at the moment," she said carefully, not looking at him, and Danny let out an unexpected chortle.

"Like my Grandad used to say to me when I asked him why someone had popped his clogs. "'E stopped breathin',," he used to say. "'Is 'eart stopped beatin',," he used to say. Well they do, don't they?"

They all ignored him as he went on cheerfully replacing the viscera in the carcase ready for the surface stitching to be done.

"Can you find a reason for it?" Hathaway persisted.

"At this stage, no." George lifted her eyes to look at him now. He was standing with his head a little tilted, looking at her with a benign expression. "I can't. That doesn't mean to say we won't find out more when we do the histology and get the blood tests dealt with."

"Nor does it mean to say that you'll find anything even then, hmm? Could it be, doctor, the way Roop reckoned it last night? A simple died-in-his-sleep, nothing at all wrong with him?"

"Could it?—Yes, it could," she said after a moment. "But I don't know. And the reason I'm a pathologist is that I have to know. I can't do with mysteries. So far this death is a mystery."

He sighed. "Then we can't send Harold here back to the Coroner with the news that we've got a simple death by natural causes so that the inquest can be easy and the body can be released for burial?"

"No."

"Hmm," he said and walked to the door to hold it open for her. "Coming, then?"

"Ready to close, doctor," Danny sang out and she stopped. She'd been about to walk to the door, not stopping to think.

"No," she said shortly. "I'm not finished yet."

"Right." I'll go and get some lunch then, and see you later." And he went. Harold gave her an apologetic look and ambled off behind him.

It was quite irrational. She was furious with him for going off and leaving her alone to finish tidying the body and putting in the great surface stitches that restored it to some semblance of humanity, or would once it had a shroud to cover the great length of the incision and its black sutures. Why should he stay, after all? He'd been present at the important part of the autopsy and had discharged his duty—indeed, hadn't even needed to do that much, since the coroner's officer was present. So being annoyed with him was juvenile. And she tried not to think of him and Harold sharing sandwiches and beer in a riverside pub while she, positively hollow with hunger, still stood here dealing with his case.

What case? she thought then, as at last she finished and helped Danny shift the body on to a stretcher to be put in its place in one of the great rows of drawers outside. They said there wasn't one and I've tried to make it into one. I'll have to climb down, of course. They were right and I was wrong and there it is. Well, at least they'll have to wait for the rest of the tests, the histology and the blood and urine work.

She went back upstairs after showering thoroughly and changing, carrying her dictaphone and the Polaroid as usual. Sheila was coming from the main hospital corridor as she arrived on the ground floor and George handed it all over to her to get the notes transcribed at once, so that she could write her report properly and very soon, and for the pictures to be filed. Sheila looked eager as she took them from her.

"You were quick," she said. "I'm not that long back from lunch. What was it, then?"

George shrugged. "Can't say. Heart failure is all I've got at present."

"Well, that's it, then. He looked as though he might have had a weak heart, didn't he?"

"It's a perfectly normal heart." George flicked a finger at the pile of pictures. "Look for yourself. Nothing to see on gross examination, certainly. I've taken stuff, though, all through, for Jerry to do some histology. Oh, and the blood samples—Danny still has them. I want all the usual, tell Peter. A full blood picture and drug screen: cocaine, benzo-diazapines, codeine, and paracetamol, of course, though I saw no evidence—healthy liver—as well as alcohol. Opiates, though again no evidence I could find. No puncture marks on the skin, nothing. Looks like a very peaceful way to go."

"Hmm," Sheila said. "Can't say I'd fancy it myself. Not at his age."

"I suppose," George said absently. "Anything to tell me about what came up while I was downstairs? Because if there isn't…"

Sheila scowled. "I'm still trying to sort out this microscope business. I can't make out what happened. P'raps you'd better have a word with them."

George hesitated. "I've had no lunch yet."

"Well, not to worry," Sheila said gloomily. "I dare say tomorrow'll do just as well."

"Tomorrow? Why not later this afternoon? When I've eaten?"

"They finish early in the other lab," Sheila said. "Remember? It's part of the cuts in our finance. We were told—it was before you came—we were told we had to lose two technicians, and they all voted to stay on but to split the available hours between them. Dr. Royle liked it that way because at least, he said, we've got some bodies around the place when we might need something in a hurry."

"Oh, dammit all to hell and back," George shouted. "How can anyone provide a decent service this way? I've got no registrar, no houseman, I have to sew up my own autopsies when I've spent so many years sewing up other people's while I learned how to do it, and now not even a full complement of lab staff!"

"I don't suppose they told you the worst when you came for your interview." Sheila spoke with a gloomy satisfaction. "They're such crooks, all of them, aren't they?"

"You're telling me," George said grimly. "Everything short of having their fingers in the lousy till. Well, all right. Let's get on with it."

In the other lab the three technicians were busy over the input from the afternoon's diabetic clinic and the demands of Agnew Byford, who was doing a teaching round in his ward and sending down blood after blood with an urgent cry for an immediate prothrombin time. As a result none of them was in the best of humors.

"Sam," Sheila said as she marched importantly up to his bench, seeming to pull George along like a fussy little engine with an important express train. "Tell Dr. Barnabas what happened over the microscopes."

He sighed and sat up more straightly. "I've already explained. I don't know. I came in after our tea break and there was this chap in overalls, with a clipboard, showed me a piece of paper, 'marked receipt' it was, told me to sign and said he had to take them away. Fault spotted by the manufacturers. So I signed and he went away."

"Where's the copy?"

The boy looked blankly at her. "What copy?"

"The copy of the receipt," George said patiently. "You should have been given a copy."

"I wasn't," the boy said, shaking his head. "I thought he had to have one. That's why I signed."

George stifled any obvious show of annoyance at his stupidity but couldn't help speaking sharply. "It was we who should have had one, to show where three very expensive microscopes had gone."

"The manufacturers," the boy said, trying to be helpful.

Sheila looked scathingly at him. "Who told me on the phone they know nothing about them, and to check with our own purchasing office here. But when I phoned they knew nothing about it either."

"Well, I'm sorry." Sam sounded sulky now. "I meant no harm."

"I saw the chap," one of the other girls volunteered, seeming to find it necessary to come to his rescue. "D'you remember,

Jo? We met him pushing them along the corridor on one of the big trolleys, on our way back. And I said it looked as though someone else was getting new ones like we had."

"Yup," Jo said, not lifting her head from her work. "I saw 'em."

"So there it is," Sheila said triumphantly. "Zeiss know nothing about it, so they say, nor does the secretary in the purchasing office, and she was so unpleasant I'm not talking to her again, no matter what."

They all looked at George now, a little owlishly, and she sighed. "All right, I'll go over and see about it. Sheila, get that work in hand, will you? And you three, next time someone wants a receipt or a docket signed, for heaven's sake come and check with someone. Sheila or Jerry, or me."

She marched back to her office, very aware now of how hungry she was. But that would have to wait. If she wasn't careful the people in the admin offices would be gone before she got there. They too seemed to work very short hours, she thought with some bile. And the sooner this silly muddle over the microscopes was sorted out the sooner Sheila would be quiet about them. She really was like a dog with a particularly juicy bone, worrying away at the details until she drove everyone mad. This surely was just an administrative cock-up. Wasn't it?

She pushed open the door of her office and stopped short. The desk had been spread with a large paper napkin which was liberally decorated with pictures of holly and tinsel and mistletoe. On the napkin stood two bottles of lager, a large round pork pie and a plate of bread and butter. There were salt and pepper pots, a small dish of mustard and a couple of tumblers. Sitting on the other side of the desk was Gus Hathaway, his head back on the chair cushion and his eyes closed.

He sat up as she came in, rubbed his nose like a sleepy child and looked at her reproachfully. "Blimey, but you took your time! Thank God I opted for this instead of something hot. Come on, for Gawd's sake. I'm starvin'!"

9

She closed the door behind her quietly, using a great deal of effort to do so. She was so angry she wanted to slam it hard enough to make the room shake.

"Just what do you think you're doing there?"

He had started cutting the pie in half, taking a good deal of finicky care to make sure he was scrupulously fair, and he looked up, clearly surprised by the venom in her voice.

"Lunch," he said. "Fixin' lunch. I told you I'd get you a sarnie. Well, I went a bit better. These are bloody good pies, you know, none of your rubbish. Old Curly down the caff makes them himself. Not many do that these days. Come on, step up, sit down and tuck in."

"But…"

"But what?" He grinned cheerfully and pushed a slice of pie on to a plate for her. It looked good; the middle pink and luscious, the pastry fresh and flaky. Her belly tightened and she pressed one hand against her waist as unobtrusively as she could to stop the sound. "Mustard?"

It was no good. Her hunger was stronger than she was. She took the pie and the folded paper napkin he gave her and started to eat, not bothering to sit down, holding the pie in her fingers. It tasted as good as it looked, and as she used her tongue to catch an errant crumb from the corner of her mouth he poured a glass of lager for her and held that out too.

"There's plenty of room to sit down," he said. "You don't

have to be so formal, you know."

"Formal!" She managed a laugh at that, though it came muffled through the pie. "You call this formal?"

"No, not really. I'm just makin' conversation. And tryin' to get you to sit down. I'm getting a rick in my neck looking at you from here. You're tall, aren't you?"

"And you're very full of yourself," she snapped, her anger coming back.

He nodded. "Yeah, I know. Tricky really. I don't mean to be, but what can you do? When most of the people you're dealin' with are as thick as the proverbial, it's difficult not to be. You're not thick, though. You're all right. So you sit down and enjoy your lunch. You've earned it."

She gave up and sat down with a thump as he took her plate from her and put another piece of pie on it.

"Try the mustard this time. It's good. And the bread and butter. Got to eat your bread and butter or your hair won't curl. As you see, I've eaten lots of bread and butter in my time. Come to think of it, so have you."

"You're impossible!" she managed. "You march in here, take over my office, make outrageous personal remarks, you're the worst kind of chauvinist, you treat me like I'm some sort of object—"

"I'll go along with the first three accusations but I'm damned if I will with the other two. If we're goin' to have to work together a lot, we'll have to make a deal to keep off the feminist stuff. I'm as sensible as the next person about equal rights and all that, but I can't handle all that fancy talk. So, yeah, I marched in and yeah, I made personal remarks. But that's because I like to be personal with people I like. And I think you're all right."

"Oh, you do, do you? Then you've got a mighty peculiar way of showing it."

"Honest way," he said, looking at her shrewdly. "I could go in for all the chatting-up lines, couldn't I? Or get all smooth and fancy and suggest I show you around, seeing as you're new in London and all that. Or I could do what I do and say what I think. I think you're all right. I like tall women with a bit of meat on their bones. I like women with minds of their own. I like you. You've got something very nice about you, you have."

She felt the pink tide rising in her face and wanted the floor to produce quantities of thick smoke to hide her from his view. But he seemed unperturbed by her obvious embarrassment.

"I'll tell you something else. It's not easy to fancy a woman you've seen slicing up a person's liver like, well, like cats' meat. But I did and I do, so there it is." He smiled then, a wide warming grin that showed uneven, very strong white teeth. "Now, can we start again?"

"I don't—I'm not sure—I mean, goddamn it, you make me feel stupid!"

"Yeah, I know. It always happens." He shook his head, seeming genuinely puzzled. "Being honest upsets people something rotten. Amazin' 'n't it? But there you go. That's how it is. Now, how about some more pie? Finish it off, eh?"

She said nothing, just held out her plate. He nodded approvingly, slapped the piece of pie on it and they ate in silence for a while. She was grateful for the chance to avoid speech; she needed to regain her emotional balance after the battering it had experienced. Only a few hours ago she'd been glooming at herself because of the way she'd reacted to the mild attentions Toby Bellamy had been paying her and how she'd been mortified to hear that he had been paying closer ones to Felicity Oxford. She'd blamed her own insecurity as the reason for reacting foolishly to the men she met. And now this! It was enough to make any woman giddy. And it wasn't just the lager, of which she'd rather recklessly accepted a second helping.

"Now, listen, about this chap Oxford," Gus said. He pushed his plate away and, reaching, took hers to pile it on top. "As far as I can see there's nothing there to make anyone think there's been dirty work at the crossroads, right? You're goin' to have to sign the cert. as natural causes, aren't you?"

All her caution came back in a great rush. The bastard! He'd been coming on to her as a way of getting his own way. He thought he could manipulate her just by turning on the charm. Well, let him rot! She wasn't going to fall for that. No way. Nor, she decided swiftly as she sat and stared at him, nor am I going to give him the satisfaction of letting him know I've rumbled him. I can play devious games as much as he can. And play them in the same suit of trumps, what's more.

"I'll tell you what it is, Gus," she said, and smiled a wide smile so full of honesty that it brimmed and spilled over. "I simply don't know. It's that feminine thing, you know? Intuition. I have this gut feeling there's something not the way it ought to be. I'd have been a lousy pathologist—in real dereliction of duty—if I'd let you think last night that there mightn't be circumstances to investigate. I'm just trying to do my job properly, that's all. And that means I still can't say one way or the other about how this case will go. Not till I've got the reports back on the histology and the blood work. I'm real sorry about that, Gus."

He looked at her with his eyes slightly narrowed, and she stared back with a wide limpid gaze. "You wouldn't be sendin' me up, would you? Talking about feminine intuition and all that?"

"Good God, of course not!" she exclaimed, mentally crossing her fingers. "I'm trying to be as honest as you are. I just don't feel right about this one."

He looked at her for a long moment and then nodded and stood up. "I believe you," he said. "So we'll have to wait and see. When?"

"Eh?"

"Wait till when? Results and that."

"Ah! Can't be sure. The histology'll take a while—got to make the slides and so forth, do the sections—but Jerry'll get on with it as fast as he can. There's routine work to be got through as well, of course, for the hospital; and we're short-staffed—isn't everybody? But as soon as I can get them I'll call you. You have my word on that. And you have to believe I'm as honest as I'm sure you are."

He looked at her with that same slightly calculating glance and then nodded. "Fair enough. I'll get back to the nick then. Talk to you again soon. Very soon." And he flicked his forefinger and thumb against his forehead in a mock tilt of an invisible hat, and went, leaving her staring after him over the wreck of his picnic. And as coldly angry as she could remember being.

She headed for the admin block as soon as she'd thrown away the evidence of lunch (with some irritation; trust Hathaway to leave his mess behind) and had checked with Jerry that he had the Oxford work well in hand. She almost ran there; time was being eaten up today at a crazy rate; already it was getting on for four and Sheila had said the admin staff stopped early. She really had to get the wretched nuisance of the microscopes being taken back for repair dealt with today.

The admin building was quiet when she got there, the usual racket of typewriters absent. She hared up the stairs to present herself at the door marked Purchasing Officer Asst rather breathlessly. The secretary inside was busy at her desk, tidying her handbag, and she looked unpromisingly at George and said at once, "We're almost finished for today. Can you wait till tomorrow?"

"No," George said. "Must sort it out now. I'm Dr. Barnabas."

"Ah!" The woman got to her feet, reluctantly, but clearly prepared to show deference of a sort to one of the consultants. It was obvious she never stood up for any grade below that level. "Well, I told your technician, actually, doctor, these microscopes, it's nothing to do with us, if that's what you're here about. Really, she does make a pest of herself, you know. It'd be a blessing to us all if you could control her."

"Oh?" George said softly in what her own staff knew was a dangerous voice, but to which this woman, a thin and rather dispirited-looking person of about fifty, with a somewhat haunted air about her, seemed oblivious.

"Yes, indeed, when the microscopes were ordered she was here every week wanting a delivery date, as if we could do anything about that! And then when they came she went on and on about making sure the guarantees were all sorted out and then the business of checking them regularly, and now she comes nagging again! But it's nothing to do with me. I don't know anything about them going back to the manufacturer. If she did that it was her own affair, not ours—"

"She did not sent them back," roared George, for the first time feeling some sympathy for Sheila. "We know nothing about any of this. Someone came, from this office, I imagine, took the three 'scopes and got them signed for and took them away for a check-up, so he said. We want to know why and where and—"

"Have you got the receipt?" the woman said.

"Sheila explained about that!" George said, louder still. "The boy who signed it didn't know to ask for a copy and we don't have one."

"Ah, well then," the woman said, as though that were the end of the matter. She took a last comforting look in her handbag before snapping it shut. "Nothing to do with us."

George advanced menacingly. "If you say that again I'll—"

"Hey, hey, what's going on in here?"

George whirled and saw a man standing in the doorway with his brows lifted in polite but very authoritative enquiry. She tried to remember who he was. She'd certainly seen him around the hospital somewhere.

"I'm trying to get some sense and some help out of this— this *person*," George said and the woman behind her yelped a protest. "I'm Dr. Barnabas, from pathology, and—"

"And I'm Mitchell Formby." He put his hand forward to

shake hers and she remembered when she'd seen him before. At the meeting about the Barrie Ward appeal. He was the one who had talked about how the actual building and supplying of the new ward would be done once the appeal had raised enough cash.

"Yes, of course," she said as she shook hands. "Now look here, Mr. Formby—"

"Oh, Mitch, please. We don't use severe titles and labels here." He smiled widely. "So what's the problem?"

The secretary broke into a rapid babble of explanation in which Sheila and her rudeness and all-around tiresomeness figured large, and Formby held up a hand at her and shook his head.

"Now, let's do this in a logical order, May. Dr. Barnabas first."

"It's about the three new microscopes," she said, launching into an account of what had happened and Sheila's attempts to sort it all out, and his face seemed to darken as she talked and his forehead creased. Even before she'd finished he'd come around the secretary's desk and was reaching for the phone.

"I just don't know what more we can do," he burst out when George had finished. "I warn them, I tell them. I put up posters about watching out for anything unusual and yet it goes on happening. Oh, hello?" He spoke into the phone. "Could I have Tim Brewer, please? Mitch Formby." He waited, his hand over the mouthpiece, and looked lugubriously at George. "You realize what has happened, of course?"

"Like hell I do," George said, staring, as he shook his head at her and then spoke into the phone.

"Tim? We've got another. What? yes, mmm. I have the doctor with me now. From pathology. Mmm. What? I'll check—Dr. Barnabas, what exactly has gone?" George told him. "Right. Three of the newer microscopes. Yup. Three, no less. Mmm. I'll check." Again he looked at George. "When did they go? And remind me how." George told him and he repeated it all into the phone. "You see? Getting very cocky, aren't they? It has to be the same lot. Different M.O. I admit, but still—Value? I'm not sure. Just hold on, will you?"

He put the phone down on the desk and went across the office to pull open a drawer of files and go riffling through looking for one of them as the two women stood and watched him. He came back and picked up the phone. "Give or take sixty thousand. What? A big one? Oh yeah—yeah. Big enough, wouldn't you say? Mmm—So when—Oh. Not till—I see, I see. OK. I'll set it up."

He cradled the phone and stood there looking down at it, shaking his head.

George frowned and spoke sharply, more sharply than she meant to. "What the hell's this all about, then?"

"What it's about, Dr. Barnabas, is theft," Formby said, and sighed deeply. "It's the third we've had in the last three months. It was electrocardiographs the first time, then it was a pair of electronic infusion pumps from ICU. They were worth around eleven thousand. Then there were the endoscopes, flexible endoscopes, four of them one after the other, starting last year, the latest only just after Christmas. I told everyone, I put up notices…"

George bit her lip, remembering there had been a bit of a fuss just after she'd arrived at Old East. Things had been stolen from the wards, notices on the bulletin boards said. Everyone had to be aware, especially if they used costly equipment. But no one had paid much attention to them and the notices were still there, dog-eared and yellowing and as good as invisible since they were totally ignored.

"They've been stolen. Our microscopes," she said flatly. "Oh, shit!"

"You may well say so," Formby said. "Ye Gods, we know we're always going to get some wastage in a place like this with so many people wandering in and out, but this gear! It used to be sheets and towels and stuff from the kitchen and the occasional bedding—they're bloody clever in these parts, they can smuggle the biggest things out—but this is getting ridiculous. Those microscopes were almost twenty thousand pounds apiece! They'll make a hell of a hole in the budget."

"I've got to have them replaced," George said swiftly. "I can't work without them. The lab simply can't function without—"

"I know that perfectly well," Formby said. "We'll have to find it somewhere, though what Region'll say I can't imagine."

"No insurance?" George said and Formby let out a harsh bark of laughter. "Would you insure anything in this place if you were an insurance company in the business of making money? Like hell you would! No, I'm sorry doctor. It's clearly another theft, even more daring than usual this time. You say he made one of your people sign a receipt? Impudent devil! You wouldn't believe the brass neck these people have, would you? Well, as I say, theft, major theft." He sighed. "They'll be in in the morning. He didn't say what time."

"Who'll be in in the morning?" George said, confused.

Formby looked at her pityingly. "We have to call in the police, Dr. Barnabas. We can't just say, 'Oh, what a pity, someone pinched our pretties. Let's go out and buy a few more,' can we? No, of course we can't. Region'll want evidence of theft, and there'll be God knows what in the way of toing and froing before we get this settled, reams of paperwork—Oh the hell with it! Just when we're up to our eyes in the Barrie Ward project, quite apart from the usual workload. I wonder why I bother sometimes, I really do. It's the most thankless job in the world."

"Oh, Mr. Formby, but it's all so important! You said that to me yourself when I got so miserable about the way people talk to me…" The secretary began to snivel and he smiled at her a little absently.

"Well, yes, May, but don't you worry. I was just expressing my—well, there it is. In the morning, Dr. Barnabas, your staff must talk to the police. The chap who dealt with us last time—nice fella, Tim Brewer—said he'll be over first thing. He's a bit tied up right now, and anyway, what's the hurry? It happened some days ago, and another night won't make a lot of odds. It's hardly a fingerprints and sleuthing job, is it? Just a straight piece of knocking off no one'll be able to track down."

"But surely the police'll be able to do something!" George said.

He sighed and headed for the door. "The only thing the police can do is confirm it's been a theft, so that we can persuade Region to cough up the money for replacement. They can't till they've got the statement to put forward to the Department. It'll end up in some corner of Whitehall eventually, and even more eventually we'll get our cash back for our microscopes by which time the chap who pinched 'em'll be living it up on the Costa del Horrible and planning to come back for a few more bits and pieces so that he can furnish his swimming pool complex."

"And what do we do in the meantime, waiting for our microscopes?" George was alarmed. "We've got a couple of clapped-out old things—one of them belongs to one of the staff, not the hospital—and they're all right for some basic work, but for—"

"Oh, don't you worry, doctor." Formby stopped by the door. "I'll talk to Matthew—Mr. Herne—and we'll see what we can do. We've got an emergency fund, what's left of it after the holes chewed in it by the last lot of robberies, and we'll buy out of that. Then we can put it back when Region come up with the replacement cash. So you can sleep easy tonight." He grinned a little raffishly. "Unless one of your staff had something to do with the robbery, of course."

"Very funny," George said coldly.

"Just an attempt at a joke," Formby said. "Forgive me. I get a bit light-headed after a day like this."

"Well, you never know," May said spitefully, and went past George to stand beside Formby at the door where clearly she felt safe. "No one's exempt from suspicion and, in my experience, people who are rude to others are capable of anything."

"May, that's enough. You go. I'll lock up."

She threw a worshipping look at him and nodded. "All right, Mr. Formby. But you see if I'm not right. You said it as a joke but I don't think it's so funny. Trying to blame other people for things that aren't their fault..." And she went clattering off down the corridor, leaving Formby shaking his head ruefully at George.

"You mustn't mind her. She's been on the staff a good deal longer than's good for her, and she thinks she owns the place. Very protective she is, fiercely so. We understand her—"

"I'm glad you do," George said frostily. "Making groundless accusations against members of my lab staff is hardly the sort of behavior I'd expect from responsible administration personnel."

"Well, never you fret over it." Formby was soothing. "I'll deal with her. Meanwhile, do let your people know that Brewer'll be in in the morning." He turned to go and then stopped. "Or..." He turned back. "Look, I don't want to be silly like poor old May, but I have to say—well, you never know, do you? I mean it could be anyone and—well, forgive me, but perhaps it'd be better if you said nothing about Brewer coming, hmm? After all, anything that makes it quicker and easier to sort this out has to be welcomed. And making sure people haven't had a chance to—well, make up tales to back each other up out of misplaced loyalty could be sensible. What do you say?"

"There's no need," George said. "I'm sure of that. So sure that in fact I won't say anything just to prove to you how wrong you are. Fair enough? Then you can apologize." She too moved as if to leave and then halted, frowning, as a thought came to her. "This policeman who's coming. Brewer, you say..."

"That's it."

"Where's he coming from?"

"From? Oh, Ratcliffe Street. It's our nearest police station. He's a sensible chap, very sound. I'm sure you'll find him most helpful. He's part of Gus Hathaway's lot, d'you know him? I imagine you do. Or will do soon if you don't already. Dr. Royle and he were very thick, I remember."

"Oh, I know him," George said bitterly. "I should have known he'd be involved with this too." And she turned and marched out of the admin building leaving Formby staring after her in some surprise.

10

George sat thinking gloomily of how much nicer a chilli dog would have been than the concoction which now lay half-eaten on her plate. Spanish rice, they called it, though it was about as Spanish as rhubarb and custard, another of the hospital canteen's less than delectable offerings today. She was hungry, but not that hungry, and she promised herself that after she'd finished in the lab this evening she'd get something from the fish-and-chip shop she'd discovered down the Highway. A swim at the leisure center and then fish and chips over the day's papers in her room; that was something to look forward to.

"May I join you?"

She looked up and then gladly pushed her chair along to make room at the table. "Please do. How are you? Haven't seen you for an age."

Kate Sayers slid into the space and began to unload her tray. "That's not surprising. I've been so hectic I've not had time to come for proper meals. Not that I'd call this a proper meal. Ye gods, the food's gone nasty since they privatized it!"

"Is that what's wrong with it?" George said. "I thought they were using left-overs from the wards."

"It's even worse on the wards. Come and see sometime."

"I should get up to the wards more, I suppose. But you know how it is…"

"Busy?" Kate was sympathetic. "I know we are."

"Uhuh. Lots of blood work for local GPs, of course, and outpatients seem to be running on double time, but there've been four post-mortems in the last couple of days, quite apart from anything else, so I'm hectic on both sides."

"Both sides? You mean the forensic as well as the hospital's pathology, of course. How could I not remember?" She put down her knife and fork and leaned towards George eagerly. "You must have got involved with this Oxford business. It'll be a PM, won't it? Seeing he died at home on his own. Or had he been seen by his doctor in the previous fortnight? I got the impression it was all very sudden and totally unexpected."

"He hadn't, and it was. Yes, there had to be a PM." She hesitated. Kate looked friendly and cheerful, if a little agog for gossip at the moment, but then who wouldn't be? And it would be agreeable to have someone to confide in. She needed a girlfriend badly, she suddenly realized. It was a lonely life without one. "I did it, day before yesterday."

"So what was it? I imagine his heart and kidneys were pretty wrecked, hmm? He looked renal to me." Kate laughed and began to eat. "But then I suppose that'd be an inevitable observation on my part."

George laughed a little wryly. "Everyone's making diagnoses. Prof. Dieter said the same."

"Oh?" Kate was interested. "What did he say?"

"Just what you did. Not that we could talk long. He was following me down the corridor on the way to lunch and stopped me to ask what I'd found. Everyone has to be in on the act, don't they?"

"Oh, blast!" Kate said. "Is that your polite way of telling me to mind my own business?"

"No, of course not. I mean—well—I didn't say anything to the Professor. I'd rather wait till the inquest's safely over. He is the Professor, after all—"

"I know exactly what you mean. But I'm not a professor. I'm just me," Kate said winningly.

George laughed and gave in. "Between ourselves, then. The inquest hasn't happened yet, remember."

"Of course!" Kate tilted her head like a bright bird waiting for crumbs.

"Well, I saw him at the site, you know? Where he died. It's a hell of a place." And she launched herself into a graphic description of the sumptuousness of the Oxford flat that had Kate enthralled. She pushed away her plate and propped her elbows on the table, clearly finding what George had to say a great deal more nourishing than glutinous Spanish rice.

"But then this policeman arrived…" George hesitated. It was really Gus she wanted to talk about, the chance to let out her spleen about him to someone, and Kate would be a comforting person to talk to, she was sure. Or would it be too indiscreet? She decided she didn't care and said, "He's the local Detective Chief Inspector. Big-deal guy, you know? I'm likely to fall over him in every damned case I have to do for the police."

Kate grinned. "Do I detect a more than professional interest? What's he like?"

"Cockney. Pushy. Big-headed."

"Oh," Kate said and reached for her coffee. "You liked him." It wasn't a question.

"I did not!" George said, then stopped and smiled a little shamefacedly. "He likes me, that's the thing. He turned up the day before yesterday to watch me do the PM—and I'd made such a fuss the night before." She filled Kate in with the details.

Kate listened, fascinated, and then, when she heard the tale of the impromptu lunch party in George's office, laughed delightedly. "He's a man of style! Sort of thing Oliver'd have done. Once." She made a small grimace. "He's got a bit stuffy lately. I dare say it's having two children to worry over. He certainly worries over them more than I do."

"Oliver? Your husband?"

"Oh, no," Kate said sunnily. "We're not married. He had a disaster the first time around and there's no way he'd risk it

again." She stopped and added thoughtfully, "I'm not sure I'd
want to now, either. I did at first, like mad. But now…" She
shook her head. "They stay or they go. Being married doesn't
make much difference."

"You're so right," George said with some fervor, and told
her about Ian. Kate made all the right noises of disgust at such
male bullheadedness and general stupidity and congratulated
her on a lucky escape, and George basked in the warmth of
feminine solidarity. She'd been right; she had badly needed a
girlfriend.

"But this chap; Hathaway, you say. He sounds rather fun."
Kate was reflective. "I'll tell you this much. There's a lot to be
said for setting your sights on men outside the trade. Doctors
married to doctors: it can work, of course it can, but I think it's a
bit too enclosed. Not healthy for the mind. Oliver's a journalist
and that makes for much more interesting conversation around
the domestic hearth. I get all the shop talk I need here, and then
go home and pretend I'm normal. Bliss."

"Oh," George said, no more, but Kate looked at her
shrewdly.

"Dear me. Do I detect another chap in the offing? But this
one comes with a GMC guarantee?"

George laughed, embarrassed. "Am I that transparent?"

"No," Kate said smugly. "I'm just very perceptive. Do tell
me all about it—"

"Room for one more?"

They both looked up. Kate said warmly, "Of course. Move
over, George," and the newcomer sat down with her coffee and
packet of biscuits. "Is that all you're having for lunch? You
need a bit more than that."

"Since you seem to have left most of yours on the plate,
I can't say I find the advice all that disinterested," the other
said and turned to George. "Hello. I hope you don't mind me
butting in."

"Not in the least."

"I'm Hattie Clements, Sister in A & E."

"I'm George Barnabas. Pathologist."

"Oh, I know that." Hattie unwrapped her biscuits. "There isn't any new doctor turns up here but the nursing staff get to know all there is to know about them! We know all about you."

"Oh?" George was a little nettled, for all she was grateful that the new arrival had deflected Kate's interest in any involvement she might have with a medical man. Making the best of a girlfriend was one thing; pouring out her entire budget of information before they knew each other a little better would be stupid indeed. "What do you know?"

"Well, we know you're called George, that you came here from Scotland though you're American, and that you're unattached. Though some of the nurses reckon you and Toby Bellamy might be an item, having seen you around in the pub and so forth. How's that for beginners?"

George was mortified, and very aware of Kate's reaction, which was one of amused understanding. "A bit too much," she said a little acidly.

"Oh, don't let it upset you!" Kate said. "Hattie's perfectly right. Everyone talks their heads off over everyone else here at Old East. I'll help you catch up. Hattie's a widow, has two children and she's being pursued, when she isn't doing the pursuing herself, by a rather delicious schoolmaster who writes novels. She can't make up her mind whether to settle down with him or not, and spends hours talking to whoever'll listen about what she ought to do."

"Kate, shut up," Hattie said amiably. "It's nothing like that, George, honestly. It's only a little bit of truth blown up into a socking great balloon. Why George, by the bye? I've been longing to find out."

"A chauvinist grandfather, feminist mum," Kate said and George blinked.

"Ye gods, is there nothing people here don't manage to find out?" she protested, and it was Kate's turn to laugh.

"You've forgotten you told me all about it," she said. "At the Barrie party, remember? That your grandfather left all his money to his only daughter's child on condition it was called after him. So your ma did."

George bit her lip. "Sorry. Yes, I did tell you, didn't I. And yes, that's pretty well it."

"What did he do when he found out you were a girl, and not the boy he wanted?" Hattie asked.

"He never did. Died before I was born. He knew he was going to. He had terminal cancer, prostate." She chuckled. "Ma said he'd have gone bananas at first, but he'd have gotten over it. He liked people with a bit of sass about them and that was why really he liked Ma, even if she was the wrong sort."

"He'd have liked you then," Kate said firmly. "Let me know how it all works out, anyway. Have to fly. Good hunting, George. See you, Hattie," and she went, hurrying away in her usual rushed manner.

There was a little silence and then George said carefully, "What have they told you about me, then, your nurses? Ah—I mean, about who I've been going around with?"

Hattie grinned. "Not a lot, don't worry. It's just that someone saw you in the local with Toby having a drink and someone else saw you in that restaurant down by the river and there it is—that's all they need to tie two people together with bonds of steel and roll them down an aisle somewhere. They should have known better, seeing it was Toby Bellamy."

"Oh?" George was studiedly non-committal. "Why?"

"Oh, you are one of us, aren't you?" Hattie said. "Gossip with the best. Lovely!"

"I've always been interested in my fellow man," George allowed, and then added hastily, "And woman."

"That goes without saying. Well, I suppose…" Hattie made a face and looked down at the table. "I wish I'd not started this, actually."

"Why?"

"It depends on how far—I mean on how right the girls were."

"They weren't right at all," George said. "Yes, we had a drink and went out for a meal a few times, but as for the bonds of steel, phooey."

"Oh, I am glad to hear it!" Hattie said with such heartfelt sincerity that George opened her eyes wide at her.

"Are you going to tell me he's the hospital bluebeard?"

"He hasn't killed anyone yet. Not to my knowledge," Hattie said in all seriousness. "But I suppose you could say…"

"Say what?" Hattie had stopped and was looking at George a little anxiously.

"Well, if he isn't any special sort of friend, I must say I'm glad. Not that it's any of my affair, you understand, but I don't like to see someone getting tangled up for nothing. Especially a foreigner. Oh, Lor', I didn't mean that the way it came out."

George laughed. This woman was an endearing mixture of candour and sharp-wittedness, very like her mother, and that made her feel comfortable. "I know what you mean. I'm a poor lost lone crittur in a strange land."

"Oh, no. I mean, it's obvious you can cope perfectly well. But the thing is that sometimes when you know something about a person you ought to advise other people about them."

"I think it'd help if you came right out with it," George said. "I'm getting very confused here."

"Oh well, it's Toby, the sort he is. He's a nice man, don't get me wrong. Very amusing, good company. He and my Sam— you know, the chap Kate told you about'—and she went a little pink with the pleasure of saying the name—" they know each other and get on very well. And that's a sort of recommendation because Sam has this proclivity for seeing through people. It's just that—" She shrugged. "Bellamy's unreliable, when it comes to women."

"In what way unreliable?"

"Well, he's had dinner at my house twice in the past year because Sam's asked him, and both times he brought Felicity

Oxford, and I had the impression that—" Again she shrugged. "Well, let's say they seemed to be on comfortable terms, you know what I mean?"

"Like an item."

"You could say so."

"It's weird," George burst out after a moment. "I just can't handle you people. Guys are so..." She shook her head. "Why didn't Toby Bellamy say to me he was just being friendly? I mean, I'm used to people saying straight out if they want to date you or if they just want to be friendly and I got the impression I was being dated. But then he goes and watches her—Felicity Oxford—at the concert like she was made of gold dust." She shook her head again. "I just don't know where I am."

"He was being friendly," Hattie said firmly. "It has to be. I suppose you're right: people in this country don't make a clear line between friendly and sexy the way you do in the States. Here you can go around with someone out of—well, because you're lonely or whatever, and then it sort of grows into something more. Or sometimes it doesn't, but you're still friends. At least that's how it's always been for me, and I imagine Toby Bellamy thinks the same way. And we go on making new friends with people even if we're serious about someone else, sometimes. I've been out to drinks and supper with some of the people here even though I'm sort of serious about Sam. It's all quite normal."

"It is in the States as well, believe it or not," George said a little drily. "Anyway, you're warning me to keep off, is that it?"

"Oh, no, not if you don't want to. I mean not if you like him. And he can be good fun, I do agree. Nice and funny. No, I was just sort of letting you know that he seems to be spoken for. He was very taken with Felicity Oxford at one time. I have to be honest and say I haven't seen so much of him lately, Sam's been too busy to consider dinner parties and I've just not bothered."

"Anyway, thanks," George said, getting to her feet. "I must be going. Got a lot to do."

"You're not angry, are you?" Hattie looked up at her anxiously. "I really meant well."

"And you did well," George said. "I appreciate it. See you around." And she went loping off across the canteen, her white coat flying behind her with the speed of her walking, pushing her glasses back up her nose as she went. She'd certainly go on wearing them for a while yet, she told herself wrathfully. To think she'd actually been considering trying out those damned contact lenses again, the ones she'd got because Ian had told her she looked so much more appealing without spectacles on her nose. Well, Toby Bellamy was certainly not worth struggling with contact lenses for. Not if he was going to play fast and loose with her the way he had.

She was standing in the lift on her way down to the ground floor when she realized how stupid she was being, carrying on inside her head like some sort of senior high school prom queen. Toby Bellamy had been friendly, that was all; he'd never said a word out of place, never made a pass, so why should she think he'd misbehaved simply because he was tied up with Felicity Oxford? She had been the one to jump to conclusions; he'd never behaved badly at all. If she'd gone into contact lenses it'd have been a waste of effort clearly, but it would have been entirely her own fault.

To hell with you, she muttered under her breath as she reached the bottom and the doors began to whisper open. She began to lecture him inside her head.

If you prefer to have an affair with a married woman who looks like a refugee from a film set, you go right ahead. Don't you think I give a damn, because I don't.

The doors were open now and she moved forwards, just as the person who had been waiting to come in did the same, and he stepped back when he saw her and exclaimed, "Well, there's handy! I was going to come looking for you."

She put her hand behind her to hold open the door to the lift though it hissed a little, and heaved against her restraint.

"You'll miss your ride," she said. "Hurry along."

"It can wait," Toby stepped to one side to let another couple of passengers pass. "It's just a routine round I'm off to. So tell me, how did the PM go?"

She looked at him sharply as the doors sighed to behind her and the lift went away. "What PM?"

"Oh, come on, George! Richard Oxford's, of course. Have you found out what happened? Did he fall or was he pushed? Was it natural causes or foul play? Was it the butler or the chauffeur or one of the other servants he had to have to maintain his glorious lifestyle?"

"I really can't say," she said. "The inquest'll be—"

"Oh, George, don't be so stuffy. You can tell me."

She looked at him very directly. "Why? So you can run and tell Felicity Oxford?"

"I should imagine she'd be told immediately anyway," he said, frowning a little. "What are you being so cagey about?"

She tried to pass him but he didn't move and she had to stay where she was. "It's not right to give out this sort of information before an inquest," she said a little primly. "Also—"

He whistled. "Jesus, so it was a dodgy one? Someone did do for him?"

She frowned. "I said no such thing!"

"You're implying it. Like crazy. Come on, George, cough up the news. Did someone get rid of the old bastard?"

"I didn't know he was an old bastard." She was icy now, staring at him hard. "Or that anyone would want to be rid of him."

He leaned against the side of the lift, leaving the way clear for her to go. But she stayed where she was. "Oh, I can imagine lots of people'd want to be rid of him. He was an old—well, let's just say he was hard to love."

"So his wife, your friend Felicity, will be happy to be rid of him, is that it?"

He lifted a brow, watching her face all the time. "Now, what has poor old Fliss done to you that your voice should take on such a sneer when you say her name?"

"I'm not sneering! I'm just reacting to your—your unseemly curiosity about a case which is none of your affair."

"Unseemly? Well, there's a handsome word for a handsome lady to throw out. Unseemly, is it? Let's just say that I think it is very seemly to be concerned about the feelings of the living rather than the sins of the dead. And I also think it'd be interesting to say the least to know whether Fliss is a rich widow by someone's direct action or whether it was the beneficence of providence. Frankly, I'd assumed he'd had an infarct or a CVA, but you made such a song and dance over it, it's obviously something more and—"

"It is nothing of the sort!" George said, a little alarmed now. The last thing she wanted was for this hotbed of gossip to seethe with the news that Oxford had died of unnatural causes when she had no idea yet whether he had or not. And, in fact, was pretty sure he hadn't. Oh, God, she said inside her head. Why the hell did I start this whole goddamned fuss? Stupid bitch you are, you know that? A stupid bitch. "I just don't know yet. I'm waiting for results of investigations."

"Then why did you imply that the death was a dubious one?"

"Because I don't know yet! That's all!"

He looked at her, chewing his upper lip, and then said abruptly, "This is daft, isn't it? We're fighting over nothing. Look, meet you tonight at the pub, hmm? You'll need supper of some sort if you've just come down from the canteen lunch, as I imagine you have. Then maybe we can start again, and sort ourselves out. No time now."

She opened her mouth to tell him what she thought of his offer, and then temporized. "I'd planned a swim and fish and chips in my room," she said. "And anyway—"

"No anyway," he said firmly. "It sounds like a great idea. I can get to the pool around'—he looked at his watch—"say, seven o'clock. All right? And then we can have our fish and chips at that place in Cable Street. It's only a few minutes walk. Great! I'll see you there then. I'll look forward to it."

The lift came down again and spilled a couple of people into the corridor. He went in and reached for the button. "Don't be late," he said, flashing a grin, and the doors closed and he was gone, leaving her trying to work out how she felt about the evening. Would she go, or send a note to his office to tell him she couldn't?

She started across the courtyard on her way back to her department, thinking hard. Maybe she was just being silly after all. Why shouldn't he be a friend as well as having an affair with Felicity Oxford? She'd heard that men often did like to have sexy relationships with married women; they were less likely to make life difficult for them. And then she thought, as she reached the main door to the path lab. But she's not a married woman. She's a widow. Maybe it'll be different now. Maybe his interest in what Richard Oxford died of is more than just the normal gossipy curiosity of the hospital. Maybe—

I will go, she thought as she marched towards her office. I will. It could be interesting to find out why Toby Bellamy is interested to know if there is something fishy about Oxford's death, and the results'll be here soon, and then—and she pushed her door open and hurried in, knowing the investigation results should be on her desk by now, and having to admit to herself that she wanted them to show something that would make her doubts more concrete. Partly to show Gus Hathaway that she was right, but now also to measure Toby Bellamy's reaction to the news.

The results were there, tucked into a neat plastic envelope. She picked them up with fingers shaking slightly with excitement.

She read them through with great care, but there wasn't a thing to show for her efforts. The blood picture, the report said, had been normal in every way. There had been no evidence of any drug or any other substance that shouldn't be there. No codeine, no benzodiazapines, no cocaine, no opiates, nothing at all unusual.

She turned to the other report hopefully and again struck out. The swabs from the nose and mouth had grown nothing startling after twenty-four hours, and though they would continue to observe the cultures nothing was expected to change there. The rectal swab showed nothing more surprising than a little lanolin and the skin swabs were just as unrevealing. The man had used soap, body cream and cologne before he'd climbed into his elaborate bed, but there was nothing else. Richard Oxford had simply stopped breathing. And there seemed to be no reason why.

And that, George thought, her forehead creasing as she concentrated, really was rather odd. There had to be some reason for this death. Her inability to pinpoint it was beginning to chafe; her whole raison d'être was her curiosity, her need to know. And Richard Oxford was blocking that. Whether it was a police matter or not was now, she decided, beside the point. She wanted to know for her own sake. And somehow she'd find out.

11

The pool was inhabited (the word "infested' came to mind, but she dismissed it) by a large number of small boys, all intent on drowning each other while being bawled at by a species of youth-club leader who seemed incapable of controlling them. She struggled her way through them for fifteen lengths before giving up and hauling herself on to the edge of the deep end, to sit a little breathlessly, watching the children being shepherded into a noisy game of water polo. She was less than fit; time she started regular exercise again. She'd got out of the habit in the Ian days, because he'd found it rather absurd that she should take the time to jog around the hospital grounds at least three evenings a week, accusing her of being a Californian health freak; which had so offended her Yankee heart—after all, her mother had come from Massachusetts—that she'd given it up. Now she was paying the price, and she patted her belly, suspecting that it was softer than it should be. His voice behind her came a little muffled against the noise from the shrieking ball players and the inevitable echo of the great roof, and she turned to peer upwards, startled at the suddenness of his arrival.

"It looks fine to me. Like the rest of you. A very agreeable sight."

Bellamy was standing in a comfortable relaxed pose that seemed natural but which she suspected was calculated to show his body to its best advantage; a calculation that had succeeded. He was flat of belly and broad of chest with none of the softening under the ribs that gave away the couch potato in the making, and he had just enough hair and just enough muscle definition to look interesting without looking self-absorbed.

He grinned at her. "How much have you done?"

"Fifteen laps."

He squinted at the pool. "It's around thirty-five meters, I'd say. You need another ten to make it the half mile or thereabouts. Race you."

"I'm not a racer," she said. "And anyway, these kids…"

But they were at last getting out, being shooed by a forceful lifeguard in a red swimsuit who was clearly as bored with them as everyone else. The pool lay at her feet, blue, glinting and attractive, with only half a dozen or so sedate adult swimmers in it and both the lanes ahead of them totally empty and inviting in the extreme.

He sat down alongside her and said, "We'll take it from a sitting start then, on three. One, two, three—"

She couldn't refuse the challenge, and almost instinctively was away, her lack of fitness and breath quite forgotten under the spur of competition, and for the next fifteen minutes. It was hard work because he was a thrifty swimmer, making every move work for him; but she had been well trained in her school days, and managed to keep up with him. She was a shade faster on the turns, which helped, and by the time she'd ended her tenth lap she was about two meters ahead. She finished in a last triumphant kick of her legs that sent spray into his face.

"You win," he gasped. "Let me make it another couple—" and was away in a strong plunging crawl that was agreeable to watch. He was certainly a well-made man, she told herself, and sat there comfortably catching her breath and letting the sense of wellbeing that exercise always gave her creep all through her. Endorphins, she thought vaguely; that's what it is. Endorphins, but to hell with physiology. Forget you're a doctor and just enjoy yourself.

"You'll be ready for food after this," he said as at last he finished and with one smooth movement twisted his body up out of the water into a sitting position at the side. "I'm so hungry I could eat even a hospital dinner. But we'll do better than that. Does it take you hours to dress and get your hair dry?"

She was up on her feet at once. "I'll be out before you will," she promised and was away, and he too went running off down the side of the pool to the changing rooms.

She came out fully dressed and with her hair tied up in a white towelling turban that she knew suited her and anyway was less trouble than struggling with a municipal hairdrier, and was standing outside in the lobby staring at the notice board when he came out, also damp about the head and smelling pleasantly of a light cologne.

"You cheated," he accused. "Didn't dry your hair."

"I win by any means, fair or foul," she said. "Apropos of which, where's my fish?"

"Ten minutes away," he promised. "Want to race again?"

"This time I'll manage a sedate walk," she said. "You can carry my gear if you like." And she handed him her bag of towels and wet swimsuit and soap and shampoo.

"So much for women's liberation," he said, but took it willingly enough as she lifted her chin at him.

"To hell with liberation. Me, I want privilege. OK, let's be clear: we pay for our own suppers, right?"

"Right," he said. "I had no intention of doing anything else."

"You're a bastard, you know that?" She tried not to laugh but it wasn't easy. "You've got a great gift for putting people in the wrong."

"I know. I cherish it. It takes years of practice. Tell you what, though, let me buy you a drink. What do you say to that?"

"If I buy a round too."

"I thought you'd get the message. Great. Here's the pub. Or d'you prefer a different one?"

"This'll do fine." It was a beautiful pub, alight with Victorian engraved glass, well-polished brass and deeply comfortable seats; to have objected to it would have been churlish.

After he brought their beers she leaned her damp head back against the leathery seat, sighing deeply and closing her eyes, as physically content as she'd been for a long time. Good exercise, a glass of good and for once really cold beer and a solid meal to come; what more could a person ask for?

"So…" he said. Behind her closed lids she did something she used to do as a child long ago; she tried to see the color of the sound of his voice. Some voices were warm and bright and golden; some were rich and brown; a few were thin and yellowish; and others had sharp dark edges that made her shiver a little. His voice was a good deep gold, which was good, but there was a darker part to it, underneath rather than at the edge. He's worried about something, she thought with a degree of surprise, and opened her eyes.

"So what?"

"What's news?"

It sounded casual but she was not deceived. "About what?"

He made a non-committal grimace. "Anything."

"Well, let me see. There's that bombing in Northern Ireland. That made the lead story on the radio news this evening as I was changing. Then there was—"

"That's not news. That's an unending saga. News is what affects you personally. News is gossip and chatter about your colleagues and enemies and friends. News is…"

She waited, and then said lightly, "The results of Richard Oxford's PM."

"Well, yes, that could be news. If it was not what you expected."

"Listen, Toby." She put her glass down firmly. "Let's get something clear here. Did you opt in on my plan for a private evening just to pick my brains over Oxford? And if so, why? I'm a reasonable soul, let me tell you, and if I know why and what,

I'm as likely to co-operate as not. But go at me deviously or try to manipulate and I don't give with the words. Is that fair enough?"

"It's positively British, it's so fair," he said gravely, holding out his glass. "I'm ready for the other half. And it's your shout."

"Trust you to guzzle it. OK, I'll get it. And while I am, think about what I said. Tell me why and maybe I'll tell you how and what and when. As much as I know, that is. But stop the fancy footwork. It annoys me."

When she came back with the beer for him and a lemonade chaser for herself he was sitting with his head back, staring up at the light. His hair had flopped damply over his forehead, giving him a rather little-boy look, and she took a sharp little breath. He really was a very attractive man; she'd have to watch herself. She tried to think of Ian as a sort of protection, but it was very difficult. She couldn't even see his face clearly in her mind's eye, just a smooth presence with fair hair, and it wasn't worth making the effort to see further.

"Great," he said. He took the glass from her and drank half its contents in one long gulp.

She pushed the remains of her own beer over towards him. "You'd better finish that as well. I'm too hungry even for the small amount of alcohol that's in half a pint."

He grinned and took the glass and emptied it into his own and settled back. "OK, ask away," he said cheerfully.

"Ask what?"

"The inquisition can begin. You told me you have to know all there is to know, so ask me questions, so that you can be sure I'm not going in for—what was it?—fancy footwork."

She looked at him over the rim of her glass for a long moment. He stared back at her gravely. Then she sighed. "I don't know where I am with you. Are you dating me or just being friendly?"

He seemed to think about that. "What's the difference?"

"If you don't know then the answer is you're just being friendly. Fair enough."

"I'm never sure what's meant by that word, dating. I thought a date was just an arrangement you made to meet a person at a certain time and place. You make it drip with all sorts of innuendo and hidden meaning."

"You know perfectly well what I mean. Don't come this 'divided by a common language' stuff with me. I've been in Britain almost ten years, remember. I've gotten my British forensic qualifications here to add to my Stateside ones, and I've worked in the NHS as long as you have, I dare say. So..."

"Hmm. Fair enough. OK, if you mean am I asking you out just to be a mate or do I fancy you, the answer is both."

"Oh," she said and drank some more.

"Well may you blush. You've pulled an avowal out of me."

"Bullshit! You're just trying to make me uncomfortable."

"And you're trying to stop me asking questions about Richard Oxford."

There was a short silence. She looked at him and then away. "You could be right. I'm just so..." She shook her head. "I don't like the feeling I'm being used. Call it captious femininity if you like, but I'm funny that way. Like I said, when I know where you're coming from and where you're going, you'll find me very helpful. Try to fool me and I ain't so nice."

"I got that message a long time ago." He drained his glass and got to his feet. "Come on. Supper. I'll replace that lemonade if you must drink it, though I'd rather be generous and consider a bottle of wine."

"You agreed, we pay our own ways."

He lifted one hand. "*Pax vobiscum*. Not another word. Come on. When we've had some food we'll both be a bit less scratchy, hmm?"

George loved fish-and-chip shops. They were her greatest find in Britain. Hamburger joints and pancake houses and kebab sellers were ten a penny, and could have been anywhere in the world, including at home in downtown Buffalo. But a fish-and-chip shop, that was quintessentially British, with delicious overtones of the tang of the Massachusetts fish fries she'd been to when she visited her grandmother's home in Fall River as a child. This one was a particularly attractive specimen, she decided. There was the same profusion of engraved glass that there had been at the pub, but here the emphasis was on bright lights and chrome which contrasted sharply with the pub's brown fug. There were bright red formica tables and chairs, pictures of the fish of the world on the walls, a good deal of clattering and chatter and above all the rich reek of frying oil and fresh fish and earthy potatoes all sharpened with the bite of malt vinegar. Her appetite clamored even more loudly, and she ordered greedily as soon as they sat down and immediately began on the large crusty roll and butter the pert waitress brought them.

Tacitly they agreed not to speak any more of the matter of Oxford's PM, chattering instead about the people around them as Toby made outrageous analyses of the couples and their relationships and very insulting remarks indeed about their clothes and styles of hair and make-up.

She laughed a lot and when the hot food came ate with great enthusiasm, swiftly despatching a large fried sole and a considerable pile of the crispest chips she could remember eating anywhere. He too ate fast and with absorption and not until they'd refused apple pie or ice cream—hard as the perky waitress tried to persuade them—and had been given large mugs of coffee, did they relax and look at each other.

"I feel better," he said.

"Mmm."

"Time to talk?"

"Uhuh."

"You first. Questions."

"Why are you so anxious to know about Oxford?"

"Natural curiosity?"

She shook her head. "Try again. You've been really pushing. This afternoon and a while back. Not in so many words, grant you. But I know when I'm being bulldozed."

He put down his mug and sighed. "OK. It's Fliss, Felicity."

She tried not to mind the intimacy of the way he said the name, tried not to care. She didn't succeed.

"She's naturally upset about it all."

George couldn't help it. She lifted her brows and said, a touch waspishly, "Really? I gathered they were divorced, lived apart—"

"They were married nearly thirty years. Still were married, in fact. They were separated, not divorced. And even then it wasn't a legal separation. Just one they arranged themselves. They were good friends in many ways."

"Interesting."

"You sound as nasty as some of the nurses around the hospital when they talk about her," he said sharply. "The fact a woman looks stunning seems to bring out the worst in other women. Whatever happened to sisterhood?"

She reddened angrily. "I'm not being nasty. I just said 'interesting'—"

"Well, maybe I was being hypersensitive in hearing a sneer there."

"You were," she said, but then had to be honest. "Well, not entirely. I have to say it doesn't sound much of a relationship to me. Married friends."

"It's better than married enemies," he said. "This way they avoided anger and hatred, kept what was good. Anyway, there she is, in her place in Regent's Park, and there he was in the palace in Docklands."

She felt her muscles tense and tried not to show it. "How do you mean, palace?"

"Oh, incredible! A double-sized flat, a drawing room so dripping with gold and glory it takes your breath away, and the bathroom—well! Amazing!"

"Really," she said, and looked down at her hands.

He stopped, then, after a moment, said, "But I imagine you know that. You had to go there, didn't you?"

"Yes," she said non-committally.

"Extraordinary place, isn't it? You must agree it's a palace."

"You could call it that." She didn't look at him. "So, they lived apart."

"Yes." He seemed momentarily abstracted, but pulled himself back. "And they were good friends. She's genuinely cut up about him. Now she wants to get on with the funeral, treat him right, you know? She can't, of course, till the Coroner lets the body go, and I wanted to find out—and I can't deny that I was pumping you—I wanted to find out for her what the situation was."

"She's a special friend, then?"

He was quiet for a moment and then said, "You could say that."

"Ah!"

"And what does that mean?"

"Nothing! Just 'ah.'"

"Look," he began, and stopped as his bleep suddenly began to clamor, making other diners turn and stare. He fumbled for it. "Shit!" he said, reading off the message. "I'll have to nip back. I've got a woman with bleeding varices in her oesophagus and she's giving us a good deal of trouble. Look, settle for supper, would you mind? I'll sort it out with you tomorrow."

"No need." Gus Hathaway had come up behind him. "Evening, Dr. Barnabas. Had a good nosh, have you? Good. Nothin' but the best here, you have my word for it. Don't you fret about your suppers, I'll look after that."

George was staring at him. "What the hell are you doing here? Can't I escape you wherever I go?"

"Doesn't look like it, does it?" He grinned and put his hands in his pockets. He was wearing the same rather crumpled suit he'd worn the last time she'd seen him, at the mortuary.

"Won't someone introduce me?" Toby said a little plaintively. "I've got to go, but if this chap's a friend of yours and wants to buy my supper, I don't mind a bit. I'm still the scrounger I was as a student. Old habits die hard."

"Detective Chief Inspector Hathaway from Ratcliffe Street Police Station," George said grudgingly.

"Toby Bellamy, from Old East. Surgeon."

"Nice to meet you, Doctor." Gus held out his hand. "Any friend of Dr. B. here, you know, any friend of Dr. B."

"Why are you paying for our suppers?" Toby was on his feet, shrugging into his coat, reaching for his sports bag. "It's kind and all that, but—"

"Because he likes to stick his nose in everywhere," George said irritably. She did not want to admit it to herself but one of the reasons for her irritation was that she'd felt a totally unexpected lift of excitement when she'd seen Gus.

"I'm entitled to be here," Gus said mildly. "Seein' it's my place."

"Oh!" Toby grinned from ear to ear. "How refreshing! A fish-frying detective. Makes a change. You're on. Thanks for the grub, it was great." And he shook hands with Gus, pumping his arm up and down with considerable enthusiasm, waved a hand at George and made for the door.

Gus sat down opposite George and said cheerfully, "Right, how about a cup of Irish coffee? You might as well. We've got things to talk about and it'll go down easier over a wet."

12

The Irish coffee was as good as the fish had been, hot, well brewed and full of flavor, and she concentrated on it as she watched him over the rim of the cup. He looked relaxed and peaceable, and very comfortable. She noticed that the staff were as comfortable with him as he was with himself. There was no undue deference, no apparent nervousness at his presence. He must be a nice guy to work for, she found herself thinking. Treats people well.

"So what things do we have to talk about?"

He put down his cup and looked at her thoughtfully.

"A special mate, is he, that Toby? Funny name for a surgeon, Toby. Sounds like an escapee from a Punch and Judy show."

"And Gus sounds like an escapee from a—a boxing ring," she retorted. He laughed delightedly.

"I like that. Always fancied myself as one of the fancy! Like to see me in puce satin shorts and big fat gloves, would you?"

"Not particularly. I don't like boxing. It scrambles brains."

"It'd never do to have scrambled brains," he said gravely.

"Couldn't keep up with you if that happened, could I?"

"What did you want to talk about?" She sounded brusque and knew it, but she didn't care.

He lifted one brow at her and became serious. "Down to the brass whatsits, eh? Fair enough. It's this Oxford business."

"I imagined it might be."

"I've seen the test results and the full report."

"Of course. I sent them to you!"

"Nothing there, eh?"

"Not in those tests, no."

"Oh! Do you mean there're others you should have done?"

She reddened at the implied criticism. "Not should have, could have. There's a second round of investigations we can do if a first PM shows no results. I've already put them in hand."

"What for? You won't get nothing out of them, neither. You know that."

"I know nothing of the sort. It's because I don't know that I'm doing them."

"I'm getting a lot of pressure to let the body go. There'll be an open verdict tomorrow if we go to the Coroner as we are. I'd rather we could go in and agree natural causes." She opened her mouth to argue with him and he leaned forward and spoke quietly. "Look, Dr. Barnabas—could I call you your first name? It's daft to be so formal when we're goin' to be workin' together. I always called Dr. Royle Ricky. The thing is, George, we sort of started on the wrong foot, didn't we? I frightened you, wandering into the flat that way, and I can see it was stupid of me to do it. Barmy, really. If I'd been you I'd have screamed the bloody house down."

"I did," she said and then bit her lip. "You could have been anyone."

"Course I could. Could have been a murderer. If there'd been murder done. But the thing of it is, I don't think there has been. I don't think you think there has been. I think you got so shirty with me—and, like I say, rightly so—that you wasn't going to let me get away with nothin'. In your shoes I'd have done exactly the same thing. But the joke's over now, surely? There's been the PM, you found nothing, you've made your point. You're the boss in this area. Now, can we get on with business? There'll be enough murders in the next few months, count on it, to keep us both more than happy."

"I don't need murders to keep me happy! I just need to know what's happened to a body. To this body. It's what I'm here for, goddamn it, to investigate."

"And very good you're going to be at it, it's obvious. But do me a favor, darling, let this bleeder go! You only had to look at him to know the sort of life he led. Probably just snuffed it the way these blokes do, and—"

"He didn't have a coronary, if that's what you're suggesting. He didn't have any evidence of any disease, can't you understand that? I thought he'd probably infarcted too, until I looked at his heart and blood vessels, but he had no more atheroma than you'd expect in a guy his age and type. Less in fact. He had a sound heart that just stopped beating. I'd like to know why."

He leaned back and sighed deeply. "If you were sitting in my seat and getting calls every hour on the bloody hour about this funeral they want to have, you'd be glad enough to let it go," he said. "I'm the last man to want to cover up anything that's the remotest bit dicey, but believe me and my years of experience, this one is not dicey. It's a straight-up death from natural causes."

"When I've done the last tests I'll let you know if you're right," she said pugnaciously.

Again he sighed and shook his head. "You're as stubborn as the proverbial, aren't you?"

"Yankee, that's me. It's a label that suits me." She stopped and thought for a moment and then it was her turn to lean forward. "I wouldn't want you to think I'm just being stubborn though. I'm not. I won't lie and pretend I wasn't furious with you over what happened at the flat that evening. But now it's different. Healthy hearts don't usually stop for no reason. I'd be a lousy pathologist if I let it go after just one lot of investigations, can't you see that? You ought to be encouraging me, not trying to push me off the case."

"You don't need encouragement," he said gloomily. "I'm beginning to wish I'd persuaded Royle to stay. You're going to be a right liability, you are."

"Well, there it is. You're stuck with me."

"I suppose I am. Listen, what sort of tests are you doing this time around? What have you done already?"

"We did the usual blood picture and a drug screen. Opiates, cocaine, paracetamol, all that stuff. There was nothing significant in the stomach contents, so I needn't check there again. Alcohol, naturally."

"Was there any?"

"You saw the report. There wasn't."

"Hmm. So what now?"

"Various things. Insulin…"

He looked interested at that. "Like the von Bülow case? Didn't he use insulin?"

"So it seems. Anyway, we'll look for it. Blood sugar and so forth. Cyanide and its derivatives—not likely. No signs of it and no smell. Digitalis, stuff like that."

"How likely is it you'll find anything?"

"How do I know? I'm looking, I'm not into divination. This is science, Mr. Hathaway, not crystal-gazing."

"I wish you'd call me Gus. And you're George—"

"And don't ask me why!" she said quickly. "If you don't ask me why, you can call me anything you like."

"Then I'll call you George. And I already know why." He smiled. "Must have been quite a lady, your ma."

"She still is," George said and scowled. "Does hospital gossip reach as far as the goddamn police station?"

"I make it my business to find out. So, you really think there could be evidence here of something?"

She sighed. He was beginning to make her feel uncomfortable. That he was an experienced policeman was undoubted, and if he was so sure there was no reason to suspect other than natural causes probably he was right. Yet, she was uneasy. It was more than her usual hunger for facts, all the facts, that drove her; it was a genuine suspicion now, and she leaned forward again, wanting to be friendly, wanting to avoid any appearance of being combative. "Listen, I'm as sorry about this as you are. Now. When it all started I can't deny I was mad at you and wanted to get even. I didn't think it'd be all that much of a problem. But the thing is that since I refused to sign the certificate after the first PM I'm obligated. I can't sign now till I've done more work. You must see that. And you're not the only one being pressured to get the thing finished with."

He sharpened. "Oh? Who's pressuring you?"

She meant to say Toby, but it didn't come out that way. "The wife."

"Oh." He relaxed. "Fair enough. I suppose Mrs. Oxford's entitled to be interested in what happened to Mr. Oxford."

"Right now I wish I'd never heard of Richard Oxford," she said. "But do let me assure you I regret as much as you do that I ever made a fuss over that one in the first place."

He beamed at her. "Thank heaven for that. We can work together then!"

"I thought we already were."

"Properly, I mean. Not having battles all the time." He reached forward, took her hand and shook it firmly. "From now on, darlin', you and me, we're on the same side, right? No more pushing things just to get your own back and—"

"Don't you ever listen?" she snapped. "I wasn't pushing it! I'm not pushing it now. I admitted that to start with I wanted to make it difficult for you, so I insisted on doing the preliminaries at the flat, but I'd have had to do the same over the PM even if that hadn't happened. I wish you'd listen! And I do wish you wouldn't call me darling. It's patronizing."

"Oh, shit!" he said disgustedly. "That word again. Social workers' babble."

"You're impossible." She got to her feet, furious again. "One minute you're trying to be friendly, and the next you come on like a—like the worst sort of—"

"Go on, say it. Male chauvinist pig."

"I wouldn't waste my time," she said with dignity and waved at the waitress who had noticed what was happening and had been watching with interest. "The bill please. For the other man and me. *He* can pay for his own coffee." She flicked a glare at Hathaway.

"I never pay," he said mildly. "It's one of the privileges. I told you I'd—"

"You will not pay for mine and Toby's," she said with teeth clenched. "And don't think that I'd ever—"

"I wasn't goin' to offer again. I got more sense than to try such a thing with a woman in a paddy. All I was going to say was I don't think I'll ever have to. So you're leavin', I take it? Don't forget your gear." He pulled her bag out from beneath the table.

She grabbed it from him as the waitress arrived with the bill, and she grabbed that too and marched over to the cashier's desk, leaving him sitting, but he followed her as she made for the door to the street and held it for a moment so that she couldn't get past.

"Tell you what, let's make it really interesting," he said. "Let's make a bet on it. Ten quid says you don't find a thing with your second round of tests. Ten quid says you have to give in and sign the certificate and let this geezer get himself properly buried. What do you say?"

"I say go and screw yourself," she snapped, and marched out, and off along the street, her bag bumping against her legs as she went.

She could feel him watching her all the way.

"You told me to check for everything I could think of as well as the list you gave me and the others," Jerry said. "So I did. It just seemed one I could have a go at. I'm as surprised as you are. I mean, old Oxford! Who'd ha' thought it? Do you think he might have topped himself in some fancy fashion because of it?"

She shook her head abstractedly, staring down at the sheaf of papers in her hand. "I've got to think about all this. Give me some time...Are there any more to come?"

"Only the immuno-assay. I did a fluorescence polarization—that was for the digitalis. I'll go and see what's happened to that. It should be ready. Apart from that, you've got the lot. And the only one that's come up with a surprise, to me at any rate, is that one." He flicked the corner of one of the sheets in her hand and then made for the door. "I'll chase Peter on the other. Fun, isn't it? Looks as though you could have uncovered a surprise at that, doesn't it?"

She shook her head and he went, leaving her staring down at the report. The words looked up at her so harmlessly: just a few symbols on a page and yet so loaded with potential meaning she could hardly cope with it.

"HIV positive," the sheet read. "HIV positive."

She riffled through the rest of the results. There was nothing else that indicated anything at all untoward. Blood sugar was normal; no sign of insulin, so that one was out. No sign of anything that could have caused this man's death when he was apparently healthy. Yet he wasn't healthy. He was HIV positive.

Of course that didn't mean he was ill, she told herself. People can be positive for years and not have AIDS. For all we know some HIV positive people may never get AIDS. There just isn't the information available yet. But this man was positive. Had he known? Had he been helped to deal with his feelings? Been counseled? And if he had known, why had he been tested? Was he living a risky lifestyle?

No drug injecting; she'd checked particularly for that at her main examination of the body down in the mortuary. It had been a routine thing to look for, but he'd not been a mainliner, though it had occurred to her when she'd first seen him that he had the sort of pouched and less-than-glowing look some drug-users get. That had been why she'd paid so much attention to the search for cocaine. He'd been just the sort of rich man to use it. But he hadn't shown any sign. So was he homosexual? The fact that he was a married man made no difference, of course, she knew that, but he did live apart from his wife. Yet never in all the gossip about the man had anyone even hinted that he might be sexually ambiguous. In a place like this, where everyone made sure they knew everyone's business as thoroughly as they could, where Oxford had been very much part of the scene, if there had been even the remotest possibility, surely it would have been talked about?

For the rest of the afternoon, as she dealt with the piles of reports she had to make to the wards and the ICU and GP clinics, the questions gnawed at her mind. Was the fact that Oxford had been HIV positive significant? Did it mean he'd had good reason to die prematurely? Did it mean—

She gave up and buried herself in her work, choosing the most complicated assessments to deal with first, the sort on which she had to concentrate hard to do at all, and that helped. So much that when Jerry suddenly came into her office in a most dramatic manner, holding out a sheet of paper with an air of suppressed excitement, she was startled.

"Well, Dr. B.!" he said. "We've got a fascinator here!"

"Eh? How do you mean?"

He came over, very portentous, set the sheet of paper before her and smoothed it out. "What do you think of that then?" he said triumphantly.

She read it and then leaned back in her chair to look at him. "I've forgotten," she said. "I can't think straight. What's the safe level?"

"I'd forgotten too, so I looked it up. At the very most it shouldn't exceed five milligrams per litre," he said. "And will you look at that! He must have had—oh, I don't know, I'd have to do the computations, but I'd guess he couldn't have had less than—here—" He reached for her notepad and started to scribble, murmuring amounts beneath his breath and then stood upright, staring down at the pad in his hand. "He must have had in excess of thirty twenty-five milligram tablets, I'd say. Maybe more."

She was still stunned. She'd pushed for this, resisted all attempts to deter her, and she'd been right. She had it so clearly in her mind she was just being stubborn and she wouldn't find anything that now she had it was difficult to take it in.

But the surprise ebbed and what came in its place was exhilaration. It was shameful to have to admit it but discovering Oxford had died of unnatural causes made her deeply content, and she was unable to keep the smile off her face.

Jerry was grinning too. "You were right, then. Everyone said you were nitpicking, but you were right!"

Her grin faded a little. "Everyone?"

He had the grace to look a little embarrassed. "Well, you know how it is. People talk."

"My God, they do!" she said with some feeling. "More here than any place I've ever been in! Anyway, you can now start some more talk. Tell 'em I was right. That they can put it in their overworked mouths and chew it! All we have to do now is find out how he got so much digitalis in him. He had no heart disease so there was no reason he should be using it, and when I looked around his bathroom I didn't see any there. Though I can't pretend I looked all that thoroughly."

"Well, it'll be a police matter now," Jerry said cheerfully. "I'll be panting to know whether he jumped or was pushed. But I can't for the life of me see how he got it in him. I mean, nothing in the stomach contents, was there?"

"No," she said, checking the reports. "No, nothing. However, as you say, it's a police matter now." She smiled beatifically up at him again. "Tell you what, Jerry. You could do me a favor. Will you phone Gus Hathaway and tell him he owes me ten quid? No more than that. Just tell him he owes me ten quid."

"Like that, is it?" Jerry said and laughed. "It'll be a pleasure!"

13

"Dammit all to hell and back," Kate shouted. "How much longer do I have to wait to get that blood picture?"

"I can't help it," Sister roared back. "We've been trying to ring the lab for ages, but the phones are continuously engaged. I just can't get through!"

"Then send someone down to get it," Kate said, calming down a little, but only a little. "I have to have it right now because I can't get this next dialysis sorted out until I do, you know that. Maybe the phone's out of order or something."

"I thought of that," Sister said wearily as she beckoned her most junior nurse. "I got them to check at switchboard. They're engaged speaking all right. Someone down there has got nothing better to do than talk all day. Nurse, go down to the lab as fast as you can and get me the reports for Daisy Blair, will you? And tell them to clear their damned phones for at least five minutes in every hour and put us all out of our misery."

"No!" the voice said in Sheila's ear with flattering amazement. "Not really! Heart, do you say! Poisoned?"

"I'm sure as I'm standing here telling you," Sheila said dramatically as she settled down to a long cozy chat. "Not that I'm all that surprised. As I was saying to Yvonne, when I told her, I always said there was something odd about the man. I mean, I read somewhere that people don't get murdered except for a very good reason and they only have themselves to blame, and that has to be obvious, doesn't it? And you only had to look at him to know."

"But couldn't it have been suicide?" the other objected.

"Oh, no, he wasn't the type." Sheila was very confident. "I mean, everything to live for, he had! Couldn't be suicide. He was too—well, you know. Larger than life. Never suicide. No, it has to be murder." She shivered happily. "Isn't it exciting?"

"I'll bet it was suicide. It's the most probable. People don't get murdered that way, do they? Not with secret potions. People get hit over the head or knifed down by the river, or mugged in pubs, that's the sort of murder we get around here."

"Well, we've got a different one now. And it's someone we know, not just a patient," Sheila said, a little annoyed by her listener's scepticism. "And I really can't waste time talking now, I've got a lot to do. I'll let you know when there's more to tell you. Let the other people in the choir know, will you? They've got a right, after all, seeing they worked with him."

By the time she'd hung up and dug out of her address book the next number she wanted to ring, someone had picked up the extension and the line was busy. She muttered irritably and tried George's line. But that was engaged too. She'd just have to wait—or she could go over to see the secretary in the Dean's office. There was still that matter of the forms for the pathology lectures to sort out, and she could ask her as well as anyone. Yes, that'd be better than the phone.

"My dear, I've just heard. I can't tell you how sorry I am."

"It's all right, Charles. I'm fine. Don't worry about me."

"But of course I'm concerned. You've had a dreadful time lately, a perfectly dreadful time. I'm most anxious that—"

"You needn't be." She sounded quite brisk. "Now I know I feel a little better. The last few days of waiting have been, well, difficult, but now at least I know."

"You don't sound unduly surprised." His voice was cautious.

"I don't think I am. After all, there are plenty of people who had ample cause to…Shall we say he wasn't as popular as he might have been?"

There was a little silence and then he said quietly, "No. I suppose he wasn't."

"Not that that means I don't care."

"Of course it doesn't, I know that."

"As long as you do."

Again there was a silence and he said carefully, "Shall we— Can we—Am I able to be of any help to you?"

"I don't think so." Was he imagining it or was there a hint of laughter in her voice? "I don't think you can be of any help to me at all."

"Well, in that case…"

"Though perhaps I can be of some help to you."

"To me? Well, I'm not sure that—I really can't say—Why should—I imagine that when it comes to the funeral there'll need to be some—"

"It's all right, Charles," she said. "This is me, remember? I'm Oxford the obliging, not Oxford the awkward." Now there was laughter there and he felt a frisson of disapproval, almost shock. To be able to display levity in such circumstances offended his sense of what was right and proper.

"Well, if you need anything, let me know. I'll be here. We'll—er, we'll both be glad to help in any way we can."

"I never for one moment doubted you, Charles," she said and hung up, leaving him sitting with the phone in his hand, wondering. Had she put an emphasis on the penultimate word? And if she had, what did it mean?

"Oh, Fliss, what a bastard it all is. How are you coping?"

"As you'd expect."

She was tired, he thought. Certainly she sounded weary rather than distressed. "Who told you?"

"Mmm? Oh, it was the police. They sent a girl in a fancy

uniform. So careful not to upset me that I was terrified half out of my wits. It was easier once she told me. It seems there was digitalis there."

"Digi—I hadn't heard that." He was silent for a while. "The policewoman told you that?"

"No. I phoned the pathologist, what's her name, Barnabas."

"Ah, yes. George."

"Whatever. She seemed a little worried at first about saying anything but I pointed out that as his wife..."

"Yes, I imagine she would be sensible."

"Is that what you call it? I call it giving in to the right sort of pressure properly applied. I'm quite good at that."

"Yes, I'll grant you that, any time. Listen, Fliss, are you sure—er—that—"

"Oh, do stop it. You know me better than this! If I put on a great act of being heartbroken you'd be disgusted. I'd be disgusted! I'm not heartbroken or anything like it. To tell the truth, I breathed a sigh of relief last week when he died. I could do without this complication, I'll grant you that, but it's been a long time since Richard actually quickened my pulses any."

He took a sharp little breath. "You're still as hard as they come, Fliss."

"Oh, for Christ's sake, do you have to talk like a cheap women's magazine? I'm practical, yes. Efficient, yes. Intelligent, yes. Sentimental, no. Now, there're things I have to do."

"Yes, of course. Can I help?"

She laughed, a short bark of a sound. "If anyone else turns up to offer help with this funeral it'll be like a state event. Either that or a positive camel of a committee-designed abortion. No, forget that. Perhaps I'm a bit more bothered than—Anyway, I need no help, thanks. If I do I know where to get it. Thank you for calling." And she hung up, crisply, leaving him with the buzzing handset still held to his ear.

***

"Not today, damn you. I'll let you know when."

"It's convenient for me today."

"Well, it isn't for me. The last thing we want is you turning up in the middle of—"

"But what the hell difference can it make? It'd be a bloody sight better than me being caught with the bloody things here. I warned you right from the start. I warned you I wasn't taking chances like that. They've been here too long as it is."

"There's been developments here. They'll be buzzing around the bloody place like—"

"All the more reason why it won't make no difference. I made a deal with you, my old mate, and I'm not buggering around with it now. They'll be there today and there's the end of it." And he hung up.

"Oh, Christ!" The man holding the phone almost moaned it. "Oh, Christ."

"Mr. Formby?"

"Yes. May?"

"Have you heard?"

"Heard what?"

"About Mr. Oxford?"

"What now?"

"Murdered he was, Mr. Formby."

"Ye Gods, May! Everyone knows that! The porter at the gate told me when I drove in, and I've been told by everyone else I've seen since I got here. I thought you had something new, like who murdered him."

"I'd tell you if I knew." She sounded hurt and he took a deep breath. No sense in upsetting her. She could sulk for a week if she was upset.

"I'm sure you would. If that's all then…"

"Oh, no, Mr. Formby. Mr. Herne wants a word—"

"What? Why didn't you say so at once? I'll go right over."

"He's on the phone, Mr. Formby."

He stopped worrying about upsetting her. "For Christ's sake, and you've kept me blathering on about Oxford? Put him through, woman!"

She put him through, and he could feel her flouncing as she did it. God help him for the rest of the week. His coffee would be disgusting. So would the pained silences.

"Mitchell?"

"Sorry to keep you, Matthew. Wretched girl put you through on the wrong line or something."

"Then you'd better get them checked, hadn't you? Your responsibility, the phones, aren't they? Now, listen, Mitchell. I'm most concerned. Most concerned."

"Oh?"

"Oxford. Murdered you know."

"I had heard." Formby made it as non-committal as he could.

"It's the money that I'm worried about."

"Money? What money?"

"For Barrie Ward, of course! What else?"

Formby let his shoulders relax. "Oh, I see. Well, I'm sure we'll find someone else to take over the chairmanship of the committee, Matthew. It's early days, that's all. I'll suggest to that woman, what's her name, the dressmaker one—Madeleine Schwab—I'll suggest to Madeleine that she approach Felicity Oxford as soon as is decent, see if she'll take over. I think she'd be best, you know, knows everyone on the committee and people are always sorry for widows. I don't want to sound too calculating, of course, but we're committed to a lot of building there and it's important we keep the money coming in. And making the best use we can of our assets, like Mrs. Oxford, would make sense—"

"Do stop! I'm not concerned about the committee! Or not at the moment. It's the money that Oxford was handling that worries me'

"Eh?" Formby was startled.

"The takings of the concert, the last big Bring and Buy and the response to that special mailshot he did. He handled it all. I've checked on the computer account and there's none of it in. The question I have to sort out is whether we have to get our lawyers on to it, or whether it'll show up once the will has been sorted out. I've never been involved with a person who got himself murdered before." He spoke with an air of fastidiousness. "So I don't know the drill."

"I can't say I have either," Formby said a little drily. "What does the lawyer say?"

"I told you, I haven't asked. I have to decide what to do about lawyers." He sounded uneasy. "The problem is, it's a lot of money. Thirty-seven thousand."

"Thirty—what?" Formby's voice squeaked its amazement. "How much?"

"It was the mailshot. He got various big names to sign it. It brought in a lot—the thirty thousand part. The rest was all the work the committee's been doing. It ought to be on the hospital computer by now."

"When did you realize it wasn't?"

Herne sighed. "I meant to speak to Oxford about it, but it wasn't convenient. I thought I'd catch him at the concert, but of course he wasn't there."

"No," Formby said. "He wasn't, was he? He was busy getting himself murdered at the time."

"I can't see how that happened," Herne said fretfully. "On his own, locked in his flat, how did he get murdered? It has to be a mistake, surely."

"Well, the police are the people you'll have to ask about that." Formby was thinking fast. "As for the Fund money…"

"Yes. What shall we do about that?"

"I think you should talk to the lawyers. At once," Formby said, putting a definite emphasis on the word you. "If I'd been at all involved, that's what I'd do. It's up to you, of course. I'm just the one who agrees spending. I don't actually handle the income."

Herne took a deep breath. "I see. Thank you for your help, Formby. Talking to you has cleared my mind a little. Yes, cleared my mind. Thank you."

He hung up.

"Carole? I'll be late tonight."

"Oh, Bear, must you? I've been looking forward to getting out. I've been stuck in all day."

"Darling, I know. If I could be there, don't you think I would? It's just that there's a panic on here'

"What sort?"

"That man who missed the concert, Richard Oxford. He's been murdered."

"Ooh? Really? What a thing! Who did it?"

"No idea. No one has, but there're problems of course, what with money and things."

"Money?" Her voice sharpened.

"Coochie, I'll tell you all about it tonight, I promise. You'll be there?"

"Well, I don't know." He could see her pouting and felt the tingle at the back of his neck. "It'll be so dismal if you're not here, but I could go over to Barbie. She's got a little party tonight and I thought we'd go on there together. But..."

"Oh, Christ," he muttered and she said, "Mmm?" in a questioning voice and he said loudly, "Nothing!" and thought hard. "I'll tell you what, sweetie. You get yourself all dolled up and I'll be home by, say, seven. How's that? The party won't get going till after that, will it? Of course not. And I'll dress so fast you'll be amazed and we'll go to Barbie's together."

She squealed delightedly. "Oh, Bear, darling, you are adorable! I've got the most fabulous dress you ever saw—"

"Another one?"

"You said I could if I wanted to and—"

"Oh, of course, of course," he said hastily. "Of course I did, angel. So, seven o'clock, hmm? Put my things ready for me to change. You never know, we might have time for a little this and that…"

She giggled. "We'll have to see about that, sweet old Bear. Maybe, if you're very good."

"Oh, Christ," he said. "I want to come home now."

She giggled again. "Got crowded trousers, angel face, talking to your puss? Ooh, you are a naughty man! Shall I see you this afternoon, then?"

"Shit, no!" He was sweating a little. "I can't. But I'll be there as soon as I can. I do love you, Carole."

She giggled again and it made his neck crawl even more. It was a sound he needed to hear. "I'm beginning to think you do, my angel. See you tonight, then. I won't dress till—oh, half past six. How's that?" And again she made that breathy little giggling sound and hung up and he sat there for a long time with the phone to his ear, listening to the buzz. It helped a little.

"Beatrice? Is something wrong?"

"No. Should there be?"

"You don't usually call me in the middle of the day."

"I had a call from Felicity Oxford."

There was a silence. Then he said carefully, "Oh?"

"About her husband." Beatrice sounded impatient. "That he'd been done away with."

"So it seems."

"You didn't tell me."

"I would have done tonight. I didn't think it worth a special call."

"Oh? I would have done. However, she's concerned about the Fund and the committee meeting. Kind of her, under the circumstances."

"Very."

"I told her I'm willing to chair it. It's tomorrow."

"It might be better to cancel."

"Oh, I don't think so. It's important to keep ahead of things.

I just want you to see to it that the agendas are printed ready and the various documents organized."

"I'm very busy just at—"

"And tell your secretary to see to it this time the tea is hot. No committee I'm running will have to tolerate the sloppiness we've had to put up with."

"I'll tell her, Beatrice. Anything else?"

"Not at present."

"Then I'll see you tonight."

"I need a favor,"

"Oh, do you?" she said sweetly. "Want me to let you off your bet?"

"Not on your nellie! I always pay any debt of honor. Every penny of it. No! I'm glad to pay up. I need some help, that's the thing."

"But you know I'm falling over backwards to help the police."

"So I'd noticed. You don't have to be that acrobatic, mind you. All you got to do is…Look, one of the detective constables tells me you took pictures of the Oxford flat that night."

"What if I did?"

"So I need to see them."

"Can't you get your own?"

She could almost see the chagrin on his face at the other end of the line. "Not the ones I want, bugger it. Some bloody idiot gave the wife permission to go in. So I don't know what's been moved and what hasn't. The dickhead said he saw no harm, seeing it wasn't a crime."

"But that's what you thought." She sounded more sweet than ever. "They say that every organization takes its tone from the head, so you can't blame your chaps if they thought it was just an ordinary death, can you?"

"I've had enough of that," he said. "No need to push the shovel an' all down me throat, is there? I've eaten enough crow as it is. But now I have to see what the place was like, before anyone wandered around unsupervised."

"With pleasure." She cooed the words with deliberate charm. "Come any time that suits you. It's always a pleasure to help a colleague." And she hung up and sat back in her chair, her hands linked behind her head, grinning at the ceiling. It had been a long time since she'd been so pleased with herself. It was a very agreeable feeling.

14

He looked again at the photographs, which were spread in a tidy pattern across her desk, and then sighed and swept them up into a pile. "It's no use. I can't remember that well. They look much the same to me, as though nothing's been disturbed, but who am I to be sure? Just a bloody copper, after all."

"Supposed to be a detective," she murmured. "Supposed to see at a glance when things have been messed about with."

"Don't you start again. You've been piling on the agony enough. You were right, I was wrong, and I've said so as handsome as I know how. Now lay off." But he didn't sound all that angry. More amused, she thought.

"I'll try not to rub it in," she said kindly. "I can understand how much you must be smarting."

"Not me." He got to his feet and reached for his jacket, after pulling down his shirt sleeves and buttoning them. "I never look back at mistakes. Only forward to success. OK, I'll take these and go and start some comparing."

"I'll get my coat. Just give me five minutes to talk to Jerry about some stuff here. I can spare—oh, an hour, perhaps."

"Who asked you to come along?" He stopped and lifted his brows at her. "I don't remember saying anything about you coming along."

She reached forward, took the pictures from his hand in one neat movement and tucked them into the pocket of her white coat. "You didn't have to. I've decided to come along."

"What for?"

She sighed a little theatrically. "To do some comparing, of course."

"There's the photos. That's all I need."

"And I've got my memory to add into the mix," she said. "And let me remind you it's a trained memory. I'm an observer. It's what pathologists do best, you know, make observations. You need me."

"Haven't you got anything else to do? They need you here, too, I imagine."

"I'm a good administrator." She smiled as serenely as she could. "So I can delegate."

"Listen, doll. I like your company. You know that. But I got the impression you weren't that crazy on mine. So what's this all about? I don't generally expect the doctor to do a follow-up at the scene of the crime. So why are you being so pushy?"

Her serenity wobbled and then melted away. "Pushy? Me? I like that! I'm not being anything of the sort. But I do know what I'm good at and I'm good at noticing things other people don't. I told you, it's what pathologists do best. It's what I do best, dammit. And since if it hadn't been for me you'd have had this chap neatly in his grave and no one any the wiser that there was a murderer wandering around unchecked, it's a bit rich to—"

"All right, all right!" He held up both hands in mock surrender. "I give in. I'll allow you to come along with me, on one condition."

"You're not allowing anything. I've told you I'm coming, so you can't make any conditions. Only I can. And the first is you wait till I sort out a couple of things." She walked past him out of her office and into the big lab, feeling him follow her but paying no attention.

"Jerry!" she called. "I gather Sheila's still over in Formby's office sorting out the reagent orders?"

"It's what she said she was doing." Jerry looked up from his microscope. "Mind you, she's been gone long enough to order a supply for the next seven years. But there it is, she's got a lot of people to talk to on the way, I imagine." He winked at Jane who giggled and put her head down over her microscope as George turned to look at her.

And then frowned. "Jane? Which microscope is that?"

"This?" Jane patted it. "It arrived an hour ago. Isn't it great they moved so fast?"

George went over and looked at it. Then she shook her head. "Who'd have thought they'd manage that? How long did you have to wait to get them in the first place? And Formby told me...Yet now they manage to get replacements as fast as this. Well, for once no one can complain. Have they all been replaced? Or is this the only one?"

"They're all back," Jerry said cheerfully. "This time I signed the delivery note and kept a copy. I put it on Sheila's desk. She'll put it through to you in the usual way, I imagine."

"Well, thank God that little business is settled," George said. "Now we can catch up with some of the backlog, I hope. Peter, let me have those livers from ICU as soon as I get back, will you? I have to go out for an hour. This murder..." Behind her Gus snickered softly but she ignored him.

Jerry looked up and grinned at her. "How does it feel to have hit the jackpot?"

"I wasn't gambling," she said repressively. "Just doing my job," and again Gus snickered.

"And trying to interfere with mine while she's at it," he said in an amiable tone and Jerry laughed. "But I dare say you're used to that, eh?"

"I'll take my bleep with me," George said, looking as though she hadn't heard a word he'd said. "There shouldn't be anything special, but if there is..."

"I'll let you know," Jerry promised and she nodded crisply and marched out, a maneuver which was rather hampered by the fact that Gus was leaning against the door and made no effort to get out of her way. But she managed it and fetched her topcoat from her office, transferring the precious photographs from the pocket of her white coat, which she shed, to its capacious inside pocket. She was damned if she'd let Gus get them in his supercilious hands, she told herself. They were hers and there was no way he was going to claim the credit for having them now.

Outside it was still cold and blustery, which made the chill bite harder. Her eyes watered a little behind her glasses and she sniffed hard.

"I'll soon have you all cosied up," he said as he strode along beside her so fast she was hard put to it not to break into a little run to keep up. "You'll feel better then. Got to look after you, haven't we? Seein' you're not used to going out and about on investigations that much—and why should you be, after all?"

She ignored that too, and went on, her head down, until at last he stopped on the far side of the car park.

"Here we are," he said, and she could almost feel the pride oozing out of him as he unlocked the car door.

What a stunning car, was her first reaction. Her father had always had a sneaking affection for old autos and she'd learned a good deal from his attachment. It was obvious that this was a very special one. Black, shining, with the unmistakable lines and trims of a nineteen-seventies model, it was clearly a much-loved object, and she couldn't help her admiration showing.

"Not bad, is she?" Gus said modestly, actually patting the roof. "She was me old dad's. He never drove her much, mind you, but he reckoned a man as successful as he was deserved a good motor, so a good motor he got. And then left it in the garage most of the time. He liked using shanks's pony or gettin' on a bus. Said it gave him a better view of his customers. As though everyone wasn't his customer anyway, seeing he sold the best fish in all London."

"It's very nice," she said, and then couldn't maintain the air of coolness any longer. "Very nice. It's a—"

"Thirteen hundred Austin Van den Plas. Original leather upholstery, still got the picnic hamper in the back, all that, but I've done a few things to the engine. She can really move now. Got twin Weber carbs, raised compression ratio, and I stiffened the suspension and put on low profile tires. She rides like a dream. Get in, then."

She did and took a deep breath of the satisfying smell of leather as she settled back into the comfort, enjoying the look of the polished wooden fascia in front of her. When he got in beside her she said impulsively, "She's beautiful!"

"I knew we'd get on well," he said. "Any woman who understands what a good car should be like has to be a woman worth knowing. Don't forget your seat belt. It was sacrilege to fit 'em, but it was the law."

The car moved smoothly, manoeuvring easily out of the hospital yard and into the mainstream of the traffic, always heavy at this time of day, and took off along the Highway. She sat and stared ahead of her, reveling in it. He looked at her sideways after a while and said casually, "I suppose you'll have to get back to the hospital this afternoon?"

"Mmm? I told you, I've only got an hour. Of course I have to go back."

"I just thought we could go and have a drink or something afterwards." He pulled the wheel around to take them down towards the river and the Docklands Development area. "Get to know each other better, like."

She turned her head to look at him. "That's a change of tune."
"Eh?"

"Back at the hospital you were complaining because I wanted to come on this trip, and now—"

"One thing's got nothing to do with the other. I told you, I like you. You're all right. Especially now I know you're keen on old cars. We could talk about engines."

"I don't know that much about engines. And anyway, don't change the subject."

"Who's changing any subjects? I just said, let's go and have a drink and talk about cars."

"As long as I don't talk about the case, is that it?" she said. "You want to turn me into a—a date so that you stop having to deal with me as an equal colleague in work? It's an old trick, that, and—"

He sighed. "There you go again. If you grow any more feminist prickles you'll end up like a porcupine. Whatever you do, you'll have to do it so carefully it'll be no fun any more." He slid his eyes sideways for a moment before returning his attention to the road. "That'd be a pity."

"Oh, God," she said disgustedly. "That stupid joke is as old as last week's cold cabbage and just as boring."

"Whoops!" I'd better be extra careful, hadn't I? You'll be having me for sexual harassment next."

"I wouldn't be such a wimp. If I couldn't handle someone like you, I wouldn't regard myself as safe going out without my mom. Do me a favor, Hathaway. Just be businesslike, will you? We can dispense with the footsie game."

"What a woman!" he said with an air of great admiration. "What a woman! All right, here we are. Equal colleague, are you? Then get yourself out of the car and up the stairs. I'll see you there." And she had barely got out of the car and pulled her coat belt tight than he'd locked it and gone zooming up the road and into Oxford's building, nodding at the policeman standing there, leaving her to follow him. She was irritated to realize how much she minded being left behind.

"It's a bit much, 'n't it?" he said when they were standing in the middle of the living room. "Looks like a tart's dream of heaven."

"I wouldn't know about that," she said. "Any more than you would. I know it looks expensive."

"Cheap, though. All this stuff…Cost a fortune, no doubt, but at the end of the day, look at it."

"Mmm," she said, agreeing with him and not wanting to say so. The room that had taken her breath away the first time she had seen it looked tawdry now. The gold leaf of the pillars seemed as insignificant as toffee paper, and the thick leatheriness of the furniture and the curtains could have been the cheapest plastic in the bleak daylight. It was like a Christmas tree the day after New Year's when the lights are dead and the tinsel is threatening to tarnish at any moment.

"Looks the same in here, doesn't it?" he said, glancing at the photographs she had taken from her pocket. "Not that you took many in here." He took them from her and she relinquished them without demur.

"I concentrated on the bedroom and bathroom. Your sergeant was in here so I didn't hang around."

"I'll ask him what he remembers. Bedroom next then, if, that is, you don't mind."

"It's what I came to do," she snapped and moved away, following her memory to the bedroom door.

Here too the intrusion of daylight made it seem diminished. The carpets looked tired and crumpled, the mirrors simply silly. The sheets had been taken away and the counterpane and blankets left folded under the pillows from which the slips had been removed. They looked almost pathetic beneath the tulle drapes hanging dispiritedly from the ceiling fitting. George looked around, making herself remember it as it had been, pulling the picture back into her mind almost as a conscious effort. It was a trick she'd long ago taught herself; she had always had a good memory, though it had never been fully eidetic—the sort of immediate imprinting that enables owners of such memories to read with their mind's eye a page only once seen—but she could bring herself very close to it. She did so now.

"Apart from the changes in the bed," she said, "the rug's been moved. It was right beside the bed, that extra thick one, and now it's been put down beside the dais. And the chair that was by the fireplace has been shifted back a foot or two."

He looked at her in silence and then down at the pictures in his hand, shuffling them till he found the relevant ones of the bedroom.

"That was some display," he said after a moment.

"I told you I was useful."

"Yeah, well, maybe. But that useful? Lady, you're incredible! Is that all in here?"

"I think…" She looked around again and narrowed her eyes, bringing back the memory so that she could superimpose it on what she was actually seeing. "Yes. It is."

"Bathroom, then."

He led the way, much more polite now, holding the door open for her. She was childishly pleased to have had so marked an effect on him. That'll show him, she thought. That'll show him.

Here in the bathroom, where there was no outside window to admit the dull daylight, the artificial light was glittering its magic, and the effect of tawdriness was absent. The room looked as exotic as it had the first time she'd seen it. She stared around and then shivered a little.

"I know," he said. "Decadent, 'n't it? That's the only word I can think of that fits."

"I know what you mean," she said absently and forced her memory to work once more, doing the same superimposition trick she'd done in the bedroom. "It all looks much the same so far. That toothglass was on the side like that, and the toothbrush on the ledge. And the smear on the mirror, I remember that too."

He was scribbling in a notebook. "Anything else?"

She hesitated. "Not with the doors closed. I looked inside though, too. And snapped that as well. Look and see."

He riffled through the photographs again, selected half a dozen and set them out in a row on the tiled edge of the washbasin.

"They're good pictures. Taken from the right angles. Well done."

"Yes," she said, not really listening, and pored over them. "Yes, they're the ones. I don't want to look though, not too much. Let me remember…"

"With pleasure," he said with some fervor and stepped back as she moved to open the cupboard doors.

One after another she stared at them: the rows of bottles and lotions, the tubes of creams, the pill bottles, all the usual bathroom equipment with the added items she'd expect to see in the possession of a man who was moderately hypochondriac. And in her experience, that was most men beyond the age of fifty or so.

"It looks undisturbed to me," she said. "I don't think anyone's moved a thing." She frowned, concentrating, and shook her head. "Do the pictures match?"

He moved forward and went from open cupboard to open cupboard, and as he moved his reflection was picked up by the mirrors and thrown from one to the other so that first he seemed to disappear into an eternal vista of repetitions of himself and then seemed to grow and loom closer like an army of one man marching. It created an odd sensation and she had to close her eyes for a moment because it made her giddy.

"They agree with you. Nothing moved. Not a thing. Hmm." There was silence as he stood and looked down at the pictures.

"Now what?" she said at last.

He looked up. "I'm not sure. I think perhaps…Yes, I'll get our fingerprints chap over. Not that I expect to get anything…" He reached into his pocket and pulled out a pair of thin black silk gloves, the sort that George wore when she went skiing, and pulled them on. "Watch me and make sure I'm careful. I want to look at some of this stuff."

Gingerly and with great delicacy he lifted some of the medicine bottles from the cupboards, picking them up by the milled edges of the caps. "Surfaces like this don't take prints so I can't do any harm here," he murmured and turned the bottles around to read the labels, one after the other. "Paracetamol:

good old painkiller. Aspirin: ditto. He must have had a lot of headaches. Multivite—well, yes, we've all got those lying around. Sustenol—what's that?"

"Male hormone," she said and he chucked his chin in a gesture of unsurprise.

"Yeah, well he was the sort as'd use that kind of thing. Looked like it, anyway. No pharmacist's label on it, just a doctor's name. I'll check on that. I imagine this is one of the Harley Street blokes Oxford used and who his GP was so sharp about."

"I wouldn't be surprised," she said. "I hear there's quite a—a good deal of that sort of work done in Harley Street."

"Quite a trade you were going to say, and perfectly correctly, too. Some of these so-called specialists are little more than meat marketeers. Makes me sick. If you'd ha' known what they got up to before the abortion act, and how much money they made—Well, take it from me, they was bad news. What's this? Amytal…" He unscrewed the bottle carefully and peered in. "Capsules."

"Hmm," she said. "It goes with the male hormone, perhaps. It's an—um—"

"I rather think I know about this. Use it when you're having sex and it blows your head off, right? Only you've got to time it right."

She was pleased with herself for not blushing. "Something like that."

"There's not much they didn't get up to, is there? What about these things?" He was picking up tubes now. "Lubricating jelly—well, we won't go into that, I think. I know enough about that. Zinc and castor oil cream with cod liver oil?"

"Useful for pruritus. Itching. Acts as a barrier cream, too."

"Mmm. And this?" He was peering at another label. "'The Cream. Use as required.' Very informative, that is."

"Show," she said. He held it out to her and she read the list of ingredients on the label. "I thought so. That's a hemorrhoid cream."

"Then why doesn't it say so?"

"Because he had it privately dispensed." She shook her head disgustedly. "He could have bought a formula much like this over the counter anywhere for a quid or two. God knows what he paid for this, just because it was specially made up—"

"Hemorrhoids," Gus said. He shook his head as he put the tube back into its place. "Supposed to be funny in some circles. I'm here to tell you they ain't."

"I'm not interested in your medical history."

"I wasn't telling you mine," he said mildly. "It was me old dad. A martyr to 'em, he was."

This time she did redden. "Oh."

"Did Oxford have bad ones? Could account for his reputation as a bad-tempered type sometimes."

"I don't know."

"Eh?" He looked at her sharply. "Didn't you look?"

"Not specifically. One doesn't usually."

"Oh, well, you can always check up."

"I suppose so. Is it all that necessary?"

"We have to check everything in a murder investigation," he said, and now he was very serious. "You know that. I have to get these pills and creams and so forth checked at forensic, have to interview all the prescribing doctors. It'll take ages." He sighed. "Could you take on some of 'em?"

"Me? Take on what?"

"You're quicker than the police labs," he said. "If I can get some of the work done by you as well as sending some of it off to our own forensic people it'll save me a lot of time. I could do with it. Seeing I was stupid enough not to listen to you and wasted all the time I could have been on the job." He smiled. "It's a bit of a cheek asking you a favor when you've already got me out of shtook just by insisting on doing your job properly and finding out it was a nasty one. But I'd appreciate it'

She was silent for a moment and then said a little hesitantly, "I think you mean that."

"Of course I do. You'll have to get used to me, you know. I'm always serious. Except when I'm joshing, and you can usually tell when I'm doing that. If you're clever. And you're clever."

"Thanks a lot. Well, I suppose I could. What do you want me to do?"

"Let me get the boys here, get the place resealed, and the man on duty relieved—he's been here all day. I've set up my incident room at the nick and you can send down there tomorrow to pick up—" He saw her raised eyebrows and lifted his hands in mock self-defense. "Sorry, sorry! I'll send over the stuff I'd like you to work on, after the fingerprinters have done their bit, and leave you to check up on it. OK? Do we have a deal?"

"Well, I suppose so…"

"Lady, you're a gent," he said, taking her hand and shaking it warmly. "I'll go and make the necessary calls and then I'll take you back to Old East. Ta, George." He flicked his thumb and forefinger in that imaginary salute at that invisible hat brim and left her standing in the bathroom surrounded by a disappearing vista of herself in all the mirrors, and feeling once again rather self-satisfied.

15

George was in the small lab, sorting through the contents of Oxford's bathroom cabinets which Gus had sent over to her, watched by Jerry who was scrutinizing her in his most birdlike manner.

"What are we looking for then?" he asked. "Is it something special? Or—"

"Everything there is to be found," George said. "He died of digitalis overdosage, but there was none in his possession as far as we could see and we have no record of his ever being treated with it. Or so the GP says. The police are dealing with the various Harley Street types he used'—she flicked one of the tubes of cream a little dismissively—"but until we hear from them, we have to check everything. He must have got it somehow. So we need to see if anything from his bathroom was adulterated in any way."

Jerry picked up a bottle of vitamins. "You mean one of these might have had digitalis in it?"

"Perhaps."

"But they couldn't."

"How can you be so sure?" George took the bottle back from him to put it in its appointed place among those she was sorting. "It wouldn't be the first time someone put a poison in something else so that a person would take it without knowing it was harmful."

"Not one of these," Jerry said very positively. "I mean, look at 'em." He picked up the bottle again and shook one of the tablets on to his palm. "They're coated. Even if someone knew how to make a pill like that—and it's obviously a machine-made one—they wouldn't be able to coat it to match, would they? And what about the size of it, anyway? I told you, he must have had around thirty of the twenty-five milligram tablets to give him the tissue levels he had. That'd make one hell of a big pill."

"Maybe it was more than one."

"All right. So he—or she, whoever the person is trying to get rid of old Oxford—makes two or three of these pills, though God knows how, seeing they're coated and all that. How can he or she be sure that Oxford'll take them all at once? People don't take three of these at a time, do they? I thought the whole thing was that they're once-a-dayers. So it couldn't have been these."

"You're probably right," George said. "I dare say it wasn't one of these, or three of them. But he took it in something, so we have to check everything."

"Maybe whoever it was came and gave it to him," Jerry said. "Gave him a nice hot drink of milk and laced it with digitalis."

"No way. Remember the stomach contents? Absolutely empty. He hadn't eaten for a long time before he went to bed. If he'd had something with milk I'd have found traces."

"Well, tea then, or coffee. Or a whisky and soda. No, dammit, not whisky. He was clear of alcohol."

"Completely. And why should he take a handful of digitalis pills anyway? Not that there's any point in our even discussing it. I keep coming back to those stomach contents. Nothing there except a bit of mucus and gastric juices and enzymes. I'd swear to it he didn't take a thing by mouth that could have hurt him within several hours of his death. If he'd swallowed those pills he'd have died before the last of them left the stomach, surely. And we'd have found them."

Jerry sighed. "It's daft, anyway," he said lugubriously. "Didn't you say the place was locked up? Burglar alarm set and everything?"

"Exactly. No one came and tucked him in with a handy dose of poison and then left him. He put himself to bed after he'd locked up—"

"Oh, I am enjoying this!" Jerry said. "It's just like being Inspector Morse."

"Except that we're dealing with a real man who died. And that's not fun, is it?"

"Oh, I don't know," Jerry said with a judicious air. "It is, really, seeing it was Oxford who's involved. Everyone thought he was a shit so why pretend about it? The way he used to prowl around sticking his nose into everything, he was such a creepy old devil. Smarmy and nosy at the same time, him and his fundraising. Just a front for meddling."

"I know," George said. "I remember taking a scunner to him when he came crawling 'round me with his 'let me know what I can fix for you' talk. So I suppose there won't be many who—"

"—won't be glad to see the back of him," Jerry said. "Right."

George stopped what she was doing and stared at him. "People around here? At Old East?" she said.

"Heavens yes!" Jerry picked up another pill bottle, the paracetamol this time. "Half the hospital, if you ask me."

"Then the person who did this could be someone we all know."

"Mmm?" Jerry looked at her, his forehead crumpled. "I suppose so. What's wrong with that? It'd be marvelous to uncover a villain here. I'd love it. You're not going to go all soggy over this, are you Dr. B.? You should find it more interesting to track down a person you might know, rather than just any old stranger. Adds a spice, I reckon."

"You would," George said, taking back the paracetamol and starting work again. "Look, take all these tablets and be very careful indeed with your readings and your recordings. I don't want the police to be able to make the smallest complaint. We're doing this instead of sending it off to the police forensic lab, to save time—"

"And money, I'll bet," Jerry said.

"Probably. Anyway, it's got to be superbly done, you understand me? I want no cock-ups."

"It'd never do to upset the Chief Inspector, would it?" Jerry said wickedly. He took the pills and carried them over to his work station. "Is this all?"

George, finding it easier to ignore his comment about Hathaway, said shortly, "You can see for yourself. That's all the pill bottles. I'll deal with the liquid doses myself. Let me have an answer as soon as you can."

The laboratory settled down to silence. Jane and Peter were still in the canteen on their afternoon tea break and Sheila was away somewhere around the hospital on one of her interminable administrative trips, and George thought, as she organized her equipment to start analysing her own samples, I'll have to deal with her. She's letting her taste for gossip get in the way of her work. It would be hard to complain to Sheila because although she was well known for her penchant for gossip and was frequently absent from the lab in the pursuit of it, she did her work with great skill and attention to detail; it was hard to find any fault in it, ever. Jane, who never stirred from her station except to go to meals and the lavatory, who never made a private phone call and whose only vice was allowing herself to be distracted by Jerry's chatter, made far more mistakes and did far less work than Sheila ever had. All the same, George thought as she measured reagents into a test tube, I'll have to speak to her.

Jane and Peter came back and she put them to work, too, on some of the samples from Oxford's flat. There was hospital stuff to get through, but nothing urgent, and the sooner she got all this out of the way, she told herself, the sooner she'd be able to see that the laboratory was working full tilt on hospital demands. But she knew that the real reason was that she wanted to show off to Gus Hathaway, wanted him to be amazed at the speed with which he got results back from George as compared with the police laboratory, and she despised herself for it. But she still did it.

Sheila came back to the lab about half an hour later and George looked at her over her microscope with an enquiring air that made Sheila look stubborn at once.

"I can't help it if these wretched secretaries take so long about everything," she said. "I try to hurry them along, but they don't know what the word efficiency means."

"Everyone's out of step except me," sang Jerry sweetly into his microscope and Sheila glowered at him.

"I'd like to see how you'd get on if you had to worry over the things I do," she said. "Dealing with that supply office is like dealing with a cloud on legs."

"All right," George said peaceably. "As long as whatever it is is sorted out…"

"Not really." Sheila sniffed. "I've told the wretched woman to write to the manufacturers now and get me copies of all the paperwork. Then I'll know where I am. I'm sick of her looking for it and not finding it. Let her go to the trouble of tracking it down and leave me to get on with my work."

"It'll make a nice change," Jerry murmured and again Sheila glared at him.

"Jerry Swann, if you want to—"

"Enough," George said loudly. "That's quite enough."

Behind them the door from the other lab opened and the young technician Sam put his head around it.

"Er, Sheila," he said. "I thought I heard your voice. Please, could I have a word?"

"What about?" Sheila snapped, now thoroughly irritable. "Can't you do anything without someone behind you all the time?"

"It's not that," Sam said and then, as someone behind him apparently pushed him further into the room, "It's something different. Not work. Well, not exactly. I wouldn't have bothered you but Tracy said I should."

One of the girls was standing behind him now and her face was set in a sort of stubborn yet excited look, and she said loudly, "It's something that you've got to know about."

"Well, what is it?" Sheila said resignedly, moving towards the door.

"It's those microscopes," Tracy began and nudged Sam. "Tell her."

"Oh, not again!" George cried and put down her test tubes, rattling them in their stand in her hurry. "I don't want to hear another word about the damned things. They were stolen, you all gave your statements to the police, they've been replaced and surely that's an end of it. Do we have to keep on and on chewing over the same old—"

"Of course we do!" Sheila cried. "I have to have all the paperwork—the order-form copies and so forth—so that I can keep the file updated. Suppose they were stolen again? If I didn't have all the paperwork, it'd be a complete mess!"

"It is anyway," George snapped. "The important thing is we've got the things. To hell with the paperwork. Life's too short to spend shifting pieces of paper from one place to another."

"But this is important!" Tracy said as Sam tried to pull on her arm and get her away.

"It's all right," he said. "I don't suppose it's anything. I could have been wrong, anyway."

"You weren't wrong," Tracy said firmly and looked at George. "The thing is, Sam looked at the microscope I got when they came back and he says it's the same one."

"The same what? How do you mean?" George said.

"He recognized it." She nudged Sam again. "Tell 'em, do!"

The boy was red and miserable, almost on the edge of tears, and he spoke directly to George, trying to ignore Sheila who was looking at him furiously. "I never meant to do any harm, it was an accident—"

"Oh, shut up about that, Sam! No one'll care about that now! Now we've got proof that—Look, shall I tell them?"

The boy nodded weakly and Tracy turned. She stood with her feet set a little apart to brace herself and her hands shoved deep into her white-coat pockets to hide their shaking. She was very excited.

"We've got definite proof that these microscopes were stolen and—"

"But no one doubts that," George cried, bewildered. "That's why the police were called and—"

"—and the ones that have come back are the same ones. The stolen ones."

There was a short silence and then Sheila asked in a slightly stupefied tone, "What did you say?"

"Sam had an accident with his, the day after it came. The first time it came, I mean. After we'd waited all those months for them. He dropped something heavy and chipped a bit of the enamel. He was ever so worried, said you'd kill him and—"

"You're damned right!" Sheila said. "A new microscope? What'd you expect?"

"So he got some touch-up paint. The sort you use for cars."

"And tried to hide the damage," George said, and made for the door. "Show me."

They all went into the big lab, Jerry and Jane following, even silent Peter being pulled from his stool in the excitement as Sam led the way to Tracy's station.

"There, you see?" he said, pointing. "I'm ever so sorry, Sheila, honestly I am. It wasn't my fault. I had one of the big weights and it sort of slid in my hand and hit the foot all sideways and there was this great chip and I thought, well, after a few months no one'll remember and it'll be all right. But then they were stolen—"

"And when they were replaced we thought they were new ones, but then I saw this mark on mine and I said to Sam, it looks funny, this bit, and he looked and said it was his microscope because he'd fixed it."

"I spent hours over it," Sam said. "I'd never have forgotten what it looked like. I never will. That's my microscope all right."

George was sitting at the microscope now and peering down at it. "Give me that hand magnifier," she said over her shoulder. Tracy handed it to her.

There was a long silence while she looked through it at the mark Sam had shown her and then she put the magnifier down and sat silent, frowning down at it.

"Sheila," she said after the long pause. "When these came back, who delivered them?"

"I don't know. I came back to the lab—I'd been somewhere—and found they were here. Jerry signed the delivery note."

George looked up at Jerry. "What sort of person brought them?"

Jerry screwed up his face. "Oh, Lor', Dr. B. I can't remember! Chap in overalls, the usual sort, you know."

"Had you ever seen him before?"

"Not to my recollection."

"Did anyone else see him?"

Jane lifted her head. "Me. Only I can't say I noticed much. Ordinary sort of a man. Said, 'Here's your microscope, sign here,' and Jerry said, 'I've got to have a copy,' and the man said, 'Fine,' and gave him one and that was it."

"How were they brought here? On a trolley or carried or what?"

Jerry pointed across the lab to one of the big trolleys they used to shift materials around the big room. "Just the usual sort."

"And he took it away with him afterwards?"

"Yes. Why?"

George shrugged her shoulders. "I haven't the least idea. I just wanted to try to see how it was. Look, Sheila, the copy of the delivery note, I imagine you have it?"

Sheila nodded. "Jerry left it on my desk. I'll get it."

George pored over the piece of paper and shook her head. It was a piece of the hospital's stationery, carrying the familiar letterhead, with "Supplies Department' printed across the top left-hand corner in black print. She put it down on the bench and again shook her head.

"It's the usual sort of scribble, isn't it? Three microscopes, replacement for invoiced items and no number to identify the invoice."

"That was what I kept telling that stupid woman in Formby's office," Sheila said triumphantly. "I said if she numbered everything that went out of there she'd be able to track the things down. She just said she did and denied her system ever went wrong, but here we are with proof."

George had picked up the sheet again and now she frowned. "Sheila, have you any other supply department notes?"

"Of course. But not to do with these microscopes."

"It doesn't matter. Let me see what you have."

Sheila went away and everyone stood around George in awkward silence as they waited for her return. George was about to send them all back to work when Sheila at last came back and put a sheet of paper in front of her.

"Ah," George said. "I was right." She felt a lift of excitement, the sort she used to feel when sitting exams and she had found the answer to one of the questions bouncing in her mind. "I knew I remembered." She ran her finger over the heading on the paper and said to no one in particular, "You see?"

"See what?" Sheila said crossly as the others leaned closer and peered.

"Oh!" It was Jerry who saw it first and he sounded startled. "It's the wrong color!"

"Got it. This lettering'—George touched the sheet that Sheila had just brought her—is in very dark blue, isn't it? And very slightly raised, isn't it? But this is black, and quite smooth." And she ran her finger over the heading on the delivery note that Jerry had signed.

"It's not a proper piece of stationery," Jerry said. "It's a—"

"I reckon it's a photocopy," George said as she got to her feet. "Jerry, Peter, all of you, back to work. Sheila, you and I must go and see Formby over this. Right now."

"My pleasure," Sheila said with great relish. "It'll do my

heart good to show those stupid people just where they've—Oh!" And she stopped.

"You've realized!" Jerry said. "Imagine that! Sheila's understood! It's not their fault, is it, if someone pinched a bit of their stationery and photocopied it to use for a theft, is it? You've been nagging that woman purple all this time and it wasn't her fault at all."

"Oh," Sheila said again, blankly this time, and then very slowly her face began to flush and Jerry laughed delightedly.

"Better if you go on your own, Dr. B." he said. "Sheila'd not be much of an asset the way things are, would she? You go and sort it out yourself. It would be better, don't you agree?"

16

"You can't expect me to say nothing about it," George said in what she hoped was a tone of calm reason. "You called the police when they went missing. Now they've come back, obviously they have to know."

Formby was sweating and his eyes had a slightly exophthalmic look, as though the pressure inside his head were pushing them outwards into a bulge. "It's not that simple," he said. "It's obvious something's gone very wrong in this office. I do all I can to keep it in order but when you're dealing with entrenched staff practices'—he threw a venomous glance over George's shoulder and behind her the wail broke out again as May found more tears to shed—"then you can't always be as efficient as you'd like. If the police are called again, it'll be a—a scandal!"

"And if they're not?"

"It won't make any difference! Oh, shut up, May, for Christ's sake! You're making enough noise to deafen the whole bloody hospital."

May let out another cry and got unsteadily to her feet. She went scrabbling for the door. "I'm not staying here to be insulted. I'm not staying. I said it wasn't my fault and now you're saying it is and—"

"No one's blaming you," George said wearily. "I told you, it's just a mix-up as far as you're concerned. The paperwork never had anything to do with what happened."

But it was too late. May was shrieking in full hysterics now. George jumped up, took the woman by the shoulders and held her firmly, trying to calm her, but she had to shout to make herself heard and that seemed to make May worse.

It was Formby who stopped her. He came up from behind his desk and, with an almost vicious twist of his wrist, slapped May's face so hard that the sound could be heard above her wails and red finger marks appeared on her wet cheeks. She gasped, hiccuped and retched, but fortunately didn't vomit, and then settled to a low moaning. Formby said loudly, "Go and lie down, May. You'll feel better later. Leave this to Dr. Barnabas and me. Go on now."

The woman fled, pulling the door open and scuttling down the corridor like a slightly demented insect. As they watched her go, Formby said in a tight voice, "Bloody woman! She drives me nearly—"

"If she's that bad at her job, shouldn't she be, well, given an easier one?" George asked. He shook his head as he went back to his desk. "And you didn't have to be so hard on her. That was a hell of a wallop."

"Oh, I know, but I have no choice when she gets hysterical. Believe me, I know her. As for an easier job, I can't. She's— it'd all get a lot worse if I did," he said. "Look, she'll get over it. I'll see to it that she…But meanwhile, this business, the microscopes…" He sat down again and put his hands on his desk in front of him. George could see they were shaking, however hard he tried to prevent it. He was sweating even more now and his face had a pallid oily gleam that was embarrassing to look at. She looked away.

"I can't see why you're not calling the police to tell them the microscopes have reappeared," she said.

"What's the point?" He tried to look casual and failed.

"The point is you're wasting police time!" she said tartly. "That's the point. I thought that was an offense."

"They're not wasting any time on us!" He managed a sort

of grin but it was ghastly. "Do you think they're looking for the thief? They know perfectly well they can't find him. They know they always get away with it. So why bother? It's simpler to say nothing."

"I can't," she said flatly. "You may think it's simpler but I think it has to be reported. In a sense I'm an officer of the court anyway. I can't ignore this." He closed his eyes and his face went so pale that she thought he was going to pass out. She added sharply, "Are you all right?"

He shook his head, his eyes still closed, and then took a deep breath. "Well, if you must, you must." He opened his eyes and now his color began to come back. "I'll call them." But he made no move towards his phone.

"When I came last time to report the loss of these microscopes you phoned your man at the station at once. Why don't you now? Or shall I? What was his name—Brewer, wasn't it? I seem to remember that. Tim Brewer."

"I'll call him," he said quickly. He pulled the phone towards him and pushed at the dial as she stepped closer. After a while he said, "Tim Brewer please…Mmm? Oh, Mitchell Formby, Old East."

George watched him. Then she leaned forward and took the phone from his hand. He tried to protest but failed, and she put it to her ear. All she could hear was the buzzing of the dialing tone.

She put the phone back on the cradle and said quietly, "It's no use, you know. You'll have to tell me. It'll be better than playing charades."

"Tell you what?" He tried to bluster and she shook her head at him, sadly.

"Why you're in such a sweat over this. You know what's been going on, don't you? You're scared because you were involved with this theft."

To her amazement he stared at her and then laughed. His face twisted painfully when he did it, but it was a real laugh.

She looked back at him, nonplussed. "Me, involved in—Oh, don't be so daft! If I were I'd do it a bloody sight better than this! It's nothing to do with me, this theft, or the return of the damned things. But I can't have the police here again."

"So the last time you called Brewer when I was here it was a real call? Not like this one?"

He looked at her for a moment, seeming puzzled. But he nodded. "Oh, I see. Yes, of course it was. They came and saw your people, didn't they? Of course it was. But I tell you, I can't have them here again."

"Why not?"

He stared at her miserably and then apparently made up his mind. "It's her." He jerked his head towards the door. "It's all because of her. I can't."

George was bewildered and let it show on her face. "Whyever not?"

"She could make so much trouble." He almost wrung his hands; certainly they were twisted tightly together on his desk in front of him.

"You'd better explain, hadn't you?"

"If I do will you promise not to call the police again? I couldn't handle it. I really couldn't."

"I make no promises of anything, Mr. Formby," George said. "You must see I can't do that."

"Oh, shit," he said. He closed his eyes and this time tears appeared under his sandy lashes and began to inch down his cheeks.

"You'll feel better if you tell me," she said as calmly as she could. "You've got this far. There's no going back, is there?"

"It's her," he blurted out, opening his eyes to stare at George helplessly. "She makes my life hell. It was a bit of a joke at first, a woman her age, but then she sort of—Well, I'd had a few drinks and I didn't really know what I was doing and you know what they say about all cats being gray in the dark."

George blinked. "Do you mean to tell me that you and…" She looked over her shoulder at the door as though the secretary were still there. "You and *May*?"

He nodded and the tears stopped, but he was staring at her miserably. "I couldn't help it. It wasn't my choice, I told you. She brought in whisky for her birthday and after the others had gone offered me a drink. I couldn't refuse, and anyway I never thought an old bag like that…But she, she…" He swallowed. "I have a problem anyway, I really do. It's very difficult for me."

"How difficult?"

"Last time they gave me a suspended sentence." He almost whispered it. "It was awful but at least no one knew it was me. I could keep it quiet, don't ask me how, there was a lot of other stuff in the news then and anyway—Well, no one here ever found out and so it was all right. Three years suspended and then she did that and she's been after me ever since and what can I do? What can I do?"

"I still don't understand," George said carefully. "What sort of suspended sentence? What for?"

"A—sort of assault, it was." He looked at her quickly and then his eyes flicked away. "Sort of…"

George sat back in her chair. "I see. Rape."

"Assault, I swear it. Only assault—"

"Only!"

"There was doubt, that was why the suspended, but if anything happens again—and she says if anyone ever asks her about those microscopes again she'll tell them it was all me, and not her at all, that I raped her—I swear I didn't, but can't you see? She's got pictures of—of bruises and—She's shown me, bruises. She'll show people, she says, if I ever—I have to do what she wants."

"Bruises?" George was lost again.

"She likes it! That's why she gets so hysterical. She likes it when I hit her, likes it when I shout at her. Oh, how can you understand? You never could. Just believe me. She's got me exactly where she wants me, because she knows about the last case. She says if the police come she'll tell them what I did to her. She pinches a few bits here and there so she's scared for herself. Stupid, really; I've covered it up for her. The police'd never find it. But she's sure they will and she says if I let them in here again, she'll tell and they give people like me a terrible time in prison and anyway there's my job...I never thought she'd try to hurt me but she says if the police come back she'll tell them and if I don't go on with her—Oh, it's all such shit..." And now he was weeping again.

George sat still, trying to think what to do. That the police would have to be told that the microscopes had come back seemed to her to be obvious, the only thing to do. She couldn't think of them wasting time searching for a thief if—

"Look, I tell you what I'll do," she said. "Do shut up and listen. I'll talk to Brewer, find out how the case is going—"

"No!" he yelped. "No, you can't do that. If you do, she'll—"

"If as you say they aren't investigating, fair enough, I'll say no more about it. There'll be no point. But if they're using police time to look for a thief..."

He lifted his head, and real hope seemed to look out of his eyes. "Honestly? If they're doing nothing, you won't tell them?"

"I must be mad," she said. "For all I know this is a complete whitewash and you're just trying to con me, and you're the thief."

"Christ," he said. "I wish I were."

And she had to believe him. It was such an impossible story that it had to be true.

Or did it? She left him there eventually and went and sat on the bench beside the scrubby flowerbed outside the admin building to think. Once she was away from him, it was easier to get some sort of perspective. She stared unseeingly at the dead leaves drifting around the naked stalks of last autumn's chrysanthemums, working it out in her mind.

Was there a connection between Oxford's death and the theft and reappearance of the microscopes? She couldn't quite see how, but there could be. There had to be a reason for Oxford to have been filled up with digitalis—though how that had happened was still a mystery that had to be sorted out, dammit—and some sort of hospital chicanery could be involved. After all, she reasoned, Oxford had spent a lot of time here, had known many of the people here; his involvement with the Barrie Ward fundraising committee had given him every reason and every chance to be well entrenched at Old East. What he had done to lead to his being poisoned was something she couldn't yet know, but surely she could find out?

She drifted into a half-reverie, in which she somehow succeeded in sorting out the whole business of Oxford's death and the microscope thefts in such a way that she showed Gus Hathaway for good and all just how superior and successful a person she was; and then, as a sharp little wind blew up with the dwindling of the afternoon, shivered and got to her feet. Dreaming of putting one over on Hathaway was silly; but the idea had its charms. She'd try to see if she could find out for herself what truth there was in Formby's claims, outrageous and ridiculous though they had been—increasingly so as she thought about them—and then see if she could find a link between him and Oxford. By the time she'd found out how the digitalis had got into the man—and surely that would emerge soon; it only took painstaking attention to detailed routine work, after all—maybe she'd have the answer to why it had been done as well as how. And that would perhaps tell her who. It would indeed be very agreeable to present Gus Hathaway with all the answers.

She walked back to the lab quickly, planning as she went. There were people she could talk to to set her on her way, she told herself, as ideas began to form in her mind. One was the young Scottish Detective Constable Urquhart and another was—and here she narrowed her eyes as she considered the possibilities, and then had a brilliant idea and was pleased with herself—the other was Hattie Clements, Sister on A & E. Both of those could get answers for her if they were asked in the right way. But first, of course, she would have to talk to Gus Hathaway. Very carefully and obliquely, of course.

She talked to Gus on the phone, as delicate in her words as she had ever been.

"The thefts there've been here at Old East," she said. "You know about them?"

"Mmm? What thefts?"

"Equipment and so forth, ECG machines, microscopes."

"Ah," he said. "Those. Yes, I know about those. One of my fellas is on it, isn't he?"

"Brewer?" she said casually. "Is he getting anywhere?"

"Why do you want to know? Have you lost something?"

"What the hospital loses I lose too," she said. "Send not to hear for whom the bell tolls…"

"Mmm. Well, I can tell you that there's not a lot anyone can do. The security in that place of yours is bloody awful. We've told 'em till we're blue, but they pay no attention. But in all fairness there's not a lot they can do."

"People walk in and out all the time."

"Precisely."

"So you're not investigating?"

He sighed. "Are you trying to make a monkey out of me, Dr. Barnabas? I got a lot on my plate. I delegate things like that!"

"But you're the DCI, aren't you? In charge of everything?"

"Not bloody likely! I've got a Super for that."

"Still and all…"

"Oh, dammit, all right! So we're not moving much on the hospital thefts, all right? I'm trying to run an incident room for this Oxford death and that comes first."

"I just wondered," she said meekly. "It's not important. Listen, I've finished the tablet checks."

He was diverted immediately. "Have you, then? And what have you got for me?"

"Not a thing. Sorry. Every one of them is what it says it is on the label."

"Shit!"

"Well, yes. Any news from his Harley Street doctors?"

"Not a great deal. He seemed to have been a reasonably healthy chap. Hadn't seen any of the ones who had their names on those bottles and stuff for almost a year. The gut chappie said Oxford had a mild go of piles and he treated him for it, gave him some tubes of cream, told him to come back when he felt the need. The others'—he sighed "not a bloody thing. And now you've got nothing either."

"I'm starting again on the samples from the body," she said. "And there's still the rest of the things in the bathroom cabinets. There were some bottles, remember, with liquids."

"I'm not too hopeful." He sounded gloomy. "Whoever did this was a smartarse who knew what he was about. Covered it up a treat. But we'll get the bugger, you see if we don't."

"I've no doubt at all that you will," she said sweetly, and then hesitated. "Look, I've had one idea about all this but it might seem a bit, well, far-fetched."

"What's that?"

"Did he have anything in his flat that was like an office?"

"An office? He had a fancy room with a desk and a computer and so on, yes. Didn't look as though it got much use, mind you. Considering he was a writer."

"Look, will you let me go after an idea I've got? Will you help me to—"

"Madam Amateur Sleuth, are we? Very nice. You tell me what you've got and leave it to me."

"It's not worth talking about at this stage," she said, leaning back in her chair and staring at the ceiling. The phone was hot and sticky in her hand and she tried to relax, afraid he might pick up her tension from her voice. "If you'll find out stuff for me, I'll see what might fit my idea and then I'll tell you if there's anything in it."

"No way." He was brusque. "This is a police matter now, ducky. No meddling, if you please."

"It was my meddling that proved it was a police matter in the first place," she said and there was a little silence.

"Fair dos," he said at length. "But I shan't do any finding out for you, all the same. You do your own if you're that good at my job."

"By God, I will," she said and slammed down the phone. "I will," she said to the ceiling. "Just you watch me."

17

She started in the A & E department and gave a good deal of thought as to how she would do it.

There were two possibilities: the direct and the devious. She opted in the end for the former; mainly, she couldn't deny, because it was the easiest. However hard she tried she couldn't think of any way in which she could get the information she wanted without coming out directly with her questions; so as soon as the lab was finished for the day she went over in the glimmer of the early evening twilight to the main hospital, following the scratched paint lines across the courtyard to Blue block. It was the time of day she most enjoyed and she stopped for a moment to look up at the big ward buildings with their shimmer of lighted windows and the theatricality of the effect as nurses and sometimes patients passed them, and thought of all that was happening there; of people being born and people being freed of fear and pain; of people being forced to look at their own mortality and of course people dying. Lots of people dying; and she considered the illogicality of fretting so much over the death of one somewhat disliked man in a world in which there were so many people, and from which he'd hardly be missed, and then thought how glad she was that it was a world in which such deaths were cause for concern; and finally shook her head at her time-wasting and hurried on to A & E.

It was full of its usual over-heated glittering clatter. The waiting area benches were filled with their regular human detritus: meths drinkers from the wasteground over towards Wapping; young tearaways who had battered themselves to interesting bloody messes on motorbikes; children with grazed knees; old women with aching joints trying to bypass their GPs and get their hands on extra painkillers; but nothing, her experienced glance told her, that was particularly urgent. The nursing staff were moving around at a comfortable speed, with none of the barely contained hysteria that characterized A & E on a really hard night; it would be a good time to pin down Hattie Clements for a little while.

George found her in her cubby hole of an office, writing her notes up for the night staff as she got ready to go home. George put her head around the door and said cheerfully, "Would I be a pest if I came visiting?"

Hattie looked up and smiled widely as she recognized her. "Not in the least! I'm nearly done and then I have to wait for my chap anyway. Care for some coffee?"

"I'd kill for some," George said.

Hattie got to her feet and went over to the corner of the room where a small percolator sat bubbling contentedly on an electric ring. "This'll be stewed to death, no doubt, but I've got used to it bitter and strong. I suspect I'm hooked on it. Will it be OK?"

"Is there any other kind of coffee?" George asked, taking the hot beaker gratefully. "How're things?"

"Could be worse." Hattie looked down at her desk. "Another five minutes of this and I'll have a chance to talk. Would you mind if—?"

"Not at all," George said, "scribble away," and leaned back in her chair and watched her bent head as she worked. They'd only talked a few times: that first occasion when they'd met in the canteen and once or twice since; but she seemed a cheerful friendly soul, and had greeted her warmly enough this evening. Would she be forthcoming? Or would she shy off and get agitated at being asked to help as George wanted her to? Well, it was a gamble she had to take.

Hattie finished her writing, closed the book and pushed it away. "That's it," she said with satisfaction. "Till tomorrow. Here's hoping nothing nasty happens in the bomb or the RTA line before I get away."

"Am I holding you up?"

"Not in the least. I told you I have to wait till my chap gets here. So, how're things with you?"

"Busy." George sipped at her coffee, trying to look as offhand as she felt was necessary. "It's a busy department anyway and what with forensic—"

Hattie leaned forwards eagerly. "Do tell. You're dealing with the Oxford business, aren't you? Any news?"

George laughed. "You're as bad as the rest of them! Dying to get a bit of information before everyone else."

"Of course I am! I'm nothing if not normal."

"Well, what do you want to know? Perhaps the best thing'd be to tell me what you know already."

"Right!" Hattie reached into her drawer and pulled out a small make-up bag. "Do you mind if I—? Thanks. Well now." She began to apply make-up lightly but with some skill. "Richard Oxford died of digitalis poisoning."

"How did that get around so far and so fast?"

Hattie laughed and looked at her over her mascara brush. "Danny."

"Oh. Yes. Danny."

"He's a popular chap at present, which makes a change for him. Most people find the mortuary man a bit less than appetizing. Now everyone wants to chat him up. He's making the most of it."

"I'll bet he is," George said a little grimly. "So, you know it's digitalis."

"But not how he got it. Or whether it was an accident or deliberate."

"I can't see how it was an accident," George said carefully. "He didn't have any sort of heart condition that would mean him using it, so it can't be an accidental overdose. Anyway, it was too much to be an accident. He must have had thirty or so tablets."

"Thirty?" Hattie stopped, her lipstick held in mid-air in surprise. "So much?"

"It was somewhat of an overkill," George said drily. "But that's the estimate."

"Suicide?" Hattie said and George shook her head.

"That's not really on. They leave notes; there's always some sort of…No. No one thinks that likely, not Gus, nor I, nor—"

"Gus?"

George looked a little uncomfortable. "The Chief Inspector in charge of the case."

"Ah," Hattie said non-committally. "A friend?"

"Not really. Why?"

"First names and all that. I'd have thought you'd call him Inspector or something."

"Modern, we are in the forensic world these days. First names all around." George made it sound flippant. "I call him Gus, he calls me ducks."

"So, if it's not suicide and it's not an accident…" Hattie packed away her make-up and leaned forward to concentrate on George. "A real murder, hmm?"

"What is it Conan Doyle used to say? When the improbable has been eliminated, whatever is left, however impossible, is the truth? Well, anyway, something like that. So, yes. It's possible. It's also *possible* that it was an accident or suicide, but I don't think it's probable."

"So, the detectives are hard at it."

George chuckled. "So'm I."

"I'm sure you are. You're the one that finds a lot of evidence for them, of course,—doing the post-mortem and so forth."

"Not only in the mortuary. I work at the scene of the crime too, you know."

"It must be rather horrid."

"It can be. But it's also fascinating."

"Ye-es. I wouldn't like it."

"No. Mind you," George said with a studiedly casual air, "not all the detecting is done at the scene of the crime or at the mortuary, of course."

"Well, of course."

"Some of it can be done by people who have nothing to do with the police or the scientist."

"I suppose so."

"I mean, your chap, he's a novelist, isn't he?"

Hattie looked pleased. "You remembered? Yes, he is. Schoolmaster still, but he says once one of his books earns enough he's giving up the inky schoolboys to get more inky himself."

"Well, he could do some of the detecting in this case."

"He could?" Hattie looked a little startled. "Are you saying you want him to do something for you? Is that why you're here?"

George made a grimace. "So much for softly softly, catchee monkee techniques," she said. "Here was me thinking I was being so clever."

Hattie laughed. "You don't have to be clever with me. If you want something, say so. What is it you're after?"

George bit her lip as she thought and then put down her beaker and leaned forward too, so that they were sitting almost head to head. "I'm puzzled," she said. "Oxford lived so high on the hog, you know? You ought to see his place, expensive isn't in it."

"Really?" Hattie was fascinated. "Go on!"

George did and Hattie listened, enthralled, shaking her head in admiration and the sort of awed disbelief that shows a listener is having a lovely time.

"And I can't help wondering," George said, "just how much of that money came from his books. I know he does well—I mean, even I've read one, but do writers really make all that much? I've heard some of them do."

"The ones who write all the inwardly-onwardly-downwardly thrusting books," Hattie said. "That's what Sam says."

George chuckled. "Yeah, bonkbusters, isn't that what they call 'em? But Oxford didn't. They're rather good adventure stories. In fact, I thought the one I tried was quite well written."

Hattie nodded. "And well-written books don't tend to sell as many copies as bad ones."

"You've hit it. So I'd love to know how many he did sell. But how to find out? That's the problem."

"Can't the police help?"

George made a face again. "I want to score over the police," she said. "They're too fond of getting all the information they want out of me and then trying to leave me out of it. It's no fun at all."

Hattie nodded in instant comprehension. "A bit of the amateur stuff, hmm, to show 'em what asses they are?"

"I'm not that amateur! I mean, I do the PMs—"

"Sorry! I mean no insult. It's just that doing the things the police aren't—"

"Well, yes. Anyway, there it is. Could you help? That is, could your—"

Hattie's face had suddenly lit up as she looked over George's shoulder, and she said happily, "Ask him yourself. Sam, this is Dr. Barnabas. George. She wants some help."

"Oh?" He was a pleasant-looking man, George thought. Bulky, a little untidy, with rough salt-and-pepper hair and a shabby sports jacket over far-from-well-pressed trousers. "Glad to, if I can. Kids are fine, Hatt."

"Of course they are! There's nothing they like better than spending the night at Judith's." She turned to George. "Makes a mother feel very inadequate when her children prefer her next-door neighbor."

"So, what do you want of me?" Sam looked at George and she warmed to him. A direct sort of person. No need for any butter on this popcorn.

She told him as succinctly as she could and he nodded in immediate understanding. "Did this chap's lifestyle match his income, that's what you want to know. You realize he might have had assets other than his immediate earnings from his books?"

"Yes, of course. But it'd be a help, wouldn't it, to know just how big an earner he was?"

"Of course. But if you want to know more about him you might have to go to Companies' House."

"Eh?"

"A lot of high-earning writers are companies these days. So they have to file returns at Companies' House. It's the law."

"Oh," George said, a little dashed. "Then finding out about his book sales won't help?"

"Oh, yes, it'll give you some idea. I'm just pointing out you may have to look further. But I'll gladly see what I can do. Who were his publishers?"

George went pink. "I should have checked on that before I asked you."

"Well, it'd have helped, but don't worry. I'll look that up. He may have had more than one, it's not all that unusual. And then I'll see what I can do. It's not easy; publishers tell the most awful lies about their authors' sales. Except to the authors themselves." He grimaced. "Mine is painfully honest. I'm not selling enough to feed a sparrow yet."

"You will," Hattie said with great loyalty, hugging his arm. "It just takes a little time to get—"

"I know. Established. Well, Oxford was certainly established. It'll be fascinating to know a bit more about how he did. Leave it to me. I've friends in a few publishing houses and, with a bit of luck, one of 'em'll be his. I'll let you know. Is there a hurry for this?"

George contemplated being polite and opted for honesty. "Yes, please."

"It'll be a pleasure. Beats trying to bash out a few useful words of my own. Hattie, the curtain's up in just over half an hour. It's going to be a bit of a rush…"

"I've gone," George said and got to her feet. "Thanks, both of you."

"Wait till you see what you get," Hattie called over her shoulder as they led the way out of the small office. "Oh, before I go, I must have a word with the night girls, Sam. Just a second…" And she darted away, leaving Sam watching her fondly if a little impatiently.

"Thanks, Sam," George said and held out her hand to be shaken. "It's good of you to be so—"

"It's a pleasure," Sam said. "Don't thank me till you know what I come up with. I'll send it over here with Hattie."

"Please," George said and turned to go as Hattie came back; but Hattie was not alone.

"The night people'll see to it," she was saying to her companion. "They've plenty of time to get the stomach washed out."

"It'll help a lot," he said. "They're rushing around there like lunatics. I can't operate till the morning, mind, but it'll give the poor devil a better night's rest if he's clean before he's admitted to the ward. Hello, George."

"Good evening," George said politely and Hattie threw her a quick glance and then tugged on Sam's sleeve.

"Come on, Sam," she said. "We mustn't be late. See you, George. Bye, Mr. Bellamy." And she positively scuttled away.

George made to follow her, but Toby Bellamy put out his hand to stop her. "I haven't seen you since, well, since we shared fish and chips. Do I owe you for that or did your friend keep his word?"

"I wouldn't have dreamed of letting him pay," she said with a lofty air.

"More fool you." He sounded cheerful. "I've learned never to say no to a free lunch. It's not true what they say. There are such things: I'll prove it. Come and have a late one with me now. To make up for last time."

"Don't you ever think of anything but eating?" she snapped.

He looked at her thoughtfully. "Only when I'm thinking of other pleasant physical experiences. How about you?"

"Oh, for heaven's sake." She turned to go and he put out one hand to stop her.

"Hey, what have I done? I'm sorry I had to rush off and leave you last time we were out, but you ought to know about people being on call, for heaven's sake! Why are you so shirty with me? Have I done something I don't know about?"

That stopped her and she stood still, trying to get her thoughts into order. Yes, she was suspicious of him. He'd been altogether too interested in what she had discovered about Oxford's death, ostensibly on behalf of his friend Felicity Oxford, and that had annoyed her, made her feel used; and there was, after all, the hospital gossip. It wasn't much fun to be pursued by someone who had a reputation around the place for being a womanizer, and it certainly had seemed to George that he fell into that category.

And yet...She looked at him again and he smiled, and once more she experienced the little frisson she'd felt that time on ICU when they'd shared a consult. He was a very interesting man, after all; men like him attracted gossip and unjust accusations of being woman-eaters the way dogs collected fleas. Besides, maybe he knew more about Oxford and his past and his money. Maybe he knew something about Mitchell Formby and why he behaved so oddly. And maybe he knew—

"I'm sorry," she said, and managed a smile. "I've been a bit busy, I guess. Makes me edgy."

"That's better! As long as it's nothing I've done."

"Not a thing."

"OK, where was I? Oh, yes. Suggesting a return to our last meeting."

"What? Swimming again?"

"If you like."

"I don't think so."

"Then supper, or—" He stopped and grinned and dug into the breast pocket of his white coat. "How about this?"

"Mmm?"

"Free tickets for the theatre. We get 'em here sometimes, and when I was in Herne's office arguing with him about bed allocations he collected a couple for himself. I couldn't see why I shouldn't have some too, so I told his secretary on my way out that I was to have a pair."

"I thought they were meant for the less well-paid people on the staff when they come in?"

"Well, who else is as badly paid as I am for the important work I do? Anyway, Herne took a pair, so why shouldn't I? Oh, come on, George! It's one of my few free evenings—Kate Sayers is on call for me for any immediate problems since she's stuck here with a dicey kidney transplant all night—so I don't want to waste it. There can be no arguments over these since neither of us is paying. What do you say? They're for that new musical at the Dominion. The reviews were great."

"Oh, well," she said, thinking of how much talking she could get out of him in the interval. "Why not? I'll just go and put on something a bit—"

"Oh, George," he said. "And here was I thinking you weren't like other women! More sense. You look fine as you are. Just take off your white coat and you'll do."

And she laughed, and agreed.

18

George sat at her desk and tried to think sensibly of the day's work. There was a good deal to sort out, after all, for the forensic work she'd promised Gus was still not finished and the demands from the hospital for routine jobs was intensifying. She'd already got Jerry going on the remainder of the containers brought from Oxford's flat, but it would be some time before she could hope to get answers from him. Not till later this afternoon.

Sheila had already poured her coffee and she poured another cup, hoping the rather dismal, thin stuff would sharpen her mind and stop her from being so silly, and she yearned for a cup of Hattie's harsh Accident and Emergency department brew. But she'd have to settle for this; it had been hard enough to persuade Sheila that she should be treated like a consultant and brought a tray of coffee each morning; to start complaining about its quality would create an uproar that wasn't even worth contemplating.

She gazed sightlessly over the rim of her cup, trying to concentrate on the best way to deal with the events of the morning. She had to call Detective Constable Urquhart to ask him to do some checking for her; that was her second line of investigating now she'd got Hattie's Sam busy. Was there anything else she could try to help her efforts to find the answer to Oxford's death before Gus Hathaway did?

But it was no good. However hard she tried, her mind kept swinging back to last night and Toby Bellamy.

It really was depressing, she told herself sadly, to discover how soggy a person she was. She'd worked all these years to build herself up in her own estimation as a strong woman, a woman of principle and intelligence and power, and what happened? The first time an even reasonably attractive man kissed her she melted and turned into a heap of overboiled cabbage. It was too dispiriting for words.

But he's not reasonably attractive, a part of her mind protested. The man's seriously gorgeous. Why shouldn't you find him worth kissing? If men are allowed to go around fancying women all over the place and acting on their feelings, why can't you? Are you a woman or a—a—and she couldn't think of a sufficiently insulting epithet to use.

But that's the point, she thought then. I deserve to be insulted. I wasn't the one who did the kissing. It was done to me. If I'd done what I wanted and pounced, it'd have been different, but I was as bad as any silly schoolgirl. One minute there we are laughing like idiots and the next he's coming on like King Kong with the hugs and slobbers, and you, damn your eyes, you just adored it. Admit it. You cooperated. You showed all the tender shyness of a crack Panzer Division in World War Two. If it hadn't been for his bleep, who knows where we'd have finished up?

In bed would have been nice, she thought wistfully. That was the trouble, of course. She was feeling deprived. In Ian's day bed had been good; well, not perfect, but good enough to start with. She had been all set to teach him some better ways, but he'd gone and behaved so—no, Ian was not to be thought of. That was a rule. If she had to think about such matters, think of Toby Bellamy.

She did, and once again the sensations came back to make her feel a lot better than she would have thought she could, under the circumstances. Stupid woman you are, she scolded herself. A pushover for the first pretty guy that happens along once you've got rid of—been got rid of—by a great blond idiot like Ian—Oh, shit!

Something would have to be done in the distraction line, no doubt about it. She picked up the phone and buzzed through to Jerry. He listened to her demands and said sweetly, "Dr. B., I promise you, you'll have it all as fast as we can do it. I'm checking every damn thing in sight for every damn thing I can think of and a few more besides. You will have the fullest of reports in no time at all. Well, not long after lunch. If you leave me alone to get on with it, that is."

She snapped the phone down, glowered at it, and then picked it up again. Constable Urquhart. Detective Constable Urquhart. He was the fellow she needed to talk to now. At the very least, he'd keep her mind off Toby Bellamy.

The call nearly ended in disaster; the Ratcliffe Street station switchboard put her through to the CID room when she asked for Mr. Urquhart, and as soon as he heard her voice he said cheerfully, "Och, it'll be Mr. Hathaway you're wanting. I'll see if he's available—"

"No!" she shouted. "No, it's you I want. In fact, I'd as soon Mr. Hathaway didn't know I'd called."

"Oh!" The young voice became guarded. "Now, why would that be?"

"For the same reason you got annoyed with him," she said. "You told me you'd be glad if I showed Mr. Hathaway I wasn't the sort to be pushed about. I remember it perfectly."

"You do?"

"Indeed I do. You also said that he can be downright nasty sometimes, and that he won't listen to other people's ideas. That he doesn't trust intuition and only wants hard evidence."

The voice became even more cautious. "I said all that?"

"You certainly did."

"Hmm. Well, and suppose I did? What of it?"

"I've been using my intuition."

"Ah." There was a short silence in which she could hear the rattle of typewriters in his office and the sound of other men's voices burring. Then he said, still carefully, "Well, now. I'm interested to hear that. But why do you want me?"

"Because I need help to get the hard evidence. You said yourself that if he gets hard evidence…"

Again there was silence and then he laughed, a soft low sound that had a great deal of real pleasure in it. "D'you know, doctor, you're a grand lady. I'll—"

"Don't call me doctor! He may be listening."

"No, he's no' listening. He's too busy bawling out Brewer to be listening to me. So, what is it you want of me?" She told him succinctly and he listened, making affirmative noises. When she'd ended he said, "Got that. Would you just spell the name again?"

"F-o-r-m-b-y," she said. "Mitchell. I don't know where the offense was supposed to have been committed. I've checked here and I can tell you he's been on the staff for a year if that's significant."

"It might be. Is there anything else you need to know?"

"I don't think—Yes! Come to think of it, yes. Oxford. Did he have a computer in his flat?"

"A word processor."

"Same thing. Look, is it still there? And all the software with it?"

"Which software? There was a good deal."

"Well, I'd like to know if there was any that dealt with money. I can't go and look, I suppose."

"If you do, it'll be noted and reported," he said. "Every visitor to the flat has to be logged."

"Can you look for me?"

"I could try. What is it you're wanting to know?"

"I'm not sure. About money mainly. I don't suppose it's that important, but I'd dearly like to know where he got it all from. Can you see if he's got a disc for his bookkeeping or whatever?"

"Well, it'll no' be as easy as finding the other, but I'll try…

And, er, doc—I mean, I wish you luck. I'd like to see you—um—showing you weren't one to be pushed about."

"Oh, me too, Mr. Urquhart, me too!" she said and hung up.

After that it was easier to concentrate on the routine of the day and she didn't think about Toby at all until she had to go over to the renal department at eleven-thirty to see one of Kate Sayers's patients. The boy had not responded to his dialysis as he should, and Kate wanted to consult on the matter of his creatinine levels, among other things.

They sorted that out fairly quickly, with Kate herself seeing the best way to adapt the boy's medication once George had discussed the vagaries of proteins in dialyzed blood at some length. Then Kate said cozily, "Any news?" and George laughed.

"You'll make me suspect you only asked for a consult because you wanted to catch up on the gossip."

"Oh, no, I wouldn't waste your time that way. But now you're here…coffee?"

"This place runs on caffeine," George said, and perched on the edge of the table. It felt less time-wasting than sitting down. "So, what sort of news?"

"The Oxford murder of course." Kate busied herself with her coffee equipage.

"If it was murder. We can't be sure yet. Why is everyone assuming it is?"

"Isn't it?"

"Honestly, I don't know." George took her coffee cup. "It looks very possible, but it could have been, well, possibly, accident, suicide…"

"Hattie told me you said it couldn't be either."

George sighed. "I know I did. But neither can I say it's murder, don't you see? It's evidence we need. If I could find the way he got all that digitalis in him then it'd be a lot easier. We're doing the checks now—I have to get back." She glanced at her watch. "Jerry promised to have it all done by lunchtime. If I nag at him it'll just slow him down, but—"

"I thought you'd do the tests for something so important yourself."

"And cause an uproar in the labs? No way! People have their own jobs to do, and I have to let them do them. It'd be like you taking over the nursing here because you regarded a particular patient as more important than another. They'd get very upset, wouldn't they?"

"I suppose so. I must say I wish everyone was as sensible as you. The admin people are so ham-fisted they create havoc."

"Oh?" George was alert at once. "Trouble with Formby?"

"Mmm? Oh, not him. I hardly know him. He's the chap who deals with the Barrie Ward building, isn't he?"

"And the major supplies. Haven't you had any gear stolen here? Like the—er—ECG machines that went from cardiology?"

"Oh, did they? I hadn't heard about that. But then, things are always walking in this place. The wastage must be colossal."

"So, if it isn't Formby who's giving you grief, who is?"

"Oh, Matthew bloody Herne! He's so pompous and so—so *slippery*. And so boring."

George giggled. "He didn't look boring last night."

"Eh?"

"I saw him at the theatre. With a somewhat overdressed creature who looked as though she'd been sprayed with polyurethane. She was the one who was with him at the concert, too."

"Oh, that's his wife. Extraordinary-looking woman, isn't she? A model, some say. I don't know. It certainly caused a stir when he first brought her here last summer."

"Oh! Then they haven't been together that long?"

Kate shook her head. "Apparently not. Was he all over her?"

George grimaced. "I wasn't actually watching them, they were a few rows in front. But he certainly seemed—what's the word? Uxorious."

"Couldn't keep his hands off her," Kate translated.

"Something like that. What's he done to annoy you?"

"Oh, it's my dialysis machine. I told him I spent hours, absolutely hours, in discussion with the manufacturers, worked out exactly what new systems we need, sorted out the prices, everything, and then when I send it all along to get the authorization signed, he suddenly announces he's got a better supplier, takes all the specifications and sends my chap off in high dudgeon. I feel such a fool. It looks to the firm as though I was the one who used all their time and expertise to sort out my problems and then took the order they were entitled to expect to another company."

"I can see that'd annoy you, but was it your own fault? I mean, did you just go ahead and deal with it all without getting the hospital's authority first?"

"No, of course not! It's taken ages to sort this out. I started on it last spring—almost a year ago! Herne told me it was fine, to go ahead. I'd been nagging for two years before that for some money to upgrade this department and he said I could have it in this coming financial year. So of course I started investigating the situation right away. I know more about dialysis equipment now than it's decent for any person to know who isn't manufacturing it. And after all that he goes and gives the order to another firm!"

"Is it one you approve of?"

Kate shrugged. "I never heard of it. It's a foreign one. I'd done my work with British firms. Not that I'm a little Englander or anything, but it seemed to be more sensible to have the gear of a company that could be fetched in a hurry in case of an emergency. I know we're in the EEC now, but I'd still rather fetch people from Birmingham or Leeds than Stuttgart or Paris or wherever, and it's easier without a language difference. I have to make sure the patients can understand all the instructions for the parts of the system they use in their own homes, and translated advice is never all it might be. Anyway, there it is. He won't be budged. It's got to be his choice of manufacturer and that's all there is to it. It's as you said. He's behaving like someone who can't trust people to do their own job properly."

"Yes," George said and looked at her watch again. "I see what you mean. But I must go. Jerry'll have that stuff ready for me soon, and if I'm not there to be impressed by his speed he'll be as mad with me as you are with Herne—and I want to know as fast as I can anyway. I'm as interested as everyone else in what happened to Oxford, take it from me."

"Promise you'll let me know as soon as you've got the answer?" Kate said. "I'm really fascinated by the whole thing, and so's Oliver."

"Oliver? Why?"

"He's a journalist! If there's a story here, obviously he'd like to have a crack at it and get some inside stuff other people couldn't get. You can't blame him. He deserves something to pay him back for all those broken nights when I'm working and he has to cope with the kids on his own."

"I'll tell you, I promise," George said as she slid to the ground. "As soon as I know, you'll know."

She went back to the lab via the canteen, so that she could pick up some sandwiches. They were never very exciting but they were better than the usual hot food; lunch on her desk might be lonely but this way it would at least be something she could actually eat.

Toby was there two places in front of her in the line-up, buying cheese and pickle rolls, and she thought for a moment of turning and scuttling away before he could see her, and then dismissed the idea as shameful and marched up to get her own sandwiches.

"Good morning!" he said, calling across the pair of gossiping physiotherapists who stood between them, and then stepped back to let them through. "How are you today?" he added as perforce she came to stand beside him.

"Fine," she said, leaning into the cold cabinets ostensibly to study in great detail the packs of sandwiches on offer. "Busy, of course."

"I know." He was richly sympathetic. "Lunch on the run. Isn't it dreadful the lives we dedicated sons and daughters of Hippocrates lead?"

She didn't look at him, wouldn't respond to the laughter in his voice. "Mmm. I'll take the tuna and cucumber," she said to the gloomy girl behind the counter. "Can I have it on wholemeal bread, please?"

"All gone," the girl said, clearly brightening at having to impart the information. "It all went at the mid-morning breaks."

"Then why don't you order more, if it's so popular?" George said, and the girl gaped at her.

"We don't get enough call for it," she said and went away in a huff when Toby burst into a loud hoot of laughter. This time George did respond to him. It was a relief to have something outside themselves to which she could.

"Last night was fun," he said, when the laughter stopped.

"Mmm. I liked the play."

"Bugger the play. I was thinking about later."

"The case you were called back for—difficult?"

"It was a perforation, had to operate right away. Didn't get to bed till gone seven this morning."

She risked a glance at him. "You look all right on it."

"It's being so near to you that gives me strength." He grinned and put a hand on hers very deliberately.

"Toby, I have work to do!" she said, stepping back. "I really can't—oh!" as a group of chattering nurses joined the queue and separated them. "I really can't talk now. Must get back."

"I'll see you this evening then. I need a swim to recover my energy and a nice early night. How does that idea grab you?"

"If that's what you need, you go right ahead," she said. "Me, I'm working late."

"I'll pick you up in the residence this evening," he said, and also made way as more and more people arrived to join the lunch queue. "I can wait till you're ready. See you!" He winked at her and pushed past on his way out, and, as he went, trailed one finger across the back of her neck making her shoulders hunch and her hair stir on her head. Oh, damn, damn, damn, she thought. Now I won't be able to think of anything else all afternoon.

19

The tuna sandwich lay ignored on the side of her desk as she sat there with Jerry beside her and the test results spread out in front of them.

"Who'd have thought it?" he said, almost jigging up and down in his chair with excitement. "Who'd have thought it? I wouldn't have done in a thousand years and I'm as devious as most."

"Mmm," George said and looked again at the report on the samples taken from Oxford's anus and rectum and then the report on the contents of container D. "You're absolutely sure?"

"Of course I am!" Jerry was indignant. "You know me better than that, Dr. B. I may fartarse about a bit, but when did I ever do a bad bit of work?"

She patted his hand apologetically. "Sorry, Jerry. It's just that it's so…" She shook her head. "Hemorrhoid cream! Who would have thought of spiking a man's hemorrhoid cream?"

"What you might call a really fundamental idea," Jerry said and giggled. "Really getting down to basics."

"Let's get the jokes over and done with, then," she said. "So we can forget them."

"Well, you can't blame me. Honestly, hemorrhoid cream: it's so easy! You could pack a lot of stuff into it, and then leave it to the poor bugger to poison himself all unbeknowing. How long would it take to absorb, do you imagine?"

"Depends on a lot of things. How it was put in—I mean was it tincture or crushed tablets? And the excipient—how much was there adhering to the mucosa, and how long does it take the active substance to penetrate and get into the bloodstream? And how vulnerable was he in terms of—" She shook her head. "It can't be more than guesswork, but I'd say it had to be as fast if not faster than by mouth. They used to use the rectal route to start anesthetics at one time and put the pre-med in that way. And people have been fed through it—babies— they can absorb a good deal of glucose and saline rectally. And why not? Mucous membrane is mucous membrane pretty well wherever it is."

Jerry was laughing again. "Oh, can't you see their faces when this gets around the hospital? There won't be anyone who'll not fall about, even the most po-faced of 'em. Poisoned with hemorrhoid cream!"

"Ah!" she said, lifting her head and staring at the wall opposite, thinking hard.

"Ah, what?"

"I'm not sure I can let you talk about this."

"What? Bloody hell, Dr. B., why not? It's not exactly a secret the chap was pushed off his twig, is it? I've heard you saying to people it wasn't suicide and you couldn't see how it could be accidental, so what was left? Now you've got your actual proof, so why not let me—"

"Because if we know for sure it's a murder then we also know for sure there has to be a murderer," George said impatiently.

Jerry frowned. "Well, of course! So what?"

"So, he probably is part of this place and there's no sense in warning him that he's been discovered."

"Part of this—" Jerry sat in uncharacteristic silence for some time and then said, "But hang about a bit, how can you be sure that he's part of this place?"

"Where do you get hold of large quantities of digitalis?" George said reasonably. After another pause, he nodded.

"It seems logical, I suppose, though you can get it with a prescription, I imagine."

"Would you like to go to a nice GP and say, 'Please give me a script for ever such a lot of digitalis so I can squash it up and put it in someone's hemorrhoid cream?' Or would you like to wander into your friendly neighborhood pharmacist and get him to make it up for you?"

"Ah," said Jerry.

"Precisely. And, of course, there's another thing."

"Oh?"

"It would be someone who knew him well. Well enough to have intimate knowledge of the state of his rear end."

"Yes, I see that. His wife, I suppose—"

"But they didn't live together, did they? It could be a lover we don't know about, and, as I say, someone here. With access to the pharmacy."

There was a little silence as Jerry thought. Then he made a little moue and said, "So what now?"

"So I hand these results to the police and see what they have to say."

"They'll say, 'Ta and go away and play, and we'll call you next time there's a murder, and you'll have to wait till we've done all our detecting before you hear another thing about it.' Where's the fun in that?"

"I've told you before, this isn't about fun. It's about a man who died."

"A man no one could stand," Jerry said. "I can't be doing with all this mealy-mouthed nonsense that suggests that because a man's kicked the bucket he's suddenly deified. He was a nasty shit before and he still is, even if he is dead. We might as well get some fun out of him. We never did get much when he was alive."

"Jerry, why are you so—so hostile to him?" She was curious, but puzzled too. Jerry had gone a little white around the mouth and seemed genuinely angry, not his usual bantering self at all.

"*Hos*tile…" He mimicked her accent and laughed. "Hos*tile* is what I am, Dr. B. You'll have to change your style a bit if you want them to be really nice to you around here."

"You're changing the subject." She was sharper now. "Why are you so angry about Oxford? Why does it matter to you that you should be able to tell the world about how he died?" Jerry got up and moved across the room. She watched him, her puzzlement deepening into suspicion. "You'll have to tell me, won't you? Now you've got this far."

"How far? I haven't got anywhere. You've just jumped to a conclusion."

"You've pushed me to it," she said, and then in a gentler tone added, "Oh, come on Jerry! I can't imagine it's anything that awful."

"I'm not sure, all of a sudden." He turned to look at her and she was startled at the strain in his face. "I hadn't really thought about it before. I mean, that it had to be someone here, from the hospital, who killed him. I sort of thought it could be someone from, well, anywhere."

"It could."

"But you said—"

"I said it would be hard for someone outside the hospital to get their hands on a quantity of digitalis. As it would be for them to get it into the tube, wouldn't it? They'd need some equipment?"

"A syringe?"

She shook her head. "Did you find any needle holes in the tube? Or didn't you squeeze it to get the sample out to test? If you did, you would have spotted any hole at once by the worm of excipient that would have emerged."

"There wasn't a hole," he said and his voice was low now. He didn't take his eyes from her.

"So the tube had to be tampered with another way?"

"I suppose so."

"It's obvious to me how. Isn't it to you?"

"No, or at least…" He frowned and then shook his head. "I don't really know. Open the end and then reroll it?"

"It'd show when you looked at it. I looked at all those tubes. They were virginal. Every one of them—except the one that had been started and that was just like the others at the base. So, as I see it, it's very possible—even very likely—that the tampering was done here in the pharmacy. They fill their own tubes there, don't they?"

"I imagine so."

"So, there you are. It's very reasonable to assume it was someone at the hospital who did it, though not absolutely certain. But it had to be someone with access to the pharmacy when no one else was in it to see what was going on. And you say that's what worries you…"

"Oh, shit!" he said and came and sat down in the chair again. "Look, I didn't do anything to the old bugger. I hated him, sure I did. I had plenty of reason. He—he treated me like a—like—He was bloody rude."

She said nothing, just sat and looked at him, waiting for him to go on. Unwillingly at first but then in a rush, he did.

"I had daft notions of going on up the career ladder at one time. Thought I'd get more qualifications, maybe go into the private sector, make myself a little bomb in my own private lab. There're people in the Harley Street setups who do that. But I had no money and I thought, Old Oxford hangs around here all the time, reckons he cares about hospitals and so forth, well, let's see what he might do for me. After all, it'd be for the ultimate good of patients, wouldn't it? So I wrote and asked for a loan. Not a gift, mind you. I didn't want a hand-out. Just a loan to get me going. And the bastard sent me the nastiest and most insulting letter you ever…Well!" He shook his head. "It really was hateful, so of course I hated him. But not enough to try to kill him! Only enough to want to make people laugh at him. Making people laugh is what I do very well. Turning that old buzzard into a hoot struck me as a great way to get my own back."

"Have you still got the letter?"

"Still—What do you take me for? Of course I chucked it. So would you have done. Called me a parasite, he did, said I was a—well, just take it from me, it was really terrible. You could see the man was a writer, I'll grant him that. He really got under my skin. I was glad when I heard he'd died, and now I know someone killed him, good luck to him, say I. I hope they never catch him."

"Until he does it to someone else?"

Jerry looked at her uncertainly. "That's jumping to conclusions again."

"Maybe. But let's face it, it's a possibility. If it's easy the first time and you get away with it, you'll be tempted to keep on doing it. I would. Wouldn't you?"

He shook his head. "You don't get me admitting I'd even think of killing a person once, let alone twice. I told you I was mad, but I just laugh at them."

"Well, OK, Jerry. But I still have to say you can't talk about this to anyone outside this office. Not till I say so."

"The others already know," Jerry said. "And that means the rest of the hospital does by now."

"Oh, shit! How can they? Oh, I suppose it was inevitable."

"We sit side by side, after all. And Sheila's in and out like a yo-yo. And with her nose for a story…"

"I'd better warn them at the station," she said. She got to her feet and swept the papers together into a bundle. "What's the time? Nearly five. They should still be there. Tell Sheila to lock up. I'll go there with this stuff now and talk to Hathaway."

"Are you going to tell him about me?"

She looked back at him sitting there at the desk, his rumpled fair hair springing around his face in a particularly endearing way and felt her own face soften.

"I might have to, Jerry. It wouldn't do to keep it quiet," she began and to her surprise he nodded.

"I'd rather you did. The sooner they know I had a grudge the better. Then they can forget all about me. Because it's obvious I couldn't have done it, isn't it?"

"Why not?"

He sighed a little theatrically. "Dear Dr. B., I'm my own best proof of innocence. Who did the lab tests that uncovered how it was done? I did! If I'd put the stuff there myself, would I, do you think, have told you I'd found it afterwards? Call yourself a pathologist? Garn! I could beat you at your own game."

She was so relieved she laughed aloud and came back to her desk to reach over and push at his shoulder. "You're a—you're the pits!" she said. "I'd have thought it through eventually, I dare say, but yes, you're right."

He grinned a little shakily. "Well, I have to say I only just realized it myself. But you gave me a bad ten minutes there."

"I'm sorry. But that's the trouble with murder. It obviously does make you get odd ideas. Even about people you like."

"I'm glad to hear that, at any rate."

"What?"

"That you like me."

She straightened. "You'll do, buddy. Now, go on. Get the place cleaned up and tell the others. I'll see you in the morning. Right now I have to go down to Ratcliffe Street."

"The nick," he said and got to his feet a little heavily. "Well, sooner you than me, thanks very much. Even though I'm as innocent as the driven whatsit, I don't fancy hanging around cop shops."

The police station was fairly quiet when she got there: just three people were sitting on the benches in the outer office waiting to talk to the duty sergeant and he, when he saw her, bobbed his head and pushed the bell beneath his high desk. The uniformed policeman who popped his head out of the inner office in response was instructed to "take the doctor up to

Mr. Hathaway sharpish. Nice to see you, doctor." The waiting people all turned and looked at her doggishly and she tried a vague smile at them as she followed the policeman up to the CID room, feeling slightly guilty. It was a knee-jerk reaction of the silliest kind, she knew, and particularly silly for a highly qualified forensic pathologist, but there it was: she never felt quite as comfortable in a police station as she might.

The lights were burning in all the offices and there was a cheerful rattle of typewriters and the sound of a great many loud voices as people called to each other from one room to another. The uniformed man ignored it all, and led her at once to a corner door on which he tapped politely and then left her. She had to respond to Hathaway's muffled call by pushing the door open herself and marching in.

"Hey, this is unexpected," he said after peering at her for a moment. He stood up. He was in his shirt sleeves and had left his tie dangling over the jacket which he had hung lopsidedly on the back of his chair. He looked tired, she thought and was annoyed with herself for noticing. "What can I do for you?"

"I've got the answers," she said, standing just inside the doorway, her hands in her deep pockets. She could feel the folded sheets plump and firm against her touch, but she didn't take them out.

"Have you, by cracky? That's a grand piece of—And looking at your face I'd say it was interesting."

"Very much so," she said. She came further in as he came around his desk to pull a chair forward for her and offered to take her coat. She shook her head, feeling safer inside its thick folds somehow, a reaction she knew was absurd but did not resist.

"You needn't have come over on your own on such a mucky evening," he said. "I'd have come and got 'em. Sent a messenger or something."

"Am I in the way?"

"Not in the least. Don't be so spiky. OK, let's be looking at it."

She pulled out the papers, smoothed them and put them in front of him. He sat down again and pored over them, his head propped up on both fists. Behind her she could hear the people outside still talking loudly, and the shrilling of phones and beyond that the noise of cars as they moved in and out of the police yard beneath the window. She felt a little dreamy, as though she weren't here herself at all, really, but imagining all this.

"Well, that was a bit of a hit below the belt, wasn't it?" he said and grinned up at her and she came down to earth with a jolt.

"Oh, God, not you too! I wonder how many variations there'll be on the same joke? And you were the one who said hemorrhoids aren't funny."

"They aren't, but I have to tell you that hemorrhoid cream used as a murder weapon is bloody funny." He pulled the papers together and tidied them before pushing them into a plastic folder and adding them to the pile of similar folders on the tray at his right-hand side. "Well, well. Now we really will have to settle down to some hard work. Old-fashioned police work, lots of interrogating, lots of watching and lots of plodding. The dull bits. You've done the magic part, shown us how it was done, and I hand it to you, Dr. B., I really do. You spotted it was a murder and now you've spotted how it was done." He stopped and stared at her for a moment, his eyes very bright and dark. "Put me out of my misery. What gave it away to you? How did you know it was a murder? Right at the start, I mean. What made you go on and on at it, all stubborn like?"

She looked back at him and then couldn't help it. She let her lips curve and said sweetly, "Intuition. Just my feminine intuition."

"Intuition!" he said and leaned back in his chair so that his face was in the shadow and the brightness of his eyes seemed to disappear. "Such stuff! Well, as I say, from now on we've got to plod and do the boring bits. Real evidence, real work.

Intuition's no use for that. Anyway, ta, Dr. B." He got to his feet and she looked up at him and frowned.

"Do you have the idea you're going to send me away now?" she demanded.

He looked a little surprised. "Why not? There's nothing else, is there?"

"There's the whole case," she said. "I'm interested! I'm not going to be pushed out now just because the pathology's all done with. Or apparently so. You never know what might still turn up."

"Oh. One of those, are you?"

"One of those what?"

"Nosy types."

"Yes." She smiled again, even more sweetly. "Ever so nosy. I want to keep on working on this one. Find out why as well as how, and who."

"Oh, I've got some ideas about who," he said. "Want to hear them?" He was watching her closely now and she was suddenly a little uncomfortable.

"Yes. If you'll tell me."

"Glad to." He went around his desk to sit down again. "Let me give you a little basic lesson in detection, Dr. B. Not that you really need it, I'm sure, but just to give you a freshener, you know what I mean? When it comes to murders most of 'em's domestic."

"Domestic?"

"Yes. That is, they're done by someone the victim knows—knew—well. They're done for nice domestic reasons. Jealousy and sex and money, all like that. In the real world, Dr. B., here in Shadwell, we get a lot of sex murders. This one may be fancied up with Docklands development gloss and lotsa dosh but I don't suppose it's all that different from the sort of cases we get 'round the council estates."

"I dare say you're right."

"Good. I'm glad you see that. So, I'm going to start in the obvious place as far as suspects are concerned."

"And where is that?"

He lifted his brows gently. "Domestically. His wife, Dr. B. His wife."

She nodded. "I see the sense of that."

"And also, of course, any—shall we say?—special friends of hers."

Her chest tightened suddenly. He was watching her so closely and seemed so intent on observing the most minute of responses in her that she found it unnerving. But she managed to look back at him calmly and raise her brows interrogatively.

"Like boyfriends, Dr. B."

"If she had any," she said and her lips felt a little stiff.

"Oh, she had them. Well, one at any rate. Very close they were. Still may be for all I know. We'll have to look into him."

"Really?"

"Mmm. Friend of yours, I'm afraid."

"I rather thought you were going to say that," she said as equably as she could. "After all, the hospital community is a small one and most people tend to know each other in it."

"But she isn't part of the hospital, is she?"

"No. But Oxford was, very much so. So it makes sense that—" She shook her head. "So you're telling me that you'll be investigating Mr. Bellamy?"

He looked almost disappointed and that pleased her. It was good to have cut across his bows this way. "It doesn't worry you?"

"Why should it? I doubt very much that he had anything to do with the man's death, but of course you have to talk to everyone. It's the plodder's way, isn't it?"

"You could say that. All right, Dr. B. There it is. I'll let you know how we get on. Not that I have to, you understand, but I appreciate the interest of a colleague. I'll be in touch."

"Yes," she said. "I'm sure you will." And walked out of the office in as relaxed a manner as she could, pulling her coat around her as she went. He sat and watched her and she knew he was uncertain of the effect he had had on her and that helped a lot.

But she still felt dreadful. So, the gossips at Old East were right. The police had already investigated and discovered that Toby Bellamy was indeed a woman eater. That meant he couldn't care less about her. How could he if he was fooling around with Felicity Oxford? And maybe, as well as that, he was a murderer? It was a horrible thought, but she couldn't banish it. And to top it all, she, stupid goddamn fool that she was, had let herself get far too fond of him. She'd done it again, but this time she couldn't run away to a new hospital. Getting over Toby would be much harder than getting over Ian.

20

He caught up with her just as she walked out of the police station and into the street, and she yelped in surprise when he pulled at her coat sleeve.

"I thought you were in a hurry for this information?" he said reproachfully. "And then ye go walking past me as though you'd never seen me before in your life!"

She blinked as she turned to stare at him in the dim light thrown by the station windows. "Oh! Mr. Urquhart!"

"Och, call me Michael, it's easier."

"I'm sorry. Did I pass you? I didn't mean to be rude. I was—I was thinking."

"Was the Guv'nor being tiresome?"

"Oh, not that you'd notice. I mean, not really. Uh—do I understand you've got some information for me?"

"I have at that," he said with great satisfaction. "It was easier than I'd ha' hoped, and I've a fair surprise for you, indeed I have."

"Tell me!" She began to feel better. "Right now."

"Well, not here!" he protested. "Now, I'm away from here in just twenty minutes. If it's all the same to you, we could perhaps meet somewhere and talk quietly. I don't really fancy bein' seen out here like this." He looked a little uneasily over his shoulder. "Not that I don't have the right to talk to anyone I choose, d'you understand, but it might not be politic, me being junior as you might say and you being the doctor an' all."

"Ye Gods, you Brits and your snobbery!"

He opened his eyes wide at that. "Nothing of the sort! Snobbery's no part of it. It's no' me, nor the others. It's the Guv'nor I'm thinking of. It has nothing to do with class, everything to do with him being the sort of man that has to be in full control all the time. He has to know what everyone's thinking as well as saying." He shook his head. "At the risk of shocking you, though I'll not be able to do that easily, you being a doctor an' all, I have to say that if he could he'd count the times we went off to the lavatory, that he would."

"Hmm," George said and nodded. "I take your point. So when and where can we talk?"

"In twenty minutes or thereabouts, like I said. I should get away easy enough. There's no big push on, on account there's not a lot we can look at at present."

"There will be now," she said. "I've found out how it was done."

He lit up. "Ye have? That's grand news. Tell me."

"Like you said, not here, not now. Where shall we—"

"There's an Indian restaurant away down the other side of Watney Street market—they call it The Eastern Raj; very clever, seeing where it is an' all that—I'll meet you there as soon as I can."

And George, thinking of Toby knocking on her door in the doctors' residence in the next half-hour, agreed.

"I suppose there's no chance one of the other people from the station'll come in and see us and tell Hathaway we've been talking? It makes no difference to me, but if it might to you."

"You're right, it would. But there's no chance. They never come in here." He made a small grimace. "They never eat, to tell you the truth. They go to The Green Man all the time and have their lunches and suppers in a glass."

"But you don't mind a drink," George said, looking at the lager beside his plate. "So why—"

"Ah, first things first! I canna be spending all my time hanging around pubs. Me, I'd sooner have a place where you eat and can get a drink than a place where you drink and can sometimes get a sandwich."

"Oh, but it's good to be with a Scot again," she cried impulsively. "I hadn't realized I missed Inverness so much."

He looked pleased and flustered and then leaned back as the waiter appeared with a plate of onion bhajis. "Well, I'm no' from Inverness, but still…"

"Eat those quickly. I'm dying to hear what you've got for me," she said, needing to relieve his embarrassment. "I can see why you wanted to eat first, but all the same it's driving me mad."

"I'm no' fair to keep you waiting, then," he said with his mouth full. "Here, you look at that. If you're sure you don't want some of these?"

"I'm sure," she said eagerly and reached for the paper he'd pulled out of his breast pocket.

She smoothed it out and read it fast and then again more slowly as he chewed cheerfully and watched with happy anticipation. She looked up at him, her forehead creased.

"I don't understand. How did you think to look for this? And you're sure it's the same person?"

He grinned and wiped his mouth with a flourish of his table napkin. "I'd like to be able to tell you it was my own brilliant idea, but it wasn't. I sent the request through to the computer operator at my friend's nick, over in Wimbledon. I thought it'd be a bit, shall we say, more discreet. We tap into the same database, you understand, but there's less chance of anyone wondering why such information is being looked for. My friend Peter never asks questions any more than I do when he asks me for favors like this."

"You're a resourceful pair," she said.

"We are that. We're ambitious, do you see? This way we help each other. And he passed it down to his clerk and it was he who got it arse about face, if you'll excuse the expression."

"Indeed I will. But you checked the proper way 'round as well?"

"Of course! What do you take me for? As soon as he sent the first printout I called Peter and asked him what had happened. He checked and came back and told me that the clerk had assumed it was written Army style, surname first. I hadn't specified, do you see."

"I can see how it happened." She looked again at the piece of paper and then read it aloud. "Mitchell, J. Formby. I suppose Formby could be a first name here in Britain. It's common at home, of course, for people to have an extra surname. They take their mother's."

"And don't forget there was also the J.—John. He just uses that as an initial both ways. And why not? Aren't there lots of names that could serve either way? My own, for a start. There are plenty of people surnamed Michael. And I dare say your name might confuse some."

She grinned. "It does even when it's the right way 'round. They expect an old man. What they get is me."

"I can see it would surprise a few. So there you are! Your man has a nasty record and a fancy way of dealing with it."

She shook her head. "I still don't see how he got away with it. I mean, when he applied for this job at Old East, he must have known it wasn't enough just to turn his name 'round. They'd have found out he had a record, surely?"

Michael shrugged. "Why not risk it? He strikes me as a man who takes risks, for all you say. He tells you this whole tale about being a sex offender and risks you going to check it out and finding it's not true."

"Maybe he didn't think I'd be able to check."

"Not him. He thought of it, but he gambled. I dare say if you went back now and told him you'd looked in the records and there was no sex offense nor any suspended sentence listed anywhere against him, he'd have another tale to tell you. The one thing he didn't think was likely was that you'd realize he'd simply turned his name around to hide a much more important offense."

"More important? Than rape?"

"More important to him, seeing the sort of job he has. And it worked, didn't it? I dare say the hospital took up references, made searches for past misdeeds, and found nothing under Formby, M.J. If they'd looked under Mitchell, J. Formby, of course—"

"They'd have seen he'd been convicted of embezzlement. Yes, I suppose it would be more embarrassing to him to have that known." She frowned suddenly. "He really has to be a bastard, you know. To pick on that poor woman to wrap his lies around, and to think that pleading a sex crime would make me be kinder to him. Jesus! What a man!"

"Well, there it is then. Yon John Formby Mitchell is a known embezzler who's worked in major businesses before, and he's doing it again. Working, I mean, in a position where he could commit the same crime as he did last time. So, now'— he leaned back in his seat again as the waiter brought their main courses—"now, maybe you'll tell me why you wanted to know. I mean, what was it about him that put you on to the possibility that he might be bad news?"

She was silent until the waiter had gone and then said carefully, "Michael, I think we may have a problem, you and I."

"How's that?"

"With your Guv'nor. The thing is, I think I now know who killed Oxford. Or perhaps did. I can't see any link between the two yet, but it has to be. There can't be two villains in the same place at the same time. It'd be stretching credulity too far."

"You're saying that this Mitchell fella did for Oxford?"

"It seems possible, doesn't it? Let me explain: there's more. He's been behind a series of hospital thefts, I'm certain of it. The system is simple. Terribly simple. He arranges thefts of expensive equipment, right? Then he draws checks from various funds over which he has some control to replace said equipment. He has the invoices made out to some spurious company or other, I imagine, and then replacement goods are duly delivered. Only they're not replacements. They're the original stolen property. Mitchell walks away with the price of the goods for very little effort. He has to pay something to the people he hires to act as his delivery men—and thieves—but the profits have to be high. Those microscopes he stole from us and then replaced cost around twenty thousand pounds apiece. And there were three of them."

Michael pursed his lips. "Hey, hey! That means he made around—well, it couldna be less than fifty thousand, allowing for any expenses he had to pay to these other people."

"And that was just one such theft. There's been a rash of them. ECG machines—I don't know what they cost, but I dare say it's expensive enough, and then there were some electronic inflation infusion pumps and I do know they can cost up to seven thousand each. I had to look up something and they were in the same catalog and I was amazed they were so pricey. And I think half a dozen of those walked."

"He's made a grand sum of money, then?"

They sat and stared at each other for some time, leaving their lamb korma cooling in front of them, and then he said abruptly, "We'll have to tell the Guv'nor, of course."

"Of course. And he'll find out you helped me—"

"—and I'll be for the high jump." He stared at her lugubriously and then said something in a low voice which made her quirk her head in enquiry.

"Never mind. I was swearing in the Gaelic. We'll have to think about how we get out of this, will we not?"

"I'll think of something," she said and was silent again for a long time. Suddenly she brightened. "I think it's time I met your friend Peter."

"Eh?"

"Peter. If *I* were a friend who had asked him to do the searching for me, it wouldn't involve you at all, would it? And your Guv'nor can huff and puff at me till his ears fall off with the tension—I wouldn't mind at all. Not at all. In fact, I might quite enjoy it."

A slow grin moved across his face. "You're a grand woman, Dr. B."

"You've said that before. Now eat your supper, it's getting cold." And she began to eat herself, for suddenly her appetite had returned in a very healthy state.

Her good temper remained with her until they'd finished their meal with a little bowl of sugared fennel seeds and cardamom-scented coffee and argued amiably over the bill, agreeing in the end each to settle their own. It was important to George that they should do that; the last thing she wanted was to have a young detective constable getting proprietorial over her. Life was complicated enough as it was. But he gave in gracefully in the end, and when they reached the pavement outside the restaurant, shook her hand cheerfully.

"I'll fix up for you to talk to Peter tomorrow on the Phone," Michael promised. "I'll explain it all to him tonight as soon as I get back to my flat—he's used to late-night calls from me—and then you can go along to the Guv'nor and tell it all to him. Though I have to say I agree with you, I canna see yet how the man's linked with the Oxford case. But that's not so important. We've got to get him sorted as a thief first, and, Doctor—" He hesitated and she looked up at him in the metallic light thrown by a sodium street lamp above their heads, at the way his face seemed to shimmer behind the clouds of breath vapour that surrounded him on this cold night, and smiled. He was an endearing lad, she thought. Pity he's younger than me—and could have slapped herself. Would she never stop noticing men this way? "Doctor, I'm grateful to you."

"Whatever for? It's I who owe you a debt for digging this out for me."

"Not a bit of it. I tell you what, you're a grand woman."

"Do stop saying that."

"And if I can do more, I will. If we can think of a decent reason for it, I'll gladly take you over to the Oxford flat so that we can look at his computer and stuff. You said you wanted to."

Excitement leaped in her at the idea, but she had to shake her head. "You're a grand man yourself, Michael, but I don't see we can do that and keep you out of it. You've been marvelous so far; let's not push our luck. I think I should be able to persuade Hathaway to let me have a look, once I bring this into him." Then it was her turn to stop and think. "Now I feel guilty about you."

"No need."

"Every need. This could have been promotion material if you'd brought it in."

"Not at all. The idea was yours. I can make the top by my own ideas, never you fear. I don't need to claim this. Good night to you, Dr. B. I'll not see you back to the hospital. It isn't far and—"

"—and it would never do for us to be seen together."

"Exactly. Our CID lads go 'round in the cars quite often. They don't come here, for this is a precinct and the cars can't get in. It's just the uniformed lads sometimes, so it's all right here. I'll make sure Peter phones you tomorrow, then. And I'll look forward to what happens when you've talked to the Guv'nor." He chuckled, a rich little sound deep in his throat. "I'll enjoy that."

The walk back to the hospital was bitterly cold and she stepped out smartly, her chin tucked into her collar so that her warm breath would not be wasted, and wondered where she'd put the furry ear muffs that she'd brought with her from Buffalo. She'd hidden them away when the fuss about fur started, but right now she'd be prepared to risk the wrath of any passing animal liberationist to be warm. Her ears were stinging with the icy air.

As she got nearer to the hospital she tried to keep her mind fixed on such matters as her cold ears, the ear muffs, the call tomorrow from the unknown Peter who was to be her ally, and what would happen when she told Gus Hathaway of her discovery. But in spite of all that, it wasn't possible fully to exclude thoughts of Toby Bellamy. Had he been angry when she hadn't returned to the residence? She'd not agreed to go out with him, of course. He'd just taken it for granted that she'd be there. Well, she hadn't been and she hoped, oh how she hoped, that he'd been disappointed and hurt.

He doesn't matter, she told herself furiously, as she made the last turn that brought her in through the hospital's main gates, slipping past an emerging ambulance and pressing herself against the wall to let another come in immediately after it. He's possibly a murderer, according to Gus Hathaway—even though she herself was convinced it was Mitchell Formby,—or rather Formby Mitchell, who was the killer—and he's certainly a philanderer. As the word came into her mind she relaxed. It was so stuffy and old-fashioned a word and she was being a silly old-fashioned person to create so much. Why should she, after all? Weren't there as many good fish ready for the tickling as she could possibly need? Michael Urquhart clearly thought highly of her, so why should she care that a worm like Bellamy had treated her badly? Modern women don't give a damn about men like him, she told herself firmly as at last she reached the walkway that led to the medical residence on the far side of the private wing. They live their own lives their own way and don't give a damn about male opinions—

"Dr. Barnabas! Dr. Barnabas!"

She stopped and turned and peered back into the darkness. Someone was running towards her and panting hard.

"Are you wanting me?" she called and stood still as the fellow came running up to stand in front of her, gasping for breath.

"Take it easy," she said cheerfully, looking at the familiar face of Bittacy, the A & E Head Porter. "You'll give yourself a coronary."

"Am I glad to find you," he panted. "I been lookin' everywhere for you, Dr. Barnabas. There's been a call out for you this past hour and gone. We tried your bleep."

She swore under her breath. "I forgot to switch it on. Sorry. What is it?"

"Police, doctor. They got a body for you, want you to come to the scene as soon as possible."

"I'll get my kit," she said and pushed past him to go back to the main hospital and her office in the lab. "Where's the body? Are they sending a car, or—"

"You don't need no car, Dr. Barnabas," the porter said, barely able to disguise his excitement. "You can walk it. It's in the Barrie Ward building. The new bit. Fell off the main roof, he did. It's a real mess."

21

She sent Bittacy to fetch her kit and set off at a run to the Barrie Ward building site, cutting through the underground corridor that led beneath Blue block to the far side of the hospital grounds. It was quiet down there and smelled of dirty laundry and disinfectant and boiled cabbage, and her own hurried footsteps echoed back at her disagreeably from the cable-lined concrete walls, sending a shiver of real fear down her back. Atavistic, she found herself thinking. I'm being primeval. It's like being afraid of the dark. You're on your way to see death and you're on your own, that's why you're feeling so apprehensive. It's silly.

But when she got there she knew she hadn't been silly. Part of her had expected and feared to find what was waiting for her.

She had to climb over piles of bricks and breeze blocks to get to where she could see a few lights and shadows as people milled about and called to each other, and she tore her tights and swore, glad of the distraction; and then picked her way over raw frozen earth to reach the center of activity beneath the skeleton of a building which stretched overhead into the blackness of the sky, showing pale squares where the spaces between the upright beams yawned into the blank interior.

"Dr. Barnabas, is that you?" someone called. She squinted into the bright light that was thrown her way from a hand-held torch. "Glad you're here. We've been waiting for you. This way, doctor." The torch wavered, beckoned and then showed the ground at her feet. She followed its beam obediently.

Someone had set up a tarpaulin hung over a makeshift frame of battening. Behind it there were a couple of storm lanterns which had been set on the ground to throw glaring beams into the sky. The shadows made by the light were hard and dense, and she had to narrow her eyes to see clearly, for the contrast between the blackness and the vivid beams was stark.

"Over here, doctor," the voice said and she followed it 'round the edge of the tarpaulin to look down at the body waiting for her.

It lay on its front in a pile of assorted rubble and was bent into a clearly impossible posture, with the left leg almost at a right angle to the trunk and the arms crumpled beneath the chest. The head was turned sideways with the face away from her, and she moved around to look at it, though she knew what she would see.

The eyes were open and gleaming in the mess of blood that was the face, but she recognized it easily and took a long breath.

"Evenin', Dr. B.," Gus said and she lifted her head and peered into the shadows to see him standing with a couple of other people. "This, it seems, is—"

"I know," she said. "Mitchell."

"—Mr. Formby," Gus said at the same moment. Then he stopped and looked at her sharply. "Here, he wasn't a mate of yours, was he? If he was and you want me to find someone else to take over for you on this one, you just say the word."

"He wasn't a mate," she said and glanced over her shoulder. "Bittacy should be here in a moment or two with my kit. I'll wait for it before I do anything. Any idea what happened?"

"He must have fallen," one of the people with Gus Hathaway said, stepping forward into the light, and she lifted her brows, a little surprised.

"Professor Dieter! What are you doing here?"

"I came as soon as I heard from one of the porters," he said a little stuffily. "Who else would you expect to see?"

"Mr. Herne, perhaps," she said without stopping to think. "He's the admin boss."

"And I am the senior medical person at Old East." He turned away and looked at Gus. "Is there any reason why I should not be here, Mr. Hathaway? Am I in the way?"

"Not in the least," Gus said cordially. "Only it's up to Dr. Barnabas who gets involved with him medically, d'you see what I mean? She's in charge of the body till after she's done her bits and bobs. When she says it's OK, and the Soco is done, I take over. But right now—"

"For heaven's sake, Professor, I didn't mean to suggest you shouldn't be here!" George said hastily. "I was just surprised. But of course it's perfectly natural now I think of it."

"Thank you," he said coldly, turning away. "Mr. Hathaway, I want to ask you..." He went over to Hathaway and began to speak to him in a low voice so George felt herself to be snubbed and was irritated. Why shouldn't she question his presence? He normally wasn't at the hospital in the evening, she knew that; he always made sure he had the best of registrars for his patients and it was rare indeed there was any need to call him out of hours. He lived...where? She had been told but had to think hard to remember, and then it came back to her. Totteridge. He lived out in Totteridge, way to the north of the city, and it took him the best part of an hour and a quarter to drive in in the morning; he often complained about it at medical meetings. Even outside the rush hour it had to be a long drive for him; so why was he here at this time of night? She set her jaw to prevent herself asking him. To be this suspicious of everybody was absurd. No doubt he had an excellent reason.

"I would like to get back to my work," she heard him say a little more loudly. "I really have to finish it today—I mean tonight—the seminar is tomorrow evening and it is most important."

"Of course, Professor," Gus said and stood aside. "I'll let you know if I need any more from you. Goodnight."

The Professor moved back towards George on his way out of the little huddle behind the tarpaulin and he paused as he reached her. "Well, Dr. Barnabas, this is a sad business, very sad."

"Yes," she said cautiously, not sure whether he wanted to say something important or just to show her that now he had delivered his snub there were no hard feelings. "I don't know yet what happened, of course."

"A fall, I imagine. Checking some work here after the workmen had gone, and fell. He was a very devoted man, meticulous in his attention to detail, cared a great deal about his responsibilities. He'll be sadly missed."

"Indeed," she said politely.

"Well, I must go. I have my paper to finish." He began to walk away, then turned to look at her closely. "You'll be there, of course. It's a subject upon which you should have strong views."

"Mmm? Er…" She hesitated. Clearly this was something she was supposed to know about; it would be far from politic to display complete ignorance. "You'll have to remind me of where and when, I'm afraid, I tend to rely on my diary as an aide-mémoire, there's so much going on." She looked up at him candidly, hoping her mendacity wasn't too obvious.

"Tomorrow evening in the Board Room." He said it a little reprovingly. "I sent a memo to all the medical staff. I really am very anxious we should be as well informed as possible."

"Of course," she said, grateful for the memory that came back in a rush of an event she had dismissed from her mind as soon as she'd heard of it, having no intention of wasting an evening on a subject she knew inside out. "The AIDS debate. Um, I'm not sure. It depends on how the pressure of work is, and I am pretty well up-to-date on HIV, and—"

"I want us to consider all the options on this one, doctor," he said heavily. "And will need your input. I hope indeed you can arrange your work so that you can get along. As you have no patient load…" He left it hanging in the air and smiled vaguely. "Well, as I say, I must go back to my office. No peace for the wicked." He looked back over his shoulder. "Poor man. I imagine you'll be contacting any relations, Inspector? Yes, I thought you would. Well, goodnight to you all. Sorry business, very sorry. I'll see you tomorrow, doctor."

Well, that explains that, George thought as she reached for the kit which Bittacy, still panting with his exertions, had at last brought. Now let's see if we can explain what happened to Mitchell Formby, or Formby Mitchell, whichever he was.

She knelt by the body and started her examination as Gus and Sergeant Dudley watched her. The Soco, a little round man in a rather crumpled navy blue suit, was standing poised to get on with his job and he watched too, and she was very aware of the audience as she began gingerly to make her examination.

The injuries were multiple and it would take a detailed PM to be sure of the cause of death, but it was clear from her initial observation that there had been more than one. His skull was severely fractured at the left temple, pushed in by some sort of hard pointed object, and had shattered into several pieces, some of which protruded from the wound. She looked beneath the body and there was a brick lying crookedly that could have inflicted it, though it seemed unsteady in its place; she would have thought the weight of a falling body would have dislodged it rather than driven it into the skull. But it could have happened…

In addition there were injuries to the chest which had penetrated lung tissue—there was brightly scarlet frothy blood at the points of entry—and the belly too was clearly demonstrating damage, for it was distended and so taut that the skin felt hard to her touch. A lot of interior bleeding as well as exterior, she noted into her small dictaphone, keeping her voice low out of a sort of embarrassment due to the watchers surrounding her. In addition the left leg was shattered at the femur. It looked as though the bone had been sheared off completely, for the limb was sticking out at an ugly angle and the lower part was white under the torn cloth of the trousers. "Exsanguinated," she murmured into the dictaphone, "major blood vessels clearly lost."

"Can you give us a time of death, Dr. B.?" Gus asked and she shook her head.

"Give me a chance, please! So far I've barely begun." But she took out of her kit the thermocouple to check temperature. She expected little joy; the night was so cold that the body was already chilled and she checked it again for rigor. Stiff and cold; normally that would mean death had occurred about eight hours ago. But on this bitterly cold night that could be grossly distorted.

She checked the temperature in the nose, the ear and then, as an extra check, the axilla. To try to take a rectal reading here would be absurd even though she was sure there would be no objection from the police to having it done; no one could see this as a sex-linked crime with evidence that could be disturbed by such an action; but she remembered all too well how Oxford had died, and knew the careful examination of the rectum at the PM was a must. So, no rectal temperature now. The other readings would have to suffice.

She took them all down in her notebook as well as dictating them into her machine and then sighed and looked up at Gus after finishing her calculations.

"I'l'd be hard put to it to swear to this but you can have an estimate if·you like."

"I'll settle for that."

"OK. Between, oh, five and nine hours. Maybe a little less, maybe more. It's so cold tonight that the readings may have been badly distorted, but I reckon you can narrow it to between those hours."

"Hmm. Not a lot of use, is it?"

She bridled. "I told you, I can't—"

"I'm not complaining! Just making an observation. Now remind me, Roop. Give me the timetable again."

Sergeant Dudley stepped forward in the light to where he could be seen, nodded unsmilingly at George and flipped open his notebook. "Body was found at nine p.m. by Thomas James, one of the night staff who lives over in Tobruk Street at the back here. He was taking an illegal shortcut through this way. He was late for work and worried about it so he was very aware of the time. He had a torch with him and saw the body that way. Didn't touch it, ran like hell to the A & E Head Porter's office—he's a night porter, is James, and has to report to him anyway. Head Porter, Bernard Bittacy, called us; call logged at nine-eleven. We got here at nine-seventeen. Took a long time to get over the rubble and suchlike. Professor Dieter turned up at nine-thirty, did the identification. At ten p.m. I talked to the staff of the supplies office on the phone—took till then for Professor Dieter to get the numbers for us. These people are being seen by D.C. Morley who'll get statements from them, but in the meantime I can tell you that the person who saw him last was May Potter, secretary, who said he left the office at half past five, didn't say where he was going. She went home a few minutes after him, locking up first." He snapped the notebook closed and looked at Gus. "That's all so far. We couldn't get on as fast as we'd have liked, since we were looking for Dr. Barnabas." He didn't glance at her and his voice was wooden. "The Soco's been here for the past couple of hours or thereabouts'—he looked at his watch—"it now being eleven-ten. That's about it, Guv."

"Mmm." Gus said and stared unseeingly down at the body. "Well, if you've finished, doctor?"

"I've finished here," she said and got to her feet, very aware of the way the tear in her tights had become a vast hole that exposed her entire left knee. "You can take him over as soon as you like."

"At least we don't need transport," Gus said. "You—er— Bittacy, isn't it? Yes. Can you get one of your agony wagons out there where the path is smooth? And a stretcher and a cover of some kind. Then we can shift this chap right over to the mortuary at once. Very considerate of him to die on the premises like this."

George opened her mouth to speak but then closed it, and moved away to the side to let the police get on, standing there with her hands in her pockets, once she'd dropped her plastic gloves back into her kit, watching them gloomily.

I've painted myself into one hell of a corner, she thought. He has to be told about the man's background and what I know, but I can't tell him now or I'll drop Michael in it. It'll have to wait, but if it waits will they go off at a tangent and waste a lot of time that they don't need to? It was a difficult situation and she couldn't see how she was going to get out of it, and then had an idea and walked over to Gus Hathaway. "Are you planning to start the investigation tonight?"

"We usually do," he said, turning away from one of the detective constables to whom he'd been talking. "Go on, Wheeler, you get on with it." He turned back to George. "There are things we can start straight away."

"It might be easier to wait till after my PM," she said. "I have to tell you the truth, I'm not at all happy about the estimation of time I had to give you. It's damned difficult in these conditions and on a night as cold as this—you understand."

He looked at her long and hard and then sighed. "You're taking back what you said, then?"

"Not taking it back." She spoke cautiously, well aware of the fact that she wouldn't be able to change her estimate, since there would be no new evidence to make that possible. "But I need time before confirming it as more definite. I really couldn't stand by it at the moment, that's the trouble. And if you start investigating along the lines of the timings I gave you, well…"

"Hmm. I see what you mean." He thought for a moment and then quirked an eyebrow. "You wouldn't be trying to get us to stop and go to bed because you're too tired to work now, would you?"

She flushed. "It makes no difference to me," she said tartly. "I won't do the PM till tomorrow morning anyway. I need my technician and he won't be available till then. I was just trying to save you a lot of trouble."

"Well." He seemed to make up his mind quickly. "Well, then, I'm grateful to you. We'll see the body over to your mortuary, cover the site and go to bed like proper people to start again in the morning. At least I don't have to set up an incident room—we've already got Oxford's going."

She caught her breath. "Do you think there's a need for that with this one? I mean, you think it wasn't an accident?"

"I wouldn't dream of saying at this stage. I have to wait for your report, don't I? But I have to think ahead to all possibilities, and I was just thinking, if it did happen to be a dicey one, and I did happen to need an incident room, at least I'd be able to double up a bit. Because if it should turn out not to be an accident it'd be logical to assume that the two were linked in some way, wouldn't it? Me, I've had too much experience to deal in unlikely coincidences, like two killers at work on the one premises for separate reasons. That doesn't happen very often."

"No," she said, and tightened her fists in her pockets. "No, it doesn't." And what happened to Mitchell here tonight has to be linked with Oxford, she thought, it has to. Oh, I hope Michael's friend phones early in the morning! The sooner I can give this man all the information I have the sooner I'll feel right. Because at present I feel godawful.

"We're ready, Guv," someone called and Gus turned and went, and slowly the stretcher bearing the exceedingly battered remains of John Formby Mitchell—or Mitchell J. Formby—was carried away over the piles of bricks and breeze blocks by a couple of sweating men, followed by a huddle of policemen. George took a deep breath and followed the little cortège. It was the least she could do, she felt, to see the man on to her premises.

"Dr. B.!" Gus called and she stopped and turned to look at him.

"Yes?"

"Didn't you wonder why we had a Soco here?"

She lifted her brows. "You had one at Oxford's place, and you were sure that was an accident."

He sighed. "It was an accident that the Soco happened to be at the station when the alarm went off. That was why he went to the Oxford flat with Roop. And it was burglary that was suspected there, of course, which makes a difference. This was an accident on a building site. We wouldn't usually bring a Soco into that first go. Didn't you think about that?"

She stared at him silently.

"I'd hardly ask for a scene-of-crime officer if I didn't think there'd been a crime, would I? And I have to say it seems to me a bit much to have a fatal accident following a murder. That's why I decided to take no chances. I just thought I'd mention it, because if you know anything that might be useful about this man, it'd be handy to hear it. Though I'm sure you'd tell me if you knew, wouldn't you? You're not the sort to hold back important evidence, are you?"

22

She slept fitfully and, waking early, was in the lab before eight. It seemed to make better sense than tossing and turning in her narrow hospital bed in the chill of her room in the residence. I'll have to get myself a flat, she thought as she washed, shivering, and hurried into her clothes. I can't go on like this. They're too mean to heat this place properly and it's the ugliest room I've ever slept in; and she closed the door behind her gratefully and went over to the lab in the thin early morning light.

The hospital was already bustling and, as she hurried across the courtyard, trailing vapour clouds of breath behind her, she could smell the morning toast and coffee and the strong salty reek of frying bacon, together with the acrid tang of the disinfectant used to swab the floors and surfaces everywhere, and felt a sudden lift of her spirits. Life was complicated at present, what with murders on her doorstep and rather more men around to meddle with her feelings than there usually were, but life here at The Royal Eastern was never dull, and for that she was deeply grateful. She could cope with anything but boredom; and she unlocked the lab and let herself in, whistling softly between her teeth.

There was a large manila envelope lying just inside, clearly having been pushed under the door. She seized it and, looking at the way her name was scrawled on the front, hurried into the main lab and switched on the kettle to make herself a cup of coffee, and then perched herself on a high workbench and tore open the envelope.

It was, as she had hoped, from Sam.

I've done some solid checking on your man [he wrote]. It was quite a fun piece of research to do, and it cheered me not a little. I thought the R. Oxfords of this world made far more money than I did, and certainly had a bigger following, but when I compared his PLR rates with mine I was greatly encouraged. PLR, by the way, is Public Lending Right. The reports they let you have from public libraries tell you just how many people have borrowed your books—it's a measure of popularity, really. Last year, it turns out, Oxford didn't make the top tranche—those authors who earn the maximum by getting something over half a million borrowings a year, and he's got seventeen titles in print—but the one immediately below. Since I was only a couple of rungs behind him, with just one book to my name, I was very chuffed.

However, it's sales that matter and here he does rather better, oddly enough. He has very big overseas sales and has sold a few film rights. I found a very helpful girl at his publishers, as you can see from the attached figures, and it was she who gave me all this as well as his PLR computer printout for last year. Highly improper, but she's a friend. I'd say his annual income from his books was around sixty thousand. A nice living by anyone's measure but by no means in the Barbara Taylor Bradford or Ken Follett bracket. They really make millions. I suppose he earned a fair bit from lecturing and a bit more from radio and TV as most authors do these days, but even that wouldn't bump him into the six figures a year group.

So there it is. He earned well enough but it wasn't great. He certainly didn't seem to make enough to support the lifestyle you described. By the way, he isn't even a company as so many authors are. He is—or was—still a private citizen and according to my little friend at his publishers paid all his income tax—he complained to her enough about what they

took which is how she knows—and as he was a man on his
own, with no children, it's my guess he paid at the top rate, too.
   I hope this is of help in your amateur sleuthing (that's
Hattie's description, not mine, so don't think I'm patronizing
you!) and if there's anything else with which I can help then do
let me know.

Yours,
Sam Chanter

She folded the paper slowly and put it back in the envelope.
So she'd been right. Oxford's money was a key issue. It had to
be obvious that he'd got it from some other source, and it was
reasonable to assume that the reason for his murder was to be
found in the investigation of that source. Which was something
she couldn't do for herself. Only Gus and his men could do that
and she felt a stab of irritation. It would have been so much fun
to find out the why of this murder on her own. She knew the
how, and that was surprising enough. Now she almost knew
the why, but only almost. It was tantalizing to be so close and
yet not be able to get nearer on her own. Unless she could get
at Oxford's private affairs and see for herself what sort of accounts he kept, she was balked.

    She took her coffee into her office and set to work sorting out
her kit and cleaning it ready for the morning to come, thinking
hard all the time, but she had to admit she'd gone as far as
she could. Gus Hathaway had to be given all the information
she had, and allowed to do his job properly. And she scolded
herself as she worked, well aware that she had overstepped
professional boundaries in behaving as she had; she should
have told him at once about Mitchell Formby. If it hadn't been
for young Michael Urquhart she'd call him right now and get
it all off her conscience.

    But of course she didn't and, with her appetite sharpened
by the coffee, decided to take herself over to the canteen for a
quick breakfast before starting the PM. Danny would be ready

for her by nine with a little luck. She left a note for him in the mortuary and then hurried over to the main hospital block.

She was sitting at a corner table dealing with a bowl of muesli and some toast and marmalade when Toby came and sat beside her.

"And what happened to you last night?"

"What? Oh. I was working."

"I told you I'd call for you and we'd have supper."

"The fact that you said it doesn't mean I agreed," she said tartly. "Anyway, it was just as well I didn't. I had to—"

"You're changing the subject." He sounded suddenly serious, not at all his usual bantering self. She glanced at him and put down her spoon. Her hand was a little unsteady, so she had to. "Are you trying to tell me I'm making a nuisance of myself? I didn't get the impression you were actually, shall we say, repelled by me. Yet when I try to take us a bit further along the road to wherever we might get to at the other end, you become untouchable. I didn't see you as the sort of woman who played hard to get, but if I'm wrong and you're a tease at heart, say so, and I'll play along as best I can. Not that I'll enjoy it, because I think that's not only daft, but positively Neanderthal behavior. But I'll do it if I must. But if I'm really up shit creek and you can't stand the sight of me—"

"Ouch," she said. She picked up her spoon again but couldn't eat. She just sat and stirred her muesli.

"Well, what is it?"

She swallowed. It really was very hard to be rational in this man's company. "I thought you were playing games with me."

"Playing—Well, of course I am, you daft object! The best game there is. A little slap-and-tickle, or come-and-be-kissed or whatever else you want to call it. What is it with you, lady?"

"According to Gus Hathaway you're a suspect for Oxford's murder." She hadn't meant to put it quite so baldly but now it was out and in a way it was a relief. She looked at him, and he sat and gazed back at her, his face quite blank.

"Oh," he said.

"Well, you asked me." She allowed herself to sound irritable. "I didn't want to tell you but if you keep on pursuing me—"

"Faintly pursuing," he said and laughed, but it was a tight little sound with little of pleasure in it.

"I don't know what to do. I thought I knew who it might be, but now he's dead and so—"

"What?" He actually gaped now. "Hold your horses, will you? You're losing me here."

She sighed. "I imagined the whole place'd be humming with it by now. Mitchell Formby—deputy to Matthew Herne, the admin chap—he was found on the Barrie Ward building site. Last night."

"Dead, you say?"

"Severe multiple injuries. Stoved in skull, belly like a drum, lungs perforated. Nasty."

"Then very dead." He took a deep breath. "And you thought he was the one who'd murdered Oxford? Don't tell me why. I don't think I could handle it. But anyway, that police bloke thinks it was me! For God's sake, why?"

"Because of Felicity Oxford," she said. She was still looking at him, never breaking the eye contact. It was the hardest thing she'd ever done, but she managed it. "He says that in every murder investigation you have to start with the nearest and dearest. And even though they don't live together, that's her. And you're...The term he used was close. Very close, he said. And you are, aren't you? And I do know—I have heard, dammit, you've got a reputation as a—a fickle type. Playing around—"

"And that's why you didn't come back to the residence last night to meet me?"

"Partly."

"Oh?"

"I had a meeting with—with someone who was getting information for me."

"Oh. About me?"

"No." She had reddened sharply at the sardonic note in his voice. "Of course not. About Mitchell Formby, if you must know. I thought—Oh, damn, there's so much you don't know and if you're a suspect—and you are—I'm not sure I should be telling you all this anyway. I should keep you in the dark so that if Gus Hathaway does find out facts that prove he's right, at least you won't be forewarned..." Her voice trailed away and to her horror she felt her eyes filling. "Did you have anything to do with it, Toby?"

He reached out one hand and held on to hers. She felt it warm against her very cold skin. "Would you believe me if I said absolutely not?"

She took a deep breath and willed the tears back under her lids. Somehow she managed it. "I'd like to."

He let go and nodded. "I see. You'd like to but you can't. Well, would it be pushing my luck too hard to ask if he has any evidence to support his belief?"

"He hasn't told me of any—" She stopped then and added impulsively, "But I—I wondered about something..."

"Spit it out," he said as she hesitated.

"You seemed to have a very, well, detailed knowledge of the interior of the Oxford flat. Talked about it as a palace and how the bathroom was so...How did you know?"

"I've seen it."

"Oh." She didn't know what more to say.

"I was a guest there," he said shortly. "I had dinner with several other people, if that's significant, and Oxford showed us 'round. He was very proud of the place. Did everything but put on a peaked cap and ask for tips at the end." He got to his feet. "But never mind, George. I won't make a pest of myself by asking any more questions or making any more declarations of innocence. You'll clearly need more than that. You don't seem able to take someone on your own estimation. You prefer to listen to others' opinions. And gossip." There was a cold edge in his voice as he said the word. "Well, that's up to you. If they take me off the suspect list, do let me know." And he pushed back his chair with a savage little gesture and went, and she sat there and watched him go, more miserable than she'd been for some time.

The phone rang just as she got back to her office. She nearly let it ring unanswered, wanting to get down to the mortuary and busy herself in work. The more detailed the work she had to do, she reckoned, the less likely she would be to think of the way Toby had looked at her, with a face that showed genuine hurt. She felt dreadful about him, quite dreadful.

"Well?" she snapped.

"Er, Dr. Barnabas? My name's Pritchard."

"So?"

"Peter Pritchard."

"Oh!" At once she was all attention. "I'm so sorry. You caught me at a bad moment. You're, um, Michael's friend?"

"That's right."

"He's explained to you what it is I wanted to talk to you about?"

The voice laughed in a resigned sort of way. "He has. There never was a geezer like him for getting what he wants, and now he wants me to help you. Well, that's fair enough. I don't see any reason why not."

"Well, I'm going to tell Gus Hathaway—Detective Chief Inspector Hathaway—that I got the information you discovered about the Mitchell man—or the Formby man, whichever he is—from you, and that I asked you because I knew you. Will this cause you any problems?"

"Oh, there might be, if he complains to my Guv'nor about me using police time for a non-authorized person."

"Oh, hell! Then I can't—"

"No, it'll be all right, doctor. There's no one else here can touch me on this computer. They all need me to do their bits for 'em, so they won't fuss too much. Anyway, it turned out it was police business, didn't it? It's going to help you nobble a thief, as I understand it."

"He's already nobbled," George said.

"Eh?"

"Accident. Or maybe not. Anyway he was found late last night in a heap on a pile of rubble on a building site here. And that stops him being a suspect for the Oxford murder, which is what I had him in my sights for. So there it is. Still, it's important information because if the death wasn't an accident...Well, either way, it has to be linked with the thefts in some way, doesn't it?"

"I'd imagine so. Look, don't you worry. You tell 'em I did this for you and there's an end of it. We're old friends, so—"

"How?"

"What? Oh, how old friends? Well, say I was a patient of yours once?"

She laughed. "Hardly! I'm a pathologist, remember."

"Whoops! Sorry. Well, of a friend of yours then?"

"Yes. Ye-es." Her lips curved. "Say you were a patient of Dr. Ian Felgate of Inverness. Saw him when you were on holiday, with a bellyache. OK?"

"Ian Felgate. Got it. Good hunting, doctor."

"I hope so. I'm about to do the PM on Mitchell Formby—or vice versa—now. I dare say Michael'll fill you in with the news when there is some."

"I'll see to it he does. Goodbye, doctor. I'll be thinking of you."

She came back to her office four hours later, her back aching with the tension that had filled her all through the post-mortem and her head aching a little. It hadn't been an easy one and having Rupert Dudley standing there in his most morose style, watching her like a lynx, hadn't helped.

Gus Hathaway was waiting for her, sitting in her chair with his feet up on her desk.

She scowled at him. "There's a chair for visitors over there."

"And I thought you were better than us stupid anally retentive men!" he said and got to his feet. "But you're as bad as I am, thoroughly territorial. OK, I'll sit here. Nasty one, was it?"

"You saw the body," she said shortly. "Not exactly a thing of beauty and a joy for ever."

"I'll grant you. You smell nice."

She was disconcerted and just blinked at him.

"Joy, isn't it? Expensive stuff! You do yourselves well, you pathologists."

She flushed. "So would you if you had to deal with a job as malodorous as mine. I like to make sure I come out of my shower smelling like a live person rather than a corpse."

"You're very much a person," he said approvingly. "Now, tell me about the corpse. I'll hold me nose if it gets too much. What did you find?"

She sat down heavily as Sheila came in with a tray of coffee and dimpled at Gus as she set it down and busied herself pouring it out. "We can manage, thanks, Sheila," she said at last. "The Inspector's got a lot to talk about." Sheila flushed and went away and Gus laughed.

"If she put any more bunting out she'd keel over," he said. "I do prefer a woman to be a bunch of thistles rather than a posy of pinks. And she's no end of a poser'

She laughed in spite of herself. "Don't be rude about my staff. Now listen, you want to know my findings."

"Accident? Did he fall or was he—"

"I can't say. I doubt anyone could."

"Hmm, I expected as much. We looked at the upper parts of the structure this morning. No slip marks, nothing untoward. There's been the world and his mate up there, and so much muck and cement dust and rubbish and mud on the wooden slats he could easily have slipped. Question is, what was he doing up there in the first place, when all the workmen had gone?"

"He signed the bills, it seems. He was the one who inspected work and agreed it was passable, so it's reasonable he should, I suppose. I gather he spent a good deal of his time there'

"Yes. So, no post-mortem evidence of what might have happened."

"A few splinters in his hands, but even those could have got there by normal means. I looked at the angles and the depth. There was nothing to suggest any violence was involved in getting them. They were in different directions, all the hallmarks of accidental splinter collection from handling raw wood. And there's enough of that about that site, I imagine."

"You'd be right. Hmm. I suppose it's the tough hard labor bit now of plotting everyone who was there that afternoon and evening and everyone who saw Formby and everyone who didn't, to see if we can find out if there was anyone who might have pushed him. And then of course we have to find out why anyone would have wanted to in the first place'

"Ah," George said and looked down at her hands.

"Now what?" He sounded resigned. "When you say, 'Ah,' like that I'm learning to be wary."

"Just as well." She looked up at him. "I've got some evidence for you." Then she couldn't help it. She smiled, broadly, hugely pleased with herself. "There might be very good reasons why he was pushed even if there's no postmortem evidence." And she took a deep breath and explained it all, from the first fuss over the microscopes to her carefully edited account of how she got the information about the man's past from the police computer database. He listened in total silence, only watching her face all the time she talked.

"Well," he said when she had finished. "Well, well, well."

"Is that the best you can do?" she demanded.

"What do you want me to say? That I'm gobsmacked? OK, I'm gobsmacked. Furthermore, I'm as sick as a parrot, over the moon and—"

"That'll do. As long as you're pleased. This should be useful."

"Oh, I love it! Useful? How's that for meiosis?"

"My what?"

"Meiosis. The verbal technique by which it is conveyed that a thing is of lesser importance or size than it really is. It's bloody enormously useful!"

"And I get a lecture in English grammar as a reward for it from a man who claims to be a none-of-your-nonsense cockney? I am indeed the recipient of no meagre recompense. That's litotes, by the way, a grammatical technique for aggrandizing something by using a negative as an affirmative."

"I'm not sure you've got that quite right," he said judiciously. "But we'll call the honors even. Have you the evidence to prove all this?"

She nodded, pulled out her desk drawer and gave him the copy of the printout from the police computer, and then after a moment also took out the letter she'd received from Sam. But she didn't give it to him at once.

"I went a bit further," she said. "When I saw Oxford's flat it seemed to me that he spent a lot of money there—so much I wondered where it all came from. And I, er, I asked a friend to check up on a few facts."

She held out Sam's letter and he glanced at it and then up at her face. "Let me guess. You've found out that he didn't earn enough professionally to live in the style he seemed to do. That he paid full taxes on his literary earnings and had no overseas stash anywhere. Hmm? And that suggests to you he had another and probably illicit source of income."

She stared at him nonplussed and then slowly put the envelope down on her desk. "Well, yes."

He smiled cheerfully. "What do you think I've been doin' all this time, Dr. B.? Scratching my ar—bottom? We've been busy, we have, me and my busies." He grinned. "We've found out much the same as you have. And a bit more besides." He reached into his pocket and pulled out a sheaf of papers of his own. "You might like to cop a look at all that."

"What is it?"

"A printout. The software that Oxford had for his computer was varied and considerable. We went through it all—like I told you, ours is a plodding sort of job. We get our heads down and just beaver away. This disc is the most significant one. Look at it when you've got time. It'll show you just where Oxford got his dosh. Not exactly who from—that's encoded material, I'm afraid, but then it would be—but how he did it. Enjoy yourself."

He got to his feet and smiled down at her. "Dr. B., thanks a lot for all your help. It's great to have you in amongst us, believe me. This case is coming along nicely with your help. I'm not saying we wouldn't have managed it well enough ourselves, but you've helped."

"Helped?" She almost snorted it. "Who had to nag you into believing there'd been murder done at all? And who—"

"I said I'm grateful." He shook his head complainingly. "What more do you want? By the bye'—he had turned for the door—"I take it he had nothing nasty tucked up his rear end?"

"Of course not. I looked for it, naturally I did. But there was no evidence I could see. We took samples but I'm pretty confident."

"Yeah. Me too. Now I've seen all that stuff." He pointed to the sheets of paper in her hand. "Anyway, check it all and tell me what you think. I'll look forward to hearing your opinion. You're good at this job, aren't you? My job..." And he tipped his invisible hat with his mock salute and was gone.

23

The Board Room, which was clearly a versatile space, had become a lecture theatre for the evening. There were rows of chairs facing a desk at which three further chairs had been set, and behind that a projection screen, and George sighed as she settled herself in the back row. That meant slides or transparencies of some sort and the lights going up and down and no chance to relax properly. God, it was a bore! She had better things to do than sit here listening to someone prosing on about a subject she knew well already; such as going over in detail the printout from Oxford's computer.

It was obvious now that the man had been a blackmailer on a massive scale. She had suspected so for some time—that was why she had so much wanted access to the computer—but she hadn't expected it to be so very organized, or so lucrative. Payments of twenty thousand at a time were entered into the accounts, though there were also much lower ones. He seemed to have been as content to take five hundred as the higher sums. Altogether it added up to a great income; the past year alone had netted him two hundred thousand.

But just as she'd settled down to deeper study of the columns of figures and letters in the hope that she might be able to tease out the identity of some of the payers, the phone on her desk had shrilled and Professor Dieter's secretary had reminded her of the symposium. She made it very clear that to miss it would be regarded as the greatest dereliction of duty. So George had locked the papers away and come stomping furiously over here; and now she muttered irritably and pulled out the writing pad she would keep on her lap to pretend she was taking notes.

The room was already half filled with quietly talking people. It was clear that they were all there as she was: because it was politic to be so. Dieter had sent out a three-line whip, obviously, George thought sourly as she looked at the faces, now familiar to her: row after row of the hospital's most senior consultants as well as the junior doctors and several of the more senior nursing staff; and she found some cold comfort in at least not being alone in her irritation. There were many glum faces.

Kate Sayers slid into the seat beside her just as she noticed that Toby Bellamy was sitting further along her own row, on his own, and she was grateful for Kate's company and greeted her with some effusion.

"What's new?" Kate said. "Tell me something interesting to help me get through the next couple of hours."

"You too? I thought I was the one who didn't want to be here."

"None of us do, but this is one of the bees he keeps well fed in his bonnet. He's always trying to get people to agree with him."

"About what?"

"Oh, he's a Duesberg disciple."

"Duesberg? Not the chap who says that HIV isn't the cause of AIDS?"

"That's the one. Mad as a hatter, if you ask me, but Dieter thinks he's got it right and goes to a lot of trouble to try and convince us that we're wrong if we don't agree."

"It's always the same," George said. "Cranks proselytizing. They need to share their fantasies, but I thought better of Dieter."

"Don't jump to conclusions. He makes a strong case. Just you wait and see."

"It'll have to be very strong to get past me," George said firmly. "The evidence is too—"

"Well!" Kate said, staring down the room. "Look who's here!"

George turned to look. The tall woman who had been with Professor Dieter on the night of the concert was standing beside the table in close conversation with Felicity Oxford, and everyone was watching them covertly, or at least watching Felicity Oxford. She was, as ever, worth looking at. Her hair was still the same polished primrose-yellow helmet with the huge bun pinned elegantly at the nape of her neck, but now she was wearing a trouser suit in deep green suede rather than the severe black she had worn at the committee meeting where George had first seen her, and again at the concert. George's mouth tightened as she looked at her; there was something so insolently calculated about her choice of clothes tonight; casual and elegant but quite bright in color and clearly relaxed, as though she were daring them to disapprove of the fact that she wasn't dressing like an inconsolable widow. Beside her the big woman in the awkward drapery looked like an ill-dressed haystack and the glint of the jewelry with which she was heavily bedecked gave her a tawdry air that underlined Felicity's glamor, and this time George smiled. This was a woman who did what she wanted when she wanted and to hell with everyone else.

"That's Mrs. Dieter, isn't it?" she murmured to Kate, who nodded.

"Doesn't she look a hoot? But don't be misled. That woman's got the mind of a man twice her size and three times her charm. She can knock Charles into the middle of next week in any debate. Fortunately, she agrees with him on this issue. If she didn't he'd be in trouble."

"Is she that powerful, then? After all, he's the Professor here and—"

Kate snorted with laughter. "Whatever he is here, she's queen at home, ducky! She's also a very assertive type— lecturer in biology at the University. When she was doing original research back in the Sixties they used to murmur she was Nobel material. But she dropped that and now she just gives her lectures and runs Charlie's life and keeps her hand in that way. And also, of course, she has the money, it seems, or so the gossip goes. And the gossip, as you know—"

"—is never wrong. Indeed I know," George said. "Well, as long as you're there to fill me in on any nuggets I may have missed, maybe the evening won't be a total write-off. Whoops! Here we go."

Professor Dieter had come in, followed by a thin lugubrious woman in a sagging gray suit and a man who looked half asleep in neat black. As the little troop arrived at the table at the front, Felicity and her companion nodded at them and moved away, and George watched them out of the corner of her eye as they came and sat down in the same row as the one in which she was sitting, with Felicity taking the place next to Toby. Her jaws tightened again, and she looked steadily ahead at the people now fussing over who should sit where at the table in front. Gus hadn't been wrong about Toby. They were close, very close, he and Felicity. It was none of her business, of course it wasn't, and why the hell should she care? But she did.

The speakers were settled at last and the room slowly quietened into an expectant hush as Dieter got to his feet.

"Welcome all of you to this important seminar in our series of Modern Medical Issues. I make no apology for returning to the question of Acquired Immune Deficiency Syndrome. It is one that is exciting a good deal of comment and work and we should be sure we keep ourselves abreast of the newest information and ideas in the field. Working as we do in a deprived area with more than our share of drug-abusers and homeless alcoholics, we are in the front line of the battle. We'll inevitably get more than our share of patients."

He cleared his throat and looked down at his notes and George felt her face tighten. It always irritated her beyond measure when people talked of high-risk groups for infections;

as though viruses and bacteria were respecters of persons, and she considered for a moment standing up to say so, but then decided against it. Better to hear the arguments before joining in, however knowledgeable she might be already.

The thin woman was the first speaker after Professor Dieter and set the agenda by defining the subjects they were to cover, and she turned out to George's surprise to be an American, by her accent from California, and that in itself made George dubious. She was as open-minded as she knew how to be, but the prejudices of her parents were inevitably part of her own and they had for as long as she could remember scoffed at the sort of lunatics who inhabited the West Coast. However, she made a conscious effort to set aside the bigotry of such a reaction and concentrated.

It wasn't easy. The woman was producing reams of statistics to prove that HIV, while it was always present in people who had AIDS, was far from the most important of the factors in causing the disease. It was due largely to drug abuse, in her opinion. The misuse of narcotics and other psychotropic drugs depressed the immune system and led to the appearance of symptoms that resulted as AIDS. Alcohol abuse was also incriminated, and she offered another string of statistics on the screen behind her to show the death rates among such people and the various organisms they harboured which could be as responsible as HIV was supposed to be.

She was followed by the man in black, who was quiet-voiced and had an accent which proved to be from Austria and who also offered statistics on the screen to support the idea that HIV was no more significant in the human host than E. Coli. "Just as we all carry this in our gut as harmless passengers and only suffer disease from it when it is transported to other body systems," he said in his carefully clipped tones and perfectly rounded vowels, "so we carry HIV. Unless we are deprived of good living, unless we abuse our bodies with drugs—and alcohol of course is a drug of damage—then we do not suffer from AIDS, whether or not we have HIV…" and more of the same as George steadily became increasingly involved in what she was hearing. She'd come under pressure, but, now she was here, she found herself getting more and more interested. This after all fell into her field of expertise, to an extent, and she knew these people were misinterpreting their data, and ached to tell them so.

"Easy," Kate whispered in her ear. "Your temper's showing."

"I've never heard such stuff!" she hissed back. "Don't these people read the work that's been coming out of the States these past few years? And there's all the French work, let alone ours."

"I know, I know. But this is like religion. They'll find figures to support their thesis just as religious people find quotes in the Bible that give them permission to treat other people like shit. Do keep your head down, ducky. It'll get you nowhere to fuss."

But George couldn't keep her head down. Dieter was on his feet now, burbling happily on about the brilliant papers that had been put before them and speaking with admiration of the concise and logical position that was being offered, and even before he asked for contributions from the floor George was on her feet.

Dieter looked gratified and said happily. "Dr. Barnabas. As our pathologist you will of course see the validity of the papers we've been offered here tonight."

"But I don't! How do you explain the high incidence of death from AIDS in Africa where the disease is clearly proven to be sexually transmitted? The presentations we've had this evening have barely touched upon that mode of transmission."

"Because it is of less significance than the other factors we discussed." The Austrian was on his feet too now. "The mode of transmission for HIV we accept may be sexual congress, but our argument is that too much emphasis has been placed on the organism and not enough on the real factors that cause the symptoms of Acquired Immune Deficiency Syndrome, which are drug and alcohol abuse, poverty, poor housing and all the other things which we know compromise immunity and permit disease to flourish. I must remind you that in the nineteenth century tuberculosis was rife, probably all the population was exposed to infection by the bacteria, but by no means all succumbed to the disease of tuberculosis. It is the same, we are convinced, with HIV. We have the virus, yes, perhaps transmitted in the sexual mode, but it is not necessarily a killing virus. This is where we are concerned with the emphasis health education puts on the spread of the virus rather than the treatment of the contributing factors such as substance abuse and poverty."

"Yes, but—" George protested and then Toby was on his feet and joining in, and to her relief he agreed with her. He spoke with passion about the risks of telling people that HIV was not responsible for their disease when it was present in every person who died of it; couldn't the posture of the speakers tonight contribute to the rapid spread of the epidemic? And then everyone was off, with one after another getting to their feet and joining in, and Dieter looked more and more satisfied as the noise levels and the temperature of the big room rose in equal degrees.

Kate sighed into George's ear at one point when she was sitting down and listening to the others, "Now look what you've done! If you'd shut up they'd have all stayed quiet and we could have gone home by now."

George shook her head. "Someone would surely have had a go," she said and Kate made a face and had to agree that she was probably right.

The symposium had been billed to end at eight sharp but it was almost half past eight before a flushed and clearly pleased Dieter called a halt. Enough people in the audience had seemed to accept his colleagues' papers and conclusions as reasonable to make him happy; and he even managed to say a few gracious words in his summing up about those people who had, like George, refused to be beguiled by the arguments.

"We'll come back to this important subject again, I have no doubt," he said. "Now I must allow you all to depart for your evening meal. I'm sure all this talk has made you very hungry." And he smiled charmingly and turned to his speakers as a gesture of dismissal.

It was more than George could bear. Despite the fact that the Oxford papers were waiting for her in her office, demanding to be considered, she couldn't leave it there. She said a quick goodnight to Kate, who fled as fast as she could, and pushed her way to the front to talk to the speakers. She had to make her points more strongly, she felt; and she joined the little cluster of people at the central table to wait her turn.

Behind her there was a little flurry as Mrs. Dieter came bearing down on the group. George made way for her politely.

"Now, everybody!" She had a high rather thin voice that didn't match her presence at all. "I really must hurry us along. I've arranged dinner for our speakers and I'm sure they're very hungry. Charles, if you don't mind..."

"But I did want to say very quickly..." George began and Mrs. Dieter turned and looked at her sharply.

"Have you met our pathologist, Beatrice?" the Professor said swiftly. "Dr. Barnabas, Dr. George Barnabas."

"Good to meet you," Mrs. Dieter said. "And now, if you'll forgive me?"

"But I really must speak about those statistics."

Mrs. Dieter looked at her again and said crisply, "Then you'd better come to dinner."

"I beg your pardon?"

"Dinner," Beatrice Dieter said as though she were speaking to a halfwit. "At our house. It's all arranged and as it's a buffet there will be room for as many as wish to come. Charles, bring Dr. Schenck and Dr. Esposito and come along. There'll be, let me see..." And she stared around and counted on her fingers. "Felicity, of course, and her friend, and you two and ourselves, and of course Mr. Herne and the Coopers and—oh, yes, you,

Dr. Barnabas, ten of us. Excellent." And she was gone, surging ahead of them to the door as people scattered to make way.

"I really don't think..." George began but Professor Dieter took her elbow and smiled a little weakly.

"I think it's a splendid idea. There's clearly much more for you to discuss with our speakers, and as the person on the staff with almost the most involvement on the nonclinical side of the AIDS story, then it is important that you get the chance to do so. And dinner won't be all that bad. We have a very good cook, you know, Filipino, and she does excellent Eastern food for these evenings. Do come along. Perhaps there's room in our car for you if you don't mind crushing in the back seat with our speakers. I'm sure you won't. It will give you a chance to speak to them immediately, won't it?"

She stopped trying. It was like being caught in a strong tide and there was little point in kicking against it with her feeble swimming strokes. And she did indeed want to challenge the evening's speakers.

It was a surprisingly good dinner in surprisingly comfortable circumstances. The drive to the house had taken just over an hour of fairly fast moving along the main roads out of London to the north, during which she had at last been able to pin down both speakers to listen to her strong views on their interpretation of their statistics, and it had not been possible to see much of the house when they'd arrived, though she had an impression of a large front garden and a great many trees as the car moved through a pair of iron gates and traveled up a noisy gravel drive to the front door. Inside the house was warm—a great pleasure to George after the long hard cold nights she spent in the residence where heating was meagre to the point of being totally absent—and furnished with an eye to comfort rather than elegance. Deep chairs, deep carpets and deep dark colors were everywhere, and there were open fires in both the drawing room where they congregated for a very quick drink

("You'll all take sherry?" Beatrice Dieter said loudly. "Yes, I thought you would.") and in the dining room where a long table had been set with food.

And it was delicious. George helped herself to plates of stuffed crab claws and small spring rolls and other Eastern delicacies and ate with real pleasure as she sat beside Dr. Schenck and talked even more of the evening's proceedings. He was a serious man who liked nothing better than discussing his own subject and they were deep in conversation when Charles Dieter came to sit beside them.

"I'm delighted to see you taking so strong an interest in this matter, George," he said with great cordiality. George blinked. So far he'd always been very formal with her. "Are you beginning to be convinced we have some justice in our arguments?"

"I'm far from convinced," George said. "I take your point about the contributory factors of poverty and homelessness— they always add to the effects of any illness, of course they do—and you may have a point about the immunosuppressive effects of substance abuse. But to suggest that the virus is not significant—"

"We're not saying that at all," Charles said. "Just that it is of very small significance in the presence of other factors."

"And we do people a disservice if we concentrate solely and wholly on the effect of the virus," Schenck put in.

"But—" George began and then stopped as Toby Bellamy came to stand alongside them. She hadn't realized until they'd all arrived at the house that he was in the party, and then discovered that he was the "friend' of Felicity Oxford of whom Beatrice Dieter had spoken when she'd rattled off the list of her dinner guests. *Had* she realized, George had told herself furiously, she would have escaped the invitation, no matter how offensive she had to be to do it. But it was too late, and all she had been able to do was studiously avoid catching his eye all evening, although it had been difficult to be unaware of his presence. She had been constantly conscious of the fact that he was there in the room, mostly sitting next to Felicity Oxford and listening to her as she talked. Now, however, she couldn't ignore him and she looked at him briefly before bending her head to concentrate on the cooling contents of her plate.

"What do you think, Toby?" Charles said, looking up at him, and Toby lifted his brows.

"I remain unconvinced," he said. "There may be a point in what you say, inasmuch as the lifestyle could shorten or lengthen the latency time between infection and the appearance of symptoms. But if you'll forgive me, Charles, I've had a long hard day and I really must be going back. Mrs. Dieter has arranged for me to give Dr. Barnabas a lift, since she came in your car."

"Oh!" Charles said and looked at George who had opened her mouth to protest. "To tell the truth I hadn't thought about the problem of getting you all back."

"I did, Charles." Beatrice came and joined the little group and, despite George's efforts to object and demand the right to call a cab to take her back to Old East, overruled them all with the power of her shrill voice, her will, and her plans.

"Felicity is staying here tonight so that we can do some important work about the Barrie Ward committee early tomorrow morning, before I have to leave for the Biological Sciences Faculty lunch. So there's room in Toby's car for Dr. Barnabas. It's all arranged. I'm sure you're ready to go when Toby here is, aren't you, Dr. Barnabas? Yes, I thought so. Well, there it is, it's all settled. Now, just before you leave you must try some of Maria's special red-bean pancakes, Toby. They are most delightful. Come along, Charles, let us leave the rest of the discussion on this matter for another day. We've all had quite enough to get on with tonight."

Which was how George found herself sitting next to Toby in his rather battered old car at midnight and parked on the side of the road under a tree in the darkness.

24

"Look," he said as the sound of the engine died when he switched off the ignition. "I can't handle this. You sulking all the way to Old East's more than any man could be expected to put up with."

"If you think I'm going to sit here and talk to you at this time of night you've got one hell of another think coming," she snapped. "I'll get a taxi." And she tried to open the door, but he reached across and held on to it.

"Don't be so stupid and melodramatic. There isn't a taxi rank for miles and you'll never get a cruising one in the middle of a suburb like this at midnight. For Christ's sake, you don't think this was my idea, do you? I wouldn't have suggested driving you back for all the world. It was that bloody juggernaut of a woman who made me."

"You'd much rather be driving Felicity Oxford, of course," she retorted, and then could have kicked herself for letting the words out, for he stiffened beside her and then relaxed, and finally laughed softly.

"Dear me! It's like that, is it?"

"It's like nothing of the sort," she shouted. "Start this car and get going at once!"

"Shut up. I'll start again when I'm ready and no sooner. So, you're jealous, are you? Poor little darling! Here was I thinking you'd just been leading me on and it turns out that you do fancy me after all! It's a pity you can't trust me as well as fancy me, mind, but you can't have everything."

"I do not—I never—I mean—Oh, will you take me back? I can't cope with this."

He leaned over again and for a moment she thought he was going to open the car door and let her go, and somewhere at the back of her mind she prayed he wouldn't. This was a long dark silent road, she remembered, and it could be a good hike to a place where a taxi might be available. But he didn't touch the door. Instead he pulled her shoulders around towards him and kissed her very thoroughly. Then he leaned back, drew the back of his hand across his mouth and said with great satisfaction, "There! I feel better now."

"I'm glad to hear it. I'm damned if I do. How dare you? How *could* you—"

"Oh, do shut up, George." He sounded amiable. "You didn't mind one bit the other night, so don't come the outraged female with me now. It doesn't suit you."

"The other night I didn't know you were a suspect in a murder and I didn't know that you were—were involved with someone else. I'm one of the old-fashioned kind, Bellamy. I want a one-to-one relationship, not to be part of some bloody man's harem."

"I said you were jealous," he said happily. "It's Fliss that's bothering you and always has been, not the matter of my being a suspect. Look, let me tell you about Fliss, OK?"

"I'm not interested."

"Well, you'll have to listen anyway. You've no choice. Yes, Fliss and I are old friends. Yes, we're on affectionate terms. But it's not what you think."

"I didn't think about you at all," she said icily. "Will you stop chattering like a romantic novel and take me back to the hospital and—"

"It's anything but romantic, you silly object," he said. "I don't sleep with her—"

"I'm not *interested.*"

"—because she's HIV positive and she reckons safe sex is

no sex. But she gets lonely and frightened and needs a little affection from time to time."

George sat and stared ahead of her through the rapidly misting windscreen and tried to get her head clear. "HIV positive?" she said after a long pause.

"You ain't got cloth ears," he said with a mock cockney accent that grated a little. "You heard me."

"Oh, my God," she said at length.

"Well, she does say that quite often, not that she's all that religious." Toby said. "But she also says she needs someone to talk to who talks back, and since I've known her a long time, I'm the one she tells."

"He was too," George said abruptly. "Richard Oxford."

"Surprise, surprise!" Toby sounded very sardonic. "Who could possibly have thought that? Where do you think she collected the virus, for Christ's sake?"

"She's sure it was…" She swallowed. "I'm sorry, I don't mean to…"

"She was never promiscuous." He laughed then, a short barking little sound. "She's never been all that interested in sex, that's the ridiculous thing. Looks like that, and couldn't care less! It's probably why she went for Oxford in the first place. These men who are AC/DC make life easy for a woman like Fliss. What you see is what you get with her. And you have to admit she's the image of the original ice queen."

George nodded in the darkness. "Yes, I suppose so. She always looks so…"

"Perfect. Precisely. Not a human woman who sweats and swears and gets her hair in a state and sometimes loses her temper. Just a piece of perfection. Me, I couldn't be doing with it. Not in a one-to-one relationship, you understand." She knew he was laughing at her and couldn't think of anything to say. "It's fine in a friend, but no use in a real set-up, is it?" He moved a little closer. "So, does that make a difference? Does that make it possible for us to use this time parked at the side of a deserted road in a more rewarding manner?"

"No," she snapped. "It's—it's late and you're still a murder suspect and—"

"Oh, piffle," he said. "Knowing what you know now about the sort of relationship there is between Fliss and me, do you think your pal Gus'll keep me on his list? I'll gladly talk to him, if I must—though I can't deny I'd rather not because it's a bit tough on poor old Fliss to have all her private affairs, not to say soiled linen, hung from the highest flagpole—but if I must I will. And then he'll know that I don't have a smidgen of a motive. Do I?"

"I'm not sure." She turned to look at him in the dimness. "Maybe you have after all. If she's a real friend and you're as angry as she must be about her being infected with HIV—"

"But she isn't angry! She accepted the fact long ago. It's been close on two years, you see. She knew he liked men as well as her when she married him and, as I say, it suited her. When it happened and she found out, she was distressed of course, but she had more sense than to blame him. She blamed herself for marrying him at all."

"I can't see why she did." George shuddered a little. "He must have been a hateful husband. He was certainly a nasty man. I thought so, anyway."

"He was good fun. And he had money. That's always been important to Fliss—she's the most insecure person I ever met," Toby said after a moment. "Tell me, are you saying he was hateful because he was bisexual? And even more wickedly went and caught himself a sexual infection?"

"No, of course not. It's because he was a—" She hesitated. She felt differently now about Toby's relationship with Fliss, obviously, but all the same, wasn't he still a suspect? Couldn't he have been a victim of Oxford's blackmail? She thought rapidly, trying to get her head sorted out, remembering all sorts of minor details. His own tightness with money: so glad to get a free supper, scrounging free theatre tickets. Was that because he too was like Felicity, inordinately fond of money? Or could it be that he had to watch every penny because he was being bled by a parasite? Maybe there was some disreputable fact about him that Oxford had got hold of and used against him? To tell him now that Oxford's blackmailing behavior was known to the police could be a very stupid thing to do. She was after all alone with this man on a remote country road where anything could happen...

"It's because he was so, well, smarmy to me. And the way people talked about him, he was from all accounts a very selfish person," she extemporized lamely. "He must have been, not to give her a divorce, and—"

"Oh, don't talk tommy rot, George! She didn't want a divorce! It suited her very well to have her income secure and, as long as she was married to Richard, it was. It suited him to have a wife when it was handy to be seen as straight, and one who closed her eyes to his life when he preferred being gay. She got what she wanted, which was security, and he got what he wanted, which was respectability. A better arrangement than a lot of marriages, take it from me."

"Have you ever been married?" she said, startled by the bitterness in his voice, and he caught his breath in the darkness.

"Long ago, when I was a student, yes," he said after a while. "It lasted till I qualified and then she couldn't handle a junior doctor's lifestyle. Like working all the hours God sent. So she went to Australia with a dentist." He laughed then. "Which was a bit like taking coals to Newcastle, wasn't it? All the male population of Australia practices dentistry, I reckon."

"So that's how you know what was right for Felicity and Richard Oxford's marriage." She sounded sharp and knew it, and didn't care.

"No. I know it because Fliss told me so."

"Have you known her long?"

"About seventeen years," he said. "I needed some money and I took some work as a model, believe it or not. They liked the rumpled type in those days. And she was running the agency."

"Good God!" She was so startled she could only stare at him.

"I know. It's not something I tell many people—would you? Anyway, that's how I met Fliss and later Oxford. It's why I work at Old East. He put in a word for me with the Board and…" He shrugged. "You know how the system works as well as anyone. It's not what you know but who and so forth. The clichés are true. That's why they're clichés."

"I see." She took a deep breath. "So you owed him, really."

"Owed him? No. I'd long since paid back anything I owed him." He sounded hard suddenly. "Looking after Fliss for him. No, George, don't go running down that cul-de-sac. I owed Oxford nothing and he had no interest in me, except as a friend of his wife's. There's no motive for me, you know. I didn't kill the man. I had no reason to. Every reason not to, in fact. Now I have to take even more care of Fliss. She's genuinely upset, for all she looks so calm. There are depths to that woman few people recognize."

"Except you of course."

He ignored the hint of a sneer in her voice. "Except me." He leaned forward and switched on the ignition. The engine coughed into life. "I'll take you back now. There's no need to sit here any longer. Obviously you aren't feeling at all amorous."

"Ha!" was all she managed. She sat back in her seat and glowered through the window as it cleared under the attack of the warm air from the demisters, and tried to clear her head to match. There was a lot to think about here; but she was too tired right now to get anything straight. But she did feel rather better than she had, and that was something for which to be grateful.

The following morning she was heavy-eyed with lack of sleep, which didn't help, since there was a great backlog of work to be done and Sheila and, unusually, Jerry were both in filthy tempers. It took her until almost noon to sort out a pile of irritating jobs and disagreements, and to pour what little soothing oil she could find on Sheila and Jerry's thoroughly ruffled heads. She certainly had no time to look at the printout that Gus had brought her, or to think about the revelations of last night.

At noon Gus telephoned. "I've got an idea," he announced. "How would it be if you came over here to the incident room and we had a bit of a talk about this case? Would you be willing to do that?"

"I'm gratified to be asked," she said, and meant it. "But I can't leave here, I'm afraid. We've got a bit of a push on, and—well, it wouldn't be politic'

He sighed. "I was hoping I wouldn't have to come out on such a rainy morning. All right then, I'll pick up some grub and come over to you."

"What?" She was furious. "You were willing to drag me out in the rain to keep your own feet dry? Is that the only reason you suggested I come to you?"

"No, not the only one. I thought you might be interested to see the progress we've made. It's quite a bit. But if you can't, you can't."

"Well, I can't."

"So I'll come to you. I told you I would. Now, I'll get the sarnies. BLT suit you?"

"I couldn't care less what sort," she said, no longer feeling gratified. "In fact I'm not sure that—"

"OK then. BLTs it is. I'll leave it to you to lay on the coffee. I might find a little something to go with it. Leave that to me." And he snapped down the phone and left her listening to the buzz of a dead line.

By the time he arrived she'd worked herself up into a state of considerable temper, but he seemed oblivious to her glare as he came in and shook his wet coat much as a dog shakes itself when it comes out of a stream.

"It's coming down like bleedin' stair rods, as my old granny used to say," he announced and then shook his head too, so that water sprayed half across the room.

"Here, go easy!" she protested as the drops spattered her. "I don't want my papers ruined."

"See what I saved you?" he said cheerfully. "I'm a good old sort after all, aren't I? Yes. Now, where's the coffee? I've got the ideal thing for a day like this." And he reached into his jacket pocket and pulled out a miniature bottle of brandy. "Share that between us and it'll warm the cockles and never make a ha'p'orth of difference to the old brain boxes. And we're goin' to need 'em. Off you go, then. Fetch the coffee."

He moved over to her desk and plonked down a large cardboard box tied with pink ribbon which he began to untie, and she, to her own amazement, obeyed him and went to fetch her coffee tray. She certainly had no intention of asking Sheila to provide it.

When she brought it back she found he'd laid out his offerings on the desk and they looked good. As well as the bacon, lettuce and tomato sandwiches, there were a couple of tubs of fresh cole slaw and potato salad, and a large dill pickle which he'd cut into neat slices.

"Thought you'd like a bit of old-fashioned New-York-style deli," he said. "We can get anything in this part of London. Just you wrap the old choppers 'round that lot. Ah! The coffee. Here we go then." And he carefully shared the contents of the small bottle between the two cups and then topped them up with the strong black coffee.

"If you're a sensible woman you won't want sugar with that lot," he said. "But in case you're like the rest of us, here's a couple o' sachets for you." He pulled them from his pocket and dropped them on the desk. "All right, tuck in, then we can do some talking."

"You're impossible, you know that?" she said and sat down in her own chair, which he had studiously left for her. "You march in here, take over, decide everything…"

"Someone has to," he said comfortably. "It's quicker that way. There's nothing wrong with all this, is there?" indicating the desk and its spread. "I asked you if you wanted BLTs and you said yes."

"No, there's nothing wrong, but—"

"Then what's to fuss over? Eat up, girl. We ain't got all day!"

She gave up. There was nothing else she could do and the sandwiches were indeed very good, and could have come from the Stage Deli in New York, and the coffee was exactly what she needed. By the time she'd finished she felt well contented.

"Now," he said, clearing the debris with deft movements. "Let's see what we've got here." He pulled a notebook from his pocket and set it on the desk between them. "I've got my own ideas. But let me hear yours first."

She looked at him curiously. "Is this a consult? Medical style?"

He peered up at her. "No. It's a discussion. Police style."

"Is it what you usually do with your pathologist?"

He seemed to consider that. "No. But I've never had such a nosy pathologist before."

"Nosy? Hey!"

"Interested, then. My God, you're a bit of a Harrier, aren't you?"

She was diverted. "Harrier?"

"Jump jet. Vertical take-off. Keep your cool, Dr. B.! Look, I thought you wanted to be involved with this investigation. After all, if it hadn't been for you being so bloody-minded we wouldn't be doing it at all."

"Well, yes, I do want to. But I was a bit surprised."

"Never be surprised by me. I do what I think's right. I walk all over the regulations when it suits me, and run things my own way. So far I've not had any disasters or failed cases, so they let me get on with it. The day I give 'em a cock-up'll be the day they meddle with my style. Till then, though, let's make the most of it. OK? OK. Now, have you looked through that stuff I left you? That printout from Oxford's computer disc?"

"Yes. And it seems to me—"

"Wait a moment. Let me be ready for this." He flipped the notebook open and took a pen from his breast pocket. "OK. Let me have your ideas and then I'll offer you mine, and we'll see what sort of a pudding we can make out of our shared ingredients at the end of it. You never know. We may solve this one just sitting here at your desk. Seeing all the donkey work's been done." And he smiled at her widely. "Fire away."

25

She was hesitant at first, but it got easier. "Well. It's obvious he was a blackmailer, isn't it?"

"Is it?"

"Stop coming on like a school teacher," she said. "If I ask a question I'm entitled to an answer. And I'm saying it's obvious and asking if you agree."

"All right. I agree."

"Thank you. Right. He was a blackmailer. He identified the people he was biting by letters of the alphabet. Nothing very remarkable about that, but I can't work out his code, I'm afraid. I mean, look here." She smoothed the printout on the desk between them. "Against this steady monthly five thousand pounds all he has is H.I. That could be anyone. I've tried to think who there is here at the hospital who might have those initials but got nowhere."

"Now why should you think that?"

"Think what?"

"That it has to be someone here."

"Ah." She lifted her head and looked at him closely. "I wonder if you'll agree with this? It seemed to me that the person who killed Oxford has to be someone who had easy access to various places here at Old East. Digitalis is a common drug and easily obtained, but it is a prescription drug and getting hold of thirty-odd tablets when you don't have a right to could be tricky—but here it would be very easy indeed. No one counts the stock of digitalis the way they count dangerous drug doses."

"But the stuff could be obtained outside a hospital."

"Oh, yes of course. All drug stores have it. But there's another thing that makes it unlikely. And that's the method of giving it to Oxford."

"Oh, yes. Our chap who really likes to get to the bottom of things."

"Please, a moratorium on gags like that? It had to be put in a cream and then in a tube and done in such a way that the user wouldn't notice it had been spiked."

"It could have been done by one of the doctors who dispensed it, of course."

"You'd have told me if you had any evidence it had been."

"Shrewd point, Dr. B. Yes, you're right there. We checked the doctors he'd visited in Harley Street and they hadn't seen him for a long time—I thought I'd told you that—and most of the tubes of hemorrhoid cream we found in his flat had been dispensed ages ago, almost a year, by John Bell and Croyden. There's no reason at all to think there was any meddling there. Anyway, I checked with them and they keep good records. They were able to prove to me the tampering couldn't have happened while the tubes were in their establishment. The place is run with the security of Fort Knox. So we can definitely scrub them off the list, and the prescribing doctor too."

"Which leaves us with Old East, for the tube that killed him."

"I suppose so."

"And the pharmacy's the place to look at. They deal with all the drugs and so on. And it's easy to get into the pharmacy here."

"It is? But what about all the alarms and special keys?"

"Oh, they're there, but I was able to get in to wander 'round during the day—no one queries one of the consultants taking a peer about—and I saw things. One was that the list of instructions for turning off and turning on the alarms is pinned to the wall near the keypad that has to be punched, and secondly there's a list of who holds what keys and where."

"Would you believe it!" He sounded disgusted. "You saw that for yourself?"

"I did."

"I ought to go down there and give them a right royal rollocking, oughtn't I? If they had a break-in and someone walked out with a lot of dangerous drugs, there'd be all hell to pay."

"Be fair. The really important drugs are in a safe and there's no way anyone can get into *that* without knowing the combination. And only two people in the pharmacy have that information, and it's changed every month anyway. They put a note of the combination in the main hospital safe to be available for emergencies, but otherwise it's inaccessible to staff. But access isn't necessary for this case. Digitalis is just on open shelves, and the equipment for filling tubes is on a bench. They make up quite a lot of stuff here for the dermatology unit. We've got a consultant who invents his own gunge, it seems."

"I see. So you say it's feasible that the murderer is someone here at Old East who used Old East facilities to help him commit his crime."

"I think so. What say you?"

He grinned from ear to ear. "Don't throw anything at me but I have to tell you I'd already worked that one out. I interviewed the pharmacist last week. I didn't realize that it was made quite so easy for intruders to get in but he did admit the security wasn't as tight as it might be."

She looked at him almost nonplussed. Then she said, "Look, am I just wasting my time here? I thought you wanted me to help, and I'm glad to do it. But if all you're doing is checking me to see if I've walked the same route you have, you can go to hell in your fancy car and not bother to come back. I've got better things to do than play silly games."

He shook his head. "I didn't mean to make it sound like that. I truly did want to talk to you about this stuff. I can't talk to Dudley, because he just says, 'Yes sir, no sir, three bags full sir,' and doesn't fancy himself a man of ideas. I'm not the bloke to go to my Super and bounce ideas off him. I like to present him with a nice finished job, know what I mean? The department's working flat out on any number of things—we've got some armed robberies we're still sorting out as well as a few con artists on the patch and Gawd knows what else—so who can I talk to, eh?" He looked pathetically at her. "The fact that you've covered the same ground as I have doesn't mean I'm testing you, you know. It just means that you really are my sort of lady. You think the same way I do. No copper could ask for more."

She looked at him suspiciously. He gazed back at her guilelessly and she sighed and gave in. "All right, I'll believe you. I shouldn't, but I will. Now, where was I?"

"Proving that the murderer was probably an Old East person, and that therefore the initials used to code the sums of money on Oxford's printout could match individuals here."

"Yes, that's right. Well, I looked at all these initials here, and there was one odd thing I noticed."

"Mmm?"

"A lot of them seemed to have the central letter H. I find that odd. Not everyone's got a middle name and anyway it's too much to expect everyone's middle name to be Harold or Hannah or something of that sort."

"You're right. I thought so too. I can't work it out at all. It's probably something very simple but they can be the hardest codes to crack, the simple ones. Because they're so easy you can't get a handle on them."

"Isn't there a general technique you can use?"

"Well, I suppose we could try it on the computer wizards at the Yard. Or on your helpful friend—over at Wimbledon, wasn't it?"

She kept her head down so that he couldn't see her face. "Mmm. Wimbledon."

"We could see if they can use one of their code-breaking systems for it. But as I say, it mightn't be much good because it looks too easy."

"Let me have a go, anyway," George said. "I'll copy the list and keep it. Is that permitted?"

"Of course. Here, I'll sing 'em out. You write 'em down and—"

"Not all of them. If I can't do it with a sample, I can't do it at all. Give me half a dozen or so to start with."

"OK. Here we go. Y.J. £2,000; S.P. £3,000; K.K. £1,000; G.J. £5,000; R.H.A. £2,500; U.H.R. £500; G.I. £5,000—"

"That'll do. I'll start on them and collect the others later if I need them. I know that if I try to deal with too many at once I'll make a complete mess of it. OK. So Oxford's a blackmailer and that was why he was killed. And that brings me to Formby Mitchell."

"Or Mitchell Formby."

"Whatever. I thought he had to be the murderer. I reckoned he was stealing the gear here and selling it back to the hospital to pocket the money in order to pay off Oxford. That was what made me sure Oxford was a blackmailer, even before I saw this printout. But then of course, Formby was killed."

"Inconsiderate of him. It spoiled a nice theory."

"Watch it, Hathaway."

"I mean it! It's maddening to have a nice neat theory and see it ruined. It's happened to me too often not to sympathize."

"Yes—" She stopped then. "OK, that's all I have to say. Now, what about you?"

He leaned back in his chair. "Well, so far we've marched the same furrow. I agree with you that the figures on that printout relate to money obtained by blackmail. We know that Oxford's official earnings and lifestyle were wildly out of step, so that's a double assurance that that's what the printout means."

"OK, now what? The man was murdered in a very odd fashion. Someone filled his bottom cream with poison—not a rare one, but an easily obtained one—and put it in his bathroom cabinet. That was because he or she expected that eventually he'd have a sore back end and would shove the cream in and hey presto, one dead Oxford."

He stopped and stared at her owlishly and she lifted her brows at him. "Well?"

"So it wasn't critical in terms of time, was it? The murderer didn't mind when Oxford obligingly killed himself—as long as he did it eventually. So this was the crime of a person who'd suffered a long time from Oxford's presence on this earth and was prepared to put in a bit longer if he had to, to cover any tracks. And come to think of it, had enough money to go on paying for that much longer, too."

"Which underlines the fact that the murderer had to be someone with a secret worth keeping."

"Precisely."

"Even if it was months before Oxford's piles started bothering him again—"

"The murderer could have counted on it being a frequent problem, maybe? Knew him well enough to know all his medical details?"

"Possible, I suppose," she said. "So, where do we go from here?"

"Well, the next question has to be who was able to get into that bathroom? The stuff had to be planted, but how and when? Once we know that we might have a better idea of who."

"Yes, I see that. What have you been able to discover?"

"Not a lot. He liked to entertain, gave dinner parties and so forth, but when he did that, he used the other lavatory for his guests and his daily help. No one ever needed to go into his bedroom. We talked to the caterers he used—they were listed in his address book. That doesn't mean guests didn't see his bedroom and bathroom—I gather he was fond of taking people over the place and showing it off. But he always did it in a crowd so there was no way someone could sneak the cream into the bathroom without being seen. It wouldn't be possible even if there was just the murderer and Oxford in there. Every time one of those cabinet doors is opened the whole room goes into conniption fits, the way the images shift and confuse you."

"I know," she said feelingly. "It made me feel dizzy."

"Quite. So, who could it have been? A special guest maybe. A lover?"

There was a little silence and then she said, "He was bisexual."

"I thought as much."

"Why?"

"HIV positive. There was no record of him ever having a blood transfusion and he never actually went abroad, in spite of the books he wrote. And anyway he—"

"Don't say he looked it. There's no way you can tell just by appearance."

"I wasn't going to say that. Don't be so prickly! I was just going to say the fact that he lived apart from his wife on close and friendly terms. I've come across that before. It's an odd thing, but women in my experience are remarkably tolerant of blokes who share their love lives with other men rather than other women."

"Watch it. You're beginning to sound like someone who trusts his intuition."

"Do me a favor! I'm quoting years of past experience. That's a very different thing."

"Like hell it is. Intuition is what that is. Past experience, common sense, a quick eye and a fast brain. Add them together and you get intuition. Women are good at it. We're clever, you see. Fast brains."

"Don't you smirk at me! I still think it's codswallop. Anyway, it's my experience that told me he was bisexual. What about you?"

"What?"

"How do you know? Intuition again?"

"I was told." She didn't look at him and she felt rather than saw him stiffen.

"Oh? Who did that?"

She took a deep breath and now she did look at him. "I need to know. You told me that Toby Bellamy was a suspect. Is he still?"

"Of course."

"Because he was having an affair with Felicity Oxford?"

"Yup."

"He wasn't."

"Oh? How can you be sure of that?"

"He told me."

"And why should I believe him? Why do you, come to that?"

"Because Oxford was bisexual. And Felicity Oxford preferred men like Oxford. She isn't interested in sex, it seems. Never has been. But clearly she did have sex with her husband at some point because—"

He was looking at her with his eyes bright and birdy again, his head to one side. "Because she's HIV positive too," he said softly.

"Exactly."

"Toby Bellamy told you all this?"

"Yes."

"And—"

She tightened her jaw. "Yes, I believe him."

"Listen, this is a hard question and if you want to tell me to sling me 'ook I'll understand. But is he soft-soaping you? Because he fancies you? I'd understand it if he did. You're a very fanciable lady."

"None of that," she said sharply. "Don't you get personal."

"Who? Me? I just calls 'em the way I sees 'em. So tell me, could it be that he's fooling you? That what he's telling you is just, well, things he wants you to believe? Like that he isn't having it off—that he isn't playing around with Felicity Oxford?"

She gazed at him with her lower lip caught between her teeth as all her doubts came thundering back on eager hooves. That night in his car she had thought she believed him. Now…

"I don't know," she said. "Isn't it hell?"

"Do you want me to find out for you?"

She looked at him sharply. "Can you?"

"I can investigate Mrs. Oxford again."

"Again?"

He laughed. "Of course. You don't think we haven't talked to her in detail already? She's the man's wife, so of course we did. That's how we know all about Bellamy seeing her so often. I have to say there's no evidence that he's wrong. She doesn't have a lot of men friends—more female ones, in fact. Very devoted to her job."

"Ah yes, her job. The model agency."

"It doesn't sound like a real job, does it? Something for a rich woman to play around with, more like. That's what I thought. But it seems to be a real business and she gets a good deal of work for her clients. Gets some of them married off, too."

"If they're good models, it's not surprising, I suppose. Pretty women always do get snapped up."

He chuckled. "This one wasn't all that pretty. More striking, really. You've seen her."

"Oh?"

"Carole Herne. She's one of Felicity's girls."

George gaped. "Matthew Herne's wife? The senior admin guy? The one who's an ex-major, or whatever?"

"That's the one."

"How unlikely—if you see what I mean. Though perhaps not. Soldiers and empty-headed females…"

"You're a mass of prejudices, aren't you?" he said admiringly. "Nearly as bad as me. I like that in a woman."

She flushed. "I'm just quoting previous experience. The sort of men who go in for learning how to kill people systematically, which is what career servicemen do, are also the sort who like women who look better than they taste, if you see what I mean."

"I told you, I see someone like me, with lots of strong opinions. I approve of it. Listen I'll settle this one way or the other for you. I'll check our Mrs. Oxford again and we'll see what we can discover about your friend Bellamy. Er..." he seemed casual suddenly. "Is it important to you that he should be what he says? Innocent and so forth; just a friend of hers?"

She thought for a while and then nodded. "Yes," she said. "I think it is."

"Then find out we must," he said lightly and looked at his watch. "Time's swift chariot, bugger it. Have you any views on who might have done for Formby Mitchell?"

She was bewildered by the sudden shift of mood. "I'm not sure. I've tried to work it out. I looked in the list for his initials only of course they're not there. But I could try his against all the codes and see where I get. Mind, it'll be difficult, not knowing which way 'round to use his names."

"Well, beaver away at it. I think it's possible that he was helping someone else raise his blackmail money. Have you thought of that possibility?"

She hadn't and did so now. "An accomplice? But what would be in it for him? Unless you mean he was sharing the cash."

"He could have been responding to blackmail on his own account," Gus said. "Try that on for size. Here's our man who's got himself in here under false pretences in a top job, handling money. Someone's found him out, the same sort of way you did, maybe, or by accident, it doesn't matter. He's being blackmailed himself and needs more money, but how to get it? Ah! He'll use Formby Mitchell to get it for him. So he leans on him to do the necessary and so makes sure that if ever the crap hits the old doodah he'll be pure as the driven. He knows Mitchell Formby won't tell on him, because he scuppers himself if he does, and anyway if a man with a record like Formby's gets caught who's going to believe him if he tries to push it on to someone else? Either way our man is safe. How does that idea grab you?"

She had listened with great concentration and now nodded slowly. "It's an elegant scheme. It could be, so how do we find out if it's all true?"

He got to his feet. "That's up to me. I'll be digging around for the next few days to see what I can see. I've also got to look more into the matter of the money Oxford collected for the Barrie Ward Fund. There's been some uneasiness over that, according to Dieter's office. The secretary there was bumbling on about it. Could be just gossip, but I have to check all the same. My chaps are going to be busy for a few days. Ah well! No peace for the virtuous like me. Nor you. So, let me put an idea in your mind."

"Please do. I've used up all my own."

"Some of Felicity Oxford's models do a bit of extra work on the side."

She frowned. "On the side? Freelance, you mean? Well, I suppose—Oh!" She stared at him. "Do you mean they were prostitutes?"

"I do. Not all, but a few. It's not that unusual, of course."

"How do you know?"

He laughed. "What a question to ask a copper! We found out! That's what we do best, ducky, find things out. Take it from me, some of her girls are on the game. High class, but all the same, they're brasses."

"Do you mean that Felicity…No. She's not interested in sex."

"I don't see that would disqualify her. Lots of the girls aren't but they still sell it. But I didn't mean Felicity herself. Think about it, Dr. B. I'll be in touch again soon. Meanwhile, have a go at that code. I'll look forward to seeing what you can do with it. Good hunting!"

And he scooped up his bag of bits and pieces and his coat, tipped his invisible hat, and was gone.

26

The only place she could think of to work on the code was the library in the old medical school. It had been some time since Old East had had its own medical students; nowadays it was attached to one of the major City hospitals and students just came for experience in particular specialities, but the library was still there, and it was a pleasant enough place to work, with its crowded bookshelves and big central tables. It was, above all, warm; the thick layers of books that covered every available space trapped warm air inside the room, giving it a comfortable frowsty air.

But finding the place to work, she decided, wasn't quite enough. She needed more information about the people employed at Old East before she could check whether their initials appeared in code. A good many were known to her by name as well as by sight now, after having worked in the place for almost three months, but she didn't know them all by any means. So she stopped in the Dean's office on her way to the library that evening after a scrappy supper in the canteen. The Professor's secretary had a reputation for working as late as she possibly could every evening (rumor had it that she charged the hospital overtime for every extra minute she put in, and was saving up to buy a country cottage) and she certainly seemed the person most likely to be able to help her.

She was indeed at her desk, her head down over a pile of envelopes she was carefully writing by hand, and she didn't look up when George came in and stood on the other side of her desk.

"Good evening, Phyllis," she said at last.

The woman looked up unwillingly. "Can I help you?" she asked frostily.

George bit back the desire to snap back that with a facial expression as disagreeable as hers it was very unlikely, and instead smiled winsomely. "I'm feeling so guilty," she said. "Professor Dieter and his wife included me in their supper party the other night, after the lecture, and I haven't thanked them. I couldn't write directly to Mrs. Dieter—I don't have the address in full—so I thought I'd drop by and see if the Professor was here to be thanked."

Phyllis looked a shade less forbidding at this display of belated good manners. "He's not here at present," she said guardedly. "You should have come during the day."

"Alas, much too busy," George said with well-simulated regret. "We're quite overrun down in Pathology. You'll understand if anyone will…"

"Well, yes, no doubt." The woman twisted her face into the semblance of a smile. "Well, I'll tell him." And she put her head down again to continue with her envelopes.

"Thank you so much. Oh, by the bye." George said it as casually as she could. "I'd be so grateful, since I'm here, if you could give me another little bit of assistance. I was at a medical meeting the other day and someone there asked me to deliver a message—a verbal one you understand—to one of the staff here, and I said I would. He said it was important. The trouble is, I simply can't remember the name of the person I was to deliver it to! Isn't that ridiculous?"

"Yes," Phyllis said and looked up again with barely concealed impatience. "I always write such things down."

"I should have done, I know that, but you know how it is— busy meetings. The thing is, I thought you'd have a sort of hospital staff directory? One that lists all the names of the staff here? I could go through it. I'm sure I'll remember the name when I see it."

"Was it someone medical?"

"I—Well, I'm not sure," George said carefully. "It might have been. Possibly one of the senior admin people, though."

"Well, if it was one of the juniors or the domestic staff of course I'd have no knowledge of them." Phyllis looked pleased with herself on this score. "I deal only with the senior people in all the departments here. I have my own office list, of course, of their extension phone numbers. That's all there is."

"Could I look through that?" George said eagerly. "I'm sure I'd find it there."

"You can't take it away."

"Oh. Well, I'll sit here then, and—"

Phyllis changed her mind. "You can take it for an hour or two, I suppose. As long as you bring it back at once. I'll be here till about ten, I imagine." She sighed heavily. "There is a great deal to be done in this office."

"Oh, I'm sure," George said and smiled winningly. "Then I'll bring it back in a couple of hours, or even less. Thank you so much." She held out her hand.

The woman hesitated and then reached into her drawer and pulled out a medium-sized stiff covered ledger and handed it over. "Don't make any marks on it," she said. "It's often used by the Professor and it has to be kept just so."

"Of course," George said and escaped, her prize clutched to her, triumphant at her own success as a detective. To have asked for the book outright, she told herself, would never have got it into her hands. Gus'd be impressed. He only has to ask and they have to give him what he wants, because he's a policeman. Me, I have to cajole them. And didn't I do it well?

She was less pleased with herself an hour later, when she had gone through the list of names with patient thoroughness and found nothing that was of any use after all. How could there have been, she asked herself crossly, when all it is is a list of names that mean little or nothing to me? And why did I ever think I'd be able to sort it out this way? She stretched her aching back and looked for the umpteenth time at her list of initials taken from Oxford's computer disc. Not that she expected it to tell her anything—and then suddenly her back stiffened as her eyes lingered on the third on the list. K.K. £1,000. A double. She reached for Phyllis's telephone list again and began to riffle through it quickly.

There were seven names which had matching initials. None were K.K., but there were two in the Ds, David Denton, an anesthetist, and Donald Dench, who was the deputy head of the physiotherapy department; two Ws, Walter Weinstock whom she knew as a medical registrar, and William Warden who was the hospital Chaplain. Then there was Frances Furlong, the Catering Supervisor, and Jo Jennson, who was the senior in the accounts department.

It might be nonsense, she thought as she scribbled as fast as she could, but equally it could be a beginning—and then she almost jumped out of her skin as a hand was put on her shoulder.

"Working very late, Dr. Barnabas!" Professor Dieter was looking down at her with undisguised curiosity. "Or is it still that list of names you're looking at? Phyllis told me you had a message for someone whose name you'd forgotten."

"Uh—yes." George blinked up at him, not sure what to do. Tell him the truth even though she'd been at pains to hide it from his secretary? But that wouldn't be wise; after all, everyone at Old East could be regarded as a suspect, even the Professor himself. And unbidden a memory rose in her mind like a bubble; Professor Dieter at the Barrie Ward building site the night they'd found Mitchell Formby's body. Could be have pushed the man to his death? And then instead of vanishing hung around the place, as a sort of double bluff? Silly bubble, she thought then, and let it burst. It couldn't have been Dieter; he'd do nothing so—well—crude, as to push a man to his death. He'd be far more subtle, surely? But absurd an idea or not, she had to take the possibility into account; and there was another, too. What would Gus say of her detective abilities if all she did was blurt out the fact that she was helping him by attempting to break a code that might find the murderer of Richard Oxford? Better to continue lying.

"I—er—yes, I was asked at the Royal College meeting last week if I'd deliver a message to someone here and for the life of me I can't remember the name. So I thought maybe if I saw it it would come back to me."

"Ah, yes, the unconscious memory, hmm? Have you had any success?" He bent closer to look at her lists and it was too late to put her hand over them.

"I've managed to remember that it was an alliterative name," she said, improvising hard. "So I noted all those and I thought I'd wander 'round to them all and ask them if the message made sense."

"You're very punctilious for what was after all just a minor encounter, I imagine."

"Well, I promised, you know, and one does like to keep one's word."

"One is impressed," the Professor said drily. "May I have my list of phone numbers back now, please? I have some calls to make."

She handed it over at once. "Of course. I'll go and see these people I've picked out and deliver the message. I can't do more. If I've got the name wrong after all, well, there it is."

"Let me see if I can help." He leaned over again and she had to let him look. "Hmm. Well, I can tell you that Mr. Denton left us a few months ago. Gone off to Bart's. Mr. Dench is still here, though I can't imagine what anyone at a pathology meeting might need delivered to him. What was the message, by the way?" He looked at her with his eyebrows up and she smiled at him in the most relaxed way she could.

"Oh, rather odd." She managed a light laugh. "He just said to say that the books were ready and, since they were wanted, to call for them and there was a good surprise in them. It's mysterious."

"Yes," the Professor said and bent his head again. "It just occurred to me you might have been told whether the person was a man or a woman. You have here both sexes, which seems a bit odd."

"Oh," George said, and her mind seemed to blank as she looked down at her lists again and then almost before she knew she was saying it, had her answer. "The trouble is those women's names there—Frances and Jo—they could be men, couldn't they? He, er, Dr. Ambrose, didn't write it down, you see. Just said it. So it could have been anything really. I just made a note of all the alliterative names. Oh well, I dare say it's a waste of time anyway. Oh, Professor, by the bye, I did want to thank you for including me in your party the other evening. It was most kind of you and your wife. I've been very wrong not to have thanked you sooner."

"It was our pleasure." He straightened up and tucked the book of phone numbers under his arm. "Our pleasure indeed. Well, goodnight, Dr. Barnabas. I have work to do, I'm afraid." And he nodded at her and went, leaving her sweating and immensely relieved behind him.

But even after all that, she was no further forward with breaking the code a couple of hours later. She tried all sorts of combinations of letters to see if she could make them match the sums of money alongside them but nothing seemed to make any sense at all. It had to be as Gus had said; a code of such staggering simplicity that it couldn't be broken except by accident, possibly based on some quirk of Oxford's that made the key inaccessible. And she put the printout sheets back in their plastic envelope and stretched her back wearily.

I must be crazy, she thought. I don't have to put myself through all this for what is, after all, none of my affair. It's Gus's job to solve this crime, not mine.

But she knew she'd go on meddling, probing, trying to find

an answer. It was almost impossible for her ever to leave even a minor confusion alone. The drive to untangle, to identify, just to know the true facts was far too strong in her. It had driven her all through her school and college years; had chosen her career for her, for what was a pathologist but an untangler of mysteries? To be faced with this mystery, involving two deaths and a code and blackmail and theft and not to try to resolve it would be to go against all her deepest instincts. And now, tired as she was, and hard as she'd tried, the mystery remained as inpenetrable as it had been when she'd started this evening. That irritated her. She couldn't just go to bed and leave it; there had to be more she could do that would be useful. After a moment's thought she pulled her scribbling pad towards her and wrote at the top of a clean sheet: SUSPECTS.

And then stopped to think. In order of likelihood? How could she know that? Better just to write them down as they came to mind and see where she went from there.

A pattern established itself quickly. First she wrote NAME in large capitals: *Felicity Oxford*. MOTIVE followed, again in large capitals. *Wife of the victim who was bisexual and who gave her a virus that will ultimately kill her*. That must have made her hate Oxford.

But hate him enough to murder him? George stopped and thought hard for a while longer and then added *Money*. Surely Felicity stood to inherit what had to be a considerable fortune? Or—and here she stopped and stared into space. Would the law step in and prevent Felicity from taking money that had been ill-gotten? Could a blackmailer's money be left to his family or was it impounded by the State? She had no idea, and she made a star at the side of the entry to remind her to check up with Gus. And maybe something else needed checking. Could Felicity have known her husband was a blackmailer?

She stopped and thought some more and then had to add, unwillingly, a new heading: COUNTER-MOTIVE. *If Felicity Oxford knew he was a blackmailer and shared his profits it was of benefit to her to keep him alive, not kill him.* That, George decided was a depressing thought and moved on quickly.

OPPORTUNITY. That had to be the next one, obviously. Beneath that she wrote *Masses.* Who better to go into the dead man's flat and plant a tube of poisoned hemorrhoid cream? No one would give her a second glance. After all, she was the man's wife, even if they didn't live together. But there was a second set of factors to be taken into account under this heading: the possibility of getting hold of digitalis and filling a tube with it in the pharmacy. Here George had to write *Moderate.* Although Felicity spent less time hanging around Old East than her husband had, she was still here often enough for committee meetings and the like. She could have managed it.

The next name she wrote in under her headings, she put there with a firm hand: *Toby Bellamy.* MOTIVE? *To protect his Fliss for whom he had more feeling than he had admitted. At the very least, she was a friend. It could be that he had lied and she was a lover.* George looked at that and then hurried on. OPPORTUNITY? *All there is. Easy access to everything at Old East. Also admits to having been in Oxford's flat at a dinner party so could have planted the spiked cream.* There was no limitation on the timing, after all; it could have been put there months before Oxford used it. And though Gus had said that guests didn't get into the master bathroom except as part of a guided tour by Oxford, that didn't mean Toby hadn't slipped out at some time and tried to do it and succeeded.

Then she looked at COUNTER-MOTIVE, and under it had to write *None*, which made Toby a strong suspect. Every means, every reason to do it, and none not to.

"Sod it," she muttered and hurried on resolutely to her next name. She thought hard, and then wrote *Jerry Swann.* It might seem far-fetched, but after all he had admitted to being very angry; so under MOTIVE she wrote *Insulted, disappointed, enough to cause murder?* Probably not, but it might be for some people. Jerry could be more sensitive than he appears.

OPPORTUNITY. Here she sighed and wrote *Every: to get the stuff and to fill the tube. Possible to get it into the flat?* Well, he might have lied and been a visitor at some time. But to the best of her knowledge that one had to be a false start. He'd never shown the least sign that he had any knowledge of the place. Which was a comfort. Under COUNTER-MOTIVE she wrote *There wouldn't be much profit in murder for this one.* Lots of worry and a little revenge, that was all. Taking it all around she thought Jerry came low on the list, but he was definitely there.

That gave her three suspects, which wasn't very much. Surely there had to be other people at Old East who belonged on her list?

She went over the entries again, reading them carefully. None of them seemed to offer her any leads and she started to read yet again; and then suddenly remembered, the thought coming into her mind totally unbidden, like another bubble. Carole. The girl who, according to Kate, had been a model, and according to Gus had been used by Felicity's agency. And what else was it Gus had said? That Felicity's girls had jobs on the side...

The bubbles came thicker and faster, solidified into hard ideas and began to click and slide into place in her mind, like the colored balls on a double helix model. Matthew Herne was the senior hospital administrator. He was the man to whom Mitchell Formby had answered. He was the man who should have spotted what Formby was when he applied for his job. Because he appointed him, he was the man who should have discovered his depradations on the hospital's equipment. He was the man who had a wife he adored to the point of obsession. A wife who might have been a prostitute when she had worked with Felicity Oxford. Who might have known about her employee's extra-curricular activities and mentioned it to her husband, Oxford. Who might have used that as a weapon against Matthew Herne, threatening to tell the world that he was married to a "bad' woman, which would be something the highly upright exsoldier would find very hard to handle, yet he would not be able to let her go, loving her as he did. His only recourse surely would have been to rid himself of Oxford, both to be free of his demands for money as well as the fear of eventual exposure of Carole. Maybe protecting her name was part of keeping her. And maybe he used Formby as his tool for getting the money he had to pay to Oxford and even possibly used him to help with his murder.

It was a beautiful scenario, and she contemplated it almost in awe at her own perspicacity. To have seen it all so clearly... Oh, it had to be Herne. She was quite sure of it. Who else had had so strong a motive, so easy an opportunity and no counter-motive whatsoever? Herne had everything to gain, nothing to lose by getting rid of Oxford. And what was more he had to get rid of Formby as well once he no longer needed to use him. He was as much a danger to him as Oxford had been; he might one day try a bit of blackmail on his own account. With the sort of history she'd uncovered about Formby it was very likely.

She almost hugged herself with pride and sheer excitement, but she didn't. She scribbled all the details as she had worked them out into her list of suspects and then leaned back in delight to study them again. And looked at the list of initials from the Oxford computer printout.

At last, she had a real lead. She had not only a pair of matching initials to try, but also M.H. for Matthew Herne. If one pair of these initials here could be made to link logically with M.H. she was home and dry. She'd have solved Gus Hathaway's code for him. All she had to do was start again on the code.

She pushed back her hair, which had tumbled into her eyes in the heat of the moment and bent her head again over the code. She had to break it somehow. Tonight. And here she'd stay until she did it.

27

She woke suddenly, sitting bolt upright and staring around wildly, totally disoriented. Around her the library stretched, quiet and stuffy, and she blinked at the walls of books and tried to rub her face with one hand only to discover it was numb and had started pins and needles that promised to hurt abominably. She shook her hand to bring back life, as memory came back too.

Dammit all to hell and back, how could she have been so stupid? She peered at her watch and cursed again. Half past two. To have struggled with that code so long that she had fallen asleep over it had been a ridiculous thing to do, especially as she had failed ignominiously to get anywhere with it. Bad as her room in the residence might be, it did at least offer a proper bed, and she'd have been better off in it hours ago. She yawned and, as her numb hand began to settle down to some sort of normality, picked up her papers and made for the door.

Outside in the corridor the medical school building lay still and dark around her, smelling faintly of formaldehyde and dust and old shoes. She stood hesitantly in the doorway for a while, trying to decide what to do. The door between this building and the doctors' residence adjoining must have been locked hours ago. It wasn't even worth going along that way to see if she could get through. It would have to be the whole boring business of going down to the ground floor, along to the door that led out to the main entrance yard, then around the private wing by the main road to the residence beyond. A five-minute walk she didn't fancy in the least.

The main yard door was locked, of course, she thought as she went padding along the corridor towards the staircase, but she had a hazy memory of seeing the keys to the building in the small porter's room that adjoined the door. She should be able to get out all right, though she wouldn't be able to lock up again. Or maybe, she thought sleepily, I could lock the door and post the key back in through the letter box.

But to her surprise the door was not only unlocked but open. She pushed on it cautiously, trying to see if there was anything wrong with it. Had someone broken in? There would be no point in anyone doing so—there was little worth stealing apart from the collection of antique medical instruments and books on the fourth floor and perhaps a typewriter or two from the various offices—but it was obvious as soon as she looked that the lock had not been tampered with. It was simply unlocked and, what was more, set on the latch, and she considered for a moment putting the latch down to close it on the other side so that the building would be secure after she left, but decided against it. There might be a good reason for this; perhaps a late-working cleaner or a porter who had nipped out for a moment and would be returning.

She emerged into the narrow entry yard, which was just big enough to let a single ambulance through, a fact that caused many daytime hold-ups and much honking in the main road outside when new arrivals jockeyed for position with emerging vehicles, and stood there for a moment to catch her breath. It was still bitterly cold, for all it was now April, and she wondered mournfully if summer ever came to London. It had been a rare enough visitor to Inverness and sometimes she had yearned for the hot summers in the States; and for just a moment, in her sleepy state, in the chill of the dark dead watches of the morning, she yearned for home like a child wanting its mother and despised herself for being so silly. And walked out into the street beyond.

There was a car parked a little way along on the opposite side of the road. She looked at it in surprise, because there was a shadow beside it that looked as though someone were there crouching down and peering in through the driver's open window, and then the shadow moved and proved to be precisely that, and she stood very still against the wall in the darkness thrown by the concrete buttress that supported the wall beside the entrance, trying to be invisible. She didn't know why, but she felt it would be politic not to be seen.

She could hear a faint murmur now, so soft as to be almost a whisper. It wasn't loud enough for her to hear words and certainly not to identify any familiar voice, and she had just decided that this was just a late-night reveler on his way home—though where he had come from heaven only knew, since there were no private houses along this street at all, or bars or restaurants or anywhere else a person could have come from at half past two in the morning—when the shadow stopped crouching and became an upright and recognizable figure. It looks like Professor Dieter, she thought, and peered again; and then the figure turned and moved away as the engine started, quietly because it was a big expensive car—a BMW possibly, though she couldn't be sure in the poor light. The figure— yes, it was Dieter, she was certain of it—waved, and a hand came out of the driving window and waved back. She looked as the car passed her going westwards towards the middle of the city and saw the face of the driver clearly and frowned, trying to think who it was. She knew him, she was sure she did, but she had to scrabble in her memory for his name. Of course, Dr. Neville Carr, the oncologist. She had little to do with him in the course of a day's work and had only spoken to him in passing at various medical events and in the canteen; but she was certain it was he, and was amused at herself for being so suspicious of this little encounter. Clearly he had come in to deal with an emergency and Professor Dieter had been asked for a consult. Even he had to get up in the middle of the night sometimes. She was about to step forward out of her shadows and greet the Professor who was now walking briskly back towards the hospital entrance, but thought better of it. To have to explain why she was standing out here at two-thirty would be tiresome to say the least; better to let him go. And she waited until she heard the latch of the door to the medical school building click and went gratefully on her way to her own building and bed. It was dreadful, she told herself as she brushed her teeth and climbed shivering between the sheets, to become so suspicious. It's as though everyone I look at, no matter what they're doing, has become an object of my detection. I ought to leave all this to Gus and stop meddling, she thought drowsily. I'll drive myself crazy if I go on this way. And yet, it was all so fascinating and exciting. She, who liked to discover the roots of everything, was tailor-made for detecting. "Tailor-made," she murmured into the darkness and fell asleep as abruptly as an exhausted child.

It was later in the afternoon that her brilliant idea came to her. All morning she had been on the point of phoning Gus Hatha-way to tell him of her great discovery and her identification of Matthew Herne as the murderer, but somehow she had been held back. There was always something else to do first, but now she had to admit it. She didn't want to tell him. Not yet. It would be much more fun and infinitely more satisfying to give him something concrete to prove her elegant solution. It couldn't be denied that all she had so far was based on what he would regard as much despised intuition. She knew it was nothing of the sort, but would he?

Solid information, she thought. Real evidence. How the hell do I get that for him? What was it the police did when they wanted real evidence? She thought about that, about all the films she had ever seen of the police at work and how they collected evidence, and it was then that the beginnings of an idea came to her. A stake-out, wasn't that what they called it?

You set up a scene in which the people you expected to give you the evidence you needed operated without knowing you were there to watch and catch them. Would it be possible to do something of the sort?

Her office door rattled and Jerry came in, walking backwards so that he pushed the door open with his rump. He was carrying a tray and on it was a plate with a large cake, which bore one fat candle in the center and was iced with virulent pink fondant.

"It's my birthday, Dr. B.," he announced. "And for birthdays in the lab we always have a bit of cake here in the boss's office. It's the only thing that keeps us going year by year. We always use this room to cut it and share it out and have a cuppa. Dr. Royle quite enjoyed it. I hope you will too."

She stood up and looked at the cake and then at the people who were following him into her office; Sheila, of course, and Jane, the trio from the big lab, and even Peter, looking as morose as usual, but still there, and she laughed.

"It wouldn't make much difference if I objected, would it?" she said. "Seeing you're here. OK, OK, have your birthday cake. Who's got a knife?"

"Me," said Danny from the doorway, as he came in at last, carrying a very large PM knife. George looked at it in some horror and then at Jerry.

"One of those? Ye gods, I knew working in a lab coarsened you but—"

"It's all right," he interrupted cheerfully. "It's never been used for anything but our cakes and suchlike. We like to shock outsiders—that's why we use it—but we tell you the truth. Now, who's going to light my candle?" He leered at George. "It's no secret, Dr. B. that I'd love it to be you."

Jane giggled and George went a little pink. She had successfully repelled Jerry's tendency to flirt with her before she'd been in the place a week, but lately he was beginning to get a little uppity again. She looked at him straight-faced and shook her head. "Do it yourself, Jerry. Much more suitable."

He grimaced as Sheila snorted with laughter, and caught the box of matches Danny chucked at him. "If I'm not there when the loving begins, start without me," he muttered as he lit the candle, but George ignored him and turned to help Sheila who was now being efficient with a teapot and mugs.

They ate and drank and laughed as Jerry chattered on in his usual way. George sat on the edge of her desk staring into space as she worked on the plan that had dropped almost fully fledged into her mind. A birthday celebration? Maybe. Unless she could think of any better or more logical reason; but she couldn't. So it would have to be a birthday party. All she could do was look them all straight in the eyes and swear she'd been born in April and hope no one remembered her personnel file in which it was clearly shown that she had in fact emerged into the world in October.

The cake finished and the teapot drained they began to trail regretfully back to work. George timed herself carefully: as Jerry collected the remains of his cake, she murmured, "Pop back, will you Jerry? I need a word."

He looked at her sharply and nodded and followed Sheila out of her office with the others, obediently reappearing five minutes later.

"I need your help, Jerry," George said, "It was your bringing your birthday cake that made me think of it. The thing is, it's my birthday next week—"

"Oh! Really? Super. Lots more cake. I thought we'd have to wait till June and Sheila's annual lie. She tries to take off an extra year every time, you know. She thinks we've all got the galloping amnesia. I'll tell them. They'll be delighted."

"No you won't," she said firmly. "Because I can't ask them all to the event I'm planning. I'll have to ask you because you're going to help me get it together, but don't go getting any ideas in consequence." She sounded severe now. "If I ask you and not the others it doesn't mean anything special. Understand?"

"I can hardly do anything else," he said a little mournfully. "Still, it's nice to be asked. Where is it?"

"That's the problem. I can't entertain in my own home because I don't have one yet, though I'll be looking for that soon. So I thought I'd get permission to use the Board Room for a private party. They do that sometimes, don't they?"

"Oh, yes. There're always things happening over there. It's a bit of extra cash for the hospital, I suppose."

"Well, I hope it isn't too much extra cash," she said, thinking of her bank balance and wondering if it would survive. Detection could be an expensive hobby. "Anyway I'm determined to do it. A dinner party, I thought, for—oh, maybe twelve people."

"What and me too? Not just a thrash? That's a bit—well!" He was pink with gratification and she laughed.

"Look, I can't deny this is enlightened self-interest. I want some help and that's why I want you. I've got a guest list in my mind." She went around to her desk to sit down and pick up a notebook. "How about...hmm." She pretended to think hard and then scribbled her list.

"Kate Sayers and her partner. They're good friends, and I owe them. I've had dinner at their place a couple of times. And Hattie Clements from A & E and her chap, Sam. They're very nice too. And I think I'll have to ask Prof. Dieter and his wife since they invited me and I owe them a return, and Dr. Bellamy'—Jerry flicked a glance at her face and snickered and she knew it but pretended not to—"and Mrs. Oxford because she's a friend of his and needs some cheering up, poor soul, after her husband's death and perhaps...hmm, well, Matthew Herne. I think his wife's a looker and you can flirt with her, since you like flirting so much. She's an ex-model."

"Don't I know it," Jerry said gleefully. "Don't we all? Look, it's very good of you to include me, Dr. B., but—"

"I told you I need help. First of all, this'll have to be catered. Are the hospital people any good?"

"Are you mad? You've eaten their stuff!"

"All right, then. Who's the best caterer in the area? If I'm going to do this I might as well push the boat out."

"There's really only one," he said after a moment. "Or as far as I know. Whenever anyone does anything special around these parts they bring in Castor and Pollux, from the Highway."

"Castor and…"

Jerry grinned. "A very pretty pair. I hope it doesn't bother you but they're really quite outrageous. All, you know…" He bent one knee and dropped his right hand from his wrist in a stereotypical gay pose. "But they cook like angels, they really do. The best parties I've been to are the ones they've done."

"Then why on earth should I care about their sexuality?" George said and closed her notebook. "OK, there it is. I'll get on to them. Do you have a phone number?"

"It's in the phone book, I expect." He reached for it and riffled the pages. "Here you are. Call them and get a quote."

She dialled the number and found herself talking to a very polite young man who didn't seem at all as Jerry had described. When she told him what she wanted he promised to send around at once a sheet of sample menus with prices and an account of all they could do.

"Just you check the date you want us, as soon as possible, and we'll arrange it. It's been a bit quiet lately—this isn't the best time of the year, and I can't pretend it is—so I dare say we'll be able to fit you in. I'll send the stuff over by hand. You're only across the road from us, really, at Old East. We know it well. So let me know as soon as you can."

Jerry went back to work, sworn to silence, and she settled down to end her own afternoon's work before getting on with her planning. But first she rang the admin office and checked the availability of the Board Room for her own private use.

Daphne, Matthew Herne's secretary, listened carefully to what she wanted and then suggested she talk to Mr. Herne.

"He's always very generous to staff," she said. "If you ask him yourself he might manage a discount." And George, who had been trying to think of how much of her own money she was going to spend on this non-birthday party, agreed with alacrity. The man may be a murderer, and she may be using the event to unmask him, but even so, she had to make the best of her opportunities.

He was very affable. She started by telling him she wanted to give a birthday party to which he and his wife were invited, and very much wanted to use the Board Room. Would that be possible and what would it cost her?

"Cost you, Dr. Barnabas? Well, let me see. When do you want it? If it's a popular day it makes a difference."

"Well, tell me what's available," she said. "As long as it's soon, it's not really vital."

"But I thought it was for your birthday?"

"Oh, it is, but I—er, I don't want to be childish. The most convenient for you'll do fine for me. If it's easier for you..." And she crossed her fingers very childishly against the lie.

"Well now." There was a rustle as he turned over pages and then he said, "Hmm. You could have April 23 if you like. It's a Thursday, and that's never a very popular day. And—er—actually it's one when I'm free too. I'm sure my wife would be most pleased to join me in accepting your invitation."

She was fulsome in her appreciation, especially when he told her she need pay nothing for the use of the Board Room, and hung up feeling oddly guilty. She'd every intention of unmasking the man as a thief and a murderer and yet she had used him shamelessly to protect her own pocket. It was disgusting, she decided, quite disgusting. But she did nothing to alter the arrangements.

She also phoned Professor Dieter's office. Phyllis told her icily she would convey her invitation to Professor and Mrs. Dieter, and became very agitated when George insisted that the polite way would be to do it herself, but in the end

consented grudgingly to giving her the address to write to.
Then she phoned Kate and Hattie, both of whom accepted with
flattering alacrity. Toby and Fliss, she decided, would have to
be approached differently later on. She didn't know quite how
she'd persuade herself to ask them but ask them she would.
After all, convinced though she was of Herne's guilt, there
were still some lingering doubts about Toby that could do with
being aired. Maybe her party would be as good a place as any
to do it, if it all went as she planned.

The sample menus from Castor and Pollux, who turned out
to be in fact called Stephen Danbo and Miles Chapman, arrived
at half past five, brought by a child of around twelve or so
who waited sullenly in front of her desk until she realized what
was expected of her and gave him fifty pence, and she read
them with increasing pleasure. Castor and Pollux seemed like
good cooks who knew what they were doing and understood
wine as well; and their prices, when she worked it out, weren't
too horrendous, especially as she was not having to pay for
the room. Altogether this party was going to be fun, she told
herself, as she settled to the agreeable task of choosing what
she should give her guests; so much so that she began to wish
it were her birthday after all.

28

I must be mad, George thought, standing in the doorway looking at the preparations for her party. Quite mad. I'm spending all this money and what for? To make a complete ass of myself, trying to do Gus's job and dig out information no one'll want to part with. Oh, shit! I wish I were in Buffalo.

Across the room the three of them were bustling about; Stephen Danbo and Miles Chapman were respectively folding napkins into elaborate turbans and setting food on the table, while Jerry fussed over the flowers that had been arranged in the center. She had to admit it looked good and took a deep breath and then realized it all smelled good too; there was a redolence of garlic and hot bread and the seasideness of fish cooked in dill.

Jerry spotted her. "Oh, you look wonderful. I knew scarlet was your color. Doesn't she look great?" he appealed to Miles who looked at George's silky trousers and jerkin and nodded a little thoughtfully.

"We'd better take those tulips out of the arrangement," he said. "They clash. Just leave the yellow and white stuff. We're almost ready, doctor. There are drinks all set over there." He nodded at a table against the window and went on with his dishing out of the salmon mousse they were having for a first course.

"I've heard of attention to detail, but this is ridiculous," George said as Stephen obediently removed red tulips from the center arrangement. "It's really not that important."

"Of course it is. It's your birthday!" Jerry said and went over to the drinks table. "You re the special one tonight, so everything has to be right. What will you have?"

George, whose guilt was beginning to rise as well as her trepidation, said, "Whisky," very firmly. Miles quirked an eyebrow at Stephen and she felt the comment even though he hadn't said a word. "I've a good head," she said loudly to no one in particular and took the glass Jerry gave her, pretending not to notice how generously he'd filled it. Anyway, she reminded herself as she drank deeply, I've got to come on as though I'm smashed.

But you mustn't actually be smashed, dummy. Just seem so. If you are in reality, you'll never get anywhere. You'll just forget what people say, if you even hear them in the first place.

Jerry went bustling off back to the dining table to continue tweaking flowers and candles to Miles's and Stephen's obvious irritation. George took the opportunity to tip her whisky back into the bottle and help herself to a handful of potato crisps to soak up what she had already swallowed. It was a matter of some regret that she couldn't drink at her own party, but after all, it wasn't her birthday.

Which was something she had to work hard to remember as the evening took off and her guests arrived. She'd completely forgotten the possibility that she would be given birthday presents and now, as parcel after parcel wrapped in everything from glittering foil and silver ribbons (Carole) to brown paper and string (the Dieters) was pushed into her hands, she felt shame fill her and make her as dizzy as whisky ever had.

"You really shouldn't," she said over and over again, and, "Oh, but I didn't want presents! Just a little agreeable company is all…"

But they smiled at her and patted her shoulder and shook her hand and the parcels piled up. She looked at them uneasily. Open them now, or save them till later?

Remember what you're here for, she told herself sternly and set to work along the lines she had planned. But it wasn't at all as easy as she'd thought it would be.

First of all she fussed over seating them and used the process to drop the first of her carefully contrived innocent remarks. "I'll sit you here next to Dr. Bellamy, Carole," she said, smiling tipsily. "I'm sure you'd rather sit next to a handsome bachelor than a husband any day." Carole was supposed to look, well, somewhat uneasy perhaps, and Matthew Herne was supposed to react in some way, but all that happened was Carole said vaguely, "Oh, thanks ever so," and sat down, and Herne, moving without any apparent haste but very definitely, sat down on her other side.

So that was one ploy up and running into the wall, George registered bitterly and turned to Felicity Oxford, who was looking stunning in her obviously very expensive little Jean Muir number in deepest purple. Once again, a nice fashion touch, George thought. Somber without being obvious as a widow's weeds. She never gets it wrong. But she hadn't waited to be told where to go; she sat down next to Matthew Herne and beckoned to Charles Dieter and the rest of the table fell into place without any help: Beatrice Dieter opposite her husband and apparently content between Sam Chanter and Kate's Oliver Merrall; and Kate and Jerry and Hattie and herself taking the available spaces left. So it would have to be in general conversation that she did her stuff, George decided, as her guests with every sign of appreciation set to work on their hot garlic bread and the salmon mousse.

It was remarkably easy to pretend to drink more than she was, in fact, or at least to hoodwink her guests. Whether she fooled Stephen Danbo, who was going around with the wine, she wasn't sure, but she wasn't concerned about him. It was the others she was after and once the main course of roast duck breasts with assorted fruits was on its way to being demolished she got going properly.

"That business of poor old Formby," she said with a bright smile all around. "Awful, wasn't it? To have another sudden death around the hospital so soon after poor Mr. Oxford..." She threw a regretful glance at Felicity who sat stony-faced and concentrating on her duck. "Well, it's a bit much, isn't it? Maybe the two were connected? That awful Detective Chief Inspector seems to think so, doesn't he? Says it could be murder."

"Does he?" Charles Dieter said sharply. "I got the impression he'd come to the conclusion that the poor man had slipped on the wet wood up there while he was doing his evening inspection and that there was no one to help him because it was after the men had clocked off."

"Oh, you mustn't believe all the DCI says," George said and lifted her glass to her lips again and threw back her head, though not in fact swallowing any of the wine. "He's a deep guy that one, deep as the Grand Canyon. He'll say anything to get the sort of stuff he wants."

"And what might he want? Why say Formby had slipped if he hadn't?"

"Well, maybe he wants people to think he thinks that." George looked owlishly around the table. They were all looking at her now. "So that the person who actually pushed him reveals himself." She looked then at Carole Herne. "Or herself, of course."

Matthew Herne lifted his head sharply. "I can't imagine he'd do anything so silly," he said crisply. "He's an excellent police officer and one I have known for some time. I can't see him saying one thing and meaning another."

"Maybe he's still got investigations to do," George said and looked fuzzily at Herne. "I mean, has he asked where you were the night poor old Formby went over the edge?"

"Of course not," Herne said stiffly. "I mean, why should—"

"Oh, but Matty, he did! You told me he'd asked you about your movements and you had this awful problem telling him!"

Carole giggled and George thought, She really is smashed. Her eyes weren't focusing as well as they might and she had a most becoming flush. "On account of you got home nice and prompt that evening so we could have an early dinner—after we'd relaxed, of course." And she giggled again and looked challengingly at George with her tongue tip between her teeth.

Is she drunk? George thought. She's straight-eyed enough now. And she doesn't seem to have had all that much. Is she just trying to establish an alibi for him? Has he told her to say that if the subject comes up?

"Not that early, darling," Herne said and his hand slipped from the table and disappeared beneath the edge and Carole let out an involuntary little yelp. He's pinched her, George realized and watched more closely than ever. "It was my usual time. I don't cheat on my work, you know, even to get home to you."

"I'm sure no one would ever check up on you, Herne," Dieter said and frowned, clearly not liking the turn the conversation had taken. "This is excellent duck, George. We must compliment you on it."

"Oh, it wasn't me who cooked it," George said, letting the grammar go hang. "I got a caterer, of course—" and she nodded in the direction of Miles who was going around with more of the lyonnaise potatoes which Oliver and Sam in particular welcomed warmly. "I got Castor and Pollux."

"Oh?" Charles said vaguely and peered in Miles's direction, but the room was glittering with candlelight now and the surroundings were rather dim so it seemed hard for him to see. "Well, they're very good. I congratulate you."

"Good evening, Professor," Miles said politely. "I have some more of the épinards à la crème for you, if you'd like it."

Charles brightened. "Splendid. I'm very fond of that."

"Yes, sir," Miles said and came around to serve him. "And the roast parsnips, sir? I rather think you like them too."

Hattie launched herself into cookery talk and the conversation steered itself away from people's whereabouts

when Mitchell Formby had fallen off the new building, and
George sat and tried to look interested as she considered. She'd
have to push a bit harder if this whole party wasn't going to
turn into an expensive shambles from her point of view. She
couldn't return to Formby's death now, it would be too obvious,
but then she brightened as she heard Kate, who was leaning
across the table to talk to Carole, say something about a new
outfit she'd seen and wanted to buy, and opened her mouth in
a wide grin.

"Hell, though, Kate, did you see the other stuff in that
fashion show? I saw it on TV as well—it was totally the pits. I
mean, no one but a hooker'd be caught dead in them. They're
so—well, they don't leave a thing to the imagination, do they?"

"Eh?" Kate was looking at her, startled, and George
ploughed on. "I mean, honestly, the sort of women who wear
that stuff...Mind you, I often wonder about hookers, don't
you? Are they born that way or are they pushed, if you see
what I mean? Do they set out to take on the life of a prostitute
because they just love sex and can't get enough of it, or is it
the money that draws them? And why do they all have such
godawful fashion sense? I never saw one that didn't look as
though she wasn't someone you'd be ashamed to take home
to your ma. And I'd love to know, can they ever be reformed?
You see these movies like—oh, I dunno—*Pretty Woman* and
all that, and they're supposed to get married and live happily
ever after, but me, I just don't see it. Once a hooker, surely—"

Stephen leaned over her shoulder and took her plate and then
they all leaned back as Miles also began to collect dishes and
the moment passed, yet again. But there had been some profit,
surely? George thought. Herne was as blank-faced as it was
possible for a man to look and Carole looked simply vague, as
she usually did; but Felicity had stared hard at George and she
wondered as conversation again picked up, this time between
Sam and Oliver and Jerry on the subject of football, whether
she'd scored a hit or not.

She had to do something better soon, she told herself desperately. They were almost ready for the dessert of a particularly luscious fruit pavlova; get past that to the coffee and people may start to go. And the way I've treated them they'll want to. She was very aware now of the tension around her table. She'd have to cash in soon or not get anything at all. She took the shortest way in she could.

"That symposium, Professor, did you get a lot of reaction?" she called down the table. He had been talking to Felicity in a low voice, but now he looked up and frowned slightly.

"I beg your pardon?"

"I wondered, did you get a lot of people coming forward to get themselves HIV tested because they were worried, afterwards? Any talk of HIV scares people, doesn't it? They start thinking of getting tested."

"That symposium was designed to do quite the reverse of alarming participants," Dieter said sharply. "We need to get rid of this notion so many people have that a diagnosis of HIV positive is akin to a death sentence, because it isn't."

"Oh, come on, Professor! Surely if you were told you were HIV positive you'd be scared? Most sensible people are." If I lose my job over this, it'll be my own fault, not Gus's, though right now I wish I'd never heard of him, she thought somewhere deep below the level of her speech. Oh, God, why am I doing this? To find out, came the whisper back from somewhere even deeper. To find out…"It's one of the things I meet over and over again. People come and ask me to do HIV tests on the quiet and then go mad if they have to be told it's positive. Yet they go just as mad if anyone ever finds out that they had a test, even if it came back negative. The fact of being tested at all is trouble."

"Is it?" Carole said, wide-eyed. "Why? If it's negative it's nothing to worry about." She shivered. "I'd hate to be told that. I'd rather not have the test at all."

"A lot of people feel that way," George said. "But they still need to know, so they come and ask me to do the tests. I've got a lot of secret ones hidden away in the lab, together with the results of all the other ones they've done there. It's something I think is interesting and I ought to hang on to them. Got them safely locked up, of course." She nodded and beamed as drunkenly as she could without becoming a caricature of inebriation and lifted her glass to her lips again. She would have liked to drink water but that would have ruined the effect. "I'll never tell, of course. But it's my guess some of these people'd go ape if they thought anyone else had found out about them, and that I had kept their old results."

"No one need 'go ape,' as you put it, if they know the facts," Dieter said in the hardest voice she had ever heard him use. "There is no proof that there is any need to fear HIV to the extent some people have been made to. It is one of my—"

"Not now, Charles," Beatrice Dieter said loudly. "I've had quite enough of this subject for some time. And we have to go now. I have an early lecture tomorrow and need my sleep. Goodnight, Dr. Barnabas. Very good of you to include us. See to it that you keep that plant we gave you well watered. It dies easily without attention. Goodnight." And she swept out, not even looking back at Charles who, after a moment, patted his lips with his napkin and stood up. "I had no idea it was so late," he said stiffly and followed her out.

"I must go too," Herne said and George looked at him and felt a lurch in her belly. He was very white, almost grayish, and for a moment she thought he was ill. But then as the color slowly came back she saw only that he was furiously angry. Or sick with fright. Or...Well, she couldn't be sure, but some emotion had him held tightly.

"Come along, Carole," he said. "I have an early start tomorrow too. Thank you, Dr. Barnabas. Please see to it that your caterers leave it all as they found it." And then they too were gone.

The rest of the party sat uneasily for a moment and then talk started once more, a little jerkily, but at least it started, and again it was good sensible Kate who was responsible, turning to Felicity to engage her in bright and rather silly conversation about gardening and George thought, She's chosen that because she thinks I can't put my foot in it there. Oh, God, will they ever forgive me, these nice people? *If* they're nice people. Which of them has killed twice? Somebody has.

Toby came and sat down beside her, where the departure of the other guests had made it possible, and murmured, "What are you up to?" in her ear.

She turned to look at him, trying to seem bleary. "Mmm? Hope you're having a nice party. I thought maybe you wouldn't come, seeing it's mine and you were so angry with me."

"I don't hold grudges. I ought to, but I don't."

"Tha's nice," she said, smiling a little crookedly and considering a hiccup.

He wasn't impressed. "You're no more smashed than I'm the Queen of bloody Sheba," he said. "What's all this about?"

She thought fast, jockeying for time. "Mmm?"

"I said you're up to something; being deliberately rude to people; setting up hares that might run. Look at what you've done to poor old Herne!"

"Poor old—" she began and then subsided, biting her lip.

"I knew you were foxing. I ask again,—What the hell are you up to?"

"None of your business." She looked covertly at Felicity, who seemed almost animated in her talk with Kate, who showed no sign of anxiety at all. "It's my party and—"

"It's not even your birthday," he said and she stared at him. "How do you know?"

"Went to find out. Wanted to check on your actual birth date so that I'd get the right present for the right day, believe it or not. Told the personnel girl it was for some research I was doing." He shook his head. "Some of 'em'll believe anything. So for the last time, what is all this?"

She gave in. "I was trying to see if I could push this case on a bit." She dropped her voice even further, though it wasn't necessary. Sam and Oliver and Jerry had returned to the subject of football and Hattie had joined in the talk about gardens and now children, and no one was paying them any attention at all. "I want to show Gus Hathaway what I can do when I'm given the chance."

He looked at her closely. "You seem to worry a lot over this Hathaway. Is he someone special to you?"

"Oh, don't be so stupid. I just work with him," she said but she was uneasy and suspected that the fact showed on her face. She'd never been any good at hiding her thoughts, dammit.

"Well, that's as may be. Just tell me, what did you think you were going to get out of that last display?"

She thought hard and then surrendered her common sense, or at least some of it. There was still a possibility that Toby Bellamy was the guilty person she had once feared he was, despite his detailed explanation of why he couldn't be suspected; still a possibility that she was playing into his hands by talking to him. But her gut instinct—intuition? jeered her inner self in Gus's tone of voice—loosened her tongue a little.

"I think Matthew Herne could have been the one who… Well, he's my main suspect."

"Matthew?" He stared. "Why?"

She sighed. "Why should I tell you? You're still one of Gus's suspects and so—"

"And I explained to you the other night why it couldn't be me, and you can't argue with that. There's no logical reason why it should be, so don't be so silly."

"I'm not being silly. I'll tell Gus. Then I'll consider telling you. Fair enough?"

"No, it's not—" he began and then Miles was behind her.

"Was there something wrong, Doctor? I was sorry to see Professor Dieter didn't finish his pudding. It's one he likes a lot, but he left so quickly."

"I'll talk to you about this some other time," Toby said, his mouth rather tight. "You're being singularly—Well, as I say, tomorrow probably, when I see you."

"Perhaps," she said as coolly as she could and turned to Miles as Toby went back down the table to lean over Felicity, "What did you say?"

"I hope everything was all right."

"It's fine, Miles," she said and smiled at him. "Everything was just fine. The duck was great. I'm sorry people left early, but it wasn't because of the food, I do assure you. Look, let me have the final bill as soon as possible, will you? I hate to leave debts unpaid."

"I will," he promised and turned to go. "I'll fetch some more coffee if people want it."

"I'm afraid not," she said regretfully as Felicity came towards her, followed by Hattie and Sam. "I think we're breaking up."

And so they were. It was barely eleven-fifteen but they were murmuring of early starts the next day and thanks for thinking of them (which made her shame come back as she remembered how devious she had been with them all) and wishing her happy birthday (which made her feel worse than ever) and as she shook male hands and kissed warm female cheeks, and a little to her surprise was thoroughly kissed on her own cheeks by Sam and Oliver, a thought nagged and twisted at the back of her mind, filling her with unease and a sense of something not quite right, something not dealt with properly, something she had missed that she shouldn't have done...

Jerry was the last to go, smiling at her broadly with what was a genuinely tipsy expression, thanking her fulsomely for including him, and threatening to topple over into sentimentality at any moment. She despatched him as smartly as she could and then turned back in some relief to Miles and Stephen who were assiduously and unobtrusively clearing the table.

"I'll be off then," she said, moving to the door and then suddenly stopped as memory exploded in her mind. It had been the sight of Miles's face that had triggered it and she hadn't realized till now what it was that had so surprised her.

"Miles!" she said. "You said that the dessert—the pudding was one Professor Dieter liked?"

"Yes, doctor," Miles said. "It seemed a pity, he hardly touched it."

"But I don't understand," she said. "How did you know that?"

Miles looked at Stephen who lifted one eyebrow a millimeter and seemed to nod slightly and Miles turned back to her. "We've cooked for him before."

"Oh!" Her hope, which had started to unfurl itself like a great green fern, faltered. "Here, I suppose. At Old East."

"Oh, no. This is the first time we've worked right in the hospital. I hope we will again. If you like what we did, maybe you'll tell other people here?"

"Of course," she said impatiently. "Of course. But if not here, where?"

"At Mr. Oxford's flat," Miles said. "His—um—his bachelor dinners, you know? Lots of times. Not that guests ever noticed us. But then they wouldn't. Richard liked us to get things ready and keep out of the way and then tidy up. The Professor wouldn't know us because we kept well back. But we know him because we saw them all. We know everyone who used to go to those parties, don't we, Stephen?" He smiled sweetly at George and she saw it, the bright and intermittent spark of malice like a firefly on a Tuscan hillside. "Oh, yes. We know them all."

29

"What's this then? A Bring and Buy in aid of the Distressed Pathologists' Home?" Gus stood in the middle of the room looking at the piles of paper and ribbons on the floor beside the desk and the goods on top of it.

George reddened and pushed out of sight the outrageous scarlet lace underwear of a very Soho sort that had been Jerry's offering. "Presents," she mumbled. "Had to get them opened so that I could sort them out."

"Presents? Is it happy birthday time? You should have said."

"Dammit, no it isn't. That is, it sort of was...It's all a mistake. Well, not exactly a mistake. Anyway, it isn't my birthday so don't you start."

"Whatever it is maybe people are trying to tell you something." He picked up the big bottle of highly scented bath oil that stood on the edge of her desk. "I wouldn't listen if I were you. You stick to your Joy. It suits you."

"Oh, shut up, Gus," she said, and pushed the piles of soap and chocolates and pot plants to one side. "I'll deal with that later. Look, I have to talk to you."

"So you said on the phone," he said and pulled the spare chair away from the wall and plopped himself down on it, turning it so that he could sit astride and rest his folded arms on the back. "Broken the code, have you?"

She grimaced. "No. It's a bastard, that code. I've twiddled and fiddled but it's getting me nowhere. Like I said, you'll have to use the computer. No, this is something else." She stopped and looked at him and then away, not sure how to go on and he laughed.

"Been playing the brilliant amateur, have you? Picked up a few clues my clodhopping coppers missed and want to save my face the way you tell me? I wouldn't worry, ducks. There's not much we miss even if you don't tell me what you're up to."

"It's nothing of the sort! But I have been thinking and—er—well, I've actually done something too." There was a short silence during which he looked at her with raised brows and she sighed and said, "Oh, dammit."

"That won't help. Whatever you've done, 'fess up."

"I'll start with the good news first. I think I know who it is who killed both Oxford and Formby."

"Ah? So you're sure Formby was killed then? He didn't slip?"

"It's not likely, is it? He was used to moving around on that structure. There was no reason why he should suddenly have an accident. And it's too much to think an accident would happen so conveniently so soon after a murder and so soon after he was shown to be a thief with a record."

"I have to agree. So where do we go from here?"

"I think…" She swallowed. "I think the accomplice we talked about—remember? You agreed that the chances were Formby had an accomplice he was stealing for or with—well, it's Matthew Herne."

He looked at her without expression. "What makes you think so?"

"There are all sorts of pointers, and something I only remembered this morning. I'll tell you about that first. You see, Kate Sayers—she's in the renal unit, uses kidney machines and so on—had to buy some gear for her department. She did all the research, sorted it all out with the rep of the British firm she wanted to buy from, sent the papers over to Herne for signing in the usual way, and he suddenly did an about face and told her he'd order it all himself from a cheaper source abroad. She thought it was just to save money, but I reckon he was about to pull another scam. I'm not sure how, but it seems likely. Maybe it's easier to get unmarked goods from abroad so no one would notice when the stuff was stolen and then returned as new gear. We would never have known here if it hadn't been for the paint on the microscope."

"I see. So you think that proves Herne was the one who was stealing and using Formby? When you told Formby you knew what was going on—"

"Formby told Herne he wanted out and tried a bit of blackmail on his own account, said he'd split on Herne unless he let him keep his job and covered up for him—"

"—So Herne killed Formby to protect himself—"

"—and had already killed Oxford because he was being blackmailed by him. That was why he got involved with the thefts in the first place. To pay off Oxford."

"It sounds seductive," Gus said after a moment. "But there's a huge hole in it. How did Herne get the digitalis into the cream and into Oxford's bathroom?"

She was silent for a moment and then grinned. "It seems a very big hole, doesn't it?"

"Well, maybe not." He got up and pulled off his overcoat. "It's getting hot in here, or I'm getting over-excited." He sat down again, walking his chair forwards in little jerks so that he was sitting closer to her. "Maybe we can find a way he could have got to Oxford's place?"

She grinned even more widely. "I think I have."

"Eh?"

"Last night, I gave a party."

"And didn't invite me? Shame on you."

"And pretended to drink too much." He was quiet now and watching her. "I thought I could start a few hares, you know?"

"Did you succeed?"

"I thought I'd failed at first. I'm still not sure. But then— well, let me tell you in order, hmm? At the party I tried to see what would happen if I talked about hookers. Herne got very bothered."

"What was the point of that?"

"I thought perhaps Oxford had been blackmailing Herne about his wife. If she really was a hooker—and it was you who put the idea into my head—"

"Then you did pick up on that? Good on you. Yeah, she was a Tom."

She was diverted. "A what?"

He smiled. "A hooker, ducks. English style."

"Oh, well, anyway, I thought that could have been what Herne wanted kept quiet."

"It makes sense. So you talked about hookers? In the middle of your party?"

"It was awful. I don't suppose any of them'll ever want to speak to me again. But it seemed to me a good way to try it."

"Did it work?"

"He got very uptight. White as a sheet, very bothered."

"That was stupid, you know that?" He sounded very sharp now. "If you really think this man killed two people where's the bleedin' sense in letting him think you know it? Do you want to be pushed off a building site or be plugged with God knows what?"

"I've done worse than that." She tried to sound flippant. "After I talked about hookers I talked about blood tests for HIV."

"HI...Why?"

She sighed a little heavily. "I thought you'd have worked that one out for yourself. It could be that Oxford was killed because he was HIV positive and—"

"I thought it was because he was a blackmailer?"

"—was using his knowledge of other people's HIV status to blackmail them with."

Gus shook his head. "That makes no sense to me. First of all, the fact *he* knew he was positive wouldn't mean he knew about other people being positive. And secondly, isn't it bad enough to know you've got HIV? I mean, what can be worse than thinking you're going to die any minute? So what if people try to blackmail you? It won't do 'em any good for long, or any worse harm to the person being blackmailed than he's already suffered."

"You're quite wrong on that second bit. Not everyone who's HIV positive's going to die any minute. The latency period—the time between getting the infection and showing symptoms of AIDS—can be ten years or more. And even people with AIDS are living longer and longer. By the time some of the newly infected people are at risk of disease there could be an answer, just as there was with syphilis and the other sexual diseases. Plenty of people were blackmailed in the past over syphilis, because that was a killer in its day. So I don't see why a man shouldn't be blackmailing over it now. And as for the first bit, well, yes, I see what you mean. But he might know someone else's HIV status because he'd passed the virus to them. He was bisexual, remember, and very randy from all the signs. That flat! He could have been thoroughly promiscuous and actually created his own blackmail victims. And anyway—" She hesitated and then frowned. "That's odd."

"What is?"

"It's a thought I just had. No, it's ridiculous…"

"You can still spit it out. There's no one here but me to laugh at you."

"I just thought…Listen, there's something else. After the guests had gone, the caterers I'd hired—well, I found out something that startled me a bit."

"Caterers?"

"They're called Castor and Pollux."

"Oh, you mean Danbo and Chapman? I know them. They do most of the local big dos."

"Yes, them. They were good. And they used to do parties for Richard Oxford."

He lifted his chin at that. "Now, that is news to me," he said softly. "I found out other caterers that he used, but not them. So they did parties for Oxford, too. Hmm. What sort of parties?"

"I thought you might ask that." She made a small face. "Pretty much what you'd expect, all-male affairs. The boys say they used to do the food, keep out of the way and had to leave before the entertainment started." She grinned then. "It was rather touching really. They were so shocked by it all. They're gay themselves, of course, but they clearly had a very low opinion of Oxford and his goings-on. He was a good customer so they put up with him but, as they said, he was a nasty piece of work. He'd have all these men to the flat, give them a great dinner and then, after the caterers had left, lay on some sort of unusual entertainment."

"How do they know if they'd left before it happened?"

"I asked that too, never fear. Once they saw someone on the way in, a strip act they knew, and he told them afterwards when they saw him in a pub somewhere that he'd never go back again. And once..." She grinned again. "Stephen, who's the pushier of the two, I suspect, hung around a little longer than he should one night and listened. All very nasty, according to him. But it isn't that that's relevant. It's who was there."

"They told you?"

"They recognized one of the regulars last night. At my party."

"So, put me out of my misery."

She took a deep breath. "Professor Dieter."

There was a long silence and he said slowly, "Charles Dieter was a regular visitor to Oxford's flat?"

"Yes."

"But according to Roop he said he'd never been there before, that night he went to see if Oxford was all right when he failed to turn up at the concert."

"I know. I was there with him, remember? He admired one of the paintings, made a big thing about it. It never occurred to me he'd ever been there."

"You have done well," he said and looked at her with huge approval.

"Delighted to hear you say so. D'you want to know who else was a regular?"

"Of course."

"Matthew Herne." And she was delighted with his reaction. He was clearly riveted by every word she said.

"So that's why you think Herne's in the frame?"

"Yup. And Dieter. It all fits, doesn't it?"

"Seems so. But don't jump to conclusions. Who else used to go to Oxford's parties? Have you more for me?"

"Indeed I have. Dr. Neville Carr."

"Who's he?"

She explained, leaving out no detail of what she had seen in the small hours outside the medical school building, and he nodded, slowly. "So Dieter had an—um—busy private life."

"It would seem so."

"Which gives him a motive, doesn't it? As well as Herne."

"With that wife, I'd say so," George said with some feeling. "She has the money, I'm told, and she's a tough lady. And if she chucked him and told the world about the fact he swung both ways, I think he'd possibly lose his professorial chair."

"It makes him a very likely candidate. Well, well, what can I say? You've been a great help." And he beamed at her.

"Umm," she said, uncomfortably. "I've done something else as well."

"Oh?"

"I've—er—well—" She stopped, not sure how to go on, certain he would not continue to be so pleased with her.

"Is this the ridiculous bit?"

"Eh?"

"You said that you'd had a ridiculous thought."

"Oh! No, that was to do with Charles Dieter." She frowned. "It's a silly sort of long shot, but it suddenly occurred to me that Dieter might be whistling in the wind when he runs those seminars of his. That maybe he's HIV positive himself and that's why he's latched on to this lunatic fringe of people who deny HIV's a causative agent in AIDS."

"You've lost me."

"Sorry." She explained as pithily as she could. "There are people—doctors—who're trying to say AIDS isn't caused by HIV but by other factors, like drug abuse and poor lifestyle. That the fact people who die of the disease have HIV in them doesn't mean it's necessarily the cause of their death. It's daft, in my book, and a lot of people agree with me."

"But Charles Dieter doesn't."

"He gets in these speakers from abroad who say it and argues with those of us who disagree. Well, why should he do that? He's a highly educated man in medical terms, he must know that he's backing a four-flush loser with that one. The best reason I can think of is that he's whistling in the dark."

"Because he's HIV positive and knows it? And wants to deny it matters?" Gus said slowly. "I think that's almost as seductive a theory as your earlier one about Herne."

"Thank you kindly, sir, she said."

"Any time." He sounded a little absent and then his voice sharpened. "You still haven't told me what else it was you did last night. This was your ridiculous thought, which I don't think is, but it doesn't end the story, I gather."

"Ah. No."

He sighed. "Is it that bad?"

"It's very stupid. Maybe I was a bit smashed at that," she admitted. "The thing is I said I had locked up here at the lab copies of all the test results for people who'd asked for HIV tests. All the old ones that had ever been done here as well as the more recent ones."

"You did what?" he said after a long, almost stupefied moment, then his voice rose to a shout. "You bloody did *what?*"

"I said you wouldn't like it. But I thought…Well, one of those people could have been blackmailed for that reason. I'm not sure now whether I don't think Dieter's as likely a candidate as Herne. Last night it was Herne I was after, so that was why I said it. It'd sort of flush him out, I thought. With a wife who's been a—what was it? Tom—he could be vulnerable. But like I said, this morning when I thought about it, I knew you'd be annoyed."

"Annoyed? Annoyed, you silly cow? I could—I could—ye gods, how can a woman be so bleedin' daft?"

"You don't have to go on about it. I admit it was unwise."

"Oh, unwise? Is that what it is, unwise? I thought you'd been daft enough when you started teasing Herne about having a Tom for a wife, but this is absolutely the end. You're not safe out without your mummy, lady."

"OK, OK. You've made your point. Now let's talk about how we use it, eh? It's done, so it's done and I don't think I'll ever take a chance like it again, if that satisfies you, but there it is. I've set a trap with nice bait. How're you going to catch whoever springs it?"

He got to his feet again and began to prowl around the room. She watched, amused. It was gratifying to have had such an effect on him. Up till now, whenever she'd tried to surprise him with information, she'd had the feeling he was at least one step in front of her, but this time she really had got ahead of him, and it was agreeable to see how much he cared that she'd stuck out her neck so far and made herself so vulnerable.

After a while she said cheerfully, "Why not sit down again? It'll get you nowhere, carrying on like that."

"I think better on my feet," he shouted, but came and sat down all the same to glare at her, and she smiled back as sunnily as she could.

"What's done is done, they used to tell me when I was a kid. No good getting into a state over what you can't cure. And anyway, maybe HIV status wasn't the trigger to the blackmail. You could be getting het up over nothing."

"We should be so lucky."

"Get you! Speaking good Brooklyn. OK, OK, you're right. I was wrong. Now what?"

"Who is there?" He reached into his pocket awkwardly and pulled out his notebook. "Let's list the damned possibilities. Then I'll know how to handle 'em. Suspects."

She reached into her own drawer and pulled out the paper she had scribbled that night in the medical school library. "This might be useful," she murmured. "I already did some work along those lines."

"Hmmph. Let's have a look." He sat and read in silence and then nodded and smoothed it on the desk in front of him. "All right. Let's start at the top. Suspects. That's people who could have killed Oxford and/or Formby, had a good reason to, and who were at your bash last night."

"They don't have to have been with me last night."

"The ones I'm worried about do. They're the ones likely to turn up here and rearrange your anatomy if they catch you on your own. Silly cow. It's the only thing I can call you. Silly cow."

"Moo," she said.

"Yeah, well—all right, suspects to be watched. Felicity Oxford, on your list and at your party. On my list too. Obviously top of it. And not only as his wife.She's on that committee too."

"Committee?"

"The fundraisers. For the new children's ward. They were there the afternoon Formby died."

Her eyes widened. "You didn't tell me that."

"I'm telling you now."

"What were they doing there?"

He shrugged. "Don't know. Inspecting where their money went, I imagine. Anyway, it turns out from what May Potter said in her statement that Formby had agreed to meet the committee on site that afternoon, so Felicity Oxford had the opportunity to push him off, if she hung around after the others had left. So she's well and truly in the frame. Now, who else? Toby Bellamy. Well, that's a comfort at least."

"How do you mean?"

"You're not letting love's young dream blur your vision."

"Don't you talk such rubbish," she said furiously. "I'm not in—I mean, there's no question of—"

"Yeah, yeah," he said impatiently. "Let's get on, shall we? Bellamy, in on all three counts. Your list, the party, my list. And could have been at the building site. We can't check all his movements that day. He said he was all over the place, but getting people to corroborate is sheer hell. That applies to a lot of people, not just Bellamy. But he belongs on any shopping list. Then there's Jerry Swann. That one's a surprise to me. But I take your point. It's a meagre motive but it's there. And he had the opportunity and the rest of it. And he was at your party. So he's in on two counts. And, of course, Charles Dieter, since he was there on site when Formby died as well as knowing Oxford's flat well. And who better to play around with digitalis than a professor of medicine? Definitely on the list. Now the rest of 'em. Matthew Herne in on three counts. Yes, he was on my original list too, lady. Don't look so surprised."

"You didn't say."

"I don't have to if I don't choose to. I had him in for the same reasons you did, apart from the bit about knowing Oxford so well. Not that tricky, was it? And his wife? Hmm. That's a thought. Why should she want to kill? How could she? Oh, in case she didn't tell her old man she had a past history that was colorful to say the least? But I doubt that. You said he showed a strong reaction when you talked about married prostitutes last night."

"Very much so."

"Then her place on the list is a pretty weak one. He already knows."

"It's worth putting her there, though, isn't it?"

"Opportunity?"

"I agree, not a lot," she admitted. "Still..."

"Well, she can go on the doubtful list." He scribbled fast. "The people who were at your party, and who heard what you said. Kate Sayers, you told me. Who else was it?"

She listed the rest of the guests and he wrote them in, then snapped the notebook shut and got to his feet. "All right. I'll get on to it, then."

"On to what?"

"Getting you covered, of course. I can't let you just wander around here all Mary-had-a-little-lambish and not have you protected, can I? Someone on this bleedin' list could be turning up to take a pot shot at you, I shouldn't wonder."

"No point, except when I'm here in the lab to give them the forms with their results on them, is there?" she said, trying to sound relaxed, though she had to admit that her pulses were knocking hard against her ears. She hadn't expected him to react quite so seriously to what she knew had been an act of foolishness. Trailing bait for murderers was never wise, to say the least of it. But she had to try to keep her head, however anxious he showed himself to be.

"Hmm," he said and stopped marching about. "Yes, I suppose so." He thought for a while, not taking his eyes from her face, and then nodded sharply. "It'll have to be a stake-out, I suppose."

"Yes," she said with some relish. "I'll tell people I'm working late and sit here and wait for whoever turns up and—"

"Bugger that for a game of soldiers." He was brusque. "If you think I'm going to let you sit here like a goat tied to the stake you're potty. No need. I'll have a policeman to do it."

"No you won't—" she began but he shouted her down.

"I do what I choose, lady, and don't you forget it. You can be in the car with us. See what happens."

She was mollified at once and to tell the truth deeply relieved. She would have hated to miss the end of the case, but at the same time was not stupid enough to want to expose herself to real harm. She had a sudden mental picture of Formby's body on the mortuary slab and the range of his injuries and shuddered. It might be a commonplace sight in her life but not when she applied the possibility to herself.

"You're on," she said. "What, when and how and—"

"Tonight and with unmarked cars and I really could hit you—you—you—" He threw up his hands in despair and went to fetch his coat which was in a heap on the floor where he'd left it. "I don't often get lost for words, but you really are the—Well, let it be. Don't stay here after the others have gone, whatever you do. Wait for me. I'll pick you up in the residence at, oh…" He looked at his watch. "Say at six? It's getting dark by then and we'll have to make a night of it. I'll behave like a nice date, then, OK?" He grinned suddenly, showing all his teeth. "And mind your manners. I only take ladies out, not silly cows. I'll see you at six." And he went, slamming the door behind him.

30

She was ready well before six, dressed in a pair of black leggings under close-fitting black boots and with a black polo-necked sweater under a thick ski jacket, also in black. She felt like something from the Addams family, but had an obscure notion that being as invisible as possible would be an asset even though she'd be hidden away inside a police car. Really, of course, she wanted to impress Gus Hathaway with her common sense, because she knew perfectly well just how stupid she had been to trail her coat quite so outrageously. Whoever had committed these crimes was dangerous, and had little to lose from trying to kill again if he or she felt it necessary; why had she been so arrogant as to think it was up to her to flush out such a person? To impress Gus Hathaway, her secret voice jeered and she almost blushed at the thought. Was there no end to her liking for male attention? Probably not, she thought mournfully and went to the residents' sitting room to wait for Gus to collect her.

There were two or three of the doctors there, mostly sleeping beneath copies of the *BMJ* or the *Lancet*, though one, a highly industrious Indian who was famous for never reading anything but proctology text books, was engrossed as usual at the corner desk. She was glad there was no one she'd have to talk to; she was nervous and was sure it showed. If one of the suspects came in and started to talk to her, she wouldn't know what to do. She almost got up and went out again to wait by the front entrance to avoid the risk, when Toby Bellamy put his head around the sittingroom door. She was sitting in a high-backed chair facing the other way, towards the fireplace where a two-bar electric fire glowed in a dispirited fashion, and saw his reflection in the mirror above it. She stiffened but then relaxed as he went away, and wasn't sure whether he'd gone because he'd seen her and didn't want to be where she was, or whether he was actually looking for her and hadn't observed her there. She suspected it was the former, and why not? She had after all refused to tell him why she had behaved as she had at her dinner party and that must have offended him deeply if, that is, he was innocent. If he was the murderer of course, it put a whole different complexion on it. She sighed and stared miserably at the fire, all too painfully aware of how complicated her feelings were getting about this man. If only I weren't so susceptible, she told herself, how easy life would be. Just death and disaster to think about, rather than life and love. Ah well.

Gus turned up precisely on time and lifted an eyebrow when he saw how she was dressed. "Commando, are we? Very nice," he murmured and led the way out to the car. "As long as you're warm. It's bloody cold out, considerin' it's supposed to be spring. There'll be a frost tonight, shouldn't wonder. It'll ruin my garden."

"Garden? You live in a flat."

"Got window boxes, haven't I? Never was a Londoner who didn't grow something around the place. Famous for it, we are. Now, settle down and make yourself at home. You'll be there a while, I reckon. There's a packet of sandwiches in the back pocket and I brought a flask of coffee."

She looked over the back of the seat at Michael Urquhart and said demurely, "Good evening, Mr. Urquhart," and he, looking ahead, said nothing but nodded his acknowledgement.

"You don't have to be so formal," Gus said as he got into the front passenger seat, next to Urquhart. "Call him Mike.

We'll be spending a lot of time together tonight so we might as well be comfortable."

"Then you must call me George, Mike," she said, as Urquhart put the car into gear and moved off into the main road traffic. "Rather than Dr. B., which tends to be used by quite a lot of people."

"Oh, get you," Gus said easily. "Very fussy, aren't we? You should ha' said sooner, Georgie girl."

"I said call me George, never Georgie. I hate that."

"Then settle for Dr. B. On account of I find it easier. Look, Mike, down there, you see? There's an alley marked 'Private No Entry.' Slide in there. You can park in easy view of the back of the path lab and not be seen."

The car went further along the main road and after twenty yards or so turned left into the narrow street Gus had pointed out, and then turned left again and rattled a little as it went over the uneven surface of a very narrow entry. It was the way the mortuary vans came in, George realized, and was embarrassed that she'd never come out on this side of her department before. She'd just accepted that the mortuary vans bearing corpses had their own special entrance, and had settled for using the usual way in from the main hospital premises. That there was a back entry was obvious, of course, but she'd never thought about it before. Had the murderer? she found herself wondering as Mike ed the car into a dim space that gave them a clear view of the mortuary entrance. There was no reason why any of the senior hospital staff should ever come this way; maybe sitting here was a total waste of time, and whoever it was would try to get into the building from the other side.

She said as much to Gus who sighed a little theatrically. "You must think I'm ever so stupid," he said. "Of course I know about the front entrance. Isn't it the one I usually use? We're here because we can't park a bleedin' great car on the other side where anyone wanderin' by can see it, and because we've got a coupla fellas there anyway. Morley and Haggerty.

They're in touch with us." And almost as though they'd been listening a voice crackled over the radio.

"We're settled in, Guv. You too?"

"We're here. Now keep quiet and sit tight. If you see anything, give us the wire. But not otherwise."

"We'd sit if we could, Guv." The voice sounded plaintive. "Only there isn't anywhere we can. It's all right for some."

"Stop whingeing," Gus said. "And shut up."

The car settled into silence and George huddled down into the collar of her ski jacket. The heater had stopped running as soon as the car engine was switched off, and now the windows were beginning to mist over a little with their breath, and Gus reached out and partly opened the window on his side, letting in a blast of cold air.

"Sorry," he muttered. "Got no choice. No use being here if we can't see anything. You all right back there?"

"I'm all right," she said. "Though I'm not sure what the hell I'm doing here."

"Same as us. A stake-out. Waiting to see if anyone turns out to pick up your bait. And I don't know why you're moaning. You're the one insisted on being here."

She pretended not to have heard that and was silent for a while. Then she said, "Wouldn't it speed things up if I went to the canteen and had supper and then very obviously went over the courtyard to the lab? I could tell anyone I met I'd be there, and—"

"Oh, what a lovely idea! Maybe you ought to run up a flag on the roof to let everyone know you're in residence, like the Queen does at Buckin'am Palace, eh? Be your age, Dr. B."

She saw Matthew Urquhart's shoulders move a little in the darkness and knew he had almost laughed and sat back again, furious. It had been a silly suggestion perhaps, but it was getting cold in here and it was already boring. She sneaked a look at her watch and was amazed. It was only half past six. She felt she'd been there for hours. They were there for hours.

They ate the sandwiches, which were rather dreary. ("From the canteen at the nick, Guv," Mike Urquhart told the disgusted Gus apologetically. "I didn't have the chance to go down to the sandwich bar.") They drank the excellent coffee. ("I go to the trouble to make my own," Gus said smugly, "it wouldn't have hurt you to make more of a try," at which injustice Urquhart looked as though he were about to burst into tears.) After that, nothing. If she spoke Gus hissed at her that they had to stay quiet, since they didn't know who might turn up or where, and it was too dark to see very much with which to entertain herself. So she sat and breathed her little clouds of mist and watched them disappear and wondered if it would be possible to fall asleep in so cold an environment, and was sure that bored though she was, she couldn't manage that.

But at midnight, she woke from a half-doze to hear Gus whisper, "I've got to go for a slash. Hold the fort, Mike," and the door of the car opened quietly and he slipped out. She lay there against the back of the seat, not moving, still not sure whether she was in fact fully awake, and turned her head to stare vaguely out of the right-hand window beside her at the various shades of blackness which were all there was to see.

Some of the darkness moved, shimmered, and became lighter and she thought dreamily, Gus, going for his pee, and wondered whether she ought perhaps to turn her head away or close her eyes, but that would be effortful and rather silly. One of the good things about being a doctor, and perhaps especially a pathologist, was no longer being bedeviled by the foolish modesty and embarrassment experienced by the majority, so she stayed as she was, still lost between sleep and full alertness.

Until the darkness moved again and this time she thought, Not Gus. Doesn't move like Gus. Not Gus. And knew whom she thought it was almost without thinking the name. It was as though he'd called her, shouted out, "Hi there, George! Here I am, it's me, here I am."

She moved then with a sharp little jerk, sitting bolt upright and staring out of the window with her eyes narrowed to get in as much detail as she could and Mike looked over his shoulder and said sharply, "Whassa matter?" and she knew that he too might have been half asleep.

"There's someone there," she hissed and he turned his own head to look where she was and then shook it.

"It's the Guv'nor. He'll be back in a moment."

"No, it isn't," she said and then the car door opened and Gus slipped back into place.

"What's up?" He stared over his shoulder at George, frowning. "What—"

"I saw someone out there."

"Me, probably. Obeyin' the call of nature," he said. "A real lady wouldn't have looked."

"Where were you? This side?" She looked out again to the right. "Because that's where I saw someone, and you wouldn't have had time to get back on your side."

Gus was immediately alert. "You saw who?"

"I'm not sure," she said and somewhere in the depths of her mind her secret voice shouted, Goddamn liar, you know you do, but she ignored it. And anyway, she wasn't sure, not to be *certain* sure.

"Keep watching," Gus said and again slipped out of the car, so quietly she was hardly aware of the door opening. Obediently she sat peering out into the darkness till her eyes began to tingle and water; but she saw nothing else.

Gus came back and leaned into the car, speaking in a normal voice. "Mike, there's no one I can see. But the back door, I left it with a marker and the marker's moved. Call up Morley and Haggerty, Morley to go in, Haggerty to stay where he is. You stay here, I'll go in. Call in for more support on your own judgement. Dr. B., you wait here." And he went.

But she wasn't going to agree to that. She moved as fast as he had and was out of the car and beside him almost before he'd turned around to move towards the back entrance of the mortuary. He looked at her and opened his mouth to argue, but then produced a half-shrug and went on, saying nothing. She followed him.

The back door of the mortuary was closed, and in front of it, on the door sill, she could see a pale sliver that seemed to be a piece of wood. His marker, she thought, that had been disturbed? Probably; and then Gus slid his hand down the panels and stopped at the keyhole. "Arrogant bastard," he breathed. "Just left it here. Stay out, for God's sake." He opened the door and slipped inside.

And for a moment she obeyed, standing still on the step as the familiar smell of the place came out to her: the pineappley reek of the Festival disinfectant Danny used to clean the place; and rubber aprons; and formaldehyde; and, deep down, the ominous stink of death. She listened hard, but heard nothing.

It was the silence which unnerved her. Had there been breathing or even the hint of movement from inside the long corridor ahead, she'd have been able to stay where she was, but the thick cotton-wool blackness was too much to bear. She moved with a sharp little action that was almost convulsive and went in, moving along the invisible corridor without any anxiety, for she could see it clearly in her mind's eye: see the trolleys parked at the left-hand side; see the rows of crates of reagents and other bottled materials they kept there; the doors that led to the shower and Danny's bolt-hole and the mortuary room itself; the rows of drawers on the right-hand side that stored the corpses; and beyond that the double-doored entrance to the lobby that led to the staircase. She imagined Gus ahead of her, visualized him moving a good deal less surely than she was herself towards the stairs, climbing them, feeling the chill that always came down from the building above, and trying to see who might be there ahead of him. And if it was who she thought she'd seen? What then? But it wasn't to be thought of. She just had to follow and wait and see.

When it happened it was so sudden and so loud that she felt her belly contract hard and for a dreadful fraction of a moment feared she'd be sick, or worse, but then she was running headlong into the blackness towards the noise.

A light exploded into vivid life. She blinked and squinted ahead, and saw the door to the staircase lobby swinging. There was a movement beyond it and more noise and a loud shriek and she ran the last few steps with legs so shaky they felt as though they belonged to someone else. She pushed the double doors open by almost falling on them.

Above her, about halfway down the stairs, there was Morley, belting as hard as he could for the bottom. At the foot of the stairs Gus was lying flat on his back, and shaking his head in confusion and trying to get to his feet; between the two of them there were two figures, one sitting on top of the other with an arm uplifted, and she stared at what seemed for an incredible moment to be a still life. There was no movement, just the whole scene imprinted on her retinas like a photographer's flash light. She tried to blink, not knowing if she could, and slowly her lids covered her eyes and rose again and with the action came movement. Morley hurled himself down the stairs to the pair of people between himself and Gus; the arm of the upper of the couple came down and made a vicious crunching sound as it connected with human tissue; and Gus was up and reaching forward just as Morley got there and pulled the upper figure away, wrenching hard at the arm which had come up again and was once more trying to connect with the body beneath.

Both men were shouting and then there were thudding feet from above and below as Haggerty appeared at the top of the stairs and almost leapt down to assist Morley, and Mike Urquhart came up behind George and pushed her aside to get to Gus. The new arrivals both had their radios clamped to them, which were chattering and rattling raucously as the men shouted unintelligibly into them; and then at last there was some sort of order. Morley and Haggerty were standing with their captive held hard between them, Urquhart was on his knees beside the figure on the ground which was producing loud and angry sounds and Gus was standing holding on to the bottom newel post of the stairs, swaying slightly and peering at the person who was staring back at him from between the two detective constables.

"Good God," he said. "Good God!"

George stared too, and wanted to speak, but couldn't. The chin that had dropped a little as Morley pulled on one arm lifted and the wide eyes looked directly at her over Gus's head, and she felt icy shock fill every part of her. She was looking at Beatrice Dieter.

From then on the noise was indescribable. Morley and Haggerty were speaking to Beatrice Dieter, cautioning her, asking her if she understood, but she stared at them woodenly, saying nothing at all; Mike was shouting into his radio for an ambulance while Gus roared at him not to be so stupid, they'd get a trolley over from the hospital main building; and the body on the floor went on bellowing as George, freed at least from the immobility into which shock had frozen her, was able to come and kneel beside it and touch with careful fingers the blood-spattered forehead.

"Toby, you schmuck," she said, not knowing how the words were coming out of her. "Toby, you dumb sonofabitch, what do you think you were doing here on your own? Are you crazy or what? Don't touch that, I'll fix it. Wait' She felt for his pulse, then ran her fingers over his head, terrified she'd find the sponginess that meant bony injury, but he was alert and far from behaving as though he had been knocked out; there was more rage than pain in the noise he was making. She took his shoulder and shook on it and bawled, "Will you shut up," as suddenly more police arrived, seeming to come down the stairs and along the corridor like a small tide.

"It's all your fault, you bloody idiot!" Toby yelled at her. "All your fault. I came here to keep an eye on you and stop you getting your head stoved in and look at me, you stupid—"

"I know," she shrieked back. "If you don't shut up, I'll hit you myself. Leave that alone, damn you, keep your filthy hands down. I'll fix it." And then there was an A & E trolley there and a couple of porters and they were pushing her aside as politely as it was possible to do and lifting him on to it.

She went to follow them as they pushed the trolley out towards the entrance that led to the main hospital when behind her Gus said plaintively, "I was bashed too, you know."

She looked back over her shoulder. He had indeed been bashed: there were three sharp lines down his left cheek where he'd been scratched and blood was trickling from them. His forehead had a bulge on it that was beginning to turn blue, and there was a graze over one cheekbone. He lifted his brows in a self-deprecating gesture and said a little awkwardly, "What's more I'd be grateful to get these scratches sorted as fast as possible. It's almost certain, you see, that Beatrice Dieter is HIV positive and I'd as soon not take any chances."

31

"Of course come in," Gus said, standing up and pulling out a chair for her. "It's good of you to come in, seein' I've been too busy to come to you. And I'm glad to see you on account of I wanted to say ta for getting my face sorted so fast. I was a bit bothered about the risks, and I won't pretend I wasn't."

"According to her it wouldn't have made any difference anyway," George said and sat down. "Not that you needed to worry. I examined her very carefully indeed." She laughed then a little ruefully. "Arguing all the way, of course. But I did, and she had no injuries at all. There was no way any of her body fluids got into those scratches, so fear you not. You're not infected, I'm quite certain."

"Hmm," he said. "Am I supposed to be grateful for that?" He touched his face gingerly. The cheek was swollen now, and his eye was puffy above it. He looked very unappetizing and she smiled at him warmly. There was something particularly endearing about Gus Hathaway in this state.

"No. You had a nasty time at her hands, and I'm the one who's grateful you've not been damaged any further, seeing it was my fault you were exposed to the injury in the first place."

"I'd like to agree with you and make you feel bad, but I can't." He shook his head. "There was no better way to sort this one. We could have gone on for ever fossicking about looking for evidence that put her in the right place at the right time and we'd never have found it. As it was you with your daft bait-trailing gave me the case on a plate."

"The way I gave you the murder in the first place." She couldn't resist it.

"Well, no need to go on about that," he said. "Listen—"

She interrupted him. "I just came to say thanks for, well, thanks for being there that night. I know now if I'd tried to go for it on my own she'd have—Well, I don't know what would have happened. And also'—she tried to look severe—"also because you've not been available on the phone when I've phoned, and the hospital's *alive* with gossip—you should just hear Sheila—and anyway there's a lot I want to know."

"Sorry about not being free to talk," he said. "But there it is, had to put the job first. Daft, 'n't it? Anyway, you're here now, so we can talk. And I've got questions, too, so listen. When you examined her, did you get the impression of a madwoman? I thought she was barking mad when I interrogated her. She looks at you so weirdly, and there's something about the way she sits. Ramrod isn't in it. On the tape she sounds cool enough but from where I was sitting…" He shook his head. "Like I said. Barking."

"Oh, you're wrong there. She's sane enough. I'm not an expert in psychiatric pathology, I can't deny—though I'm going to do some work in that field. It'll be useful—but I'd say she was well aware of what she was doing, and that's the definition of sanity. She's got some mad ideas of course, but she's not alone in that."

"Like HIV doesn't cause AIDS?"

"Yup. That was why she was so afraid her own HIV status would get out."

He sharpened. "She said that?"

"Not in so many words," she admitted. "But it's obvious, isn't it? Why else would she go to such lengths to keep it quiet? She wasn't scared of the infection itself because she'd swallowed her husband's theories hook, line and the rest of it.

But she must have cared about it for other reasons—social, maybe? I don't know, of course, but—"

"There's a good deal to this case that you don't know about," he said, and grinned at her, and then winced as the movement hurt his stiff face. "Like for example how she found out she was HIV positive at all."

"I hadn't thought about that." She was annoyed with herself "But you're right. Why on earth would such a woman get herself tested? Unless…Did she have an affair with Oxford? Is that how she got it? It seems unlikely, but maybe not." She brooded for a moment. "You never can tell about people's sex lives. The most dreary-looking wimps turn out to be very exotic sexual athletes and gorgeous creatures who look like walking hormone banks are as potent and randy as—as dead fish."

He looked interested. "Really? Give me a for example. Or tell me what you think I'm like."

"I'll do nothing of the sort," she said primly. "You tell me how she found out she was HIV positive."

He sighed. "It wasn't easy getting this stuff out of her. She's got a sharp lawyer who wanted her to stay shtoom, but she wasn't having it. She wanted to tell us stuff, but only what she wanted to part with."

"If you'd let me be there when you did the interview, I bet I could have got her talking. She talked to me in her cell when I examined her there."

"Be your age, ducks! You know you're not allowed in on police interviews. Haven't you forgotten PACE? Police and Criminal Evidence Act?"

"Of course I haven't. But I still wish I could have. You could have had me there as an observing police surgeon if you'd wanted."

"I didn't. You'd have meddled. Asked questions."

"Of course!"

"So I was right not to. Anyway, she did talk when she wanted to. Her lawyer couldn't prevent her. And I know a good deal about it all now, to add to the material we'd already collected. The rest, the bits I'm not sure about, we reckon can be filled in before we get this one to trial. But we've got a case."

"So tell me! 'More matter with less art.'"

"Hamlet. Act two, scene two." He grinned and again winced. "OK. She's known Oxford for a long time. She was the one who got him on board to help the fundraising, it seems, and they became very friendly. It was because of this charity that her old man went to the dinner parties, by the way. He used to go to them and leave before the entertainment, it turns out. It was just—oh, a political thing. So your Castor and Pollux got it somewhat wrong, didn't they? Anyway she knew Oxford and I mean that in the Biblical sense. She slept with him. She gets very agitated when she talks about him. I don't think it was all it might have been for her. Anyway the test. Her old man got hold of this theory about HIV not causing AIDS and she got interested too. She's a biologist, remember, not a doctor of medicine, but one of her specialities it seems is immune systems in animals and the epidemiology of animal infections. Did you know that? There, you see! You don't know everything! Anyway, as I say, she got interested. Then about two, three years ago he said he'd do some research, take a lot of bloods, test 'em, and see how many people who were supposed to get AIDS didn't. He needed controls, though."

She nodded, suddenly seeing it all click into place. "Of course he did. Whatever bloods he took from people known to be positive or thought to be, he had to have a matching set of people with no risks at all."

"And he asked his wife to be one of the controls."

"And she agreed?"

"Yes. But she told Oxford she was going to, and he warned her not to, seeing he knew something she didn't. She was— well, incandescent with fury when she told us that. She would be, wouldn't she? He insisted she have a test done separately first; and it turned out she was positive. So she was frantic."

"In case her husband found out?"

"Exactly."

"But I thought it was the other way about! He was the one who always let her get her own way, she was the one with the money, the hard and tough one. Everyone thought she was the controller, not him."

"She adores him," Gus said and shook his head. "It's like you said. You never know about other people's lives. She says he's a great man, a very important man, and she'd do nothing to lose him or even upset him, and when I asked her why, in that case, she slept with Oxford, she got cagey. I got the impression—it's only an impression, mind, not hard evidence—that great man though her Charlie is, brilliant though his mind may be, when it comes to more earthy matters like sex he's not quite up to scratch. Oxford got her fuddled with cannabis one night—yes, I know it sounds all very old fashioned and Sixties, but she's a Sixties girl, after all—and there it was. She slept with him. And when Oxford told her she might be positive she thought Charlie'd find out what she'd been up to. And she was terrified."

George shook her head. "I still don't see it. If she knew she was positive and refused to have the test—"

"But she didn't," Gus said softly. "That's the point. She couldn't. Her precious Charles would have been very put out if she'd refused, and she didn't know what to do. So she made a deal with Oxford."

"What sort of deal?"

"To arrange for her blood to be taken and tested, but the records to be falsified. So that Charles would never know."

"But how could Oxford arrange that? I mean—"

Gus shook his head sadly. "The people in that hospital of yours—Oxford really had as tight a hold on some of them as you could—well, it was Royle."

She stared, blankly, unable to place the name for a moment and he said gently, "Your predecessor."

"Good God!"

"He was being blackmailed by Oxford too. So he did what he was told."

George got to her feet and began to wander around the office. Gus stayed sitting at his desk and watched her happily, enjoying the way she moved but enjoying her puzzlement even more. "I never found a hint of that," she said. "No one ever said anything about Royle that..." She shook her head. "Have you talked to him? Or haven't you had time?"

"Not yet. But Roop'll be on his way to Spain to interview him tomorrow. He retired to one of those awful seaside places, poor bugger, like Eldorado." He shook his head. "Imagine having to live somewhere like that when you've lived in Shadwell so long."

"Yes," she said and looked at him sideways, and they both laughed. "But you think it's true?"

"Oh, it's true all right. And when you said that you had the blood test results in the lab she went spare, she said. Well, not in so many words, you understand, but upset enough. She'd gone to all the trouble to get rid of Oxford and Formby Mitchell and then you go and ruin it all!"

"She admitted to killing them?" George said with some awe and he nodded.

"Just like we worked it out. Knew about Oxford's rearend problems—they were close, after all!—and decided to use digitalis to deal with him. Got it from the pharmacy, filled her own tube of cream there too. I have to check with them, but it seems a couple of years back, which was when all this business started, she'd arranged via Charles to use the pharmacy to make up some tubes of cream for some of her animal testing at the University. No one remembered when I questioned 'em at the pharmacy; all new staff since then. They've got a bloody fast turnover."

"Not unusual in hospital departments," George said.

"Right. Easy as pickin' blackberries for her, it was."

"But why should she kill Formby?" George said. "It seems over the top, to put it at its lowest."

"She had to. He knew all about her involvement with Oxford. She told me. I tell you, once she started telling there was no way I could stop her. She dotted every T and crossed every I. And drew fancy scroll-lines 'round 'em. He and Oxford were oddly close, it seems. When a man pays as much blackmail as Formby did, he gets to be a favored pet of his bloodsucker. Well, that didn't surprise me. It's a bit of criminal psychology, that is." He looked pleased with himself. "I learned all about that yonks ago. Anyway, there wasn't much Formby didn't know about Beatrice, or so she said. And even if he hadn't, she couldn't take any risks, could she? So when she saw him after the committee's outing on the building site, on their own, and he told her he thought it was she who'd done for Oxford, she did, she said, the only thing she could. She pushed him off the walkway." He shook his head in some wonderment. "She was amazingly cool, giving us all this. You'd have been fascinated."

"I'm sure I should. Chance would have been a fine thing," George said. "I'd have loved seeing her in full flood."

"I know. But you'll have to take my word for it. Amazin' wasn't the word. She'd got it all worked out, you know. That's why she wasn't too worried about telling us all there was to tell. She's got no fears about how it'll all turn out for her. Told me as cool as you please that once they get her to prison she'll have time to write her book. It's going to be the greatest book ever, she said, full of scholarship, that will finally prove everything Charles says about HIV and AIDS is true, and he'll be so pleased and happy when she gets out. It won't be long, she said, because of course she'll get time off for good behavior, and naturally she'll be paroled early, an intelligent woman like her, so taking it all 'round things could be worse. It was an incredible performance." He shook his head reminiscently. "Like I told you. Mad."

"Maybe, maybe not. Maybe she really does believe—Well, never mind. Listen, Gus, what about May?"

"May?"

"Formby's secretary. I told you all the stuff he told me about her when I found out the scam he was using via the microscope thefts."

His stiff face moved into a painful grin again. "She should be so lucky!"

"Eh?" "She'd have loved all that to be true, I imagine, but it wasn't. Airy-fairy persiflage on Formby's part, that was, designed to fool you."

"It didn't." She tried to sound indignant, but then had to be honest. "Well, perhaps a bit." She sighed at her own stupidity in letting Formby fool her so successfully and sat down again on the chair in front of his desk. "So we've got all the answers? Beatrice was responsible for everything?"

"No, Oxford was." He was silent then, staring out of his window at the gray April sky pressing against the grimy panes. "It's not for me to make decisions about how evil people should be dealt with, but that man was as foul as they come. He was blackmailing people left right and center. He deserved what happened to him. If I had my way I'd let her off what she did to him. What she did to Mitchell Formby was different. He was a nasty bit of work, but not horrible with it, know what I mean? He was just a stupid bugger who thought he was clever and got caught. So she can do time for him and welcome. But not for Oxford. Christ, but I hate blackmailers!" There was a fire in him that startled her. And then warmed her. It was a sentiment she could admire.

There was a short silence as they both sat thinking and then she said suddenly, "I'd almost forgotten. The code. We didn't need it after all."

He looked at her blankly for a moment and then laughed. "Oh, yes, the code. It was like you said. Like I said too, of course. Very simple. She knew it. There wasn't much that wicked old besom didn't know. Oxford used to tell her a lot, I gather, she was sort of a confidante as well as someone to play games with under his fancy mirrored ceiling." He laughed again. "I have to say imagining what those two looked like when they were fooling around ain't easy."

"I'd rather not try," George said. "The code. How simple? I swear I tried everything I could, and most of my ideas were very simple indeed."

"I'll show you." He leaned forward. "Give me that file there—the one on top of the tray—yes, that's it." He riffled in the file for a moment or two and pulled out a sheet of paper. "Here it is. Now look. Y.J. £2,000; S.P. £3,000; K.K. £1,000; G.J. £5,000; R.H.A. £2,500; U.H.R. £500; G.I. £5,000. Looks impossible, doesn't it? But just look at the sums rather than the initials. Look especially at the ones that include a half-thousand—five hundred. See what I mean?"

She looked and then said, "They're the ones with the H in the middle."

"Got it. Try H for half."

"Oh, no! It can't be that easy. Can it?"

"It can and it is. Look, all you do is look at the number of thousands owed and move that number in the alphabet. So Y.J. owes £2,000? Fine. The real initials are two letters back. Which gives you, um, W.H. Then you look at the ones that are less than a thousand, OK? This one—U.H.R. £500. For people who owed less than a thousand, he went the other way in the alphabet. So we have to go forwards to read it, which gives us V.S. as the proper initials—leaving out the H of course because that means just a half, five hundred."

"Well, it sounds all right," she said dubiously. "But how will you prove it?"

"We already have. It's been three days, remember, since we arrested her. Lots of time to get ourselves together. We've interviewed all the people on the hospital staff who have these initials. Several of them are here—like the one who appears as K.K. She's Jo Jennson in the accounts department. She'd been up to a bit of naughtiness on her own behalf, squeezing cash out of the system, and Oxford found out. Don't ask me how—I don't know yet. But she had a boyfriend and he liked to talk a lot, and he was one of Oxford's dinner party crowd, so—anyway, however he did it he was having a great time with her, getting her to go on with her tricks to his benefit. And he milked her hard. She was relieved, really, to pour it all out. She'd been scared witless when he was killed, thought whoever did it could have started a bit of blackmailing on his own account and was going almost potty waiting for the ax to fall, as it were. We—ah—I'm not sure we'll follow this up too hard. Like I said, I hate blackmailers, and Jennson's had a nasty fright. She will go and sin no more, take it from me."

"And Mitchell Formby? He was paying blackmail, so why wasn't he on the coded list?" She bent her head to look again. "Because he isn't, is he?"

"No, but that's because this isn't the only disc, remember? Oxford had several for much larger sums of money. He was lazy with this one—they were such small sums, in his estimation, that he didn't even bother to disguise them all that carefully in his records. This was an easily breakable code, after all."

"You didn't manage it till Beatrice told you, though, did you? So don't be so full of yourself."

He grinned. "Nor did you, lady. Anyway, our computer chaps have been working on all the other discs. They found Mitchell Formby there. He was worth over two hundred thousand a year to Oxford, would you believe? He really was stealing wholesale."

"No wonder the hospital's always so short of money!" George said. "How could he get so much from stolen gear?"

"It was more than that. He had a padded payroll, too, Beatrice said. Lots of non-existent people were paid salaries that went right into his pocket, and so on to Oxford's. It all mounts up, I suppose."

"And Herne?"

Gus shook his head. "Not a thing against him. The only complaint about the chap is that he's got his pants on fire for a wife he's ashamed of. Poor devil. The only sin he commits is to skive off early to get in the sack with her. No, he had nothing to do with any of this. He's even put in to Oxford's lawyer already for money he reckons Oxford owed the Barrie Ward Fund and had held on to. He's the soul of virtue in every department except when it involves his personals. Poor sod." He shook his head. "You've got to feel sorry for a bloke who's led by his balls the way that one is. But otherwise, good as gold."

"Hang on a minute," George said. "You mean that Oxford collected money for the Fund and kept it in his own account? But surely he knew he'd be caught if he did that? And anyway he was so rich already, why—"

"He just loved money. For its own sake as well as for what it bought him. He hung on to every penny as long as possible, according to Beatrice, so he could earn interest on it."

"Ye gods," George said, awed. "It must be hell to like money that much."

"Yes," Gus said and then laughed, though it stretched his face and made him wince. "Maybe I ought to give all mine away to protect my soul from getting the infection."

"Maybe you should." She was only half joking.

He shook his head. "I'll have to think about that. Anyway, that's all about Herne, and his Carole. She was clear too. Just a rather greedy featherhead."

She swallowed, not wanting to ask the next question, but knowing she had to. "And Felicity?"

"Felicity," he said and sat silent, brooding for a while. She watched him and waited, wishing it didn't matter so much that he gave her the sort of answer she wanted to hear. Then he sighed. "There's nothing against her. She knew what he was up to but she had no part of it. There's no sin in that, nor any crime. She's got what she wanted out of it all, though."

"And what's that?" She tried to sound light but it wasn't easy. This was not what she had wanted to be told.

"Money, ducks. A lot of it. She felt much as he did about it. Likes it lots. He'll have left—God, I dunno, it runs into millions, according to the computer chaps. Even after they've taken death duties and so forth off it she'll be comfortably settled."

George frowned. "Can a person benefit from the money left by a blackmailer?"

"Yes," Gus sounded hard suddenly. "Yes, she bloody well can. Don't think I haven't tried to find out and do something about it, but the thing is he was never caught or tried in his lifetime, she was in no way involved though she suspected his activities, and we can't prove she knew, nor can she be tried for that. So no crime's officially committed and she gets the lot. Sickening, isn't it?"

"Yes," she said and thought for a while. And then had to ask him the hardest question of all. "And what about—er—" and could go no further.

"Your friend Bellamy is of no interest to anyone in this case," Gus said. He didn't look at her, but kept his head down as, moving carefully, he put the sheet of paper with the computer disc code on it back into his file. "There's nothing but what you see with him as far as I can tell, though he was there at the lab of course. That was a bit of a facer."

"He wanted to protect me," she said in a small voice. "He heard me do that stupid thing at my party."

"Which we found out for ourselves. Yes. So, there it is. No one else has any involvement in this. Not your Jerry Swann, nor Neville Carr, whose only problem is he's gay and doesn't want it known. It was all down to Beatrice. Who'd ha' thought it?"

"Ah," she said and left it at that and then smiled at him. "Not me," she said, and there was another long silence. She stretched. "Got a cup of coffee for me?"

"What, now? It's almost time to knock off for the day! I got a better idea. Give me another half-hour and I'll be clear here. I'll take you to the best fish-and-chip restaurant on the patch and give you the best bit of halibut you ever had. What do you say to that?"

She got to her feet. "Sorry, Gus. Not tonight. I—er—I have a date."

"Oh. Anyone I know?"

"None of your business!" she said. "You've no right to ask."

"Course I have. Aren't I battered to hell and back, all because you couldn't keep your big mouth shut at a party? Don't I deserve a bit of attention from you in consequence?"

"You didn't go and hang around the lab on your own just to keep an eye on me, and you didn't get battered as badly as—"

"As your date did, right?"

"Well, so what if it is Toby? I don't have to ask your permission to go out with him, do I?"

"No, of course you don't. It's just that—Oh, well, Dr. B., I'll be seeing you around, I suppose. Next case, eh?"

He stood up, came around his desk and walked to the door with her. "Give my regards to Bellamy, then. Lucky sod. But there, I dare say I'll get over it. I'll spend the night crying into my beer, and dream of the might-have-been. Yes, Roop, what is it? Can't you see I'm busy?"

Dudley had put his head around the door and was regarding them both with a somewhat owlish expression. He came right in and looked from one to the other. "Well, this is handy, I must say. Saves me putting out a call. We've got a real beauty for you, doctor. Two this time."

"Two?" Gus said. "Two what?"

"Bodies," Rupert said, grinning from ear to ear. "In a basement down the river end of Wapping High Street. Been there a couple of days, I shouldn't wonder. Shall I get you a separate car, doctor, or will you go down with the Guv?"

She looked at Gus and he looked at her, and he lifted both

hands in a gesture of helplessness. She sighed and shoved her hands deep into her pockets. "I'll go with the Guv," she said. "And you, Roop, can bloody well send for my bag to the lab. Because surprise, surprise, I don't have it with me."

"That's what I like about you, Dr. B.," Gus said as he held the door open for her with elaborate ceremony, even a small bow. "You sort of bring life's surprises with you. Well, shall we go? Pity about poor Dr. Bellamy having to wait for you, 'n't it?" She threw him a withering glare and marched out.

And Gus followed her, but not before he'd muttered into Dudley's ear, "Tell them to call the hospital and tell Dr. Bellamy that she's working all night, will you? And if you want me, later, I'll be at my place with the doctor. Eating halibut. See you, Roop!"